BLUE IN BOSTON

Blue in Boston

FAY SMITH

Fay Smith

Contents

ISBN: 979-8-9873348-8-1
EISBN: 979-8-9873348-0-5

Cover design by: oliviaprodesign
Printed in the United States of America

Trigger Warning

Please only read further if you are concerned about triggers. While it is my hope that you would go into this book open and wholeheartedly, your mental health is top priority.

This is a dark and dramatic romance, sprinkled with humor. My characters are raw and authentic, the beautiful as well as the ugly. They are kind and sometimes cruel.

There is dark content in this book to include military violence, violent sexual acts, malicious sexual acts, physical abuse, and abuse of power; more than just the acts, you will find the mental state of the characters as they deal with this abuse and PTSD (Post-traumatic Stress Disorder). There is also explicit sexual language.

My characters are strong, and process what they are going through to create an outcome; if any of these subjects disturb or trigger you, then this might not be the book for you.

Chapter 1

Jenna

I only had a half hour for a lunch break, so why did I choose to spend it in the damned department store? I should have waited until after work, when I would have a little more time to find the right dress. Why did I wait until Friday at lunch to even look? The event was the next day, for christ's sake.

Oh yeah, because I'm broke, and it depresses me.

The evening wear department was subtly lighted, making everything seem a little darker. Jenna picked up a hanger with a dress on it, holding it in front of her with a frown on her face, contemplating. She turned the tag over to see the price and gagged, putting the dress right back on the rack.

$2800? Who the hell shops here, the Rockerfellers? Crap, and now I have only ten minutes before I have to get back. This was a mistake.

Jenna swept her eyes over another rack of dresses, noticing a man at the next rack. She continued to sift through the hangers, but snuck peeks out of the corner of her eye. He was tall, with dark hair and blue eyes. His navy suit was tailored to fit him like a dream. She couldn't see his feet, but she was willing to bet he had expensive leather shoes, shined to perfection. He was tall and broad, built like a linebacker, the stuff of fantasies. She was always hyper-aware of her surroundings, and his presence overwhelmed her senses; not necessarily in a bad way.

She wondered what he was doing buying dresses. Maybe a gift for his wife or girlfriend?

God, why don't I have guys like that to buy me expensive dresses and take me out? Maybe because I'm not willing to play dumb to keep a boyfriend?...

The thought made her frown again.

As he moved to another rack she moved closer to where he had been, and caught a lingering whiff of his aftershave. The smell sent shocks through her in all the right places.

Holy shit, he smells like sex on a platter. I seriously need to get some soon if I'm sniffing after strangers in the store.

Looking at her cell she realized she was running out of time.

This high-end department store is too rich for my blood; I never should have come in.

She shrugged defeat and turned to head back to the escalators. The man stood behind her, staring at some dresses, deep in thought. Jenna raised an eyebrow. As she started to walk past, the man looked up, seemingly seeing her for the first time.

"Miss, do you have this in a size two?" he asked, his voice deep and sexy; holding a dress out to her. It was low cut, gaudy hot pink, with sequins. Jenna stopped, shocked. She wondered why he thought she worked there, and then realized she still had her gold name tag on from the coffee shop where she worked. Her uniform was a white button up shirt with a black pencil skirt, so it seemed an obvious mistake.

"I'm sorry, I don't-," she mumbled as she went to pass him, but he stuck his hand out, blocking her exit.

"Look, I don't have time for laziness. I need a dress for my... daughter, and I'm in a hurry. Be a good girl and hop in back and see if there are any there," he said insistently, with obvious aggravation.

What a pretentious prick. 'Daughter' my ass. Jenna huffed a chuckle under her breath.

"Well?" he demanded, his voice louder, the dress still clutched in his hand. "Are you just going to stand there or-"

"Yes, I am," she answered calmly. "Because you're, ... what... thirty? Thirty-five? What kind of an asshole buys a dress that sleazy for their fifteen year old daughter? Are you pimping her out?" She narrowed her eyes at him.

His jaw dropped as his eyes opened wide, his eyebrows climbing for his hairline.

"How DARE you?" He hissed. "Haven't you ever heard 'the customer is always right?' I'll have you fired for this." His jaw was clenched, and his face was turning red with anger.

"Yes, I have, but that doesn't mean the customer isn't also an asshole. Good luck with getting me fired... and with your 'daughter'." Jenna made air quotes with her hands as she said 'daughter' so that he would get the point that she wasn't buying it. With that she gave him her back and continued to the escalator.

Prick.

Great. Now I'm going to be late from lunch on my first week.

She sighed and shook her head as she headed back downstairs and out onto the street, back to the coffee shop where she worked.

◆ ◆ ◆

Max

The NERVE.

He watched the girl, "Jenna" according to her name tag, stalk away from him to the escalator. As she stepped into the brightly lit escalator area, he could see that her hair didn't just look blue, it was blue. He knew kids did that stupid shit with their hair, but she appeared closer to his own age.

When did the employee standards here drop so low? He wondered, as he headed to the nearest register. He had been shopping here for years, and he saw Doris at the register, folding sweaters. The elderly lady looked up and smiled as she saw him approaching.

"Good afternoon, Mr. Thurston. Anything I can help you with today?" She smiled at him sweetly.

"Yes, I want to file a complaint about your new employee, Jenna. She was rude and totally out of line."

He was still seething, but kept his composure while talking to Doris. She had always taken good care of him, and more importantly, she never asked any questions. She looked back at him with concern in her eyes.

"Mr. Thurston, I'm sorry, we don't have any new staff in this department. It's just me and Rachael, and Rachael is out on leave today. Can you describe the person you spoke to?" Doris was like a grandmother figure, sweet but professional, always.

"You couldn't miss her, Doris. She had blue hair," he answered.

"Oh, no, then. She couldn't be employed here. Our dress code forbids wild hair colors, tattoos, or piercings that show. I'm sorry you experienced that, Mr. Thurston. Is there something I could do to help you?"

She always went out of her way for him; he bought enough that her commissions were always good. He shopped for all of his girls here. Max looked down and noticed Doris's white name tag; not gold like Jenna's.

She really didn't work here. Her parting comment made more sense, now.

Suddenly the whole situation seemed funny to him, and he laughed in spite of himself. He could appreciate that she was a spitfire, even if she had pissed him off. He hadn't had a woman talk to him like that in... he couldn't remember how long.

"No, Doris, but thank you. I really have to be going, but I'll be back next week to pick up a few gifts." He winked at her, and smiled when she blushed.

"Oh, okay then," she answered. "We get a new shipment on Tuesday. Would you like me to hold out a few things for you?" she asked.

"You're the best, Doris." He smiled his million-dollar smile for her, and she smiled dreamily at him.

Yup, still have it. He chuckled as he turned and headed back to the escalator. He thought of the woman who had just been here a few minutes prior, with blue hair of all things.

Damn, she was hot, even the freaky blue hair. Curvy and strong, not the starved-skinny he saw on so many women. Her arms and legs were toned, she clearly worked out. And she had the most interesting shade of hazel eyes with gold in them. How am I supposed to pick out clothing for someone when I can only imagine taking the clothing off of someone else? It's a good thing she doesn't work here. If I had to see her every time I came in, I'd have to have her sooner or later, probably right in a dressing room. I'd give her something for that sassy mouth.

He adjusted his slacks as he rode the escalator down to the first floor.

◆ ◆ ◆

Jenna

The bell over the door continued to ring as customer after customer came into the coffee shop and got in line to order. Jenna was working the cappuccino machine and filling orders as fast as she could. The damn milk frother took too much time. She had been lucky, it was so busy that no one noticed she was late getting back from lunch, but she regretted not having eaten now that she was slammed with orders. It was going to be a long afternoon.

Hours later Jenna stood on the green line train headed home. The train was packed, and as it stopped every few hundred feet, the short trip took forever. Her feet and back ached and she was tired. She hoped that her roommate, Andrew, was home, and that he would be willing to drive her to a thrift store to get a dress. She hated having to ask him, but this was her life now.

She looked out the windows of the train, through the crowds, and considered what had brought her to Boston.

Well, she had to live somewhere, didn't she?

After she had gotten out of the military she had gotten married, but that didn't last long. She was too strong willed to play the role of the submissive wife.

She had traveled all over the country, but never really found someplace to call home. In the end she came back to Massachusetts, where her mother had been born and raised, and where she had attended school. It wasn't home, but it was roots. If only her mother was still alive, maybe it could be home again.

Her best friend Andrew lived in Alston, a suburb of Boston. He was rockstar gorgeous, with long blond waves of hair and a firm jaw line, as well as a body to die for; not that she'd get it, he played for the other team. They had gone through high school together, and hung with a few other girlfriends as a pack. He was a sports massage therapist, by trade, and doing very well. Andrew was like a brother or a best girlfriend for her. They shared a love of bodywork and martial arts, learning and practicing together whenever she had been in town. He was the closest thing she had to family now.

He had always told her that he had an extra room, anytime she wanted to stay; she finally took him up on it. It was nice having someone to come home to again. She didn't know if she would make this her final destination, but she was glad to have the option.

The train lurched to a stop, and the doors slid open. A wave of people headed for the nearest exit, and Jenna moved with them. She still had a mile to walk to Andrew's house, but at least she was close. She pulled her coat around her to ward off the chill in the winter air as she broke away from the crowd and down the street. She knew once the snow fell she was going to regret having come back. She fucking hated snow.

She reached the house and climbed the steps to the porch and the front door. Andrew's car wasn't in the driveway, so he wasn't home yet. A frustrated frown pulled at Jenna's lips as she fished the keyring out of her purse and unlocked the door. She dropped her purse on the table by the door and kicked her sneakers off before falling onto the sofa.

Her feet, legs, and back hurt. She was technically a disabled veteran, with fused vertebrae in her back from an IED explosion that had taken out the rest of her squad, so too much physical work really took a toll on her. Long days at the coffee shop were starting to add up in her pain bank, and she didn't do painkillers. She'd seen too many of her brothers and sisters in arms become addicts to that shit. She'd rather feel the pain. And today she was.

Andrew had offered to give her massages for her pain, but she didn't want to take advantage of him. That's how he made his living, as one of the best Sports and Pain Management Massage Therapists in the greater Boston area. He ran New Alternatives Spa, and was doing very well. But for Jenna money was still tight, and she wouldn't accept treatments unless she could pay him. He was so kind that he gave everything away, and she couldn't be one of the people who used him. Her stubbornness frustrated him on a regular basis, but he still loved her.

She was kind of stuck with the service industry; she knew she really didn't have the option to take an office job. Her PTSD gave her zero tolerance for the bullshit of customer service. Entitled demanding bitches made her lose her mind. You can only tell a customer to "shut the fuck up and wait your damned turn" so many times before they have to fire you. She had been in Boston for three weeks, and the coffee shop was her third job thus far.

It seemed to be a good fit for her, because her customer interactions were less than five minutes; but she had to be on her feet all day. Yes, she did have disability income from the VA, but it was never enough. If she wanted to start over somewhere else, she would need a nest egg. She was a free spirit who loved to travel, so she never seemed to get ahead anywhere she landed.

As she stared at the wall she considered the charity event Andrew had asked her to attend on Saturday night, the one she needed the dress for; he wanted to network badly for his spa. He was so close to meeting the numbers he needed to expand, and the event might be just the opportunity he needed to make those numbers. She shouldn't have accepted his offer to go, knowing how short on cash she was, but he seemed so desperate to have someone go with him that she didn't want to let him down. Now she had to find a formal dress to wear, and she had to hope the thrift store had something decent and in her size. She groaned to herself.

I could have stayed in Las Vegas. I made killer money, and never lacked for attention. And it never fucking snowed there....

The door opened and Andrew bustled into the living room. "Sorry I'm late, Baby Girl, but you would not believe the day I had. Hey... are you okay?" His wild dramatics came to a quick stop as he saw her slouched over the sofa.

"Yeah, Drew, I'm fine. It's just been a long day. I'm beat, and I still need a dress for tomorrow." She looked up at him and smiled weakly.

"Well then, you are in luck, Girly-Girl. Let me put my stuff away, and I know just where to get a dress for you. I'm taking you to dinner too." He smiled brilliantly at her. He was a good looking guy, even Jenna appreciated his model-worthy physique.

"Noooo, Drew, I don't want you spending money on me, we can eat here." She started to sit up off of the couch.

"Not a chance, Sweetheart. You are doing ME a favor by going to this event, so you are going to let me spoil you. Besides, if I pick the dress, you can't buy something cheap and horrible. No self respecting gay guy wants to be seen with a woman who looks cheap and horrible." He smirked at her as she grabbed a throw pillow from the couch and flung it at his head.

"Speaking of cheap and horrible," she started, as Andrew began putting his bags away, "I had the most interesting experience at Lady Saks today." Andrew turned his head to her so she could see he was listening. "Apparently some douche thought I worked there and demanded that I 'stop being lazy' and help him find a truly trashy dress in a size two for his 'daughter.' Dude, he was maybe thirty-five. I don't know what his kink is, but I really don't want to."

"So what did you do?"

"I tried to tell him I didn't work there, but he insisted. So I asked him if he was pimping his 'daughter' out with that dress."

Andrew's jaw fell open and then he burst out laughing. "You did NOT."

"I did," she said with smug satisfaction. "He said he was going to get me fired. Phhhttt." This elicited another round of laughter from Andrew, and Jenna joined in. "I wish I could have seen the look on his face when he found out I didn't work there. Rich people..." She grimaced.

"You don't have to tell me, Love. I work with them all day long." Andrew chuckled. "Entitled pricks, but I will say this; they tip better than poor people. There, my stuff is put away. Get your shoes on, woman, we're going shopping."

Andrew hopped up with a flourish and pulled Jenna up by her arms. In no time at all they were out the door looking for the perfect dress.

◆ ◆ ◆

Max

Max was already grumpy, before he had even started getting ready for the charity event. He had stayed up late with Mia, the woman he hired for female company, but rather than the release he needed, all he got was attitude and lack of sleep. It didn't help that the blue-haired beauty had graced his dreams, but at least he had found release there. Now he was aggravated and behind schedule, and he was just not in the mood for bullshit.

"But I've already worn this one." Mia whined. She ran her hands down her green satin gown and stomped her foot like a child as she stared at her reflection in the mirror.

"Baby, that was in Los Angeles. No one here has seen it, trust me. It will be fine." Max straightened his tie, his temper already flaring. Mia started to grumble, but he shot her a glare through the mirror, and she instead set her mouth in a tight white line and said nothing; but her narrowed eyes spoke volumes. Max rolled his eyes and refrained from grumbling out loud. He didn't need an argument right now before they left. He didn't need one at all, actually.

Spoiled bitch. I should just end it, she's not worth the aggravation. Hell, the sex isn't even good anymore. I'm tempted to just go solo and not have to deal with her attitude all night. I'm getting too old for this shit. She's supposed to help me relax, not give me drama.

"Let's go, we're already running late," he bit out as he turned and headed for the door without waiting or looking back. He could hear her spiked heels ticking quickly behind him on the polished wood floor. He almost wished she would just stay home.

Twenty minutes later the limo pulled up to the large hotel, and doormen opened the door for him. Max stepped out, and right into the crowd, leaving the doorman to help Mia get out of the car behind him. She was smiling her biggest fake smile at the crowd and the photographers, but shot him an angry side-glare as she caught up to him and weaved her arm into his, linking elbows. Max just continued walking.

It was going to be a long night.

◆ ◆ ◆

Jenna

"How far is this place?" Jenna asked as she stomped up the street in her spike heels. They had to park several blocks away from the hotel, and her feet were already killing her before they even got to the event. Andrew kept her arm in his the whole way, afraid she would topple over and ruin her beautiful new dress. He had a friend who was a dressmaker, and had given him an amazing deal on the blush creation that she wore. It had a strapless bodice that hugged her from her chest to her hips before fanning out into a mermaid skirt. There was a slight gold shimmer to the pink fabric, and it was a work of art: more so on her amazing body. She wore a tiny delicate gold chain around her neck with a single solitaire: cubic zirconia, of course, but it sparkled nonetheless. She really looked like a goddess; or would if she could only stop stomping like a truck driver in the ridiculously tall gold heels.

"We're almost there, Jenna. Slow down, small steps. I shouldn't have to teach you how to walk like a lady." He chuckled.

"Yeah, well I shouldn't have to teach you how to defend yourself and change your oil, but here we are," she shot back. He only laughed harder and hugged her arm.

"That's why I love you. You're well maintained and violent." He smiled broadly, and despite herself, she smiled back. They strolled through the doors and followed the crowd to the ballroom where the event was to take place.

As Andrew gave the man at the door his invitation, Jenna looked around the old ballroom. It was magnificent, like stepping back in time. Marble columns in tans and blacks rose to meet an arched ceiling with murals and a gigantic crystal chandelier. There were gold-gild borders on everything. Thick red carpeting bordered a parquet wooden floor, and drapes of red velvet framed huge windows. The room was already filling with men dressed sharply in nice suits, and ladies in beautiful gowns. Waiters circulated with trays of champagne.

How can they hold a fundraiser in a place that probably cost a fortune to rent? Jenna wondered to herself. The world of money was a complete unknown to her.

She tugged Andrew's arm to let him know she was going to the ladies room, and carefully staggered off to the side as gracefully as she could, which wasn't very graceful. Once in the bathroom stall she struggled to scrape down the tight undergarments Andrew had insisted she had to wear to keep her 'lady bits contained.'

Fucking torture devices was more like it. Let's face it, mens' bits were more obtrusive than ladies'; it was another conspiracy, like heels, to torture women.

As she struggled she heard the bathroom door open and two voices enter.

"It's complete bullshit," said the first voice, as another stall door opened.

"I agree," said the second, entering another stall. "he can't just jerk you around like that. But at least Thurston is exclusive with you. Marcus won't even get a divorce. The last time I brought it up he didn't see me for weeks, and then I had to 'make it up' to him. He enjoys punishment."

"Exclusive isn't enough." The first voice shrieked. "I'm not allowed to be with anyone else, not to get my own needs met, and I get zero security from him. Christ, it takes half the night just helping him get it up lately. What if he dumps me next week? If he wants to be 'Daddy', he needs to put a ring on it already."

"Girlfriend, you have to get your needs met. I have an arrangement on the side, nothing public, just hardcore sex. I can put you in touch. As for Thurston, be careful there. If you push too hard he will dump you. You need this income. You need to play the long game."

Toilets flushed and the stall doors opened as the two newcomers washed their hands at the sink and continued talking. Jenna finished up, squeezing the tight bodice into place, and stepped out to wash her own hands, and the other girls turned to her: surprised, at first, and then with a sneer as they looked her up and down. Jenna tried to ignore the blond and the brunette, but couldn't help seeing that the blond was wearing the awful hot pink sequined disaster from the department store. The brunette wore a tight satin green dress, and her silicone boobs were practically leaping out of the top. Jenna stepped around them and left, finding Andrew waiting outside the door for her.

Andrew took her arm gently as he moved inside the room and into the stream of circulating bodies. Jenna stopped a waiter and took a glass of champagne; she knew Andrew was in recovery, so she didn't grab one for him, and instead pulled him towards the bar for a ginger ale. He smiled at her for her thoughtfulness. They looked out for each other, always had.

Someone in the middle of the room got on the microphone to announce that hors d'oeuvres and drinks would be served for the next hour, and that there was dancing. After that the auction would begin. Music played, and people mingled and danced.

"Which charity is this supporting?" Jenna whispered to Andrew.

"I have no idea, I'm here networking." He smiled back at her conspiratorially. "Wanna dance?"

They put their drinks down and Andrew led her to the floor where other couples were already moving. He moved her with ease and she laughed when he spun her. He moved her around him again and then spun her out again; only to have her smack into a body as it moved right into her path.

"Oh I'm sorry," the man rushed to apologize, and then stopped dead when he realized who he had collided with. Jenna was face to face with the asshole from the department store. He looked just as good as he had then: same rugged features and dreamy blue eyes, but his suit was black with a crisp white shirt. He looked edible, and completely shocked at seeing her. Electricity seemed to shoot between them for a startled moment. His aftershave made moisture pool between Jenna's legs instantly.

Jenna giggled, and winked, before rushing back to Andrew and pulling him further into the crowd of dancers. "Do you know who that was?" she whispered.

◆ ◆ ◆

Max

Holy fuck, it's her! What's she doing here? I wouldn't have recognized her, except for that blue hair. God damn, she looks amazing; that gown leaves nothing to the imagination.

He was instantly semi-erect as he watched her retreat into the dancing bodies on the floor.

In his rush to duck Mia he had run smack into the hot girl from the department store from the previous afternoon. They had been nose to nose, and now she was gone again. He hadn't been able to stop thinking about her, and now she was here, somewhere.

"Max, for fuck's sake, wait up." Mia's whining voice came up on him. His erection instantly withered. She clutched onto his arm, as she smoothed her green dress down and fixed her dark curls.

"Max," Mia whined, pulling his attention back to her. Her eyebrows were pulled down into an angry petulant pout, clearly upset that he had been looking away from her at another woman. "I have had enough. I can't keep chasing you around like this. I think we need to have a talk about where our future is going. This isn't working for me anymore."

And suddenly he couldn't take it any longer.

"Mia, come with me," he gritted out through clenched teeth. He stormed out of the ballroom, and then out of the hotel door onto the sidewalk, off to the side, out of earshot with her in tow. They stood on the street, away from the main door activity, and Mia looked absolutely pissed.

"Mia, it isn't working for me either. After tonight I don't want to see you again. We are done. I'll have a cab take you home."

"What the hell are you talking about?" she demanded. "What the fuck is going on?" She was furious, and having none of of it. "I am not leaving, and this is NOT over." Again she stomped her foot. "I expected a ring, Max. You owe me this."

"Keep your voice down, or you will have a lot of trouble finding any clients in the future. I am done with your whining and drama. I will give you a good reference if you go now, quietly. If you make a scene you will never work in New England again. I mean it." His jaw was tight as he held on to her arm with a death grip. His eyes were cold with rage.

Mia turned narrowed eyes on Max, as she clutched her purse in her hands tightly. He could see the wheels turning in her head; she hated not getting her way, but if she pushed it right here it would only make the situation worse for her, and she knew it.

"I have had enough of this, Max. I am going home. I suggest you think about this long and hard. No one is going to give you what I give you. Call me when you are ready to discuss our future." She turned and stepped to a cab waiting by the curb before shooting one last glare over her shoulder. Max stood unaffected. She growled as she flung the door open, shoving inside quickly, and slamming the door behind her.

Max watched as the cab pulled away and into traffic. A great sense of relief filled him.

She's finally gone. I should feel sad, shouldn't I? But I don't. I don't want to deal with Mia anymore.

He knew that it probably wasn't over for good, she'd probably haunt him for a while, but he had ways of ensuring she stopped.

His thoughts snapped back inside, back to looking for the hot little body in the blush dress, the body that was so soft when he slammed into it by accident. He wondered how it would feel to slam into it on purpose. The body with the strange blue hair that filled his wet dreams the night before. He had to find her. She had to be his.

Chapter 2

Max

Monday morning signaled the return to the reality of his responsibilities. Max gripped his briefcase as he headed down the sidewalk to his client's business. He was a partner at Thurston, Creed, & Lowe, one of the largest corporate law firms in Boston. It was unusual for him to go out on a client visit, but this particular client had been with the firm for generations; the sweet old man held a place in Max's heart. So when he needed representation, or help, Max would stop down and visit him in person. This client was a rare exception.

He still had more than thirty minutes to kill, as traffic had been surprisingly light, and he had found a parking space quickly, so he ducked into a coffee shop to read his paper and wait. He found it bustling with mid-morning traffic, most of the tables taken, and very little standing room.

Max stood in line and let his mind wander as orders were taken and filled ahead of him. Saturday night had been a bust. At least he got rid of Mia, but she had texted him all Sunday, trying to get back into his good graces.

Not going to happen.

He never got to talk to Jenna. He had seen her dancing with a good looking guy, who looked like a surfer or a model in a suit.

I guess some women like the disheveled look. Were they a couple?

He had looked into him: Andrew Lark, a sports therapist. If he couldn't find Jenna again, maybe he could track this Andrew guy down for info. At least he had a lead.

He couldn't quite put his finger on why she had this effect on him. It was rare for him to see a girl and want her badly enough to pursue her; it was usually the ladies pursuing him, which is why he resorted to hiring Mia in the first place to be his "date" for public appearances. But like most professional dates, it could only last so long before they started getting attached, or entitled. He didn't need a relationship; he needed company at events, and a warm body in bed every now and again. He didn't have time or energy for more than that.

"Can I take your order?" Max realized he was at the front of the line and looked at the kid behind the register who waited impatiently. He looked up to see what this place called their specialty coffees, and that's when the flash of blue caught his eye behind the counter to the left.

Jenna. It was her!

Jenna was working the cappuccino machine, dropping shots of coffee into cups, and loading foamed milk on top of them. She was completely absorbed in what she was doing and never noticed him. A huge smile spread over his face.

"Sir?" the impatient cashier asked.

"I'll have whatever she is making." Max pointed to Jenna.

"Double macchiato, okay, that will be $5.95 please." Max pulled his card out and stuck it into the card reader. The cashier stepped over to the back counter a few minutes later to pick up his order and bring it back, and Max pulled out a twenty and wrapped it around his business card. Jenna never looked up. "Would you give this to Jenna, please? After I leave?"

The cashier took it from him with an aggravated look and placed it next to the register as he took the next customer's order. Max headed for the door, carefully looking over his shoulder; Jenna was still whipping out coffee drinks fast, and had apparently not seen him.

Well, now I know where to find her. This day is turning out much better than I had planned.

◆ ◆ ◆

Jenna

CRACK! Her longstaff smashed violently into Andrew's before she twisted it over his in a disarming maneuver, but he anticipated it and moved with it, leaving more space between them. They were both wet with perspiration as they circled each other again, their breathing ragged. She saw him launching his next attack and side-stepped, bringing her bo up sharply. It connected with his ribs, but not hard, as he managed to get his body out of the way at the last second.

Her shift at the coffee shop had left her body aching, and her mind almost numb during her train ride home. At first she hadn't wanted to go back out to the dojo to train, but she knew she needed it. This was therapy for her, both mental and physical. As she spun through the next movements, swinging her bo around his as he launched attack after attack, it allowed her mind to stop its endless chatter. Nothing existed except their movement.

As they circled again, her thoughts crept back to the business card she had been left by a customer. She hadn't seen him. *Maxwell Thurston...* she wondered it if was the same "Thurston" the woman at the event had referenced. She wondered if "Daddy" had put a ring on it?... And she chuckled to herself.

Suddenly the air was forced out of her lungs with an exhaled 'OOF' as Andrews's bo connected hard with her solar plexus, pushing her back several feet.

"Focus, Kitten," Andrew chided. His smile was smug.

Damn. Either he was getting better, or she was really off her game. It was rare for Andrew to land a solid shot.

"Break," she called, one hand up, as she headed off the mats for water.

"Oh, sure, NOW you want a break, when I'm finally getting the upper hand," he gloated, but he looked dog-tired, with sweat rolling down his face. She knew he was getting sloppier as he got more fatigued; it had been a lucky shot.

Her breaths were heavy and labored. She wiped the sweat off her forehead and emptied a bottle of water with one swallow. The clock showed that they had been sparring for almost two hours, that was probably enough for the night. Exhaustion would work against her. Right then, a hot shower and bed sounded like the perfect way to end the day.

Tuesday was her day off, and was largely uneventful. She filled it with weight training, and Andrew had finally worn her down and insisted she get a massage for her back. They had argued for hours, but in the end Andrew's logic, and her own pain, had her sprawled out on the massage table. She had laid there, boneless and oiled up, just letting her body and mind unwind in a way she never seemed to be able to achieve. It was the rarest of gifts for her, and she treasured it. Peace. Silence. Tears had tracked down her cheeks. Later that night she slept like a baby with no nightmares of explosions or dying friends.

Upon her return to work on Wednesday, she found out that her mysterious Mr. Thurston had been by and left her another tip, even though she hadn't been in that day. This time he left a greeting card as well. She almost chucked the card in the trash, but her curiosity got the better of her. Slicing the envelope open, she pulled the card out and read it.

"My Dearest Jenna,

I know you don't know me, but I would really like you to. Could we meet sometime? Perhaps for lunch or dinner? My treat. I have included another card for you, this has my private number on it, please don't share it.

Warmest regards,

Max Thurston"

Jenna looked at the card, unimpressed. She already had lots of guys who asked her out, and she wasn't interested. Honestly, she felt too fucked up to be in a relationship, and if she wanted someone to fuck she wanted to be the one picking, not the other way around. She was nobody's sex toy. She dropped the card and business card into the trash and got ready for her shift.

The week flew in a blur, and Friday's shift found her at the cappuccino machine again. It was mid-November, and the holiday shoppers made Boston's streets a lot busier than usual. The air outside was frigid, and the little shop was filled to capacity with people looking for hot drinks and a place to thaw. Jenna hadn't received any more cards or tips from the mysterious Mr. Thurston.

He gave up awfully easy. Not that I wanted to go out with him, but damn, not even a little fight in him. Probably some pretentious twat that just assumes all girls fall naked before his fat wallet. He's got nothing I want...

Jenna was focused on the coffees she was making, and lost in her own thoughts, when Lou, her coworker, tapped her on the shoulder. She turned from her last cup to see him sticking his thumb out in the direction of the back counter, a smirk on his face.

"Wha-" She turned to the counter to see an enormous arrangement of red roses; it was monstrously large. "Nooooo." She frowned as she made her way to it; the small card was addressed to her. She pulled the small note card out.

"My Dearest Jenna,

I am so saddened that I have not heard from you. The fault is mine. Perhaps I have not impressed upon you enough my sincerity in wanting to meet you. You fascinate me. I wish only for an hour of your time, and if you do not wish to know me, then of course I would respect that and cease all communication; but please allow me sixty minutes of your time. I have not seen a person as refreshing as you in as long as I can remember. Will you let me take you out, please?

Respectfully,

Max"

She noticed he had written his personal number on the bottom of the card again. The romantic in her was curious, but the overriding logical side of her wasn't swayed by the expensive purchase. It was still too impersonal, sending notes instead of showing up in person... not that she wanted to encourage him to show up in person... but she couldn't help but smile just a little bit. Although not enough, and completely unwanted, he was putting in some effort.

◆ ◆ ◆

Max

Max took a sip from his glass of scotch, looking over the desk in his home office. The weekends were the hardest. During the week he was scheduled to the hilt: back to back meetings, clients, and court. Weekends were unscripted, lonely affairs. He often brought files home to work on to make his work week lighter, but it left him exhausted and empty.

He could hire some girls to keep him company, but he hated waking up alone, and he wouldn't keep them overnight, lest they become too attached. It's not that he wanted a relationship, he didn't, but he did want some of the things that came with it. But no woman he met would put up with being at his beck and call, around his hectic schedule, without wanting something in return. Money was the easiest exchange. Marriage was off the table. It made for a lot of solitary time.

He had really hoped that Jenna would call him. She excited him the way the other girls hadn't been able to for quite a while; just the thought of her made him hard. While there was a good chance that if he got her to go out with him, he'd end up fucking her, there was still some lingering doubt.

That made her even hotter. She wasn't a 'sure thing.' She was a challenge that he wanted to meet, and conquer. He remembered how she had put him in his place at the department store with the skilled detachment that was usually reserved for lawyers in court. Yes, she had pissed him off, but she had turned him on too. He wanted to challenge her, debate her, and then fuck her into blissful oblivion. He imagined she would be a wildcat in bed, and he was so hoping to get a chance to find out.

The card hadn't impressed her, and he wasn't surprised. It was lazy. He knew she would require more effort than that. The roses hadn't impressed her either, and he was kind of glad that they hadn't; he didn't need another woman seeing him for gifts, although that was convenient. He was equally frustrated by, and enjoying, this challenge. He knew she was a higher caliber, more cerebral; he just needed to find her angle. Sooner or later, he'd find what it took to get her to agree to meet him, and then the game was on.

◆ ◆ ◆

Jenna

Jenna drank her gin and tonic and stared at the flames in the fireplace. The weekends were always the hardest. Andrew was out with his friends at an LGBT event, and Jenna was left with her thoughts. She had no other friends in town yet, and she really didn't have money to blow going to bars or clubs. It was cheaper to just drink at home, quieter too.

It was times like these that she missed military life; you were always surrounded by your military 'family.' At any time of the day or night, someone was awake, so you could choose to be by yourself, or to be with people, but you were never really alone.

Here she felt alone. Everywhere she had felt alone.

Maybe she just needed to get laid, let some of the tension off. She'd have to ask Andrew if he had any non-gay friends with good cocks who were looking for friends with benefits. She didn't want a relationship; she had been independent long enough that she didn't want a man "taking care of her" or expecting her to feel obligated to him because he was born with a dick. She had her own money, she protected herself, and damn it she'd rather fuck a vibrator than be expected to swoon over some idiot.

She picked up the tiny card from the table beside her. He wanted her. If he was the same "Daddy" as Thurston from the event... *Just ewwww...* She wasn't going there. But she didn't know for a fact that he WAS the same Thurston... Regardless, no. A card and flowers are cliche', even if they are huge fucking flowers that now take up most of a kitchen counter.

If that's all he's packing in his game, he can take his ball and bat and go home.

At work, Jenna wiped down the frothing arm before it could become clogged with milk. The machine was a bitch to keep clean. It was already Friday again. The weekdays had come and gone in a blur of coffee orders, dojo time, and quiet nights with or without Andrew... mostly without. The man was a workaholic. She set her rag aside as Lou called her over to the register.

A courier had just delivered a letter for her, and she watched as he made his way back out of the shop. Lou held the envelope up to her with a smirk; she was the talk of the shop with her secret admirer. One of the girls had asked for the business card, saying that if Jenna wasn't going to take advantage of the opportunity, someone should: namely her.

With a roll of her eyes Jenna took the envelope to the back room to read it in private. Once there she allowed herself the smallest of smiles as she opened it and saw the familiar handwriting.

"My Dearest Jenna,

I apologize for neglecting you for so long. My week has been hectic, but that is no excuse for leaving you to worry that I have forgotten you. Quite the contrary. I have thought about you often, and fondly.

As you have not called me, I can only come to the conclusion that you are not yet ready to meet me in person. And that is understandable, as I am still a stranger to you. I thought perhaps I could tell you some things about myself, and then I would not be such an unknown.

First, I am one of three brothers; one lives here in Boston, and the other lives in London. We are all lawyers, as we all hatched from the same type of reptilian eggs.

Second, I love coffee. Hot or iced, doesn't matter. I know that what I'm about to confide may shock you, but I don't like Dunkin Donuts coffee. I don't care how 'New England' it is; it is a poor representation of what we can offer. If I have lost you because of that, I will understand; think of me whenever you drink your dishwater coffee.

Third, I love a good adventure: in print, or in real life.

Fourth, I have extraordinarily large hands and feet. You know what that means... yes, big gloves and shoes.

And Fifth, I believe that beauty is not to be found in the external appearance, but rather in the mind, because that is where true passion lives. I would rather a passionate debate than an apathetic exchange of small talk. Bring the fire if you want to impress.

I would write you poetry, but to be honest I am not a poet, and I don't really write poetry well. I am no John Keats. I could quote other poets, I'm sure, but I can't be sure that they have felt the burning curiosity I feel when I think about you. And even if they had, I'm not sure that their flowery prose would improve upon my sharing of my feelings with you. If you are at all like me, it would probably just annoy the fuck out of you. Poetically speaking, of course.

As I have not heard from you, I must continue to endeavor under the impression that you still want to hear from me. Otherwise, you would have called to simply ask me to desist. So upon this impression I shall continue to admire you from afar; until such time as you would agree to meet with me.

Until our next...

Warmly,

Max

Xoxo

P.S. Please find my private number below; in case you *lost* it."

Jenna read, and re-read the letter three times, laughing harder each time.

Reptiles... big shoes... OMG where does he get this stuff? And then there was the stuff about adventure, and passion... Maybe he's not the same Thurston?

Later that evening Jenna sat in her bed staring at the letter. If she was being honest, he had finally crossed her barrier of interest, although only just. She did want to hear from him again; but the comments at work were getting too invasive. Her eyes lit up as an idea entered into her mind, followed by a sly smirk.

◆ ◆ ◆

Max

The office was busier than usual, with the winter holidays coming soon. It seemed the courts wanted to cram as many cases in as they could before they would shut down for the holidays; which meant everyone had to bring their 'A' game. Max picked up the phone call transferred from the receptionist, and prepared for a heated conversation with a difficult client, just as the clerk from the mail-room dropped his mail into his in-basket.

As he listened to his client rant and demand, he sorted through the envelopes, mostly holiday cards, until he came to one he didn't know. The return address said simply "Jenna."

She had mailed him a letter!

His eyes lit up and a smile bloomed over his face, his conversation completely ignored, as he tore into the envelope. Finally, his client ended the call so that he could turn his entire attention to the letter.

"My Dearest Max,

I have to admit, I do not know what to make of this current situation we find ourselves in. You are correct, I know very little about you. You could be a serial killer; or a cereal killer... either way, too messy for me.

If you were trying to impress me, then I have to admit that the first few cards were... lacking. Especially for a reptilian bigfoot who is not Keats. You only received a 2.5 out of 5 for creativity. Please tell me that you had your assistant arrange those, without a lot of supervision. I would suspend disbelief and let you throw her under the bus for the sake of continued conversation. They did not warrant a call, nor a reply.

And then the roses... they were lovely, I won't lie, while they lived: fragile and temporary indeed, no matter how well intended. That's not to say I am looking for permanence, but rather... They were very impractical, don't you agree? Especially considering how much you must have paid for them."

Max began to sweat. Was she insulting him? Did she like them or not? He really couldn't tell.

"I share your opinions about both adventure and passion, and even about Dunkin Donuts coffee. (Dishwater is insulted, I will have you know.) So I will share something about myself, and perhaps that will satisfy your curiosity. Who knows, it may negate any further need for correspondence, or meeting.

I am fiercely independent. I rely on no one but myself. I cannot be bought, rented, or managed. I have opinions, and I speak my mind. I will not be shushed. I trust my gut.

I do not say this lightly; enter at your own risk.

If I may ask, presuming you still wish to pursue correspondence, How is your '*daughter?*'

Best regards,

Jenna

P.S. I hope your Thanksgiving holiday is wonderful. Any future correspondence can be sent to the PO box listed below. I don't need my coworkers in my personal business, although Holly was very interested in calling you, if we do not pursue anything further."

Holy shit! She wanted to keep talking. It worked.

Max smiled like a giddy school boy before immediately opening his laptop to start drafting a response. Letters like these couldn't just be whipped from the top of his head, he wanted to really consider his message. He typed away with a huge grin on his face.

◆ ◆ ◆

Jenna

It was Friday afternoon, and Jenna kept her eyes peeled on the shop's door. She went through her day distracted, and she paused every time she saw a courier or delivery person.

For fuck's sake woman, get a hold of yourself.

She admonished herself silently after stopping to watch another courier go on their way. She rolled her shoulders, sighing out her disappointment, when another courier walked into the shop and straight to the cashier. She ran over to intercept him before the cashier could sign for the letter.

The envelope was addressed to her, and in the return address position was simply written "Not Keats." She rushed into the ladies room to read it in private, as the rest of the staff had already gathered around her and were nosing in to read it.

"My Dearest Jenna,

Thank you for advising me to enter your box at my own risk. I will bear that in mind. You should probably check it.

Warmly,

Reptilian Big Foot (RBF) Not Keats (NK)"

Warmth rushed over her cheeks as she smiled wide. Instantly, her practical side tried to squelch it.

For all you know, he's that depraved "Daddy" figure. He only wants you because you're a challenge. He just wants to fuck you. He's used to just buying call girls, he only wants one thing from you. Once he fucks you he'll never talk to you again.

Jenna shook her head to clear out the negative talk; even if it was all true, right then, right there, she was just so happy to think that someone wanted her. Someone wanted her enough to pursue her, and appeal to her mind. She didn't want a relationship either, so she couldn't judge him if he didn't.

But she did notice he hadn't answered the question about his "daughter." It dulled the shine she was feeling just a little.

Jenna ran for the PO box. She had bolted out of work as soon as her shift was over, and for the first time that she could remember, she drummed nervously the whole train ride home, impatient for it to be over. Finally, she slid the key into the lock and turned it. Opening the door she found a small package. A part of her wanted to tear it open there and devour the contents, see what he had written back; another part of her wanted to smuggle it back to the safety of Andrew's house, away from prying eyes. She did the latter, scurrying the whole way.

Jenna sat in her bedroom and sliced the packing tape on the package. She pulled out the note, and noticed a gift-wrapped package underneath it. She read the letter first.

"My Dearest Jenna,

I cannot begin to tell you how happy you have made me by responding to me. I was beginning to think that I had lost my touch. Ridiculous, I know. But in the face of such a fierce woman, even the most confident of us can become insecure.

Yes, I agree that my earliest attempts to contact you were sub-par. I will take your wise advice and blame my incompetent assistant, who is a man, by the way; let's not be sexist. I have had him flogged and thrown into the basement/mailroom until he repents. I hope this meets with your approval.

As to the practicality of my gift; well, I have to admit that I wasn't thinking along those lines when I got them. I wanted something beautiful, audacious, and impressive, but I couldn't find anything that even compared to you, so I got the flowers. I have included another, more prac-tical, offering in this package, that I hope speaks to you more. I have no doubt you will let me know if it does not.

As to your independence, well my dear, it was your fire that attracted me. I see a passion in you that burns red hot, and a part of me wants to know if you will drive me to the greatest heights I have ever imagined, or you will burn me to the deepest pits of despair. Perhaps you will do both. One thing is for certain, time spent with you would never be boring.

To answer your question, I do not have a daughter. I have two sons from a previous marriage, but they live in Europe with their mother, I see them a few times a year. I also have no current spouse, partner, girlfriend, boy-friend, or concubine. I do have a pet rock, but you may not pet it. I don't think we are there yet as a couple.

What about you? What is your current romantic situation? Are you already madly in love with a poet and un-available for star-crossed correspondents? Or might I be able to tempt you out of your comfort zone to meet me in a very public place for a very practical meal of your choice? If you don't scare me too much, I might even be willing to get drunk so you could take advantage of me: no promises though.

I would like to thank you for giving me access to your box, especially sight unseen. I hope it wasn't too small, and that my package fit, not that there's anything I could have done about it; I couldn't make the package smaller. It is what it is. If it's a problem, I would be more than happy to help you make your box bigger.

I'm relieved to know that you no longer need to flaunt me in front of all of your co-workers. Please hang on to Holly's number, in the event that you decide never to meet me I may need sympathy sex, as long as you're not too attached to her, as I'd ruin her.

Might I remind you that you do have my personal phone number, the one which goes directly to my cell phone, which no one else has access to answer. In the event that you ever wanted to speak with me prior to the two days the US Postal service takes to deliver each of our responses between us, you could call or text. Just putting that out there.

Know that I will be anxiously awaiting word from you.
Warmly,
Max
RBFNK
xoxo"

Jenna read the letter twice with a huge smile on her face before putting it to the side. She already enjoyed his sense of humor, even if he was a little cocky. She lifted the gift out of the box and began to unwrap it. She couldn't imagine what the hell he would send to her, what he would see as practical.

When she tore the gift wrap off she just laughed out loud. In her lap sat a survival and emergency kit: complete with knife, can opener, compass, first aid supplies, flashlight, fire starter, and various other tools. She couldn't stop laughing. Really, it was exactly the sort of gift she liked. He had nailed it. This was just too much... she was going to have to call him now.

Chapter 3

Max

Max sat alone in his office. It was Friday night, and coming up on seven o'clock, and he was just wrapping up and getting ready to go home. Not that he was in a rush, there was no one there either. He threw some files, his wallet, and his phone into his briefcase and locked his office.

A half an hour later he was home. Having already stripped off his shirt and tie he brought his briefcase into his home office. As he was getting ready to go back to his room and shower he heard a muffled notification noise and started patting down his pockets for his phone. When he remembered he had thrown it into the briefcase he picked it up and opened it again quickly, shuffling the files out of the way until he saw the light of the screen.

An unknown number had texted.

"Unknown: Are you available to chat?"

He responded,

"Max: Depends, with whom?"

Three dots lit up the screen, and finally an answer popped up.

"Unknown: Mammalian, Tiny Feet, Might be Keats"

HOLY FUCK, SHE'S TEXTING!!!

Max's pants tented so quickly it was almost painful. He rushed to his bedroom and launched onto the bed, sitting up against the headboard. Something about it felt like he was bringing her to his bed.

He immediately responded.

"Max: Well, I was going to wash my hair, but I don't want to be rude, now do I? I can be available for you."

"Unknown: I don't want to interrupt your grooming. I can't imagine how much prep time a sasquatch takes. Don't let me disturb you..."

"Max: Well, now you have my attention. Did you get your package?"

A series of three dots flashed to the screen, then disappeared, then flashed again. This happened a few more times, and Max started to worry that maybe she hadn't liked the gift after all. Maybe she was just texting to tell him to stop. Anxiety started to gnaw in his stomach as he watched the dots appear and reappear. He hadn't realized how much he wanted to continue chasing her, he wasn't ready to be faced with an end. Finally her answer came through.

"Unknown: I did. I wish I had understood how big your package was going to be. It was jammed in my box REALLY TIGHT. I mean it totally filled it. At first I couldn't even get my fingers around it, I had to really work it. I just kept pushing it and pulling it, in and out. After a bit of back and forth wiggling I got it to rock pretty smoothly, and then it shot right out. Thanks."

Max reached into his pants and was stroking himself as he re-read her message. He was seriously ready to blow.

Who the fuck was this woman?

If he'd had any reservations before, he knew he absolutely had to have her now. Max suddenly found it difficult to text back.

"Max: Well I'm glad you got it. I really wanted to give it to you myself, in person. Did you like it, at least?"

"Unknown: Max, you have no idea. It was the perfect gift. Maybe we should meet?"

"Max: Say when and where, Tiny, I am there."

"Unknown: Hmmm… How about Graff's in Kendall Square, tomorrow night at six?"

"Max: I can be there in twenty if you want to meet tonight?"

"Unknown: Actually, I'd rather wait… How will I know it's you tomorrow?"

"Max: I'll know you."

"Unknown: Well that's not fair. What if you're an ogre, and I want to run?"

"Max: I'm not an ogre. I'm bigfoot. But if you disagree… Well, you can get truly shitfaced, so you don't notice as much, and I can wear a bag over my head. The package is worth it."

"Unknown: I don't know…."

"Max: Where's your sense of adventure?"

"Unknown: All I can say is, the package had better be worth it."

"Max: ;D"

◆ ◆ ◆

Jenna

WTF, here goes nothing.

She typed the long message into the text box, filled with sexual innuendo and suggestions. She knew he just wanted to bang her, and right now she could really use a good night of sex. So why not? If he never called her again, well, that would be ok too. He was funny, and it was fun getting the cards, but that stuff never lasts anyway. Better to have the sex and get it over with before she started hanging around with him and getting attached.

She hit 'send' and waited. And waited… and waited.

He's wanking. I bet you he's wanking right now. I should totally ask him…. No, I'm not going to to do that.

When his response came back, still carrying the innuendo, she smiled. Some guys were turned off by assertive women, not that she thought he was one of them. Others just took it as an opening for instant gratification and dick pics galore. But Max responded, keeping the dialog open, witty and sexual without being crass.

Jenna bit her bottom lip.

Should she ask to meet? What if he was "Daddy" Thurston? What if he was a creeper?

But her gut didn't give her that feedback, and she was really good at assessing people.

Fuck's sake, just do it!

She hit 'send' and watched as their dialog set the place, the time. It was on. They were going to meet. And with any luck, she'd be ending her dry spell tomorrow.

Please God, don't let him be an ogre. And let him have a huge package for me!

◆ ◆ ◆

Max

At five forty-five Max was sitting at the bar and starting to sweat. He'd gotten to the restaurant an hour before they were supposed to meet, he'd been sitting at the bar watching the door. He hadn't been this nervous in years, if ever. This was so unlike him.

It's just the thrill of the chase, that's all. Once I bang her, I'll forget all about her. Better just to get this shit over with before she starts getting all clingy and talking "boyfriend material."

His knee bounced nervously on the bar stool as he sipped his beer. He checked his watch for the hundredth time. And then he saw her.

She stood in the doorway, waiting by the hostess station, looking around... for him. He left his unfinished beer on the bar and went to greet her.

Holy fuck she looks amazing. Even in a winter coat she looks damn hot. She makes me want to peel back all those layers and find the soft warm juicy center. Uggghhh... I'm never going to make it through dinner.

He stood behind her, took a deep breath and then tapped her on the shoulder.

"Tiny?" He held his breath as she turned around. Her eyes went wide, and then he saw the mask of control slip into place, her face expressionless.

"YOU?" was all she said.

Shit. She remembers me.

"I owe you an apology for my behavior that day in the store. I was rude and out of line. I absolutely deserved to have my ass handed to me. I have no excuse. I'm really sorry. Please forgive me."

"Is this all some sick control thing, because of that day in the store?" she hissed.

"No, this is me apologizing. I was wrong, and I can admit it. I can also admit that I was crazy impressed with how you handled yourself, although I was too pissed at the time to say so." He chuckled. "Please, Jenna, please let me apologize."

◆ ◆ ◆

Jenna

He wasn't an ogre. He was the fucking hot asshole from the department store. The one I ran into at the charity event. The one I want to grudge fuck. And he's standing right there in my space, his fucking aftershave making me high. OMFG I'm not going to make it through dinner. I'm going to enjoy hurting him though, and making him beg for more.

Max stared at Jenna with a hint of desperation in his eyes, like he thought she would turn and bolt any minute. He didn't know her well enough. Jenna runs from no man. She let him sweat it out for a beat or two before finally nodding her head. Max smiled at her, but she saw the sweat on his forehead, he wasn't as aloof about this as he was letting on.

They got seated near the back, in a quiet section, and picked up their menus.

"So, Max, can you explain to me why you had a 'daughter' a few weeks back, but don't now?" She smiled up at him pleasantly.

To her surprise, he smirked back at her. He'd known to expect this. He was a lawyer, after all. Damn reptiles.

"I could try and bullshit you, but I won't. I like you Jenna, and I want there to be nothing but honesty between us. Can we agree on that?" He stared pointedly into her eyes, and she nodded, meeting his look head on.

"You knew when I told you that it was a lie. I had a girl for the night, we had an arrangement. I waited too long to get her a dress, that's why I was in the store that day. Honestly, I was so unhappy. I was sick of her. We did nothing but argue. I broke up with her Saturday night, during the charity event where I bumped into you."

"Because she demanded a ring?" Jenna asked deadpan. Max's eyes got wide and his brows pulled forward in confusion.

"Yeah... how did you know?" he asked.

"I met her in the ladies room with one of her friends. They were talking shit about their 'Daddies.'" Jenna confided with a slight smirk.

Max closed his eyes and inhaled deeply before opening them again. "Jenna, I'm so sorry for that. I don't-"

"She said you couldn't keep it up. Is that true?" Jenna asked, smirk still in place. She was enjoying watching him squirm.

"Come over here and check for yourself," he offered, his jaw tight. "Jenna, I don't like to talk badly about anyone, but the dynamic between she and I was really toxic. There was no way good sex was ever going to happen between us. I really wish you would make your own determination, and not just take her word for this."

"I might." Jenna smiled. Now maybe he understood how she felt in the department store. Their karma was balanced.

"Oh, really?" It was his turn to look surprised. A small smile spread across his oh-so-kissable lips.

Down, girl!

The waiter showed up and they ordered drinks and an appetizer before Jenna picked up the conversation again.

"Yeah. I would like to understand this whole 'daddy/daughter' thing though...," she said to him. Max groaned and looked away before coming back to her.

"You go right for the balls, don't you?" he said with a laugh.

"Every time," she replied with a smile.

"Uggh... It started as a joke. I used to tease her that she was using me like 'Daddy Warbucks' from 'Annie', and I guess she had some daddy kink. I don't know. I hated it when she called me that. That was one of the things that killed anything between us."

"So how many other girls are you currently seeing?" Jenna asked conversationally, sipping the gin and tonic that had just arrived.

Max just laughed. "You waste no time, do you? Are you sure you're not a lawyer?"

"All mammal." She laughed.

"I'm not seeing anyone right now, Jenna. I was exclusive with Mia, so because we broke up I have no girlfriends now. Just like I told you in the letter. How about you? You haven't told me anything remotely horrifying about your sex life yet. I feel cheated." He chuckled, and she joined him.

"Sorry, I have nothing horrifying to offer. I've been in a drought for the last three years."

"THREE YEARS?" Max coughed and sputtered his drink, looking like his eyes were going to bulge out of his head like a cartoon.

"Yup. Three years. I've got no 'Mommy' stories to share." She giggled. He narrowed his eyes at her, but his smirk was still present.

"Do you want some 'Mommy' Stories?" He laughed.

"Oh, Sweetie, I'm not that kind of 'Mommy.' I'd break you." She laughed back.

◆ ◆ ◆

Max

Dinner was going really well. After Max learned what Mia had been saying behind his back, and he got a chance to tell his side of the story, things progressed... well. Jenna asked a lot of questions, but she never had an air of judgment around her. It was refreshing. It certainly wasn't what Max was used to at all. He was really getting his hopes up that he'd have her under him by the end of the night.

After they had finished their dinner and sat sipping their drinks, Jenna seemed to be pondering something.

"Spit it out," Max encouraged, smirk in place. "I can see you chewing on an idea over there."

Jenna smiled. "What are we doing here, Max. What's your end-game?"

"Right for the balls." He chuckled again. "Damned if I know, Jenna. I'm not a relationship kind of guy, you need to know that. I'm scheduled to death. I can't do family events, I'm lucky if I can manage to live my own life. If you're looking for a Mr. Right that will lead to a wedding and 2.4 kids, I'm not it… That's the honest truth. But if you're looking for Mr. Right Now, I'm your guy."

Jenna waived the waitress over, "Check please."

Max's disappointment was obvious. He was gracious about accepting it though. He took the bill and paid it, and helped Jenna up, leading her back to the door and out of his life, his shoulders slightly slumped.

Maybe he could get her to see him again? Probably not.

"Where's your car?" she asked once they hit the cold air of outdoors.

"Over there." He pointed to a lot. "Do you need a lift?"

"Yeah, I mean, I don't know where you live."

She looked at him confused. He looked back at her, just as confused.

"Max," She looked into his eyes and wrapped her arms around his neck, "do I scare you?"

A smile spread across his face and he wrapped his arms around her. "Umm, no, should I be scared?"

She just smiled slyly. "I seem to recall you saying that if I didn't scare you, you might get drunk and let me take advantage of you."

Max threw his head back and burst out laughing. "I made no promises."

◆ ◆ ◆

Jenna

She had him right where she wanted him.

"Well that's a pity. I was hoping to verify your reptilian origins, but if you're too tired, or too scared of me, I would understand. I'm a lot of woman, not every guy can handle all this." She smirked up at him cheekily.

He smirked right back at her. She had no doubt whatsoever that he saw right through the reverse psychology, and the hunger in his eyes was her answer about where this was leading.

Good. I need a good fuck, and an amazing orgasm.

"At the risk of being forward," he began, and then licked his lower lip, "would you like to come back to my place for coffee?" He brought his face closer to hers and she could feel his breath warming her face against the chill of the night.

"No," she answered.

His smile fell immediately, replaced by a look of shock.

She continued, "But if you want to ask me over for a nightcap, and then fuck me silly, I'm in."

She was rewarded with a million-dollar smile and he brought his mouth down over hers in a searing hot kiss. Within seconds his tongue swept into her mouth, meeting hers, and the kiss grew demanding and heated, tongues dueling. She wanted to ride that tongue. They just stood there making out like horny teenagers clinging to each other on the sidewalk. Before they could get too carried away, or freeze to death, he pulled back and looked at her.

"Well, if that's what you want... I should tell you, it wasn't Dunkin Donuts coffee I was offering though, just so you know."

"Cock before coffee," she said and wrapped her fingers into his as she pulled him toward the lot where his car was. She felt him stiffen immediately, and knew her words had the desired effect.

"Such a dirty mouth, for a mammal." He grinned at her as they walked.

"Life's too short for small talk. I'm going right for the big package." She held his entwined hand up to make a show of examining the size of it.

◆ ◆ ◆

Max

The ride home took far too long. It took all of Max's will-power to keep his hands to himself, he had to be satisfied with rubbing his palm up her thigh. He didn't want to scare her off, not when he was so close to the finish line.

He brought her into his brownstone and took her coat like a gentleman. After putting it in the closet he turned and was slammed into the wall by her body. Although she was a full foot shorter than him, she wrapped her arms around his neck, driving her fingers into his hair, and pulled his face down to hers to attack his mouth with her kiss.

FUCK!

He was hard instantly, his pants unbearably tight. He wrapped one hand in her hair as he returned the kiss and all of its heat, and used the other hand to grab her ass and grind it into his hardness. She moaned as he continued to grind her against him. He felt himself getting close and slowly, begrudgingly, pushed her away. He didn't want it over this quickly.

"I promised you a nightcap," he said deeply, his breath harsh, his eyes half lidded. "What would you like?"

"What would you like to see me drink?" she asked him in her own bedroom voice. He groaned and winced, his cock was already way ahead of him.

Shit, he needed to slow this down.

"I have some good scotch," he suggested, trying to entice her to step away before he lost control and ripped their clothing off. Fucking in the foyer wasn't ideal, but he'd do it.

"Sounds good." She finally stepped away from him, a knowing smirk on her face, as she took in his home. He could see that she looked impressed, but she didn't say anything as he poured drinks and handed her the glass.

He indicated the couch with his hand as he took his first sip, and she gracefully sat down. Seeing her sitting there, sipping her scotch, his mind suddenly went foggy.

Should I sit next to her? Should I keep some distance between us? What would she prefer? Damnit, I feel like a fucking teenager here.

She patted the spot beside her, ending his internal dilemma. He smiled down at her, as he sat, making sure his leg was touching hers. He stretched his arm over the back of the sofa beside her, his eyes never leaving hers.

She turned suddenly, putting her drink down on the side table, and turned to face him. Her hand came up to cup his face, and she was again on his mouth, in his mouth, all hunger and savagery. He shuffled his own glass down quickly, and brought his hands to tangle into her hair roughly, meeting her demands.

Her hands came down and started unbuttoning his shirt. Desire overwhelmed him. He was normally the one who had to instigate anything, it left him feeling slightly on edge, but also highly turned on. She made short work of his buttons, and pulling his shirt out of his pants roughly, she slid it over his arms and off of him, to puddle on the floor.

Mouths still locked, he reached for her waist and slid his hands underneath her blouse, pulling it up quickly. Their faces parted for only a moment, so that he could pull it over her head, and throw it over his shoulder.

Her hands were already on his belt, unfastening it. Then the button was released, and he felt the zipper slide down against his hardness. He moaned loudly into her mouth as her hand brushed over his cock. She pulled her head back from him, kissing down his jaw and neck, her hand gently brushing his cock before taking it firmly in her hand through his briefs.

"Max, do you want me to suck this cock?" she asked against his ear, as she nipped his earlobe. His cock jerked in her hand in answer.

Holy fuck did he love it when she talked dirty! She was going to be the death of him.

"Baby, do I. My cock has been weeping for you for weeks. It's all I can think about, seeing your mouth on my cock, with my hand fisted in your hair."

She slowly slid down his body, kissing her way from his collar bone, nipping his nipple hard. He groaned loudly as she flicked her soft pink tongue over it. But he couldn't wait; he brought his hands up to her ribs and gently pulled her down, down where he needed her so much it hurt. The head of his cock was already pushing out of his briefs, a drop of his pre-cum waiting. He was throbbing with need.

She moved with him willingly, the lace of her bra sending shivers over his abs as she pressed her body firmly down his. He looked down to see her glorious breasts in the black lace, taunting him in the darkened room.

Holy shit! He'd never had a woman he'd just met move on him so quickly. He'd been expecting to have to work her into it slowly, and instead she'd just blown his mind. Should he be worried that she seemed so eager? Should he-

He didn't have time to consider any further though, as she fished his cock out of his briefs. He hissed and threw his head back as her hand circled his girth, now free of his clothing. He groaned out loud. He knew he was big, he didn't expect her to be able to take it all. He was going to have a really hard time holding back and not hurting her. She was making it very difficult to restrain himself.

"Oh, my, Max. You do have an anaconda down there. Soooo big...," She purred as her tiny pink tongue shot out to lick his moisture from the tip. He groaned again, and his hands flew to the back of her head, entangling in her blue hair.

"Blue...," he groaned. "I want to feel your mouth on my cock. Suck me, Baby. I need you."

"So forward, Mr. Thurston," she whispered as her lips kissed the underside of his shaft. Her tongue snaked around the head, and then licked him broadly from base to tip. He groaned again.

"Don't tease me, Blue. Fucking suck my cock. NOW." His eyes clamped shut and he groaned as he felt her hot mouth descend on his cock. He resisted pushing her head down over him, it took all of his willpower. It felt so fucking amazing. He looked down to watch as her head bobbed up and down on his cock, sucking on the upstroke. The sight of her looking at him while she sucked him off nearly had him coming right into her mouth. She fucking knew what she was doing, she was no stranger to a cock.

As his hands grabbed her hair in what must be a painful grip, she adjusted her head back, taking more of him in. With each bob of her head she took more and more, until he felt his cock hit the back of her throat, and her nose was buried in his trimmed pubic hair.

"That's it, Blue, suck my cock. Oh my fucking God you are amazing!" He was groaning and panting, his abs contracting, and a light sheen of sweat was building over his muscles as he watched her take all of him into her throat greedily.

It was too good. It was too much. He tried to pull back, to make it last longer, but she clamped an arm around his thigh, locking him in place. He felt her other hand cupping his balls, and that did it.

He cried out, unable to stop. "FUCK, Blue, I'm gonna come. FUCK!!! AAAAAARRRGHHHH!!!"

His balls started to tighten, there was no stopping it now. He thrust his hips animalistically, pushing his cock deeper down her throat, his hands holding her head firmly in place as he fucked her mouth with force. She groaned around his cock, and he felt his body go rigid. He held her head over his cock as he buried it in her throat. Bliss overcame him as he felt his hot fluid shoot out, filling her throat. He thrust a few more times, feeling himself empty inside of her. He released a long groan as he rode out the orgasm, until he finally came to and realized he had her locked over his cock. She took it all, swallowing him, and running her tongue over him to clean him thoroughly.

He released his hands quickly, letting her move back and breathe. He was still panting.

"I'm sorry, Blue, I hope I wasn't too rough. I lost control. You ok?" He was concerned. He liked it rough, in general, but not a lot of women could take that.

God, I hope I haven't fucked this up already!

He reached under her chin to bring her face up to his, and was shocked by the satisfied smile she wore.

She liked it? Holy shit! She liked it rough! His cock started to harden again. This was like a gift from Heaven!

Chapter 4

Jenna

He was concerned. Did he think he hurt me? That was fucking amazing! If he fucks my pussy half as well as he did my face, I'd die a happy woman. He is hung like a god.

Jenna smiled up at Max, her body language reassuring him that everything was, in fact, spectacular. His cock was already starting to inflate again, and she licked her lips in anticipation. His eyes zeroed in on her mouth as she did, and he quickly pulled at her, trying to get her back up to the couch with him. She let him.

She climbed up on his lap, straddling him, his erection pressed between their bellies. He leaned his mouth down and devoured hers, tasting his own fluids on her tongue. His hands worked behind her to unclasp the bra and pull it forward away from her body, freeing her heavy breasts.

She was self-conscious suddenly. Her breasts were real, no silicone, and they were large. They were no longer perky like her twenty-year old self. Max didn't seem to notice. His hands were on them immediately, kneading and massaging. The pad of his thumb traced small circles over one nipple, sending electric shocks right to her core. She moaned deeply into his mouth.

He pulled his mouth back, diving down to take the nipple into his mouth and suck hard. She screamed and threw her head back as shivers ran through her. She wrapped her arm around his head, locking him over her tender nipple as he nipped and sucked at it. She could feel tremors building between her legs.

She pulled herself back from his mouth. He moved to pursue her nipple, but her arm held him away. He looked up at her with raging desire, his eyes half-lidded with unbridled lust. She gently scooched backward, off of his lap, until she was sitting on the couch facing him. As she did she pulled her skirt up, over her hips and belly, opening her thighs to reveal her naked swollen pussy, already glistening with moisture.

"Let's see if you can give as good as you get, big boy," she said with a purr.

Max's eyes were glued to her pussy, his pupils dilated, his breathing coming out in rough huffs. His mischievous smirk returned as he brought his eyes up to meet hers.

"Why, my dearest Blue, where are your panties? Were you just assuming I was going to take you home and ravish you? That's awfully presumptuous, don't you think?"

"Not assuming, Max. Just hopeful. And a good girl scout is always prepared, right? Now, are you going to eat my pussy or are we making small talk?" She gave him a wicked smirk, as she brought her fingers down to stroke herself, and open her lips so he could watch.

She had shocked him yet again. His eyes were glued to her fingers moving over her clit, and into her wetness. She noticed his cock was standing at full attention, thick and beautiful. She moaned as she moved her hips under her own fingers. It wasn't until she drew her hand out that he moved. He shot his hand forward to grab hers, and then brought her fingers into his mouth to suck them clean, groaning.

With his eyes locked on hers now, he lowered himself between her legs and pushed them wide. He ran kisses up her inner thigh, nipping occasionally, and then running his tongue over the area. Her breaths were coming out in short pants as she watched him. Her need was evident.

"Max, Baby, I need to feel your tongue in my pussy. I'm already wet for you. I want to fuck that tongue, Baby." Her voice was sexy and dark, and Max couldn't resist.

His mouth descended on her mound and she moaned. He ran his tongue through the folds, tasting her, before he brought it up to circle her clit in delicate sweeps. Her hands clamped down on his head, pushing his face into her, as she circled her hips up into his open mouth. She groaned out her satisfaction.

"Yes, Baby, right THERE... Yes! Harder! Harder, Baby! Make me scream!"

◆ ◆ ◆

Max

His reaction was immediate, he launched onto her clit like an animal devouring prey, flicking and sucking hard. She threw her head back and screamed, "YES! YES!" He was fully hard now. She was so fucking erotic.

He slid one finger into her and nearly came again at feeling her wet tightness gripping him back. He groaned into her clit, and then inserted another finger into her. Her hips went wild under his mouth, her nails were digging into his scalp. He continued to stroke his fingers in and out, pressing against her walls, stretching her, preparing her.

"MORE! Harder!" she demanded, her body contracting around her hips as they tried to fuck his mouth and hand from below. He slid a third finger into her, ramming his hand into her harder, sucking her clit. He could feel her muscles tightening around his hand, he knew she wouldn't last much longer, it made his cock ache to fuck her.

"MAX!" she demanded, looking him in the eye, "Give it to me! HARDER! FASTER! Make me come on your mouth! Oh my God it's soooo GOOD!!!"

Her eyes clenched again as he rammed his fingers into her repeatedly, his knuckles hitting her entrance hard. He was worried about bruising her, but the overwhelming sight of her taking him in, sucking and grabbing his hand hard, had him acting on basic primal instinct. He pounded his fingers into her slit again and again, curling his fingers until he found the spot.

She screamed out instantly, her body electrified. He felt the tightening of the rings in her channel as they milked his hand tighter, and tighter, as her pleasure spiraled out of control. He kept up his relentless pace, pounding into her, punching her g-spot with his fingers, and he latched onto her clit with his teeth and sucked hard.

"AAAAAAAAAAAAAAAAAAAAAAAHHHHHHHHHHHHH"
Her body went rigid with an unrestrained scream, her back coming off of the couch, her hips thrust onto his hand and into his mouth, as her pussy squeezed his hand with a death grip. She fell back onto the couch as aftershocks sent her into small convulsions, her pussy still greedily sucking his hand back into her, not wanting to let it go. He continued to stroke her, more gently, as she rode the waves out.

She had a large sated grin on her face, when he finally pulled his cramping fingers out of her tight wet core, and sucked them all clean. Then he brought his mouth back down to her to lick her clean as well, which elicited several more moans and more writhing beneath his mouth.

"So, Blue, you tell me... do I give as good as I get?" He looked up at her with a smile.

"I'm not sure Max, I've forgotten what you got. I may have to start over to be a fair judge," she whispered huskily.

Max laughed and brought himself up to sit beside her on the couch.

"But if we start over, we won't move on to other things," he said to her, kissing the side of her mouth. She turned her head, kissing him deeply, with all of her wetness coating his mouth and chin.

"Yeah, I want to fuck that big cock, more than I want to suck it right now. No being lazy, either, I expect you to fuck me, and fuck me hard. I want that cock hard and fast. I want you to fuck me until I scream, and then fuck me more," she said to him fiercely. His cock leaped. He had never had a woman talk so dirty to him, not someone who wasn't paid to. She was incredible, and she made his balls ache in a way no one ever had.

"Yeah, I'm gonna be balls deep in you, Blue." His hand was stroking himself in preparation, and he noticed her eyes watching him, hungry.

"You like that, Blue? You like watching me? Do you know how many times I have jerked off these last few weeks imagining that pretty mouth sucking me off, or imagining boning you to the mattress until you begged for mercy? Are you ready to take it? Do you think you can handle it?"

Jenna moaned low. Max grabbed her thighs and pulled her flat onto the couch before pulling his pants and briefs all the way off. He went to pull her skirt, which was bunched around her waist, but she slapped his hands away and pulled him down. He brought himself over her on hands and knees, so she could just feel his head at her wet entrance. She moaned again, trying to lift her hips into him for friction.

"No, Blue, not until I say so, Baby." Max reached down into his pants pocket to pull out a condom package. Tearing it open with his teeth he handed it to her.

"Put this on me, Blue."

She dutifully reached between them and rolled it down over his hard length, and then stroked him a few times before he slapped her hands away.

"No, Blue, we do this my way. I want you to take it. I want you to feel my cock fill you. You *will* scream my name."

He leaned down and kissed her fiercely as his hand grabbed the base of his cock and guided it to her wet entrance. He continued to kiss her, as he plucked her nipple with his other hand, and he sank inside of her with a swift jerk.

"AAAAAAAAAAAAHHH!" Jenna froze, her eyes open wide with pain.

"Blue, are you okay?" He stopped, frozen in terror that he had hurt her. He waited for her to answer him, but she only closed her eyes and breathed deeply. "Jenna, do you need me to stop. Talk to me, Baby."

"No." she whispered, as she wiggled her hips slightly, "I just needed a moment to adjust to your damn reptilian anatomy. It HAS been three years for me." Her cheeks were clearly flushed with embarrassment.

Max's cock and his pride swelled a little. "Take your time, Blue, you lead." Damn, he wanted to dominate her, but he would never risk hurting a woman.

◆ ◆ ◆

Jenna

Holy shit he was HUGE. How the hell did he even fit?! It was humiliating!

She looked down to see that he wasn't even all the way in her. *What the fuck?* Slowly she moved her hips, occasionally wiggling a little, until finally she was rocking onto him and moaning. He rocked with her, matching her pace and force. He was a sex god, hitting her in all the right places. She felt full, stretched. The more they rocked, the deeper he slid, until finally she could feel his balls slapping into her body. The pleasure was overwhelming, throwing her mind into a blissful fog. She couldn't think straight. All she knew was her pussy clenched around his massive cock. Euphoria!

She felt his thrusts becoming harder, his breathing more erratic.

"That's it, Max. Fuck me with that cock. Fuck me hard!" She groaned out.

She didn't have to tell him twice. He picked her knees up and threw them over his arms, lifting her hips so her ass was off of the couch, and then he launched into her with a pistoning motion. Hard, Violent, Fast. He was all animal. She wrapped her legs around him, screaming and writhing from the overwhelming sensation of his massive cock slamming inside of her, punching at her g-spot. She couldn't see straight.

He fell down over her, his arms straight, her hips still raised as he slammed his hips into her. It was brutal and violent. His eyes were pure lust. His breathing was ragged, and he was wet with sweat. She could feel him getting harder and harder within her, even as her muscled walls clenched around him, dragging her higher and higher with him.

There was no dirty talk, only groaning and cursing as they flew at each other, fucking for dear life. She looked into his beautiful blue eyes, sweat dripping off of his face and onto her body. Their gaze was locked, intense, as their bodies plunged together. Tighter. Faster. Harder.

Max straightened. "No! No! NOOOO!...AAAAAAAAAAAAAAAAAAAAAARRRGH!"

His body arched rigid, his head thrown back in a primal scream, with his cock slammed deep inside of her. She felt the telltale jerking of his cock, as it unloaded into her, and then she was frozen right along with him, her body clamping down on his cock as wave after wave of pleasure pulled her over the edge, screaming with him. He continued to pump through their orgasms, heaving breaths.

Finally, he collapsed on top of her, with his cock still buried inside of her, and took her face in his hand. He kissed her deeply. Not the hungry frenzied kisses of earlier, but a kiss full of gratitude and wonder. He worshiped her mouth and stroked her cheek with his thumb.

"Not bad for a mammal," he murmured with a small smile.

"I'm pretty sure my mammal just ate your anaconda," she replied with her own smile.

Max threw his head back and laughed, which sent her into aftershocks, as his dick was still deep inside her.

Four hours later Jenna lay sprawled over Max's body on the sofa, completely sated, sore, and tired. They had fucked all over his house, everywhere except in his bed. He was completely naked, she still had her skirt wrapped around her waist and hips, but nothing else on. She smiled contentedly against his chest and listened to his heart beating. She couldn't remember being this happy.

"Why dye your hair blue?" he asked, looking down at her. His fingers stroked her hair gently, tenderly, and he placed a kiss on her forehead.

"Oh... I guess it was just a statement of who I am. I don't fit in with corporate America. I'm not your average woman. I always felt like I didn't belong, so I changed my image to match that. I like the blue, actually." She smiled a small smile as she looked up at him through her lashes.

"It's growing on me," Max admitted. "It's just so unusual. I mean, I see kids do it, but not usually people our age."

"Well, that's because they don't feel free to express who they really are. They are tied to their identities as mothers or wives, coworkers, or friends... I'm free. I identify as free first and foremost."

"Then why don't you dye your bush to match?" he asked her with a smirk.

"Because no one has had a need to see it in a while. You can if you'd like." she shot back, and immediately winced.

There was no guarantee she'd ever see him after this night, she shouldn't assume.

Max simply laughed, apparently not noticing the moment of distress crossing Jenna's face. He leaned down and kissed her tenderly. She cracked an eye open to see that his were closed as he kissed her. He was in the moment, sharing the tenderness. There was no heat, no lust; only caring as he cupped her face gently and worshiped her lips.

This was not what she had expected to happen.

◆ ◆ ◆

Max

Max was aware of pressure on his bladder and moved to try to ease it. A gentle moan made him open his eyes. He had fallen asleep on the sofa with Jenna on top of him, and he suddenly really had to use the bathroom. He very slowly and carefully turned onto his side, so that Jenna would gently fall onto the sofa itself, as he pulled himself out from under her carefully. He didn't want to wake her.

Her blue hair spilled out over the cushion, and he watched as she breathed in evenly and peacefully. He stood to go to the bathroom when he heard her suddenly gasp loudly and then groan. He looked down to see her body trembling, her eyes flickering beneath her closed lids. She made distressed noises like whimpers, and eventually worked up to words as she started to struggle and thrash in her sleep.

"No. No. NO! NOOOO! WILLIAMS! WILLIAMS, GET THEM! WILLIAMS GET UP! NOOOOO! TAKE COVER! WILLI-AAAAAMMMMMSS!"

Jenna startled herself awake, almost falling off of the sofa. Her face was wet with sweat, and her heart was racing. Her eyes were open and wild, scanning the room fearfully. Max slowly lowered himself to the floor beside her as she seemed to realize where she was and what was going on.

"Blue, are you okay? It was just a nightmare. I'm here, Baby." He reached out to hold her, and she jerked away from his hand, her eyes still wild.

"It's okay now, Baby. I'm here. Do you want to talk about it?" he whispered softly.

"N-no. No. I'm good," she said, pulling herself together. "I'm fine, Max. it's ok. Just a nightmare." She gave him a smile that didn't reach her eyes.

"Remember what I said at dinner, nothing but honesty between us, Blue. Are you okay?" His face was serious, but compassionate. He wouldn't force his comfort on her, but he knew damned well she wasn't alright.

Jenna took a deep breath and blew it out. "I will be, Max. Thank you. I just need to get my bearings. Thank you." She reached out and hugged him, but Max could tell it was a little stiff, a little forced.

She wanted him to believe she was okay... maybe she wanted to convince herself too?

"If you say so, Baby. Look, I'm going to run to the bathroom, I'll be right back, alright?" He watched her intently until she looked up at him and nodded, and then he headed down the hall before he embarrassed himself.

He walked back into the living room talking, "Hey why don't we... what are you doing? Blue?"

Jenna was up and dressed, looking for her other shoe.

"Oh, I was just getting ready to go home." She looked embarrassed, and went back to searching.

Anger rose in Max's chest. "You don't have to go, you could just sleep here."

"No...," she answered distractedly, finally finding her missing shoe under the coffee table. "I didn't want for this to be awkward. I know you don't do relationships. I'll just go home, thanks." She retrieved her shoe and staggered a little on one leg as she put it on.

"Were you just going to sneak out without saying goodbye?" There was no hiding the anger in his voice.

"Max," She breathed out, "look, I knew what this was going into it." She looked down sheepishly.

Good. She should be embarrassed. Does she have any idea how cheap this makes me feel, having her sneak out like some whore. I thought we had a connection.

But he didn't say any of those things. His anger burned in his chest.

Clearly it was just sex for her. Or, she was embarrassed because he had caught her in a vulnerable moment after her nightmare. That was still no excuse to behave like a teenager and run off.

Jenna walked over to him and put her hands on his chest. His jaw was tight, and he was trying really hard not to bark at her. He didn't understand why he was so angry with her, but he was.

"Max. It's for the best, I promise." She reached up and kissed his cheek. Suddenly it hit him.

She's leaving! I'll never see her again! NO!

"Will I see you again?" He didn't like the way it came out cracked and needy, but he didn't want to see her walk out of his life.

"Of course, silly. Who else would I let feed my mammal?" She smiled up at him playfully. He tried to grin, but there was still a cold edge of fear in his blood.

"When?" he asked quietly.

She just smiled. "Are you getting clingy on me, Mr. Thurston? Give me the date and time, I'll be there."

He should have felt reassured, but he wasn't. "But not right now?" he bit out.

"No, Baby. I'm all tapped out. I need a shower and some recovery time. We'll talk soon." She turned toward the door.

"I'll drive you." He reached for his pants and threw them on in record time.

"Max, you don't have to-"

"I'LL DRIVE YOU," he bit out, louder. There was no way in hell he was letting her out that door, into the cold, late at night, looking that hot, by herself. He pulled his arms through the sleeves of his shirt, and threw his coat over it without even buttoning.

Jenna said nothing, and just stood and waited until he placed his hand at the small of her back and brought her to the door.

Max sat on his sofa, nursing another glass of scotch. He had dropped her off at her house... Andrew's house. She had told him at dinner that Andrew was her roommate, and he couldn't help the sick feeling he had dropping her off, knowing she lived with another man. Did they share a bed? Were they fuck-buddies? She had said they were just friends, but he remembered the guy looking at her like he KNEW her at the event. His blood boiled at the thought of her rushing home to kiss him, to climb into bed with him, while Max's semen was still running down her thighs.

Had he just been played? No... She wasn't like that. At least, he thought she wasn't.

He had hoped for a wild night of sex, but he had never imagined himself enjoying her company so much. She was smart, sexy... dirty even. He hadn't expected that. He loved talking to her. She wasn't whiney or clingy, she didn't expect money or gifts; in fact, other than sex, she hadn't asked him for anything. She'd offered to pay the check at dinner. She seemed to accept him for who he was; even liked him for who he was. He wasn't ready to let her go.

If she thought he was going to bang her and ghost her, she had another thing coming. He was just getting started.

Chapter 5

Jenna

Jenna rushed around the house, grabbing her keys while trying to get her earrings in. She had to leave soon, or she'd be late for church. As she ran out the door to Andrew's car, she wondered if the church would burst into flames when she entered, considering the sinful activities she had participated in the night before. Not really, she didn't believe in sin, but it amused her.

She drove out of the neighborhood, and made her way to the Spiritualist Church she attended every Sunday. She couldn't help the goofy grin that spread across her face every time she thought of Max.

Max, with his face between her thighs... Max hovering over her as he pounded her hard... Max hammering into her from behind. His cock was like a drug. He had made her so happy.

As she pulled into a parking spot, the reality of the situation started to sink in around the edges, muting the joyful high she was experiencing.

Enjoy it for what it was. He got what he wanted, he's not going to call you. Don't get your hopes up.

But he'd asked to see her again. He'd seemed really upset that she was leaving, which confused the hell out of her. She'd rather leave of her own free will, then face the prospect of him hinting that it was time for her to go. She was sure he would have kicked her to the curb soon after he came back in the room. And she wasn't going to sleep on his sofa, knowing that he was all hard and adorable in his bedroom a few doors away, only to face the walk of shame the next morning, either. Better that she left on her terms, her dignity intact.

As she walked up the steps her phone beeped in her purse. She pulled it out quickly to silence it before the service and saw a message from him.

"Max: I hope you slept well. I can't say I did. I had a cold anaconda on my hands all night. Do you have any idea how hard it is to get any sleep with an unhappy anaconda? It's pretty serious."

Jenna smiled wide.

"Blue: Oh, my poor reptile! I can see how serious that is. He's so big, if he gets a cold it might be fatal. You might need to warm him up."

A response popped up immediately.

"Max: I tried, Blue. I did. No amount of friction seems to work. Maybe if you talk to him?"

Jenna burst out laughing. A couple passing her on their way into the church stopped to stare, but then resumed their walk.

"Blue: I guess I can try. Look, I'm doing something now; can I get back to you later?"

"Max: Of course, I just hope he can hang on that long. It's really sad, seeing him like this."

"Blue: I'll get back to you. Xoxo"

She turned her phone off and headed into the service.

The service had been great. Andrew had introduced her to this church, and it was like finding home. She was not religious, not by a long shot, but this church was... different: unconventional, like her. They taught that everyone is responsible for their own spirituality; that you don't have to go through a priest, a rabbi, or a minister to talk to God. And a part of their service is messages from loved ones who have passed, as the ministers are also mediums.

She had never bought into any of that psychic crap. But at her first service, she had gotten a message from one of her friends in her squad, one of the women she saw blown to bits. There was no way the medium could have been faking it: she gave Jenna evidence that only Jenna and her friend knew. She had wanted to believe it was fake, she had wanted to deny it could be real, but in her heart she *felt* it. She knew Brady was in a better place, and that was really the beginning of her finding peace.

Every Sunday after church she volunteered. Jenna dipped her brush into the paint and then wiped just the tiniest bit off to give it an edge. She was painting a mural over the altar for them: an Omnist symbol, with a Tree of Life, surrounded by many different religious symbols. She found peace at the church. There was no judgment, and all views were welcome. It was her sanctuary. It also let her express her artistic side.

It was late before Jenna got home. Her back was aching from reaching up to paint and climbing the ladder. She was going to have to face the reality that she wasn't a spring chicken anymore. Andrew saw her dragging herself in, and diverted her right onto the massage table, where he spent the next two hours working on her back muscles. She was out cold for the night.

◆ ◆ ◆

Max

It was eleven at night, Sunday. Jenna hadn't called all day, like she said she would. He had texted her twice, but had gotten no reply. Disappointment swirled in his gut.

Should he text her again? No. He didn't want to seem desperate. Was she trying to lose him? Had he read it wrong? Why was she ghosting him? She seemed so distant when she had answered, before she disappeared.

He wasn't a clingy kind of guy. Not at all. Usually he was the one making a hasty exit. But he really liked her. He had somehow gotten his hopes up that there could be something with her... and then she started playing stupid games with him; first trying to sneak out, then not calling. A part of him was really offended. Another part of him thought of all of the women he had used for sex, promising to call, and then ghosting them. Was this his Karma?

Was she really just not into him, and too polite to say so? What the fuck was he supposed to do now? He sipped his scotch and scowled out the window into the night sky.

Monday morning found him in his office; he hadn't worked on any files over the weekend, so he was up to his eyeballs in paperwork and calls. At one o'clock he took a break to grab something to eat, grabbing his cell phone he saw that he had a missed message.

"Blue: I am sooo sorry I didn't get back to you. I was at church when you messaged, then I volunteered, and hurt my back, so I got a massage when I got home. That knocked me out. How's the anaconda?"

Max saw red. She hurt herself, so she got a *massage...* at home... with Andrew. The thought of Andrews hands stroking her oiled body sent a rage through him. He wanted to fucking kill that man.

And then she just fell asleep, while he sat like a moron waiting for her to message all night? She couldn't even message to say she was alright.

He didn't need this kind of drama. He put his phone back in his pocket, so he wouldn't say anything he regretted later, and went to get a sandwich.

The afternoon was just as hectic. The office was short-staffed, due to the holiday season, and paperwork was piling up. He had to go over three cases that were going to court the following week; when he finally put them down it was nine o'clock at night. He had a headache from sitting over the desk and computer all day, and his energy lagged. He hadn't gotten enough sleep the night before.

He made his way home, had a quick bite to eat, had a quick shower, and then headed to bed. He paused briefly before turning out the light, and considered sending Jenna a message, but decided he was just too tired for drama. He didn't want an argument when he needed a good night's sleep. He'd message her later.

◆ ◆ ◆

Jenna

It was Wednesday morning, and the morning rush was dying down. Jenna wiped down tables. Her heart was sad.

He must have been mad I didn't get right back to him, but fuck, I was hurting. He's got to understand I have a life. I can't be at his beck and call, especially when he's the one who said he "doesn't do relationships." I can't deal with "needy" right now. If he's going to be petty like that, then it's better he moves along.

She scrubbed the table angrily with the rag, a deep frown on her face, as if she could clean him out of her mind and heart. She didn't want it to hurt that he hadn't returned her messages over the last three days. She didn't want to admit that she really liked him, or that she really wanted to see him again. She didn't want to admit that he did things to her body no one else had ever been able to do. Because what she really wanted didn't matter. It appeared to be over before it started.

And it hurt.

As she rounded the corner to get more cleaning spray Lou tapped her on the shoulder. She turned to see Max standing in front of the register, his hands in his pockets. Her heart immediately lit up, right before she clamped that motherfucker down hard. She wasn't getting her hopes up for a moody bitch.

"Hey," she said. It was warm and hopeful, but wary.

"Hey yourself," he answered with a warm smile. "I was hoping I could take you to lunch today."

"Oh... well, I...," she started to say, before Lou cut her off. "Her lunch break is at noon."

Max smiled his panty-melting smile and nodded to Lou before turning back to Jenna.

"See you then, Blue?"

"Yeah," she answered weakly. What was she supposed to do, make a scene at work? She did want to see him again, but she wanted to clear the air before they went any further also.

It was noon before she knew it, and Max was walking back into the shop. She took off her apron and headed for the door with her coat and purse in hand. Max opened the door for her and they headed down the street.

"What do you want for lunch?" he asked, his lips tipping into a small smile.

"If I'm honest, you," she answered deadpan, and kept walking. He jerked to a stop, and then scrambled to catch up with her as the shock wore off.

"That can be arranged, Sweetheart," he purred into her ear.

"Not if we're not talking it can't," she said, bringing her eyes to his for the first time. She didn't say it with a snarky tone, it was more matter-of-fact. "What's going on, Max? Why are we not talking?"

Max stopped and pulled her into his arms. She resisted at first, but slowly warmed and melted into his embrace, hugging him back. It just felt right being held by Max Thurston.

"I didn't hear from you on Sunday. I got worried. Then I got mad. Then I heard that you had a massage, probably with Andrew I'm guessing. Then you went to sleep. I sat up late waiting, like a moron, getting more and more angry and jealous.

"When I went to work Monday, all hell was breaking loose. I've been working twelve hour days, and falling into bed at night. I had court this morning, which is why I'm in this neighborhood, and I realized what a shit I was being.

"I can't very well be clingy and needy about you, when my schedule is like this too... So I'm sorry. I don't want to play games, Blue. I don't want drama. I want to see you again. I enjoy your company. That's what's going on with me. What about you?"

Jenna stood, stunned into silence. She had never met a man who could articulate what he thought and felt so succinctly. She was impressed, and felt a little unprepared, as she only just got the inside scoop.

"Well... I... Wow. I am impressed you can just come out and say that.

"I am truly sorry that I didn't get back in touch with you Sunday, Max. Please believe that. I was hurting pretty bad. I normally refuse to let Andrew massage me, but I was pretty desperate. Once he worked me over, I was done. It wasn't my intention to ignore you. The pain takes a lot out of me.

"I didn't know what was going on with you after that. I'd like to say that it didn't bother me that I didn't hear from you, but I'd be lying. That's not to say that I don't understand, now that you've told me what's going on; but yeah, I enjoy your company too. I missed you.

"No games, Max. No bullshit. Promise me that if you're upset, or jealous, or just sick of me that you'll just tell me. Promise you won't ghost me, or punish me by withholding communication. I don't deal well with that. I will do the same for you."

She craned her head back to look up at him.

"Promise," he said, before bending down to cover her mouth with a kiss that made her toes curl.

"So what do you really want for lunch?" he asked as he held her in a tight hug.

"Anaconda." She smirked.

◆ ◆ ◆

Max

Max grabbed her hips in his hands and rocked them back over his cock, repeatedly. Jenna was on her hands and knees with her chest on the floor and her ass in the air. Max was slamming into her hard, the wet sloppy sounds of his cock pulling out and crashing back echoed through his living room. Jenna was groaning deep and long, and clawing at the carpet like an uncontrollable animal.

"Give it to me, Max! Fuck me HARD!" she demanded over her shoulder. He slammed his hips into hers, driving his cock even deeper, and felt his balls slamming against the backs of her thighs.

"So fucking tight! Goddamn, you have the perfect pussy!" Max groaned loudly.

She wailed and pushed her ass back against him.

"Harder... OH GOD!" A long keening groan rose from her chest, growing in volume, until it became a scream of release as her pussy clamped down tight around Max's cock. The milking sensation of the muscular rings grabbing his cock and sucking it into her body pulled him over the edge with her. With one final thrust forcing his cock deep inside her, his back stiffened as his balls constricted, his cock jerking inside of her. Her muscles sucked him dry as he spilled in her, emptying himself. He pumped her through their release, groaning softly, before collapsing on top of her, breathless.

Holy fuck she was hot. She was, hands down, the best sex he had ever had. He was never going to let her go.

He kissed her neck tenderly, while his hand stroked the cheek of her ass underneath him. She turned her head to the side and took his mouth with hers. It was their tender 'after fucking' kiss, sweet and reverent. He slowly pulled out of her, missing her snug walls instantly, and pulled the condom off to dispose of it. Then his hand went back to massaging her ass cheek.

As they kissed, he ran his hands over her ass, down her sides, and up her lower back; until his fingers felt a thick line of flesh running across her lower spine. Raising his head he looked down to see a web of deep scar tissue across and around her lower back.

"Blue, what happened here?" he asked.

She immediately stiffened underneath him, and her hands flew to her skirt to cover the scars. "Surgery," she said curtly, staring at the wall, her face devoid of emotion.

"Blue... What's going on here? Why are you upset?" He continued to rub his hands over her body, over the skirt where she had covered herself. "I don't care if you have scars, Baby, I love your body."

Jenna's eyes flicked to his for a second, uncertainty in them, before she closed them. He thought she wasn't going to say anymore.

"I was in the army, over in Afghanistan. The humvee we were in hit an IED. They had to put my lower spine back together as best they could. I spent two years in rehab after that. It's really hard to talk about."

Max circled his hands around her and pulled her close, but she still seemed closed off.

"Max, I don't want your damn pity." She breathed out.

"Good, because you won't get it. This is my admiration. You went through a traumatic, fucked up situation, and you're still able to be here with me now. To be incredible. I don't know that I would have been able to get through that as well as you did. Can I kiss your scars?"

Max could see the moisture gathering at her closed eyelashes, as she nodded. He swept his mouth down her back, moving her clothing off of her. He kissed and licked over her scars lovingly, holding his hands around both of her sides.

"Blue, you amaze me." He breathed against her back, and she seemed to relax and settle.

They spent a few more minutes there, just enjoying the comfort, before Max's alarm went off.

"Uuugggh, Baby, I have to go back to the office. Do you need me to drop you back at work?" he groaned.

"No," she mumbled sleepily, "I have the rest of the day off. I opened today." Her eyelids were still closed, and she looked close to sleeping right there on the floor.

Max groaned again, imagining just staying here with her, but his caseload wouldn't allow for it.

"Blue, you can stay here and sleep if you want, Baby," he said quietly, but her soft breathing told him she was already asleep. He chuckled to himself. She was damned adorable sprawled out on his rug, naked.

He gently and carefully rolled her onto her back, and then lifted her to take her to his bedroom. As he did, he noticed more scar tissue on her lower abdomen. His heart broke for her. He wondered if that was what her nightmare had been about. How did he not know she was in the military? Now he had a whole new topic of conversation with her. She was blowing his mind more and more every day.

He tucked her into his king sized bed, and left a note and a bottle of water on the bedside table for her. The note told her he would be home after work, and to call him if she needed anything. Then he kissed her on the forehead and padded quietly out of the room.

As he got to his front door the realization hit him: Jenna was the first woman to ever sleep in his bedroom. He'd fucked a lot of women there, but he'd never allowed any of them to sleep there. He wasn't sure how he felt about that, but he didn't have time to consider it. Work called.

Max sprinted out of the office at five thirty. He wasn't even sure if Jenna was still at his place, but he was hoping she was. His week had been very stressful, and the teaser he had gotten at lunch was nowhere near enough to undo all the stress his body was feeling. Only hours of having his cock sunk into Jenna seemed to do the trick.

He unlocked his front door, and put his keys in the bowl on the small table. He hung his coat, and slid his suit coat off as he walked through the house.

"Blue!" he called as he hunted for her. The kitchen smelled amazing, and he could see pots going, and his oven was on. It was a good guess that she was still there! His heart beat harder. He hung his suit jacket over a chair and pulled his tie loose, before unbuttoning several of his shirt buttons.

"Blue!" he called again, but there was no answer. He could faintly hear noise at the other end of the house. He climbed the stairs toward his bedroom, and he could hear muffled music. He walked through his bedroom, and the music was louder. The bathroom door was half open, and inside he could see Jenna, wrapped in a towel, dancing around to music she was playing on her cell phone while she lip-synced in time.

Her hips swayed seductively, her ass barely covered by the towel. Max's cock sprang to life with approval, as he watched her shaking her ass and grinding mid-air to the rhythm. She froze suddenly, catching his reflection in the mirror and screaming. She jumped and turned like a cat, her hands over her heart, and the towel spooled down around her and puddled at her feet on the floor. Her face flamed red hot, as she scrambled to pick it up.

"I don't remember giving you permission to use my towels," Max said, stepping in to snag the towel out of her hands quickly with a smile. She instantly covered her breasts and groin with her hands, squealing.

"Uh, uh, uh... My little wildcat. I love every inch of this body. You will not hide it from me, not ever. I would be a happy man if you would strut around here naked all day for my eyes alone."

He stepped closer to her, bringing her into a hug, and running his hands up and down her back and ass. He bent over to kiss her deeply, to let her know how she affected him. Well, the hard bulge in his pants helped. He pulled her ass so that her crotch was pulled tight against his hard desire.

"How are you feeling my sexy wildcat?" he whispered against her ear.

"Hungry." She panted. Her lips searching out his chest, nipping and licking as she went. "It's not fair that I am so on display, and you are still hiding in your clothes." She pointed out.

"Hiding? Is that what you think? Well, then, please take them off of me. I would love nothing more than to meet you in your nakedness," he spoke into her hair, his hands riding up the center line of her ass, making her squeeze her thighs together.

She didn't waste a moment, ripping his shirt off of him violently. She unbuckled his pants, unbuttoned them and unzipped them in record time. She shoved them down with his briefs so that he stood nude before her, his cock hanging heavily between his legs, hard.

Before he could say another word she dropped to her knees and was on his cock with her mouth sucking and pulling. His head fell back with a loud groan, his hands fisting in her hair.

"Holy fuck, Blue!" His breathing was instantly ragged.

She worked his base with her hand, pumping him hard as she sucked him in, hollowing her cheeks.

"Damn, Baby... That's soooo goood.... Aaaaaaahh... I love the way you take my cock." He brought his head down to watch her, to see his cock disappear into her tight mouth as she took him all in. As always, just seeing her sucking him off was enough to make him blow. He groaned loudly.

She adjusted her angle so that she could take him further into her throat, slamming her face into him over and over, fucking his cock with her mouth almost violently. Max held on to his self control. He couldn't watch her, or it would be over. He was hanging by a thread.

"That's it baby, suck my cock! Take it down your throat! That's my dirty girl! Do you want me to come down your throat, Baby? Do you want to drink me down?"

She moaned loudly around his cock, and it undid him. His hands grabbed at her hair as his hips flexed into her face hard. There was no thought. Only her soft hot mouth vibrating around his hard cock, the head punching the back of her throat over and over as he pistoned it into her.

"Fuck... Blue... Fuck! FUCK! AAAAARGHHHH!" He roared his release, his cock lodged deep in her throat, spilling into her. His hips jerked and he pumped in and out a few more times until he was emptied. He was heaving breaths like he'd run a marathon, his whole body spent. He smiled wide and looked down at his precious Blue to see tears in the corners of her eyes.

He dropped to the floor instantly, cradling her face in his hands.

"What? Blue, did I hurt you?" He felt like a dick instantly.

"No, Baby, just the gag reflex. I'm fine," she assured him. He wasn't convinced. He looked her over, trying to find where she could be hurting, waiting for her to admit that he had done the unthinkable.

"Babe... I love it when you lose control. Please don't ever stop doing that. I want it. I want all of it. I want you to fuck me like you hate me, and fuck me like you love me. I want you to fuck me with everything that you have, until there's nothing left, and then I want you to fuck me again. Promise me you'll never hold back." She leaned into him and ravaged his mouth with hers. His erection was already standing at attention.

Damn. I think I just fell in love with this woman.

Chapter 6

Jenna

Max had his head between Jenna's legs as she was perched on his bathroom vanity with her knees over his shoulders. He rammed three fingers into her soft wet pussy, stretching her, hitting her g-spot with precision. His lips took her clit in, sucking and nipping while she wailed and screamed, her hands buried in his hair. She was a wildcat.

Her hips bucked to ride his hand as he pounded her harder and harder. She dug her nails into his scalp, chasing her release.

"Oh my fucking GOD Max! Just like that! YES! YES! Harder! Give it to me!" Her eyes were clenched in bliss.

She had always been a very sexual creature. She loved sex. She saw nothing wrong or shameful about it. But Max seemed to bring out her inner nympho. She couldn't get enough of him. She would love a day of nothing but riding his cock until she couldn't walk again. It was amazing.

And when he ate her pussy, HOLY SHIT! This man clearly knew his way around a pussy! There was no awkward fumbling, no misguided fiddling. The man played her like an instrument, and she roared.

It was only minutes before he had her screaming, her body convulsing over his fingers.

"MAX!   OH   GOD,   MAX!!!   MAX!!!! AAAAAAAAAAAAAAAAAGGGHHH!" Her body convulsed, her mind lost in a fog of sexual euphoria. Max had to hold her hips to keep her from careening off of the vanity. When he finally withdrew his hand from within her, he licked it clean, and then leaned back down to lick her from bottom to top, sending her into another screaming round of orgasms.

She couldn't get enough of him. She could never let him go. No one had ever made her body respond the way he did. When he stood up, she was boneless, a huge grin on her face.

"I told you I'd make you scream my name," he whispered proudly.

"Did I? I don't remember that. You may need to refresh my memory," she panted.

He was about to retort when her phone alarm rang out.

"OH!" She looked up at him with big eyes. "Dinner's ready!" She hopped off of the vanity in front of him and sped into the bedroom before he could grab her.

He found her in the bedroom, pulling on a pair of his sweat-pants, with one of his t-shirts already on. He snaked his arm around her waist and pulled her into him.

"I have what I want for dinner." He nibbled on her neck. She giggled against him before pulling away.

"No, Max. I have cooked you real food. I need you to eat. You're going to need your strength." She smiled at him slyly, and his cock jumped. She reached out her hand, grabbing his cock, and pulled him down the hallway toward the kitchen. He grabbed a towel out of the linen closet on his way by.

Once in the kitchen she pulled a roast out of the oven and turned off the pots on the stove. She shuffled and strained, she sliced and organized. Max wrapped the towel around his waist and sat and watched her with awed look.

She was so natural, so in her element. She felt perfectly at home in his kitchen... and his living room... and his bedroom...

and his bathroom... a niggling feeling started to rise in her belly. A feeling like maybe she was making herself a little too comfortable... maybe overstepping her welcome. She shot a look to Max, but he was sitting watching her like she was a goddess.

"Plates?" she asked.

Max got up and opened a cabinet, pulling out plates. Then he went to a drawer and pulled out silverware. He set the table while she put everything together, and then brought it over to him.

Rule number one: if you expect a man to fuck you all night, you'd better feed him well.

◆ ◆ ◆

Max

I can't believe my fucking life. Holy shit.

Max watched Jenna bring bowl after bowl to the table. There was a roast, and vegetables, homemade bread, and salad. He was a bachelor. He was used to eating out, or living on protein shakes. It was too time consuming to cook. He had a housekeeper a few days a week, and she would sometimes cook, but other than that, it was rare to get a home cooked meal.

What had he done to win the lottery and have this hot wildcat in his home?

Jenna sat across from him, and he served her a plate before taking his own. She seemed pretty preoccupied staring at his bare chest, and he tried not to preen with pride.

His Blue liked his body. Well, it was hers to do with as she wished. He would make sure that she got to work it over later, after dinner.

They ate and chatted, laughing and teasing. He loved to hear her laugh. And she was so damned smart, she kept him on his toes. He didn't know what he was feeling, but he knew he wanted her. He wanted all of her. For himself.

"Let me ask you something, Blue," he said, pointing with his fork. She looked up to meet his eyes.

"How do you feel about being exclusive?" he asked, popping a green bean into his mouth.

"Exclusive?... How do you mean? Like not sleeping with anyone else... or not dating anyone else at all?"

She always answered in a way that didn't seem judgmental; she just seemed to be collecting facts and trying to put things together. He liked that about her. No drama.

"Exclusive like both: no dating or sleeping with anyone except each other. How would you feel about that?"

He chewed his food, and watched for her reaction. She chewed, and seemed to consider for a moment, before taking a sip of wine.

"Well... I feel confused to be honest. You said you weren't into relationships, so I didn't think we were dating. I thought this was just fucking for you. So I guess I would have to ask, if we became exclusive, would that mean that we *are* dating, and not just fucking?" Again, no judgment in her tone whatsoever.

"Let's say that if we were exclusive, we would be considered dating, and we would be agreeing not to date or fuck anyone else. How would you feel about that?" Concern was growing in his belly. What if she said no? What could he do about it? But the thought of anyone else touching her made him crazy.

"Well, if you put it like that..."

She seemed to consider for another moment. "We've only known each other for a very short time. I would be concerned that you hadn't thought this all the way through. I say that because I don't want to start dating you, exclusively, only for you to become bored a month from now and drop me."

"But who's to say that if I was dating someone else at the same time as you, that I couldn't become bored with you anyway? Not that there's much likelihood of that." He challenged back.

"True enough," she answered.

"Let me ask you this, seeing as we have only known each other for a short time, would you be ok with it if I was fucking someone else right now also?" His tone was casual, curious.

"I shouldn't have a say in the matter, as I have no rights to you, but truthfully, if I found the bitch I'd probably take her head off," she answered matter-of-factly.

"So that's a no." He chuckled. "So, Blue, I'll just ask you outright: would you like to date me exclusively? No other woman would lay a hand on me, and I would expect that you would not engage in sexual activity with anyone else either."

"Just to be clear, that would mean that we are no longer just fucking, but dating, correct?" she specified.

"Correct." He winked at her.

"Hmmm... What requirements would you have of me, if we were dating, and not just fucking? I need to know what I'm getting into." She put another piece of potato into her mouth and chewed.

Max wiped his mouth on his napkin. "Well, to begin with, we would need to get together on a regular basis, or as regular as it can be considering our schedules. We may even consider sleep overs, to make the transition time easier. Scratch that, we would definitely need sleep overs. We would get out and do things: dinner, movies, dancing. I don't know about you, but I would also like your company sometimes when I have to attend events, I'd like to introduce you to my friends and colleagues, and I'm open to meeting yours. And of course, since neither of us will be getting any from anyone else, we will probably need to have loads of sex. Then there is maintaining our animals... I would expect you to look after my reptile, and I would, of course, spoil your little mammal." He smiled at her politely.

"Hmmm... okay... I understand all that. What I'm not hearing is housekeeping, cooking, laundry, shopping... what are the expectations there?"

Max laughed out loud.

"I have a housekeeper a few days a week, anything else I can take care of for myself and you can do likewise for yourself. I don't need staff, Blue, I want to date you. I want you to be mine and mine alone. I need that."

"What changed?" she asked. "You started out telling me that you didn't want a relationship... but it sounds an awful lot like what you're asking for now."

He sat quietly for a moment.

"I don't know what changed, to be honest. I have never wanted a relationship before, I never had the time nor energy for one. But when I'm with you, I find myself wondering if we could have one. You are the only woman I have ever met who's made me want more.

"I don't want to be needy or clingy, but I can't stomach the thought of you with someone else. You bring out a primal side of me, a side that wants to dominate you, own you, keep you all to myself. I know I can't do that, not realistically, but I can ask you to keep it between us, that is, if you feel the same?" He raised an eyebrow, hoping that she didn't see the nervous vulnerability behind his calm bravado.

"Max, if I saw another woman lay a hand on your cock I'd break it for her. The hand, not your cock. I get it. You make me weak in the knees, you make me wanton in a way I haven't felt in a long time. I can't have you sharing that cock with anyone else, it would destroy me. I'd have to kill her, and I'd wind up in prison.

"And I like the way you dominate me. I have never met a man who I would allow to do that before, I've always been in charge and in control. I find with you, I don't worry about it so much. I like it. I love the way you take me, and claim me. You're assertive without smothering me.

"I don't know that anyone will ever really own me. That's something that I'm just not willing to give up. But I think I can handle dating.

"Full disclosure: I should probably warn you that I'm a little bit fucked up, if you haven't already noticed. I have PTSD. I have night terrors. I can be violent, although I haven't been in a long time. I am very protective, and I guard my personal life. I don't usually want a relationship because it means too many questions, too much drama, and giving too much of myself away. I'm being honest now, you need to know this going in. I'm not easy to be with."

Max stared at her. She was incredibly easy to be with. She was the most comfortable woman he had ever spent time with. How could she think that she was difficult?

"Are you going to boil my anaconda?" he asked, deadpan.

"No, but I might gargle with him," she answered, equally deadpan.

"Very well, I accept your terms of engagement, if you will accept mine. Can we consider ourselves exclusive, hereafter?" he asked as he raised his wine glass in a toast.

"Exclusive, hereafter," she repeated.

◆ ◆ ◆

Jenna

"Jenna: Hey, Drew, I just wanted to let you know I'm spending the night at Max's. I'll be home tomorrow after work. I need to catch you up."

"Andrew: You mean Max Cox? The guy who ghosted you for three days? I'm sure there's a story here. As long as you're ok Baby-girl. Call me if you need me."

Jenna smiled at his text. She loved that Andrew understood and respected her. He was family to her.

"You ready?" Jenna heard him ask. She turned to see Max grabbing her coat out of the closet, as she slipped her phone into her purse.

"Born ready!" she answered with a smile.

They had dinner at a trendy restaurant downtown, and then Max took her to a store for "essentials". He insisted she should have toiletries at his house as well as Andrew's, to make sleep overs easier. She giggled as he scoured the shelves for a toothbrush, toothpaste, and other necessities for her. It warmed her heart that he really wanted her in his space, something he had warned her he would never want. Hell, it was something she had never wanted either... actually, it was just something she hadn't wanted for a really long time.

They swung by Andrew's house so that she could grab a few changes of clothing, and her makeup, and were back at Max's a few hours later. Jenna smiled as Max seemed to delight in putting all of her items away in the bathroom, her toothbrush proudly displayed beside his. He put her haircare items in the shower, and put the rest of her bottles in the medicine cabinet. He also cleared some space for her in his massive closet to hang her clothing.

As he puttered with putting things away she strolled around the house. It was incredible to her: hardwood floors, decorative dark wainscotting, and embellished molding everywhere. There were marble fireplaces in the living room and master bedroom. There was a crystal chandelier in both the front entryway and the dining room. It screamed old world wealth. The kitchen was the only room done completely over; it boasted the most modern and best appliances, a chef's stove, and granite countertops. The house was decorated tastefully, but with an unmistakable masculine air. It definitely fit Max.

She felt an arm snake around her waist as she stood pondering, and smiled up at Max as he pulled her body into his. She could feel his erection pressing into the small of her back.

"I have one more thing to give you," he whispered into her hair.

"Well then," she whispered breathily, "you'd better give it to me."

Her eyes matched the hunger in his. He wrapped his fingers in hers and led her silently up the stairs and into his master bedroom. He pulled her directly to the king sized four-poster bed and sat her down on the thick velvety comforter in shades of navy and gray, matching the rest of the room.

"You have to be naked to get this gift." He purred suggestively.

"If I've already had it, it doesn't count as a new gift." She smirked up at him, but stripped off her sweater, bra, and pants anyway.

He unbuttoned, and pulled his shirt off, still standing in front of her.

"Take it out," he told her.

She didn't have to ask what "it" was. She reached forward eagerly and made a show of slowly unbuckling his belt, pulling it through the loops and letting it clang to the floor. Then she unbuttoned his pants, and slowly unzipped them, keeping pressure on his hard erection beneath as she did. Max hissed his approval.

Once his pants fell to the floor, she slowly inched his briefs down. His cock sprang free in her face, and tied around it was a red ribbon. She laughed up at him.

"You can't gift wrap it after I've already had it." She smirked up at him through her eyelashes.

"You haven't. I guarantee." He smiled back down at her.

As her hand went to stroke him, she felt something cold and metal brush against her hand. Looking down, she saw a key dangling from the bottom of the ribbon, under his massive cock. Her eyes opened wide in shock and she looked up at him.

"Now you have your own key, Blue. You can let yourself in if I'm not here. I'll give you a code for the alarm system too. I want you here, in my bed, as often as I can get you, whether I'm fucking you, or not." The look in his eyes was tender, and he reached down to stroke her face.

"M-Max... are you asking me to move in with you?" she asked. There was no inflection, no indication as to what she thought about that.

"Blue, I'm giving you access. We're exclusive, and I want you with me. Let's just see where it leads. I don't want to rush this. Let's not label it. How does that sound to you?"

Jenna could see his inner dialog all over his face. She could tell this was hard for him; he wasn't used to intimacy with women, but he also wanted intimacy with her. Truth be told, she felt it was way too early to consider moving in with him, but she did like the idea of having easy access to him. This was a nice starting point; she would keep her stuff at Andrew's, and stay here if she wanted. If things got to be too much, she could just go home. She liked that. No pressure!

"That sounds perfect!" She smiled up at him. "Now, I'm going to swallow your cock."

Chapter 7

Jenna

"So then what happened?" Andrew asked, hanging on her every word.

"Then I gave him the best blowjob of his entire life, and we had sex like animals for hours. Then we slept for a few hours before we both had to go to work. I couldn't even get out the door without him eating me out like a starving man, though; my nether regions tingled all day at work!" Jenna laughed.

"I'm telling you, Drew, he's just as much of a sex maniac as I am! I don't know if I'm going to be able to handle it!"

"And you're okay with being exclusive?" he asked as he took another bite of pasta. He had surprised her with dinner when she got home from work, dying to hear about her sexcapades with Max. She shared everything with him.

"Yeah, I mean... I guess. It's not something I was looking for, you know. But at the same time, holy fuck. He's hot, and he's so sweet. And he makes me want to fuck him like a filthy whore." She laughed again.

"So is this just your pussy speaking, or is this your conscious decision, to be exclusive?" He looked at her pointedly. Andrew wasn't judging her or criticizing her, she knew he was looking out for her, the way they did for each other.

"I made the conscious decision to do this, Andrew. I could have said no, and kept fucking him. But I don't want that dick in anyone else. He's mine," she stated possessively, taking another sip of her wine.

"Surprisingly, I'm ok with it. Despite how we met." She grimaced, and he laughed. "He's been nothing but good to me. And we have a pact of honesty. If it goes South, we discuss it, we don't just run." She looked away as she said it.

Andrew knew about her abandonment issues, he knew she had lost people she cared about, and that she wasn't really over it. And like a good friend, he accepted it and didn't make a big deal out of it.

"As long as you're happy, Baby-Girl." He smiled at her as he gathered the dishes. "You have tomorrow off, yeah?" he asked.

Jenna nodded.

"Well then why don't you head over there now and fuck him raw? At least one of us should be getting some." He smirked.

"Oh, no... Tony?...," Jenna's eyes mirrored the disappointment she saw as she looked at Andrew's sad face.

"He doesn't deserve this cock," Andrew answered flatly. "It's ok, though, I have a date tomorrow night with an underwear model. He may be worthy." Andrew smirked slyly.

"You know what they say...," Jenna said loudly, "The best way to get over a guy..."

"Is to get under another one." They both finished in unison, laughing.

◆ ◆ ◆

Max

Max dropped his keys in the bowl beside the door and hung his coat up. It had been a long day in the office. It was always a tough time of year, Thanksgiving was next week, and with Christmas just a few weeks away; work was piling up.

Christmas. Fuck. What am I going to get Jenna?

He normally saw his boys for Christmas, this year they were coming to him. Was it too soon to introduce them? He felt like it was too soon. He wanted her all to himself. He didn't want to have to explain it later if something happened and they didn't work out.

But that's not going to happen. We ARE going to work out. Fuck. This is why I don't do relationships. I can't deal with fucking worrying about shit that hasn't even happened yet.

His heartbeat picked up, and worry pooled in his gut; he blew out a slow breath to calm himself down. Maybe he should call his shrink again. He'd stopped making regular appointments years ago, when it seemed he had a handle on everything, but this new 'development' was stressing him the fuck out. He hadn't tried to make a relationship work in a long time, maybe he needed some guidance through this. He put a note in his phone to make an appointment the next day.

A sharp knocking sounded on the door behind him, and he smiled. *Jenna had arrived!* He rushed to the door and threw it open, only to see Mia standing on his doorstep.

"I told you not to come here," he stated flatly, his face falling. He noticed that Mia saw the change in his demeanor.

"Daddy, I-"

"Don't fucking start with that shit, Mia. We're done. You are humiliating yourself. Just fucking go."

He was losing his temper with her. He had already called her employer to make it understood he didn't want anything to do with her, but she wouldn't stop trying to contact him. She had even sent him flowers at work. It was embarrassing.

"It's fucking freezing out here, Max, just let me have five minutes, and I promise you'll never hear from me again." Her eyes were wide with crocodile tears. Max knew she was a manipulator, she knew he hated seeing a woman cry.

"Five minutes. But nothing you say will change things," he stated through clenched teeth, his jaw tight.

She stepped into the foyer, suddenly happy, tears gone, and shut the door behind her quickly.

"Max... I love you. I can't live without you-" Max groaned loudly with disgust, rolling his eyes, but she powered on, "We had something good between us, Baby. I can't live without you in my life. I want to come back. We don't have to get married. Can't we just go back to the way it was?"

Mia threw her arms around his neck, trying to pull him down to her, as Max tried to push her back and put distance between them.

"Mia! NO. It's over. I have a girlfriend now."

Mia froze. "WHAT?! Since fucking WHEN do you have a girlfriend?!" she shrieked. "I AM YOUR GIRLFRIEND!"

Max just stared at her, a vein in his neck ticking. He just wanted her out of his house, out of his life, like yesterday.

Mia stormed up to him as he looked down at her, nose to pissed off nose.

"Can she give you THIS?!" she demanded as one hand grabbed his cock through his pants, and the other snaked around his neck, pulling him down so she could slam her mouth over his.

Max's hand grabbed hers over his crotch, trying to pull her off, as his other arm pushed at her shoulder.

There was a loud gasp from the door, and when Max finally pried Mia off of him he saw Jenna's blue hair disappearing out the door quickly.

FUCK!!!!! Fuck! Fuck! Fuck!

"JENNA!" he screamed as he ran after her. She was storming down the street, head down. Fuck it was cold out, he had run out of the house without a coat.

"JENNA, STOP!" he screamed again. People on the street stopped to stare at him as he ran past.

"Jenna!" He caught up with her and got in front of her.

"Fuck off," she said, obviously crying, as she went to move around him, not even looking at him.

"No," he said, putting his arms on hers to stop her. She pushed them away, but didn't move. "You promised. No matter if we are upset, or jealous, or want to end it; no ghosting. We talk." he implored.

"You want to talk now?!" she yelled. "What the FUCK was that, Max?! You were holding her hand on your dick. Are you going to tell me 'it's not what it looked like?' Because I'm pretty sure it is EXACTLY what it looked like!" she was shouting, tears streaming down her face, and everyone on the street was stopping to watch the show.

He stepped in closer, and she stepped away from him.

Fuck!

"Blue, she came on to ME. I was trying to pull her off of me when you came in. I told you, she and I are over. YOU and I are exclusive. Nothing happened, and nothing will with her. You are the only one I want. I will get a restraining order on her right fucking now if you want. I'm being honest with you. You know I'm telling the truth." He was furious that she didn't trust him, and desperate for her to believe him at the same time.

Jenna stared at the ground, tears rolling down her cheeks.

"Blue, think about it for a minute. I gave you a key yesterday. Would I have had someone else over, knowing you could walk in and catch me at any time? I gave you that key to PROVE to you that you are the only one. Don't doubt me now. Don't be upset, I can't bear to see you upset." Max reached his hand out, tentatively, to stroke her cheek; when she didn't move to stop him he cupped her chin and pulled her into a tight hug.

She didn't move. She stood stock still in his arms, stiff.

"Blue, Baby, let's get inside..." He started to guide her back to his house. The people on the street all resumed what they were doing, their entertainment gone. Jenna looked up at his front door and seemed to come to her senses.

"No. Max, I need to leave." She had a panicked desperation in her wide eyes.

"Blue, Honey, it's ok…"

"I'll call you…" Jenna took off running down the street, away from him. This time he let her go. She needed space, and he'd give it to her. He knew she had heard his reasons. He knew she had to realize it was a big misunderstanding.

Didn't she?

◆ ◆ ◆

Jenna

Jenna sat on her bed in the darkness. It was ten pm, and she had to work the next day, but she couldn't sleep. The vision of that woman with her face latched onto his, and her hand grabbing his cock… no, *his hand pulling her hand onto his cock*… It was too much.

But what he said… about the key…

No, it didn't make sense. Why would he give her a key, and then invite someone over? He was expecting her. He wouldn't have had someone over when he was expecting her to show up any minute: not unless he wanted to be discovered. So why give her the key at all. For that matter, why ask her to be exclusive?

Did he freak out over it, and try to sabotage it?

But if he had sabotaged it, why would he run after her and try to fix it?!

Jenna moaned through another round of tears. She was just so hurt and confused.

Goddamn it. THIS is why I don't do relationships. I don't need this fucking stress or drama.

On her bedside table her cell phone beeped, an incoming text. She blew out a breath. It had to be Max. Slowly, she reached to pick it up and read it.

"Max: Blue, Baby, are you okay?"

She stared at the phone numbly for a few minutes before responding.

"Blue: I don't know, Max."

"Max: Baby, I can't stand to see you upset. Can you please come over? We don't need to talk. We don't need to have sex. I just need to take care of you, to make sure you're alright."

"Blue: Why would I do that?"

"Max: Because I made a commitment to take care of your mammal, and it's suffering right now. Please. I promise, no sex. We don't even have to talk, unless you want to. Please let me take care of you. I hate to see you hurt."

"Blue: Max, it's late."

"Max: I'm coming to get you. Be there in fifteen."

Jenna stared at the screen. She was terrified; not of Max, per se, but of how attached she had become to him.

How had she gotten this attached?

She didn't really believe he wanted anything to do with that girl, she knew how he really felt about her, but seeing him looking like he was being sexual with ANYONE else... it cut her deeply.

She knew he hadn't planned it, it had just happened. But it made her aware of how fragile she really was. What if he did meet someone? What if he got tired of her? And he would, wouldn't he? She wasn't young and beautiful; she was fucked up.

Yes, he gave her a key, but he made it clear she wasn't moving in; not that she wanted to... but that was a whole other issue. He gave her the key, he could take it away.

He could take it all away.

Her blood felt like ice in her veins, until she slowly went numb. She felt like a zombie, feeling nothing.

Dissociation. That's what the shrink called it when they sent me to mandatory psychiatric counseling. It's amazing that I can remember these random factoids, when I can't feel a thing...

Knock, knock, knock

Andrew stuck his head into her room, the light from the kitchen flooding in behind him.

"Uh... Max is here to get you," he stated. "Are you ok? Do you want me to tell him to leave?"

She stared at Andrew for a moment, devoid of emotion, and finally shook her head no. She dragged herself up silently, grabbed her purse and phone, and headed for the door.

◆ ◆ ◆

Max

Jenna looked terrible as she stood in the doorway, putting her coat on. Max expected anger, or sadness... he was not prepared for the void that faced him. It was like she was on drugs, she just seemed to look through things, without seeing anything, including him.

He looked to Andrew, who was standing behind her, and mouthed "Is she ok?" Concern filled his eyes. Andrew looked back resolutely, and once Jenna stepped onto the porch, Andrew put a hand on Max's elbow to hold him back so he could whisper in his ear.

"She's really fucking fragile right now, Max. She means the world to me, so don't you fucking hurt her or I will end you. Do you understand?" Fire burned in Andrew's eyes, and Max had no doubt he was dead serious. They watched Jenna walk down the stairs in silence.

Max bristled internally at the threat, but let it go. "She means the world to me, too, Andrew. I won't hurt her. Not now, not ever." They held a look between them for a moment, before Max rushed after Jenna to usher her to the warmth of the car.

"There you go." Max settled Jenna into his soaking tub. She had been silent the whole drive home, staring through the windshield, her face blank. Max was starting to panic a little. Jenna leaned back and closed her eyes, exhaling deeply as her body relaxed into the heat of the water.

Max gathered a few items and then stripped his clothing off. He climbed into the other end of the tub, and Jenna opened her eyes to watch him, expressionless. He placed a bath pillow behind her. He knelt down between her legs, pulling each one open so that her calves rested on either side of the tub, her pussy exposed to him. She just stared at him.

"How is my favorite little mammal?" Max cooed, looking at her pussy. He gently petted her wet mound softly, not in a sexual way, but in the way you would pet a kitten.

"What are you doing?" she asked him. It was the first sign of activity he had seen from her, and he delighted in it silently.

"I told you, I need to take care of my mammal. You go back to sleep, I got this," he answered her, reaching down to get something beside the tub.

"You said no sex," she stated flatly.

"Yes. No sex," Max answered, spraying shaving gel onto his hand.

"So what are you doing?" she asked, sounding more curious, and less stoned.

"Woman, you are distracting me. My mammal has needs, and I intend to see them fulfilled. I'm not having sex with you, so don't worry. Just lie back and snooze. Let me take care of my favorite mammal."

With that he lifted her hips until they were on his kneeling thighs, another bath pillow under her lower back, lifted above the edge of the water. "My poor little mammal need some loving. Don't you sweet thing?" he spoke to her mound in baby talk.

Max snuck a peek to see Jenna watching him, her eyes curious and unsure, and he bit back a smile. He rubbed his hands together to create a lather with the shaving gel and then spread it over her mound gently. There was nothing sexual in his movement, it was more affectionate and loving. Jenna watched, life slowly returning to her eyes.

Next he picked up a razor. He looked at Jenna to check in with her, but she held the same curious expression and said nothing.

"My sweet mammal has been neglected and needs some grooming, doesn't she, Baby? Don't worry. I'll take care of you," he cooed again, looking at her foamy mound.

Slowly and gently he worked the razor over her mound, leaving strips of bald flesh where her soft bush had been. He even gently pulled her lips open to get every last bit of hair, until she was finally smooth and hair free.

"There you are my sweet mammal! I can see you now!" he crooned, talking to her pussy like it was the most precious baby in the world. He pushed back and leaned down, holding her hips out of the water, and placed a tender kiss just above her pussy, on her bare flesh.

Jenna's eyes were aware now, a spark of interest lighting in them, but she still said nothing.

"Next your massage, my sweet mammal!" Max announced. Jenna raised an eyebrow. Again, Max fought to keep the smile from coming to his face, and instead reached for a small bottle of oil he had floating in the hot water beside him.

Max gently parted the lips of her soft pussy and poured some warm oil right over her clit and let it seep down into her lips. Jenna moaned softly, her eyes closing and a small smile lifting the edges of her mouth. Next Max took the warm oil and drizzled it all over her mound and around her thighs.

He put the bottle back into the water and then gently patted her mound, before reaching with both hands to gently massage small circles into her lower abdomen. From there he moved down to the crease of her legs, and down her inner thighs, stroking and massaging the muscles. He wasn't a masseur by any means, but he knew what felt good. Jenna moaned more loudly, and he watched her upper body slump deeper into the hot water, her hips still propped above it.

He worked his hands back up her thighs and gently massaged her slick mound. He gently plucked her pussy lips with his fingers, pulling them out, and letting them slide back between his fingers. Jenna moaned again, louder. He reached in to stroke the oil through her folds, trying to keep the motion sensual, without being overtly sexual. He could feel her unfolding in his hands, her wetness rising to the surface.

"Max," she whispered.

"Shhh," he insisted. "I'm busy right now. Go back to sleep."

He continued to stroke his fingers through her folds, and her hips rocked up into his hands involuntarily.

"Max…" She groaned, more loudly.

"Woman! I have obligations. I don't have time to chat with you right now. Can't you see this mammal is suffering?" he asked her playfully.

"Put it out of its suffering." She groaned, her eyes half-lidded and full of lust.

"I intend to, Baby." Max worked his hands through her folds, and down her innermost thighs, working towards the base of her ass, kneading and massaging deeply now. Jenna groaned again, her hips bucking upward with desire for more of his touch. Grabbing the bottle of oil, Max coated her mound again, holding her lips open so it would drip all the way down, and catching some in his hand. He pulled that hand between the cheeks of her ass, coating her puckered hole in the back, lingering as he ran a finger around the rim.

Jenna groaned loudly, her hands clutching the edge of the tub.

Max worked faster circles, and then gently began to apply pressure, pushing his finger into her ass. Jenna's eyes flew open.

"Will you calm down, up there?" Max asked her playfully. "This is my mammal to please."

"I don't-," Jenna started to say, but he cut her off.

"Blue, Baby, I need you to trust me. I know what your mammal needs right now. I am not going to hurt you. I promise." He held her look, as he slowly pressed his finger a little deeper, her ass tightened around him, refusing him.

With his other hand, Max gently reached up and stroked her stiff clit between his fingers. She moaned and twitched immediately, her breath coming out in short pants.

"Theeeeeere's my beautiful mammal! Come out and play my sweet, sweet girl!" he cooed to her throbbing pussy.

As he worked her clit gently, she slowly relaxed her hold so that he could push his finger a little deeper into her ass. He worked her gently, pushing the oil in and stretching her walls as he flicked and pulled at her clit.

Jenna started writhing under his hands, groaning, her hands in a death grip on the sides of the tub.

"That's it, my little Mammal... give it to me, my precious!" he cooed.

"Max!" Jenna groaned loudly. "Max I need you! Make me come! Aaaaaahhhh" Her eyes were screwed shut as the sensual feelings overtook her.

"Is that what you want, Baby? You want me to feed this beautiful mammal of yours?" he asked seductively.

"FUCK! Max! Give it to me!" she screamed.

Keeping his finger moving in her ass, he slid three fingers into her pussy hard, he pushed his body back and lifted her hips slightly so he could bring his mouth down over her clit.

She screamed with pleasure and her hands flew to the back of his head. His lips sucked her clit in hard, as he rammed his three fingers deep inside her, spreading her out with the oil; his other hand triggering her ass.

Jenna was completely taken under by the sensations, having both entrances filled while he sucked her clit exquisitely. She bucked and groaned loudly, pulling his head down onto her as she ground her pussy into his face and fucked his hand. He had never seen anything so beautiful as Jenna chasing her release with him; his eyes were glued to her face, entranced.

It wasn't long at all before he got the telltale signs that she was going to come, and come hard. He upped his pace, punching into her pussy harder, hitting her g-spot over and over, twisting his finger in her ass, and nipping and sucking at her clit.

"That's it, Baby! Give it to me! Give it all to me, Baby!" he encouraged her as he groaned into her clit.

Her back arched out of the water as she screamed, her shattered release gripping his fingers tight, pulling them into her body. Her pussy milked his hands hard as wave after wave of pleasure moved through her limp body, until she was finally a whimpering mess of sensation again.

He slowly withdrew his hands, washing them thoroughly, and then turning his attention back to her. He ran his tongue through her folds, moaning with pleasure as he tasted her juices in his mouth.

"So fucking sweet, my little mammal."

He pulled out a cloth and soaped her up, top to bottom, cleaning her entire body with massaging strokes. She was jelly in his hands. When she was all cleaned, he gently helped her to stand, and wrapped her in a thick towel to dry her off; then he picked her up and carried her into the bedroom, where the sheets had already been pulled back for her.

He placed her in bed lovingly, pulling the blankets up to her chin, and kissing her lips softly.

"Do you need anything, Baby?" he whispered to her.

"Only you," she whispered back, her eyes closed, her body already falling asleep.

"You've got me, Baby. You've got me." He climbed into bed behind her, spooning her, and wrapped his arm around her waist. Her soft warm body made his balls ache, but at that moment, he just wanted to hold her close more than anything else.

Chapter 8

Jenna

Jenna woke to find the room filled with sunlight. She looked around groggily, and realized she was in Max's bedroom. As if sensing her awareness, Max's arm tightened around her waist, pulling her ass snug against his erection, and he released a deep sigh in his sleep. Jenna smiled.

Then she panicked. There was too much light in the room. Picking up her phone, she realized he was late for work. SHE was late for work. She rolled in his hold, gripping his shoulder and shaking him.

"Max. Max. You're late, Baby. Wake up." She shook him again.

Max groaned and stretched, pulling her closer again, before slowly opening one eyelid, and then the other. He smiled a dopey smile as he looked into her eyes.

"Morning, Blue," he whispered. His hands started to roam over her.

He was so fucking adorable with his hair all mussed and half awake. I could wake up to this every morning for the rest of my life.

"Baby, we're late for work," she whispered urgently. He rolled onto his back and pulled her on top of his naked body. His cock hard and poking into her belly.

"We're playing hookey today." He smiled up at her.

"Wha- But you said... your caseload-"

"Will wait until tomorrow. I called you out sick too. I needed to be sure that you are okay first, Blue. How are you feeling?" His tone grew more concerned, and he reached a hand up to brush her messy blue hair out of her face. His eyes searched hers.

Jenna's face flushed with embarrassment. Andrew was the only person who ever saw her lose it. She never let anyone see her in less than perfect control. She felt a little foolish, and very vulnerable.

"Blue?" he prompted again gently, his lower lip pouting just a little bit as he fussed over her.

She sighed deeply. He'd already seen it, so there was no denying it. "I'm okay... now," she admitted.

Max pulled her down for a tender kiss, stroking her hair, and sending shivers over her skin. Being so close to him, naked, was already starting to affect her nether-regions. She would rather distract herself with that.

Max looked at her, but said nothing. He didn't push for an explanation. But she suddenly felt like she should tell him. He had taken care of her, he deserved to know. It was just so hard to get the words out. What if he decided she was psycho? What if he didn't want to deal with her baggage? What if he left her? They hadn't been together that long, what if it was too much baggage too soon?

But he did deal with my baggage. And he's still here...

She looked at his lips, unable to meet his eyes, as she started talking. "I... I can get overwhelmed, emotionally. When that happens... I.... I dissociate. I stop feeling. I go numb. It's terrifying, because my mind is still fully functional, I just can't feel anything."

She concentrated on looking at his lips, afraid to look into his eyes.

What if he was disgusted? What if he looked at her with pity?

Her heart pounded in her chest.

God, I hate being this way. Well, better that he knows how fucked up I am now. Cut his losses, get it over with. Rip the bandaid off.

Moisture started to gather on her lashes, and she dropped her head to his chest. His arms tightened around her immediately.

"Well, it's a good thing I know how to get through to your mammal then, isn't it?" he asked softly.

Jenna burst out laughing, a nervous-relieved laugh, and Max brought her chin up so that he could take her mouth again. His kiss was loving, comforting, and devoted. She moaned softly against his lips and his body came to life underneath her.

She was suddenly overwhelmed with the need to have him inside her: in her mouth, in her pussy, it didn't matter. She needed to make him come. She needed to have that power over his body. She pulled out of his arms and crawled down him quickly, trailing her tongue down his toned abs as she went.

"Blue, wha- OOOOOOOOOOOOHHH God!" Max groaned and spread his legs for her, giving her better access. "Fuck, Baby, you could wake me up like this everyday!"

Jenna looked up to see him pull a pillow under his head so that he could watch her as she bobbed up and down on his cock, taking him deep into her mouth. Her hands twisted around his shaft, lubricated by her saliva, and her other hand caressed his balls. She was going to fucking town on his cock, and he was completely at her mercy.

"God, Blue, I love to watch you take my cock. Do you have any idea how much it turns me on watching you?"

Spurred on by his reaction she took him deeper, hollowing her cheeks, stroking him firmly.

"Holy   fucking   shit   you're   good   at   that! AAAAAAAAAAAHHH.... Baby...I'm gonna come if you're not careful.... BLUE!" Max was thrusting his hips up at her mouth in time with her rhythm, his hands holding the back of her head, as he fed his cock into her warm mouth.

Jenna wasn't listening. She just wanted to feel him lose control, to make him blow in her mouth, to feel him drain down her throat, unable to stop. She doubled her efforts, mashing her nose into his pelvic bone to get him all the way inside of her, sucking him for dear life.

"FUCK! BLUE! AAAAAAAAAAAAAAAAAAAAAAAAAAR-RRRGGGHHHH!" He thrust up, hard; his hands clamped down on the back of her head. He was so deep that her throat gagged around him a little, and she had to try to calm herself to keep from choking. She felt his cock spasming in her mouth, felt the heat as he shot his juices down her throat. Then his hips thrust a few more times, emptying him at last into her mouth, and she could breathe again.

Mission accomplished.

Max lay back, panting, stroking his hands through Jenna's hair.

"Baby, you are just way too good at that. Holy fuck. I think you sucked my brain out through my cock." He chuckled.

Jenna snorted a laugh. "Yeah, well, there are advantages to having a gay roommate," she said cheerily.

Max's head came up sharply. "Andrew is gay?" he asked.

"Yup!" she answered with a smile. "and nobody teaches how to give good head like a gay guy!" She laughed.

Max went still. "You didn't... I mean with him?..."

Jenna burst out laughing again. "Oh my God, Max. You can't be jealous of a gay guy. NO. I did not practice on him... he coached me in ... theory." She finished with a sly wink.

Max pulled her down heavily on top of him and kissed her deeply. He had her all to himself today, and he didn't want to waste a minute of that time talking about her gay roommate. He made love to her, gently and tenderly, then they went for another round, this time brutally hard and fast. She loved that he could give it to her hard, that he didn't think of her as fragile. He left her sore and bruised in all of the best ways, and she wouldn't trade it.

◆ ◆ ◆

Max

They spent their day off together having a fuckfest, until he took Jenna to work out with Andrew. It didn't seem like such a bad idea, once Max knew he was gay.

Max sat in his car, on his way to pick Jenna up from the dojo, and his thoughts kept drifting back to their day together. He could not believe how fucking lucky he was. He loved rough sex, and he had always had to water it down to accommodate the women he was with. Even some of the professionals just couldn't handle him; between his size and his violence.

But Jenna was like a goddamned angel. She would egg him on to go harder, faster. When he was sure he would be hurting her, she would bark at him to give her more; it was like she couldn't get enough either.

He had given her a few bruises, and it had gutted him, until she told him to stop being a pussy and give her more. He didn't want to believe that she really liked it that rough, but she genuinely did. He could let go with her, he could be himself to the fullest. He had never felt so free in his life.

And she didn't judge him for it! She didn't call him a freak or a monster, didn't cry afterwards and take it all back. She didn't whine about the bruises, in fact she wore them like a badge of honor.

As if the sex wasn't amazing enough, their time out of bed was equally amazing. They went out, talked, laughed. She was as smart as a tack, and observant. She was so refreshingly different from the young self-centered girls that he had dated.

Not dated... hired. I never dated them. It was a business transaction. He mentally corrected himself. He *dated* Jenna. She was strong and self confident, beautiful but humble, and sweet but assertive. She didn't want his money, she wanted him: all of him.

Fuck. She was the whole package.

What the fuck does she see in me? The asshole who harassed her in the store? The rich guy who hires dates? The absent boyfriend who works too much? What the fuck do I have to offer a woman like that? How do you hold on to perfection like that?

Max's GPS announced his arrival, and he pulled into the parking lot of the small building with the martial arts sign. There was only one other car, and the building seemed mostly dark; concern started to creep into his chest. He got out of the car and made his way to the door to find it unlocked, that didn't please him at all. It was dark and late, anyone could walk in and hurt her. He was suddenly very protective.

Walking in, he took in the large main room; it was strewn with mats, and there were banners hanging on the walls with different asian symbols. On one wall weapons were hung, and against another was some sort of small altar. Most of the lights were out.

A loud cracking noise shot from the back, and he made his way around the room and down the hallway. The building was bigger than he had initially thought, as it expanded backwards. He could see the light coming from a room at the end, and the noise seemed to be centered there as well. He quietly made his way down, and peeked into the room to see what was going on.

His heart seized.

He saw Jenna laying on the mat on her back, a man was straddling her chest, head down, choking her. She thrashed, but the man pushed his bodyweight down on her, keeping her in place. Jenna's face was red with effort. Before Max could rush in, Jenna was launching the man into the air with her legs, and she was back on her feet. She ran at him full force, a wooden knife in her hand. She brought it down hard, but Andrew brought his weapon up to meet it.

Holy fuck, it was Andrew! Wait?! Andrew was choking her?! What the hell?!

Andrew swerved with his staff, shooting Jenna's weapon out of her hand. A smug smile flashed across his face, as he moved to hit her with his weapon, but Jenna was faster, and caught him right in the nose with an uppercut.

The fight ended as Andrew brought his hands up to his face; blood rained down his shirt and onto the mat. It was then that Andrew saw Max standing in the doorway, his jaw on the ground. Unable to get the words out, Andrew just made a gesture toward the door with his bloody hand, as Jenna tried to check his nose. Andrew walked to the door, pushed past Max, and headed for the bathroom.

"Oh, hi!" Jenna smiled at Max. She seemed so normal, not like she hadn't just had a guy choking her and disarming her.

"Hi?" Max stood frozen in the doorway, trying to figure out what was going on. A part of him wanted to go caveman at what he had just witnessed, but Jenna didn't seem bothered in the least, as she mopped the blood off the mat with a rag.

"What was that?" he asked, conversationally.

"The sparring?" she answered, "Oh, several different arts together. Andrew and I spar a few times a week. It's good to keep the skills up." She was smiling at him as if this was a normal thing, getting choked and punching your best friend.

Suddenly her sexual preferences made a lot more sense, if this was what she did for fun. He had a whole new appreciation for her limitations, or lack thereof. His dick was hard instantly, and he couldn't wait to get her naked again at the thought of it.

She glanced at his obvious arousal, smiled at him wickedly, and prowled toward him. She kissed him deeply, letting her hand run down the bulge building in his pants. He grabbed her shoulders roughly, his tongue sweeping into her mouth, battling with her own. Her other arm snaked around his neck, tight. The kiss was deep and heated, and promised wrath. When she finally pulled back, she smiled at him with hungry eyes, and damned if he didn't want to be her prey right then. He had never been so terrified, and turned on, simultaneously.

"Let me check on Andrew, then we can go," she whispered to him. He could only nod, and watch her walk out of the room, before adjusting himself and breathing deeply.

He remembered Andrew's threat when he picked Jenna up the other night. He was never one to avoid conflict, but he realized he had drastically underestimated Andrew. He would have to make sure he never got on his bad side.

Jenna had showered and changed, and they sat in the darkened restaurant enjoying dinner together. Jenna had a deep purple bruise blooming on her arm, but other than that, there was no sign that she had been fighting like a ninja only an hour before.

Max watched her smile, she was so easy to talk to. But he wanted to ask her more about herself, and he wasn't sure she would be open to sharing. He considered his words carefully.

"Blue, Baby. I have a question I want to ask you." He smiled at her, and sipped his scotch as she looked up. "You remember when I brought you over to my place, when you were... upset? You said you were overwhelmed. What was it exactly that overwhelmed you?" His voice was soft and gentle, curious.

"Oh..." She took a deep drink of her gin and tonic. "Ummm... It's kind of embarrassing. Are you sure you want to hear it?" She definitely looked like she'd rather talk about anything else.

"Baby, I want to know everything about you, but especially what upsets you. Because I never want anything that upsets you to happen between us. And I want to know how to be prepared to take care of you if I need to. You don't have to talk about it if you don't want to, but for the record, I'd really like to understand." He smiled at her and took her hand in his, brushing his thumb over the back of it.

Jenna blew out a breath, and seemed to consider. Then her eyes met his in her no-nonsense way. "Well, it obviously started seeing Mia wrapped around you like an octopus. It looked like you wanted it." She held her hand up to silence him. "I know you didn't, now, but at the time... I guess my head went to the hamster wheel, spinning, spinning, spinning... but getting nowhere. I went down my list of logical facts, and emotional notions; in the end I realized that it hurt seeing you in what looked like a sexual situation with someone else. And it was too much right then."

Her eyes flicked away fearfully, even though her posture was straight and confident.

Max caught what she wasn't saying. *"I realized you could hurt me."*

She cared about him!

His heart swooned.

Max composed himself, so that his joy over this revelation wouldn't look like he was enjoying hearing about her pain.

"I can understand that, Blue. That's why I asked you to be exclusive with me. It would hurt me deeply to think of you willingly being sexual with someone else, while we are together. I can understand why you reacted the way that you did." He squeezed her hand reassuringly. "Just please don't run from me Baby. I will give you space, time, comfort... whatever you need; just please don't ask me to be okay with not knowing if you are alright. That's all I ask."

Her eyes met his, and there were so many emotions: gratitude, fear, understanding... many he couldn't put words to. In the end it was the tenderness in her eyes that grabbed him by the heartstrings. When she looked at him like that, he would do anything for her.

◆ ◆ ◆

Jenna

If I wasn't already falling for him, I sure as hell was then.

Jenna looked into his eyes. How could he be so patient and understanding; especially when he had first told her he had zero tolerance for drama.

I caught him in a compromising position, doubted his explanation, and then ran away like a child. And what did he do? He came running to get me, to take care of me, to look out for ME.

Hope soared in her heart. Maybe, just maybe, he would see her crazy, and he would be able to handle it. Even though no one had been able to before; maybe he was different. She was almost afraid to hope.

"I have another question for you." He smiled warmly at her, and she nodded.

"So there's this charity ball coming up next week. The timing is awful, but it is for the FoodBank. They provide food for families and for the homeless. Would you go with me?" Max looked at her with hope in his eyes.

"Sure." She smiled.

"Really?!" He smiled broadly, but was clearly shocked.

"Of course, it's a part of my exclusivity clause. I have to attend events with you and whatnot." She laughed.

Max took her hand and kissed the back of it. "I don't want you to go because you feel like you *have* to." He kissed her again. "I had hoped you'd go with me because you wanted to."

Jenna laughed. "Max, after seeing me in the dojo tonight, do you really think you could make me do anything I didn't want to? Yes, I will go with you... willingly."

Max's face lit with a megawatt smile. "Fantastic! We can go shopping for a gown this weekend!"

Jenna's face dropped. "Shopping for a gown? Can't I just wear a dress?"

Max smiled warmly. "Baby, it's a black tie event. I don't expect you to have a couture gown at home. I'd love to buy you one."

"What if I don't want one?" she asked, and there was a slight edge to her voice.

"Blue, talk to me. What's the matter here. Are you upset about me buying the gown, or asking you to wear one? I'm not sure what's upsetting you." His brows drew down in confusion, but his words were calm and assertive.

"Max, I'm not a barbie doll. I ..." She huffed, and then stopped and looked down, her face scrunched in discomfort.

When she spoke again, her normal calm tone was back and her eyes met his. "I'll be honest, Max. I don't want to be like the girls that you went to these events with before. I don't want this to be a transaction where you feel the need to spend a lot of money on me for my company. It makes me feel cheap."

A pained look swept across Max's eyes for the briefest of moments, and then it was gone.

"Blue, Baby, That's not what this is, I swear. You could never be like those girls. That's why I am no longer with them: I'm with you.

"I asked you to go with me, and I said I didn't want you to feel obligated; there is nothing transactional about this. I love your company, and I am so damn proud to finally have a good looking woman with a brain to go out with me, that I want to show you off everywhere. If you didn't want to go, I would go alone if I had to. I would never insist on you attending if you didn't want to. But I'd love your company.

"I asked to buy you a gown because all of the other women will be wearing them. Like I said, I don't expect you to have a ten thousand dollar gown hanging around your house, and I would never expect you to go in anything less than any other lady there. This is about your comfort. I have plenty of money, it is literally nothing to me to buy you several gowns if they would make you more comfortable. I would never want for you to feel self-conscious, because some of those people are downright ruthless. If I didn't think they would try to attack your confidence, I'd tell you to go in jeans and be comfortable. But they'll be dressed to the nines, and I'd love to make that available for you too. I don't ever want you to look around and feel like you don't have what it takes to be there, because you do. And for the record, I never offered to buy those other girls couture gowns; I've never offered to do that for anyone but you.

"I'm not trying to buy your affection, Wildcat. I already know how gorgeous you are. I want to make every other man at that event jealous when they see you walk in on my arm. I admit, it is completely and utterly selfish of me. But the choice to go is yours, and yours alone."

Jenna chewed over his words in her mind. "You were shopping for Mia in the Department Store." It was a statement, not a question. She remembered the off the rack dresses, they were expensive, but they weren't couture expensive, they were simply overpriced.

Max nodded, a small smile on his face, as he watched her put it together.

"Okay, I'll agree, on one condition," She looked at Max. "we go to the designer who made my dress for the last charity event."

Max raised his glass. "Deal." He smiled a wicked smile.

Chapter 9

Max

Weekends were quickly becoming Max's favorite days. He spent most of Saturday balls deep in Jenna, gasping and thrusting like animals in heat, stopping only for hydration, food and showers. He couldn't believe how much she turned him on.

She had suggested that she could wear the same gown to the Foodbank event as she wore to the last one, the event where she slammed into Max and fried his brain. That golden blush creation was etched into his mind forever. He told her that if she wanted to wear it again, he was fine with that, and it hit him. Mia had whined about having to wear a dress a second time, like they were disposable, like his money was hers to spend. Jenna would have worn an everyday dress, except she didn't want to stick out like a sore thumb. She couldn't give a shit about spending more for the sake of spending more.

Jenna was so very different from all the girls Max used to be with. She asked for nothing but his body and his time; she was never demanding or sulky. When he tried to approach her about buying her things he thought she might like, she talked him out of it, in some cases arguing. She could be a stubborn pain in his ass, but at the end of the day he smiled. He knew for a fact she wasn't with him for his money or social standing.

They stood in the small shop looking at gowns. The designer friend of Andrew's was amazing, the gowns were unbelievable.

Jenna looked at one after another, looking at their tags and then moving on. They were never going to get a dress if she couldn't get over the sticker shock. He pulled her aside gently.

"Blue, Baby, I need for you to understand something. I come from money, lots of money. The people at this event all come from ridiculous wealth, that's why we are invited. They want us to donate. I am expected to show up looking like I have money, and for me it's no big deal. I'm used to this.

"I know you're not used to this, but it would make me so happy to see you on my arm in a dress worthy of you. I mean it when I say I don't give a fuck about the price. Pick whatever makes you feel the most beautiful, and there is no amount of money in the world that would be too much. Please. Don't look at the prices, just pick the dress that makes you feel the best."

Jenna looked up into his eyes, her own conflicted. Finally, she blew out a breath and nodded, heading back to the rack and picking out three gowns to try on. Max smiled broadly.

She stepped out of the dressing room in the third dress, and Max held his breath. She was incredible. It was made with a shimmery blue metallic material that showcased her amazing breasts, hugged her waist, and skimmed over her hip, with a slit up one leg to her thigh. There was ornate bead work on the bodice, and it was a work of art on her body. He wanted to pull it up to her waist and take her right there.

She looked at him with big eyes, holding out her hands for his opinion.

"Blue, I don't know if I can get you that dress. All I can think about is tearing it off of you. I don't know if I can last a whole evening." His eyes skimmed her up and down, his pants tented with obvious approval.

Jenna giggled, her cheeks flushing pink. "Then this is the one." She turned slowly, checking her reflection in the three-way mirror. "Now I just need the lingerie to go with them." She smiled at Max innocently and batted her eyelashes.

Max groaned and rubbed his palm down his face. She was going to be the death of him.

◆ ◆ ◆

Jenna

Jenna clipped the garters to the thigh-high stockings and then slipped on her high heeled shoes. She hated those fucking things, but they made her legs look incredible, as long as she didn't have to walk in them. She liked that the broad lacy garter belt covered most of her scars, she felt sexier when they were covered.

After spending the day fucking, gown shopping, lingerie shopping, and then shoe shopping she had called it quits. Max wanted to get jewelry for her too, but she wasn't having it. She'd rather wear his semen than diamonds. She had sent him to get take out, while she prepared for his return.

She heard the door downstairs close, and arranged her satin robe, open, around her as she sat on the bed seductively. She was still a little sore, but she would never let that stop her from having him inside her anyway she could.

"Blue?!" His voice drifted up. She sat patiently. "Blue? Where are you, Baby?" She heard his footsteps on the stairs, and her tummy fluttered. "Blue?" The bedroom door opened, and his eyes grew wide as he took her in, sprawled out on his bed in her new lacy underwear and stockings, heels on.

"I've been waiting for you..." she purred.

She smiled when she saw his erection immediately punch his pants out in front of him. His eyes were dilated, and his breathing was suddenly heavier.

"You have, have you?" he asked in a deep husky voice, as he made his way toward the bed slowly, never taking his eyes off of her body.

"Stop right there," she said. He stopped, his eyes flicking up to hers, his tongue swiping over his bottom lip.

She kneeled up onto the mattress, letting the thin robe slide down her arms and pool around her. She brought one hand up under her breast, stroking it gently as she maintained eye contact with him, or tried to, as his eyes were fixed on her hand and breast. She tweaked her nipple and moaned softly. Max started moving toward her.

"STOP," she said forcefully, and he reluctantly dragged his eyes back up to hers, his need evident.

"Undress. Slowly," she commanded. Her other hand moved down over her panties, stroking in broad strokes over the lace.

"Blue, I am going to fuck you so damned hard." He groaned as he unbuttoned his shirt casually, dropping it off of his body. When she didn't say anything, he then undid his pants, shucking them off with his briefs. He bent slowly and made a show of slowly pulling off each sock, and then tossing them aside. Then he stood back up before her, completely naked, his cock primed and ready to go with his juices already seeping from the head.

Keeping eye contact with her, he reached down and stroked himself in front of her. She couldn't help it, her eyes tracked his hand, and she licked her lips.

"You like this, Blue? You like watching me pleasure myself?" he asked, pulling more firmly, a soft groan vibrating out of his chest.

"I do, Baby." She smiled up at him. "In fact, I want you to come all over me." She sat back so she was kneeling with her ass on her ankles, and she leaned back onto straight arms as she watched him stroking himself. He slowly made his way onto the bed. At last he was kneeling right in front of her, his legs spread wide around hers.

"Is this what you want, Blue? You want me to stroke my own cock and get off all over you?" His hand moved firmer, faster.

His cock was engorged and dark, the first few drops leaking from the end to splatter on her.

"Cover me in it, Baby," she urged him.

"I need to see you too, Blue. Warm that pretty pink pussy for me," he countered.

She let her fingers slide under her lacy underwear and shuddered with a groan as her fingers traced quick circles around her clit. She slid two fingers inside herself, and gently stroked them in and out. The sounds of her wetness as her fingers plunged, and the wet shuttling noise of his fist on his cock filled the otherwise silent room.

Jenna rolled her head back, her eyes closed in bliss. "Babb-byyyyy..." She groaned.

"Fuck! Blue, you are too fucking hot. I'm not going to last, seeing you like that, with your fingers in your hot wet pussy. It's all I can think about. I want to pound that pussy, Baby!"

Max's hand flew over his cock, the "thucking" noise of his movements becoming louder and louder. Jenna straightened so that she could reach out with her hand and caressed his balls, while her other hand still worked her pussy. She lined her body up right in front of his cock.

"Give it to me, Baby," she commanded.

And right on cue Max's head fell back, his back arching, a roar tearing from his lips. "JENNAAAAAAAAAAAAAAARRRRGGGHH!" His cock erupted in his hand, his semen splashing out in warm spurts all over Jenna's lacy garter belt and onto her bare skin below it. It splashed her hand and her mound.

Max brought his eyes back down to watch as he stroked the last of his fluid out and onto her. She pulled her hands in to rub his fluids all over herself, over the outside of her mound, and she purred with satisfaction.

He launched his body on top of hers, tackling her to the mattress, his mouth devouring hers as his hands claimed her pussy. Rubbing hard, he pulled her panties to the side, before thrusting inside her with three fingers. He groaned into her mouth when his fingers hit her warm wetness and eager open pussy.

Jenna pulled her mouth away, even as Max chased it with his.

"Baby, I need you to lick me. I need to feel your tongue on my pussy. Get me ready for that big cock, Baby," she ordered him seductively.

It was like his mind was overloaded. He reacted immediately, climbing down her body, ripping her panties down, and attacking her pussy in an open-mouthed kiss. His tongue lapped at her folds deeply, groaning in need, until finding his way back up to her waiting clit. Jenna arched off the bed, her hands thrust into his hair painfully, pushing his face down onto her clit and grinding her hips into his mouth.

Max thrust three fingers into her waiting well, deep, making her groan loudly. Her hips bucked to fuck his hand and he punched his fingers inside her again and again, curling his fingertips to hit that spot. He smiled against her clit as she screamed and bucked, riding his hand from below.

"YES, BABY! Right THERE! FUCKING HELL! Max, Give it to me!" She was completely consumed in the sensations, slamming her hips back into his hand, holding his head firmly on her clit. He took her clit between his teeth gently, and then closed his lips and sucked hard.

Jenna screamed. Her back bowed high, her body frozen in rigor, even as her muscles trembled with the action. He felt her orgasm leaking onto his hand, and drip down between her legs, as her body grabbed his hand firmly, crushingly, trying to suck his hand into her. Then she fell back onto the mattress, heaving and panting as wave after wave washed over her body.

Max pulled his hand out of her, and brought his mouth down to suck the juices out of her, to lick up her sweetness, all the way down her thighs, and between the cheeks of her ass. He gently lifted her hips, so that he could lick her all the way in the back, tonguing her puckered hole.

Jenna screamed again, another orgasm tearing through her, and he felt the warmth of her fluids as they ran down his face and onto his waiting tongue. He cleaned her again, and then put her hips back down onto the bed.

"One of these days, my little Wildcat, I am going to fuck that perfect ass of yours. And you are going to fall apart all over my cock," he whispered seductively.

"But not today." She smirked at him. Then she pulled herself up, rolling until she was on her hands and knees before him, and sank her chest down onto the bed so her ass and waiting pussy were in the air. "Right now you are going to fuck my pussy hard with that big cock, until I scream your name. No condoms. Do you understand me?" She looked over her shoulder in challenge.

Max froze.

"Blue, Baby, believe me when I say I want your pussy wrapped around my naked cock, but I don't know that it's a good idea yet." His words were calm, but his body was freaking out; whether it was from arousal or fear Jenna couldn't tell.

"Fuck.My.Pussy," she ordered him again.

"Blue, I'm not doing this without protection. Not going to happen." He sat back, putting space between them.

"Have you always worn condoms?" She asked, her logical rational face in place.

"Always," he answered immediately.

"So what's the problem? You're clean, yes?" He nodded. "I haven't been with anyone else in three years, I'm clean. I can't get pregnant, Max. Is that what you're worried about? That I would trap you?" Her eyes narrowed slightly.

"I never said that." He barked. "I just don't want to be irresponsible. I already have two kids, I don't need to be accidentally making another one." His brows were drawn down, and the muscles around his eyes tightened in anger.

"You think I DO want to make a child, with someone I've only known a month? Give me some credit, Max." She snapped back, rising up to face him.

"I've only known you a month, how the hell would I know?" He countered, his voice louder, heated.

"Because I'm telling you, Max." She pushed her body up against his, getting her face right into his, her hands pushing against his chest. "I don't. And I can't. So you take all this pentup bullshit anger, and you fuck my pussy hard. NOW!" she roared as she shoved him.

She saw it in his eyes the moment he snapped.

His body moved on instinct, throwing her down onto the mattress in one burst, and thrusting his cock deep inside her. His hand came to her throat and clamped down hard. He slammed his hips into her with rage, fucking her as hard as he could, fucking all the emotion that he felt. His hips rocketed into her with force, and he could feel her hip bones hitting against his.

Jenna groaned and writhed beneath him, trying to bring her hips up to meet his as they crashed into her with violent force. Max held her hip down with his free hand, forcing her in place, as he rammed himself into her mercilessly. Deeper. Harder. Faster. He was primal, unthinking.

He felt her core gripping him tightly, crushing his cock into her. She was screaming his name as her back went rigid beneath him. He slammed his cock deep inside her, falling onto her and latching onto her shoulder with his teeth, biting hard as he roared. His cock exploded inside of her.

Jenna saw stars, a fog of euphoric haze clouded her mind. She felt Max's cock, still pumping out its release deep within her, and there was a searing pain in her shoulder... even with the throbbing pain that was starting to replace the intense sexual pleasure in her lower body, she could only smile in satisfaction.

Max stiffened on top of her, looking down at their joined bodies, and then looking up at her. There was terror in his eyes. He moved to push up, but Jenna held him in place.

"What the fuck was that?!" he demanded, anger burning in his eyes.

"Baby, I needed for you to let go. I needed for you to give me everything you had. I'm sorry I picked a fight; I just wanted you to know I can handle it. You can take me as hard as you want, Baby. I love when you do." She stroked his hair as she spoke soothingly to him.

"Jenna,... that's fucked up." He pulled out of her arms quickly, shaking his head and climbed off the bed, making his way to the bathroom, closing the door hard behind him.

Jenna sat up against the headboard, her knees pulled up to her chest. Tears burned in the backs of her eyes.

I know... I told you I was.

◆ ◆ ◆

Max

Max paced back and forth in the bathroom. It was all so fucked up. He had never lost control like that with a woman before. He was starting to bruise, he could only imagine what she looked like. Why the fuck had she done that?

Fuck! He could have killed her!

Was it even true that she couldn't get pregnant?! What if she lied? What if this was all some masterplan after all?

Panic started to grip his chest, and his breathing became more labored.

Tap, tap, tap

"Baby, come out of there and talk to me..." Her voice was quiet on the other side of the door. Max just stood staring at the door. What could he even say to her? He wasn't sure he could even look at her.

"I ... I'm taking a shower. Give me a few minutes," he called back, and turned the water on immediately, so that he couldn't hear her response. He stepped under the spray and wiped his hands down over his face.

What the fuck had he gotten into? She was right, they had only been communicating for a month, and had only been to-gether a handful of times. What the hell was he doing becoming exclusive, giving her a fucking KEY to his house? He was think-ing with his dick, that's what he was doing! And look where it got him!

His mind and emotions started to spiral as he washed him-self, and tried to make sense of the situation. He looked around the bathroom, as if he was going to find answers, and finally shut the water off. He couldn't hide in the shower all day.

Do I want to break up with her?

The thought hit him like a sledgehammer to the gut.

He needed some space. He needed to think.

He toweled himself off, and opened the door to the bed-room. Jenna's bra, panties and stockings were strewn on the bed with a note. Max rushed over and picked it up.

"My dearest Max,

I am so sorry that I've caused you distress. Please know it wasn't my intention; I had really hoped you would have enjoyed the experience of cutting loose. I see now that I may have hurt the sensitive side of you which does not enjoy violence. I am truly sorry.

I have dealt with a lot of violence in my life; I have learned to channel it, use it for something better. I know this may sound fucked up to you. In fairness, I did warn you that I am fucked up. I'm so sorry, I thought you might be able to handle this too. I see now, it was unfair to ask that of you.

Please know that I was honest. I can't get pregnant. The same surgery that fixed my back also removed some essential parts to make kids; it's not an improbability, it's an impossibility. I don't want you worried about that aspect of what I did, on top of everything else.

Please know that this is not me running away. This is me giving you space. If you want to end things with me, please just be courteous and tell me.

For what it's worth, this has been the happiest month of my life. So, thank you for that.

Warmly,

Jenna (& Mammal)"

She left?... Max stood in his room, holding the note. What the fuck was he supposed to do with this?

Chapter 10

Jenna pulled into traffic, being extra cautious as it was Andrew's car. He always made the car available to her on Sundays so she could go to church, even if he couldn't go. She knew her eyes were puffy, but she had slathered enough makeup onto her face to hide the worst of the dark circles.

She had gotten home late from her... fight (?) with Max the night before to find Andrew out, not surprisingly. And he was still sleeping as she was leaving for church. She really needed to talk this out with him; he didn't judge her, he understood her. She just needed a friendly ear to give her perspective. He would tell her if she crossed a boundary.

Had she really fucked up what she had with Max so soon? She thought he was different... Tears started to build up, and she swiped her gloved hands to her eyes. She didn't need to wash off all of the concealer she had spent all morning applying.

Why had she done it?! Why did she have to go and ruin a good thing? She wasn't ready to let go of Max, but she may have just pushed him away for good. She couldn't forget the look of disgust on his face. *"Jenna (not "Blue") that's fucked up."* She immediately wanted to cry again.

She swiped her eyes again, angrily.

Nope. Just nope. I told him what to expect. If he can't handle me, he doesn't deserve me. Fuck him.

She stepped on the accelerator, hard, and made her way on with her day.

◆ ◆ ◆

Max

Max pulled the laundry out of the washer and put it into the dryer. Some of Jenna's panties and t-shirts had gotten mixed in with his whites. He stared at the wet laundry in his hands for a moment, and then flung them into the dryer.

He didn't know what to think. Was she that badly broken? Was she into masochism? Bondage? He wanted to say no, but the truth was he really didn't know. He didn't really care if she was, he could live with that; he was more concerned that she had some sort of pain fetish, that she got off on people hurting her. Or worse, raping her. That he couldn't live with.

And he couldn't reconcile how his sweet Jenna, the strong woman who was so in control, could want a man to hurt her. He couldn't be that man. Was she that woman, though? Was this a misunderstanding? It all just didn't add up.

And he couldn't just walk away from her. Already his heart was aching from not waking up with her, not seeing her smile. How the fuck had he gotten so attached so quickly, and to someone he apparently didn't even know?

He had to know more. He had to find out what had happened, and see what kind of person she really was. He wasn't willing to end this relationship without knowing, because right up until the night before she had been perfect for him. She had been what no other woman had ever been before.

Max sat in the diner with his sunglasses on. It had taken him a half hour to find her church online, she had given him just enough information to do a search and find the only

Spiritualist Church near her. He saw the same car he had seen at the dojo, probably Andrew's, and he wondered if Andrew was there with her. Only one way to find out.

He had parked in the lot of a diner across the street, and was sitting inside by the window, watching the church from his hidden spot. The service had clearly ended, as a stream of people came out the doors, some still stood in clumps talking. Very soon the parking lot of the church was empty, except for Andrew's car and another.

Max left money on the table to cover his bill and made his way across the street. He walked into the big double doors, into the vestibule. There was another set of doors leading into the main hall, one of which was propped open. He didn't know why he felt the need to sneak, but he walked quietly, staying tucked out of sight and peered into the church hall.

She was there. Jenna stood on the third step of a step ladder with a small paint brush in hand, making tiny strokes with her paint onto the mural which was coming to life on the wall behind the altar.

"Bye, Jenna!" A male voice called out.

Jenna turned and smiled at the man putting his coat on at the front of the church.

"Bye, Mark! Tell Joanne I hope she's feeling better!"

"I will. Don't you stay too late now," he called as he moved toward the side door.

"I won't. I'll lock up. Bye!" Jenna turned back to her work.

Max watched as she leaned her hip heavily against the step ladder. Her left arm was stretched out to steady herself against the wall, but her hand wasn't flat; it was grasping. Her right hand trembled as she brought it up for the next pass.

Max watched as she suddenly stiffened, a small groan escaping her lips, before slowly and carefully climbing down the step ladder one stair at a time. She dipped her brush in the paint, and then climbed back up the stepladder like an old and fragile lady. Periodically she would stop, bracing her back with a groan and a wince. He could see this was killing her.

Why was she doing this? Why were they letting her? Couldn't they see how much this was hurting her? Why didn't they just hire someone?

Max stood in stunned silence, just watching. Her work was beautiful, but each wince caused him to hold his breath. He realized she had music on, when she started to sing along; it sounded like eighties synth pop. He had always been a classic rock kind of guy, but he recognized the sound from the radio and some clubs.

She sang a song of things which were precious and fragile, things which should have been taken care of better, things which were left unsaid. He could hear the heartache in her voice.

Was she singing about him?

He backtracked to his car, not knowing what to say or do. Why was he even there? What had he expected to see, to learn? His phone rang, and his caller ID told him it was Marcus from work.

He and Marcus had started hanging out a little over a year prior; Marcus's father was older, and also one of the partners in the firm. Marcus was married, but it was he who had given Max the number for the agency where he would hire his girls. It had never occurred to him to ask how Marcus had it; some things were better left unknown.

"Marcus," he greeted soberly.

"Max! Hey, how have you been? I stopped by your office last week and they told me you were out. Everything ok?"

"Yeah, everything's fine. My girl was sick, so I stayed out to take care of her." Max kept his eyes on the lone car at the church parking lot.

"Oh no, is Mia ok?" Marcus knew about Mia, just like Max knew that many of the girls he had hired over the last year seemed to already know Marcus when he introduced them.

"I'm not with Mia anymore, Marc, I have a new girlfriend." Max bit out. Even thinking about Mia pissed him off.

"Oh... When did this happen? This new girl, is she from the agency?" Marcus asked, suddenly curious.

"About a month ago, and no." Max said no more. He suddenly didn't like the way this conversation was turning.

"Oh, well, I hope she's feeling better. Look, I'm calling for two reasons. One, Louise in HR is giving me fits. She can't find a place to book the company Christmas party this late; every place is already booked. Would it be ok if we just held it in the offices again? It would be easier to get catering, than to find a place," Marcus started.

"So long as we don't have couples drifting off into the offices again to fuck, that's fine. Up security for the night," Max answered, still watching for Jenna to emerge.

"Great, will do. The second thing is, Peters and Thompson are going to Cali in January for a golf tournament with me, we need a fourth. You in?"

"I'm going to have to get back to you on that, Marcus. Send me the dates, but with the holiday pushback, you know we're going to be in court almost every day in January."

"Max, it's on a weekend. You get days off!" Marcus teased.

"Yeah, to go over my briefs for the following week. I'll think about it. That's the best I can do right now." Max was trying hard not to lose his patience. He didn't know what it was about Marcus that was irritating him, but he was getting under his skin.

"Well, don't take too long man. I'll catch up with you later. I'll send you the dates and info. See ya." The phone line went dead.

Max looked up to see Jenna slowly making her way to Andrew's car. She wasn't standing up straight, and her face was flushed as she blew out heavily. Like she was in pain. She opened the door, and slowly climbed into the car. Once inside she let her head fall back on the headrest and closed her eyes, blowing out her breaths. After a few minutes of this she looked down and seemed to be fiddling with something.

Max's phone beeped.

He looked down to see a text from her.

"Blue: Max, are you alright?"

It crushed his heart just a little to see that one sentence from her.

"Max: I'm not sure, to be honest."

He felt like shit. A part of him wanted to just forget it ever happened and take care of her; but a part of him couldn't even think of looking at her the same way again.

"Blue: Max, Can I come over please? We don't have to talk. I won't ask for sex. Can I just be with you? I need to know you're alright. I won't create any drama, I promise. Please?"

He could see the tears rolling down her cheeks as she stared at her phone. It made him feel like a creepy stalker, knowing what she was doing. He didn't know how to answer. He wasn't really ready to be with her, but he did need to have the conversation.

But what if the conversation confirmed his worst fears? What if it meant they were over?

He froze in his seat, staring at his phone. He wasn't ready for it to be over... but maybe it already was, and he just didn't know it yet. He wouldn't know until they talked, so the sooner the better.

He looked up to see Jenna with her hand over her mouth, tears flowing down her face, and her shoulders jerking with her sobs. It was killing her. She did care about him; that much was true.

"Max: Yeah, Blue. I think that's a good idea. Meet me at five?"

He watched as she clutched at her chest in relief, brushing tears from her cheeks.

"Blue: I'll be there."

He waited until she had pulled out and away before he started his car and headed for home.

◆ ◆ ◆

Jenna

Max opened the door and ushered Jenna in. She was overwhelmed with the desire to grab him in a hug and just inhale his male scent, to anchor herself in him; but she knew that's not what this visit was about.

"How are you doing, really?" She looked up at his tired face. It took all of her self control not to reach up and touch him.

He let out a humorless chuckle. "I've been better, come on." He led her into the living room; the same living room where they had first had sex. She couldn't look at the couch without seeing him stretched out over it naked, so she turned away quickly.

Max pulled her onto the sofa beside him, and put his arm around her, but his body language was wary. Jenna died a little inside to feel him so close to her, but not *with* her. She plastered her warmest smile into place, even though she knew it didn't reach her eyes.

"What can I do for you, Baby? Tell me what you need." She put her hand on his thigh, and then pulled it back again with a jerk once she realized what she had done. His lips quirked up at the corner, and he took her hand in his and placed it back on his thigh.

"No sex, and no conversation... You want to watch a movie?" he suggested casually. Jenna could still see the hurt in his eyes, but he was trying.

"I'd love that." Her smile was more genuine this time.

He vetoed romantic comedies, she vetoed war movies, so in the end they watched a mystery drama with the lights low. Jenna made popcorn while Max poured them each a glass of scotch. The movie wasn't great, and the plot was fairly predictable, but both of them sat staring at the screen, not moving.

Finally Max turned to Jenna. "I know something you can do to help me," he said quietly. She immediately turned to face him, her face serious and intent. "My reptile is cold." He smirked.

"Y-you're reptile?" She looked at him with confused eyes. She didn't want to assume what he was asking her for, and fucking it up worse.

"Yes, it's your responsibility to care for the reptile, and he's cold. I thought you might let him warm up inside you, and maybe we could chat?" His eyes were playful, but Jenna still felt that edge of wariness coming from him.

"Of course, Baby. There's nothing I wouldn't do for my reptile. Is there, sweetie-boo?" She turned her attention to his crotch, gently stroking him through his pants as she cooed.

"Enough of that." He laughed, as he undid his pants.

"Oh, wait!" Jenna exclaimed, and rushed up the stairs. "I'll be right back." A few minutes later she reappeared with the bottle of lube in her hand from his nightstand.

"You said no sex." He laughed.

"Yes, but my little reptile isn't getting in without a little help. I'm not proud," she stated defiantly, and Max threw his head back and laughed.

"He's not a *little* reptile, and you know it." He chuckled.

"Damn straight he's not. Lube it is!" She fished him out of his pants, and was relieved to see he was semi-erect; at least he didn't hate her. She kneeled between his legs and cooed baby talk to his cock as she rubbed her lubed hands all over it, until he groaned and pulled her away.

"Enough of that, Woman, climb on." He pulled her forward. She stopped to slip her panties off under her long skirt; then pulling her skirt off, she kneeled, straddled over him, on the sofa.

"You've never needed lube before," he said curiously.

"Yes, well, I haven't been in that kind of mood all day, I'm just trying to help things along," she answered, her cheeks coloring as he chuckled.

"Damn, have I mentioned how much I love seeing your bald pussy?" he asked, his eyes glued to her as it hovered over the head of his cock.

"Have I mentioned what a bitch it is when all that hair grows back in?" She teased.

"We'll get you laser," he said, then seemed to catch himself. Jenna didn't miss the wince.

So he wasn't sure about a future anymore...

Her heart squeezed in her chest.

Jenna took control of the conversation before it could suck her under. "Oooooh, my poor sweet anaconda. I can't let you be cold, Baby." She slowly lowered herself, holding him positioned beneath her opening. She got as far as the head before he just seemed to stick and go no further.

Max hissed, his head falling back. She lifted, and dropped again, but couldn't seem to get him inside of her. She was quickly becoming embarrassed, and Max was starting to groan.

"Damn woman,... so fucking tight... I thought you said no sex!" He smiled at her.

That did the trick, apparently seeing him smile opened her enough that she sank down another several inches onto him, making him jerk and groan again. She pulled up, and then slammed herself down hard, taking all of him into her. There was a slight burn as he stretched her uncomfortably, but she wasn't stopping until he was fully inside of her. Not for anything.

Once his cock was seated deep, she stopped and looked to him. She had no idea what to do next. His eyes were closed, a slow moan leaving his open mouth. He looked like he was in paradise. He finally opened them, and took her in.

"You wanted to talk?" she suggested quietly, anxious to see where this was going, one way or the other.

"I did.. I do," he answered, still seeming a little distracted by how tightly her pussy was squeezing his cock, his face flushed. Jenna sat uncharacteristically quiet, waiting.

"Blue, can you walk me through what you were thinking last night? I need to understand how you were seeing it." He spoke calmly, gently.

Shame spiked through Jenna, and it surprised her. She didn't do shame, nor regret. Not usually. She didn't give a fuck what guys thought of her. But at that moment, she suddenly felt dirty, or bad; as if his opinion of her would make or break her. It terrified her.

She steeled herself, and began talking; slipping into the matter-of-fact persona that she used to interface with the outside world.

"Well, I knew I wanted to surprise you. I wanted to take control in the bedroom. When you offered to masturbate on me, well, I went with it. I enjoyed that too. And then after you ate me out, I wanted you inside of me.

"I don't know, I guess I kind of went with the moment. I wondered what you would feel like, inside me, bare. I know I'm clean, and I figured you wouldn't be putting it in my mouth if you weren't; so you're clean... and I can't get pregnant... so I guess I thought you'd be happy about it too.

"Then when you weren't, I saw that it was pushing some button of yours. I went with it. I thought I could finally get you to lose control, to loosen up, and stop holding back on me.

"You're always worried about hurting me, but honestly, Max, my body is pretty tough. I take a beating weekly with Andrew, and you'd be hard pressed to hurt me worse.

"I don't know, Max. In that moment, I thought you would enjoy it, because I wanted it. I didn't think it would fuck with your mind like this. I sometimes forget that other people haven't lived my life, they're not used to some of my ideas. But the way you looked at me, afterwards..."

She stopped and looked at him, waiting for some response. She didn't want to sink herself further.

"How did I look at you?" he asked, clearly curious.

She looked away. "Like you were disgusted with me," she whispered.

Max sat quietly for a moment, and Jenna was doing her best to shove down the tsunami of emotion threatening to break out any minute.

"Let me ask you this...," Max asked, pulling her eyes back to his, "Do you have a pain kink? Do you get off on people hurting you?"

Shock registered in Jenna's eyes. "That's a thing?... No, I don't think I have a pain kink. I don't like being hurt any more than you do. I think I just have a higher pain threshold than most people do. Like... for instance, you mentioned anal the other day, right?"

Max nodded, his brows drawn down in confusion.

"Well, the first time you do anal it hurts like hell, right?" She looked at him.

"Well, there are preparations that need to be made... but there is some discomfort, yes," he answered slowly.

"And once those preparations are made, it's pleasurable, right? I mean, some women prefer that to regular sex." She looked at Max, who was still clearly confused about the turn of topic.

"All I'm saying, is that to an outsider anal must look brutal. You might think that only a masochist would let someone do that to them. But to the woman who loves it, it's what she likes the best, and no one else's judgment matters." Her eyes searched his.

"I like it really rough, but not because it hurts, it doesn't. Because it works for me. When I have sex I am all-in, I completely let go; I wanted for you to experience that too, I guess." She looked down as she spoke.

"But we could have had a conversation about this first." Max answered her gently.

"True. But to be honest, I still think you would have been guarded with me. I regret doing it the way that I did, but I'm glad that you did get to experience it. Did you enjoy it?" she asked sheepishly.

"Well, to be honest, it was probably the best fucking sex I've ever had... right up until the moment that I felt like a steaming pile of shit." There was no anger in his voice, but Jenna winced.

"Blue, I need to know, I need to understand... are you this way because you've been abused or beaten? If you're going to expect me to rape you because that's what you need, I just can't do that."

Jenna looked up at him with horror in her eyes, her mouth hanging open.

"Is THAT what you think?!" She gaped at him for a moment. "Max, no, no, no. I haven't been traumatized into being a sexually deviant. And I can promise you, for a fact, that you will never, *ever*, rape me." She spoke defiantly, her eyes ablaze with anger.

"Have you ever been raped?" he asked gently.

"Have you?" she retorted.

"Blue, please..."

"Max, most women have. Eighty one percent of women in the US experience rape or sexual assault in their lifetime. You can almost guarantee that almost any woman you've had sex with have been raped or assaulted at least once in her life, if not more than.

"So yes... Once, when I was thirteen. There were three more attempts over my lifetime, but those were unsuccessful because I sent them to the hospital."

"Mother of God...," Max muttered and tried to pull her close, but she pushed him back.

"My sexual preferences are not because of those experiences. I *choose* to engage in this sexuality because I genuinely enjoy it, not because I've been conditioned to expect it."

"I don't need your pity, Max Thurston. I can take care of myself. You will *never* rape me, because I would never *let* you. If I ask you for rough sex, it's because I enjoy it, and I thought you did too.

"I promise you that if you did anything that I was uncomfortable with, or that did hurt me, I would put a stop to it. I'm not a martyr. I don't do abuse or neglect.

"I'm sorry that I pushed your buttons, I'm sorry if I made you feel like shit. I should have thought it through, I should have had a conversation first. I see that now."

A raw ache was building in Jenna's chest. She was sure that this was the end of them. She didn't feel the need to open herself any further for a man who was about to toss her aside, regardless. She was already mourning the relationship that she had hoped to share with him, but she couldn't make him stay. She could feel the numbness starting to seep into her from around the edges, and this time, she welcomed it.

Chapter 11

Max

Jenna was shutting down, I could see it in her eyes. She had opened herself up and made herself too vulnerable, and her body was closing her off to protect her. To protect her from me.

"Blue, Baby..." Max pulled her chin gently so she was looking at him. "Thank you for helping me to understand. I think I get it now. I mean, how could I ask you to do anal, but get upset because you like rage fucking? As long as I know you won't ask me to hurt you, because that's something I never want to do. If you'd like, we could try that again, sometime... maybe role playing?" He smiled up at her hopefully.

Jenna's eyes were still somewhere between focused and losing focus as she nodded.

"We've both had a hard day, haven't we, Baby?" He sat up to hug her, rather than pulling her to him. "I think we need some reptile/mammal bonding, how do you feel about that?"

Jenna smiled at him weakly. He could see she was still insecure, still worried. He kissed her tenderly, and she returned it, her arms coming up to wrap around him tightly. He ran his hands down her back and over her bare ass.

"How is my little Muffy?" He cooed as he reached between them and gently circled over her clit.

"Muffy?!" she asked him, raising an eyebrow.

"Hey, my mammal to care for, I get to name it." He smiled back.

"So, do I get to call your anaconda Cocky?" She smirked back.

"Not if your mouth is full, no," he answered, laughing. "Besides, this little Muffy loves my attention, don't you Muffy?"

Jenna responded to his hand on her clit by clenching hard on his cock, which immediately had him rocking his hips up into her in response, and before they knew it they were fucking hard on the sofa, slamming their hips together while kissing desperately, devouring each other.

They were both so strung out that it wasn't long before both of them were screaming their releases, and panting on the sofa.

"I think you like Muffy, more than you like me." Jenna panted on his chest.

"No, Blue, Muffy is a part of a package deal; I chose you, and Muffy comes with... often if I have anything to say about it." He looked down and placed a kiss on her forehead.

"Do you realize it's been exactly one month, this weekend, since I met you in that stupid department store?" Jenna asked, looking up into his eyes.

He smirked down at her. "What a complete tool I was that day. How the fuck did I ever convince you to go out with me?" He chuckled.

"That's easy," she answered, chuckling, "you didn't. Your anaconda did."

◆ ◆ ◆

Jenna

It was Wednesday night, and Max was working in his home office. He and Jenna had dinner together when he got home from work, and then he disappeared into his office to finalize and review paperwork. He was sitting back in his chair, going through his notes, when there was a knock at his office door.

"You don't need to knock, Blue, you can come right in anytime," he called.

She pushed the door open and strolled in. She had changed her outfit, and wore a short tight pencil skirt, and white button up blouse that showcased her amazing breasts like a picture frame. Her hair was pulled up into a french twist, and she wore tortoise-shell glasses, as well as a pair of super sexy high heels, that she could barely move in. She held some manilla files to her chest.

"I brought those files you requested, Mr. Thurston," she said in a super sexy voice, and then she dropped them in front of him on the desk carelessly and leaned her ass against it, crossing her leg high so that he could see up her thigh and into her tight skirt.

Max chuckled. "You did, did you, Miss Jones?"

"Yes." She nodded, bobbing her head. "For example...," She picked one of the folders up, and then let it drop from her fingers onto the floor. "Oops, I'll get that!" She squealed, as she turned and bent to retrieve the file, her ass in the air right in front of Max. Her skirt was so short that he could almost see her pussy. He closed his eyes and groaned.

Jenna snapped back upright. "What's the matter, Sir? Did I forget anything?" She put her finger on her pouty lips as if she was thinking, and batted her eyelashes at him.

"Yes, Miss Jones, I think you have forgotten something." He played along with a chuckle.

"Oh no! I'm so sorry, Mr. Thurston. What do you need me to do?" She looked up at him through her lashes making doe eyes.

He grinned wide, and then schooled his features to look serious. "Miss Jones, do you understand how distracting it is for me when you come in here with your tits on display..." He reached into her blouse and fondled a breast, pinching her nipple and making her squeal. "... and your tight little skirt?..." He brushed his other hand over her ass, drawing his fingers up her thighs until he reached her sex and froze.

"Miss Jones! Where are your undergarments?!" he asked in mock outrage.

"Oh, Mr. Thurston... I had to throw them away! They were so wet they were chafing!" Jenna answered dramatically, pouting her lips out.

"You know what I think?" Max demanded.

"No, Sir...," Jenna replied dutifully, looking contrite.

"I think you planned on seducing your boss today. I think you came in here, flashing your beautiful tits and luscious ass, in an effort to coerce me into having sex with you." He put his hands on his hips as if he was serious.

Jenna smiled, and had to school her features to stay in character.

"OH NO, SIR! I would NEVER do that! I know that sleeping with the boss is completely off limits!"

"Miss Jones, you are lying to me. And you know what happens when you lie to your boss, don't you?" he asked her in a deep voice.

"No, Sir, I don't." She shook her head desperately.

"You get punished. That's what happens. Now... Are you ready to tell the truth, or will you take your punishment like you deserve. Either way, I will get the truth out of you today."

"No, Mr. Thurston, I swear-," Jenna protested.

"Fine, do it the hard way. Miss Jones, you will lie over my lap, and pull your skirt up to expose that fantastic ass to me. Do it now."

"Oh, I don't-"

"NOW!" he ordered forcefully.

Jenna tottered over and laid over his lap as he sat in his chair. He ran his hand over her skirt, and then caught the edge with his fingertips and slowly peeled it upward until her ass was bare.

"Miss Jones, I already have the evidence of your deceitful plot. Your pussy is already dripping for me. This is your last chance to come clean."

"Mr. Thurston, I would never-"

-CRACK- "OW!"

Max's hand came down hard on Jenna's ass cheek, leaving a red hand print, which he promptly smoothed with the flat of his hand. Jenna whipped her head back to look at him, shock in her eyes.

"Are you ready to confess yet?" he asked her pointedly.

"NO. SIR," she replied.

-CRACK- "AAAAAhhhh!" This time her hips wiggled on his lap as he stroked her ass where he had spanked her. He let his fingers run over her mound, without entering, and she squirmed harder.

"How about now? Are you ready to confess that you wanted to seduce me? You wanted me to fuck you with my big cock and make you scream my name?"

"No, Mr. Thurston."

-CRACK- CRACK- "Aaaaaaaaaaaaaaaaaaahhhhhhhhh!"

Jenna squirmed herself on Max's erection, each smack was making her hotter and hotter. She just needed the friction between her legs to help it. She clamped her thighs tightly.

"Are you trying to get off while I punish you, Miss Jones? Is your pussy throbbing for release right now? Are you imagining my big hard cock pressing between those pussy lips and into your tight little body? Yes... You are so wet. I bet you just want to sink down and ride my cock like a bad girl, don't you, Miss Jones?"

"Mmmmmmmmmmm" Was the only noise Jennna could make, other than whimpering.

"Miss Jones, I am going to give you one opportunity to redeem yourself, and only one. Stand up." Max helped Jenna get back on her feet, her face was flushed and heated lust filled her eyes.

"This is your one chance for forgiveness. Get on your knees. Get on your knees and suck this big cock until I come down your throat. Do you understand?" Jenna nodded at him eagerly.

"Well, what are you waiting for? Suck my cock, Miss Jones." Jenna dropped to her knees undoing his pants as quickly as she could. He spread his knees to give her easier access, and tilted his chair back slightly so he could lean back and watch her.

In seconds she had him out of his briefs, her hands stroking him greedily. "OH! Mr. Thurston! Your cock is SO BIG! I don't know if I can fit this all in my mouth!" She sucked his balls into her mouth before moving on to his shaft, running her tongue over the length and around the head. Max groaned loudly.

"Miss Jones, you are not here to be a prick tease. Suck.My.Cock. Make it good, and all of this can be forgiven." He grabbed a handful of her hair and dragged her face down over his shaft, pushing himself deeply into her mouth. He groaned out loud, and she groaned as well, around him. She felt his shaft expanding immediately, becoming engorged in her mouth.

"You like that, Miss Jones? You like when I fuck that pretty mouth with my big cock?" His voice was thick and deep, his eyes were half-lidded with desire.

"MMM-HHHHmmm" She moaned as she nodded, his cock still stuffed in her mouth.

"All right then, Miss Jones, I want you to take it, and take it all. Swallow me whole, Miss Jones." With that he used both hands to fist in her hair and fuck her face with force. He slammed his cock down her throat, groaning at the sensation. Jenna was groaning too, and the vibration in her throat, around Max's cock, sent him into overdrive.

Soon his hips were coming up off of the chair, until he was almost squatting in front of her, pounding his cock down her throat.

"FUCK... BLUE... So fucking good! AAAAAAHHH!" He fell completely out of character as he watched her rounded mouth devour his cock again and again, while she looked on with big eyes.

"BLUE!!!!" He threw his head back, his body arched stiff, his cock lodged deep down her throat as he spasmed through release. He spilled into her, and then resumed pumping his cock back down her throat again and again as he rode the orgasm out, emptying himself.

Jenna followed him as he tried to pull out, sucking him in, grabbing his ass with her hands to feed his cock back into her hungry mouth like she was starving. Her tongue swirled around him, and up him, until Max was completely overwhelmed with stimulation. Finally he pulled away from her, his cock too sensitive to touch.

"Fucking Hell, Blue!" Max fell back into his chair, his eyes wild, his cock laying red and wet between his legs heavily. He was heaving for air, his chest and shoulders contracting as he tried to get deeper breaths.

Jenna looked up from the floor. "Am I forgiven, Mr. Thurston? I swear, it won't ever happen again!" She pouted her lips and looked up at him through her lashes.

"No..." Max gasped. "I'm sorry... Miss Jones, ... but that's not... good enough... I think.... I need to ... teach you ... a lesson." His breathing was finally starting to come under control.

"Oh, no, Mr. Thurston! I'll do ANYTHING!" She mock pleaded.

"Damn, you're good, Miss Jones." Max chuckled out of character, and then he schooled his features.

"Remove your clothing, and lie on my desk on your back Miss Jones. Don't make me ask you twice." Max removed all of his work files quickly, while Jenna stripped out of her blouse and skirt, flinging her bra off at the last minute, and then hopping onto the desk, and lying back, her legs hanging over the edge in front of him.

"Like this, Mr. Thurston?" she asked.

"Just like that, Miss Jones." Max stepped in front of her and picked both of her knees up, and spread her legs wide so that he could see her pussy. "Now, I want you to pleasure yourself. I want to see your fingers make that beautiful little cunt all creamy for me. Show me, Miss Jones."

"Oh, I don't know..." She started to play argue.

"Miss Jones, you are only making your situation worse for yourself. I want to see you pleasure yourself to my satisfaction. If you do a good job, you will be rewarded." Max sat back down in his office chair, her pussy right in front of him like a gourmet meal.

Jenna's fingers moved through her lips, stroking her clit, diving into her folds. She squirmed her ass as she gasped and moaned her pleasure. Max was already stroking himself back to full hardness again, watching Jenna get off in front of him. He reached forward, pushing three fingers into her, making her gasp and jump. She felt her pussy grab at his hand as he sunk it in and out, again and again. Finally he withdrew his hand, and Jenna whimpered her disappointment. He transferred her wetness to his own cock, and began to stroke harder.

"Miss Jones, you are a very lucky lady indeed," he announced, as he stood over her. Her eyes were glued to where his hand was stroking his own cock. "I am going to give you what you came here for. I am going to fuck you with this big cock. I am going to fuck your pussy so hard that you will never forget it. And when you come, Miss Jones, you WILL be screaming my name.

"Roll over, bend over the desk so I can fuck that hot juicy pussy."

Jenna rolled and scooted her ass to the edge of the desk. Max kicked her feet wide, so that her pussy was open for him.

"Mr. Thurston…" She panted. "I've never had a cock that big before! Be gentle with me!" She mock pleaded, a sly smile on her face as she looked over her shoulder at him.

Max chuckled under his breath, struggling to stay in character.

"Well, Miss Jones, you should have thought of that before you came into my office with those fucking amazing tits…" He slid his hand under her chest to pinch her nipple, and then he massaged her breast roughly. "…and this hot little ass and wet pussy in my face!" He smacked her ass hard again, and she groaned and jumped; but he put a hand onto her hip to hold her still as he used the other to line his cock up with her moist entrance.

He stroked the head of his cock up into her folds and back down again, Jenna squirmed like a crazy thing, trying to find purchase so she could shove her pussy back onto him. He held her down as he slowly tortured her pussy.

"MR. THURSTON!!!" she finally screamed in frustration. He brought the head up to bounce against her asshole and she froze on the table with a gasp.

"You don't get this today, Miss Jones. Only the best girls get this." Max pulled his cock back down to her weeping pussy and lined it up.

"PLEASE! Mr. Thurston." Jenna was squirming and begging.

"Do you want this cock?" He asked casually, as he swept it through her folds again, rubbing it against her clit.

She screamed and bucked, "FUCKING GIVE IT TO ME!"

"Then TAKE IT!" Max rammed his cock into her deep with one solid thrust. Jenna screamed and howled, trying to bring her hips up and back to meet him, but he literally had her pinned to the desk. He leaned over her and gave it to her good, slamming into her hard. Jenna roared and wailed, throwing her head back in ecstasy.

"You like that cock, Miss Jones?!" Max demanded as he pounded into her, harder and harder.

"I fucking LOVE that cock, Mr. Thurston!" she screamed, and it was shortly after that that her pussy started grabbing, milking, and crushing Max's cock deep inside of her, sucking all of his come out of him. They locked up blissfully together, him deep and hard inside of her, screaming their releases. And he had been right.

When Jenna came, she was screaming Max's name.

◆ ◆ ◆

Max

Ever since their little chat, life between Max and Jenna had gone back to the roller coaster ride it had been. They both dragged themselves, exhausted and sleep deprived, through work, and they lived for the evenings when they would spend time together.

Max was making an extra effort not to be the workaholic he usually was; on the rare occasions that he did overwork, Jenna was usually around, bringing him food or coffee. She made no demands on him and just let him know that she cared.

It was the Saturday of the Charity Ball for the FoodBank, and he had brought Jenna to get pampered: waxed, spray tanned, and hair and makeup. That gave him time to get ready on his schedule.

He usually hated these events. He preferred to give to charities quietly, to not be in the limelight, but he knew that people expected to see him give, and that he set the example for others. It was a necessary evil, but he didn't enjoy it. There was something so wrong about a glamorous ballroom, expensive food and drink, and ridiculously expensive clothing... all in the name of raising money. If they had a backyard barbeque, and donated everything they would have spent on the party, they'd never run out of food.

This time there was a thrill running through him; this time he would have Jenna on his arm. He would have a woman he was proud to be seen with: a smart woman, a beautiful woman, his woman.

His woman? Where the hell did that come from?

He wanted to show her off, dance with her and only her, have great conversations over drinks… do the things the other guys got to do with their dates, and not just some woman they hired as a stand-in. For the first time, he was excited to be going.

The driver had brought Jenna back, and Max looked over as she walked into the room. His breath caught in his throat. Jenna was a vision in her metallic blue dress, her skin flawless, her blue hair blown out and falling around her shoulders. She smiled at him shyly, and she was the most beautiful thing she had ever seen.

He was on her in seconds, his hands wrapped around her, his nose buried in the curve of her neck, kissing her tenderly. She giggled as she wrapped her arms around him.

"You look incredible," he whispered as he looked into her eyes. Her joy was palpable. He would buy her a different dress for every day of the week if she could look this happy for him forever.

Forever?…

He brought his head down to kiss her and she murmured, "My lipstick…"

He kissed her on the cheek and then whispered in her ear. "…Will be all over my cock at the end of the night." She giggled again and he added, "You think I'm kidding?" He pulled back to give her a smirk, his eyes full of lustful mischief.

"Does my reptile need more attention?" she cooed.

"Always," Max responded, kissing the back of her hand and then turning it over to place a kiss in the center of her palm. He felt her shiver.

An hour later the limo pulled up to the hotel. The driver opened the door for Max, and he held his hand for Jenna. She put her hand in his, looked up at him, and his heart swooned. He helped her out and put a protective arm around her waist, walking her inside, letting everyone know she was his. He felt like the king of the world.

He guided her over the red carpet and through the velvet ropes which kept the press and the uninvited away. Max knew that Jenna was nervous, but no one else would ever guess it. She walked tall, back straight, head up. He looked at her and she smiled at him. It was like nothing else existed in that moment, and losing all thoughts he leaned in and kissed her right on the lips, tenderly. Cameras snapped, flashes burst behind his eyes. He didn't care.

Max felt as proud as a peacock as he walked through the ballroom with Jenna on his arm. He could see some of his contemporaries stopping and openly staring, he just smiled. He knew she was leaving with him.

They made their way to their table, and introductions began for the other couples seated with them. He knew Bruce and Melinda Hannaby, they owned a large supermarket chain up and down the Northeast.

Beside them was a younger man, probably early twenties, with an equally young date. His suit was loud and overstated, and his date was preoccupied with making pouty faces and posting them on social media. They were apparently influencers, 'new money.' They didn't talk to each other, and they didn't even pretend to want to talk to anyone else at the table; the guy took off to find his friends, and the woman spent her whole time scrolling on her cell phone.

The other two couples were older. Max discovered that one of them worked for the state, possibly the Department of Education. The other couple were both Professors at Harvard.

Dinner was uneventful, speeches were heard and applauded. When it came time to dance, Max was giddy as he asked Jenna to join him. The music was light and romantic, and he held her far too close as they swayed under the dimmed chandeliers. He couldn't remember being happier.

They danced to the next song, and then the next, and finally Jenna needed to sit down. Max knew she wasn't used to wearing heels, and her feet must be killing her. Max kissed the back of her hand and led her back to her chair. Once she was seated, he excused himself to go to the bar and get them drinks, smiling from ear to ear.

◆ ◆ ◆

Jenna

The table was largely empty, and Jenna decided it would be a good time for her to use the ladies room. Her feet were killing her, but she was deliriously happy otherwise. The event wasn't bad at all, and she was in love with her new gown. She felt glamorous and wanted.

She made her way into the bathroom stall, and began her inevitable wrestling match with the tight elastic waist trainer while trying to hold the dress up. Honestly, it was ridiculous. She was getting really frustrated, and considered just yanking the panel to the side so she could just pee, when she heard the door open and voices enter.

"I see Bill Blars actually brought his wife this time." The first voice snickered.

Oh no... not again... Jenna froze.

"Mia, I saw that Max is here... with someone new!" A second voice taunted.

"Shut the fuck up, Ashley. We're just on a break, that's all. He's going to marry me. He won't stay with her for long. I know what he likes, no other woman will put up with his sexual needs for long. I'm the only one who gives it to him like he likes it."

Jenna's heart thumped loudly in her chest. This was the little bitch she saw trying to grab Max's cock at his house.

A third voice chimed in, "I don't know, Mia. He seems pretty attached to her. He never looked at you like that."

"Because he was being a gentleman!" Mia shrieked. "She's clearly just his fuck toy! His hands are all over her, for fuck's sake. I guarantee that once she knows how rough he is, she'll run as fast as she can."

Something in Jenna snapped. She smoothed her dress, took a deep breath, and swung the stall door open with a bang. The three women at the mirror jumped and shrieked. Jenna stormed up to Mia and got right in her face.

"You dumb bitches should really learn to make sure the bathroom is empty before you talk shit. Just so you know, Mia, he's never going to marry you. I'm living with him now, and I'm not just his fuck toy. I give it just as hard as he does; so if you're waiting for me to go running, you've got a long wait.

"Oh, and one more thing. I EVER see you lay a hand on MY man again, and I will fucking end you."

Jenna straightened up and walked out of the bathroom calmly, like the queen she was, leaving the sniveling bitches behind her to gawk.

She got back to the table and sat, her rage was palpable. Why the fuck was that woman still trying to get her claws into Max? Just the memory of her wrapped around him in his doorway made her want to commit violence.

It was then that Max returned to the table. He took one look at Jenna, her face flushed and her jaw tight, and he realized something had happened.

"Tell me," he said.

Chapter 12

Max

Max put the drinks down and turned Jenna to face him.

She stared at him for a minute, her jaw grinding. She had fury written all over her face. Max had no idea what had happened, but she looked close to coming unhinged.

"Do you want to leave?" he asked gently.

"I think that's a good idea," she said and got up quickly, gathering her purse. As an afterthought she turned back to the table and picked up the tumbler of scotch Max had just gotten for her and swallowed it in one gulp, grimacing at the burn down her throat. Then she picked his up and did the same. He placed his hand on her lower back and led her from the ballroom to pick up their coats.

They sat in the living room, still in their formal wear, although Max had untied his bowtie. He shook his head.

"I can't fucking believe her. So then what did you do, Blue?"

"I completely lost my mind," she stated over her new glass of scotch. "I stormed out there, got in her face, and told her that if she was waiting for me to run off she was going to be waiting a long time. I told her I was living with you, and you were never going to marry her... Oh, and I kinda told her that if she ever laid a hand on you again, I would end her." A slow blush spread across her cheeks. She swallowed her scotch quickly.

Max threw his head back and laughed. "I love my possessive little wildcat!" He chuckled and leaned down swiftly to kiss her on her scotch-laced lips.

He hoped to hell she didn't catch his slip with the "L" word.

Jenna kissed him back with passion. Her hands began to claw at his shirt and slacks. Max stood, pulling her with him. "Upstairs," he urged, and they both raced for the stairs.

Once in the bedroom it was a frenzy of clothing flying, teeth, and claws. They came at each other like wild animals engaging in a battle to the death, each fighting for dominance. They roared, clawed, and bit, digging teeth and nails into flesh.

Jenna launched onto Max's cock while he was still tied up with getting undressed. She wrapped her arms around his waist to hold him while she devoured his cock from base to tip, deep throating him, moaning, and working him until she thought he would explode.

Max finally managed to pull out of her hold. He grabbed her and flung her on the bed, jumping after her to land across her with his mouth over her pussy. He dropped his body weight onto her, to keep her from moving or shifting as he sank his fingers into her ass cheeks and ate her out with abandon. She struggled and thrashed underneath him, groaning and cursing, trying to reach his cock, but he kept her arm pinned until he made her scream and shatter in his mouth.

Max pinned her down on her back and was thrusting into her with everything that he had; he had to physically restrain her to keep her from trying to flip him and climb on top of him. It was the most bizarre, primal heat he had ever experienced. Everything male in him rose to the front of his brain to dominate and claim Jenna, and she fought him every step of the way, while simultaneously screaming out her pleasure. He bit her shoulder hard, and she dug his nails into his back and raked them down. That spurred him on more, he only fucked her harder.

Their rutting built and built, pulling them higher and higher. Max's hand was around Jenna's throat, not choking her, but asserting dominance. Jenna was raking her claws up Max's ribs. There was no thought, no awareness other than their sexual release, and their dominance. Jenna bit Max's shoulder, hard, and he screamed as he forced his cock deeper into her, harder and faster, until at last they were both screaming, heaving, sweating... and then falling on top of each other completely spent. They were both scratched all over, with small bruises blooming, and a few cuts.

"Holy fuck..." Max groaned. "Are you okay?" He turned to look at Jenna as he tried to bring his breathing under control. She turned to look at him, still heaving in big gulps of air.

"Round two?" She smiled devilishly.

◆ ◆ ◆

Jenna

There were only two weeks left until Christmas. It was Sunday, and Jenna had already been to church, painted, and had dinner with Andrew. It was now ten pm, and she was getting ready to go to bed, and she still couldn't figure out what she was going to get for Max.

What do you buy someone who's rich?

She wanted to get him something special, something thoughtful, but the man had more money than God. Seriously, what were her chances?

Just then her phone beeped.

"Max: How is my Muffy today?"

"Blue: You only love me for my mammal."

"Max: Not true. But I do love your mammal... You want to come over, Blue?

"Blue: Yes, but I won't. It's already late, and it's colder than a witches tit outside. I'll see you tomorrow after work?"

"Max: I feel like that's a challenge. I feel like I need to find a witch, just so I can feel her tit."

"Blue: You do, and you die. And then Muffy will be heartbroken."

"Max: Well, I could never do that to Muffy. Goodnight my dearest Blue."

"Blue: Goodnight, Max, sweet dreams."

"Max: Only of you, Baby. Only of you."

Jenna looked at her phone in amazement. Max had really become more tender since their talk. He had always been attentive and thoughtful, but there was something... more. He was more possessive, more committed. He had slipped and used the "L" word a couple of times... never the full three-word-phrase, but still. He was clearly feeling it, even if he couldn't say it. The tenderness in his eyes when he looked at her spoke volumes.

Jenna was happy with the way things were. She didn't feel a rush for him to declare his undying love for her; that was usually the cue for the end. She couldn't lie; she had feelings for him. Deep feelings. But she was choosing not to look at them, not to label them; she'd rather just live in the moment and 'be' with him.

Life was shitty, and people leave all the time. She went into every interaction knowing that tomorrow is never promised. She refused to worry about how she would feel 'if' instead just enjoying the moments that she had now. She felt like she was on borrowed time, and she didn't want to waste a moment of it being unhappy about something that may or may not happen in the future. Right now is all you get.

The work week went by in a blur. There was already a small dusting of snow on the ground, and the weather was frigid. Jenna was grateful to be able to stay at Max's place, and not make the commute home to Alston every day. Waiting for a train in freezing weather was the worst.

Max and Jenna had settled into a quasi-routine. She either made him dinner, or he left her a card to order delivery. She had dinner ready for him when he got home, and they discussed their day like normal couples. It really felt like playing house; it was comfortable. As the weather got colder, they went out less and less, opting to stay in for a movie, or marathon sex. Or both.

It wasn't long before it was Saturday again, the day of Max's office Christmas Party. Jenna had agreed to go with him, after all, those bitches from the events wouldn't be there. These were his co-workers and their spouses. How tough could it be? She was curious to meet the people he worked with.

Max surprised her by buying her a short beaded black dress with spaghetti straps to wear; it was incredibly sexy and chic. A part of her wanted to refuse it, but the larger part of her wanted to wear it in front of him all night and make him beg to tear it off at home that night. The sex fiend won.

Max parked in an underground garage and escorted Jenna to the elevator. When they stepped out into the top floor of the building, the party was already in full swing. The lighting was lower than it would be during business hours, and the music was playing loud. The large room was decked out with streamers and Christmas pictures, and there was a tree with gifts in the corner. People danced, mingled, chatted, and ate.

Max introduced Jenna to person after person as they floated through the room. He was in his glory, and Jenna could tell he was happy. He was dragging people over to introduce them to her. She just chuckled at him. He seemed so proud. Finally he pulled her to the back of the room.

"Jenna, I want you to meet my brother, Ed, and his wife Joelle." Jenna shook their hands.

"I didn't know your brother worked with you," she said to Max, looking between them. They were clearly related, although Ed looked older and less muscular.

"I didn't want him to steal you away from me, that's all." Max chuckled, and then kissed her on the temple. "Oh, I need to go say hi to a few people. Will you wait here for me?" He was gone before she could reply.

"Would you ladies like drinks?" Ed asked. Joelle immediately said yes, so Jenna said yes as well. "Rum and coke for you?" Ed looked to Joelle, who nodded. "How about you?" He turned his eyes to Jenna, and it was like seeing another Max. She stuttered for a moment before finally blurting out "Tanqueray and tonic with lime, please." Ed smirked and left the ladies to go in search of drinks.

Joelle turned to Jenna. "I need a drink to get me through these damned things. They're always so stuffy."

Jenna just nodded, not knowing what to say.

"So, Jenna, what do you do for work?" Joelle asked. There was no snark in her voice, but Jenna wasn't sure she could trust her yet. Still, no point in lying.

"I'm a barista," she answered.

"Really?" Joelle looked excited. "I was a bartender when I met Ed. Don't tell anyone, it's supposed to be a secret, but I bartended at a gentleman's club. That's where I met him."

Jenna smiled. She liked this woman. "Really?!" she asked with a sly smirk, and Joelle nodded vehemently.

"You and I should get together sometime for a girl's day." Joelle suggested. "Let me give you my number. Since you're in the family now, we girls got to stick together."

"I've only been dating Max for a month and a half." Jenna laughed.

Joelle laughed as well, "Oh, Honey... you are DATING Max. You're a unicorn. Max doesn't date. And Max doesn't bring girls he likes to business or family functions. You are the first. You're family now." Jenna smiled, but her mind was reeling, trying to understand everything she had just heard.

She was the first girl he had brought to the company Christmas party. She was the first. It suddenly felt a little overwhelming.

Ed returned with their drinks, and Jenna swallowed half of hers before a man sidled up beside her.

"Hey, you must be Max's new girl! Hi, I'm Marcus!" He grinned smoothly, but Jenna got an immediate reaction in her gut that told her not to trust him.

"Yes, Hi. I'm Jenna." She shook his hand and noticed that Joelle and Ed had moved a little farther away to talk with someone. Her eyes scanned the room, looking for Max.

"He's told me all about you, I'm so excited to meet you in person." He smiled in a way that was probably supposed to be charming, but it turned Jenna's stomach.

"Where is Max?" she asked aloud, her head craning to find him.

"He's right over here, in his office. I can take you." Marcus smiled warmly.

While Jenna wanted to jump on the chance to find Max, she didn't want to be alone with Marcus. Something was setting off warning bells in her body. But if he was taking her to him...

"Sure, lead the way!" He took her hand and turned and walked. Jenna tried to pull her hand back, but he was moving, pulling her along with him. She was instantly angry at his touch. Turning a corner, he led her into a conference room.

"His office is right through that door." He pointed at the other side of the room. Jenna ripped her hand out of his and jogged for the door, pulling it open. It was empty inside. She turned to find Marcus right behind her, blocking the door.

"He's not here, I'd better get back." Jenna tried to side step, but Marcus moved into her way.

"Actually Jenna, I have a job offer for you." He smiled at her like a predator.

Jenna stood still. She understood predators.

"What do you want?" Jenna asked flatly.

"Well, I thought I might offer you a side job. I'm heading west for a few weeks, and I need some company. Whatever Max is paying you, I'll double it."

Jenna saw red.

"And if Max isn't paying me?" She spit.

"Boy, you really suck at negotiations, you know that?" He chuckled at his own joke. "Look, Sweetheart, the way I see it your career path has an expiration date. Who's going to hire you when your tits sag, and your face is wrinkled. You need to make as much as you can while you're still in your prime." He smirked and reached a hand up to touch her hair. She batted it away.

"Didn't you say you were Max's friend? Why would you try to steal his girl?" She crossed her arms in front of her and cocked her head.

"Please, we're all just renting them anyway. He won't care, trust me. I loan him my girls all the time. Hell, I even stopped seeing Mia so he could see her exclusively. You're his now, but you could just as easily be mine." He reached out and grabbed her crotch in his hand like he owned it. The look in his eyes was a challenge.

And that was the final straw.

Rage tore through Jenna as she launched at Marcus. He tried to defend himself, but she had too many years fighting stronger faster opponents. When her fog lifted and she finally stopped, he was laying on the floor, badly broken, bleeding, and wailing. Panic hit her.

This was Max's company! This was Max's friend! Oh, shit! What did I do?!

She ran from the room, away from the party, toward where she remembered the elevators being. Instead of waiting for the elevators she took the stairs down, two at a time. She pushed out of the double doors to the building and into the frigid

Boston night with only her clutch in her hand and no coat. She ran.

◆ ◆ ◆

Max

"Mr. Thurston, we have a problem." Eric from Security stood in the doorway looking serious.

"Do we have a few receptionists making the 'naughty' list?" Ed laughed.

Eric didn't even crack a smile. "Sirs, I think you need to come see this."

Ed and Max were suddenly dead serious as they followed Eric back toward their offices. When they reached Max's they saw Marcus, propped up in one of his chairs, his face a bloody mess.

"What the hell happened?" Max asked in shock.

"What the fuck is wrong with that girl of yours?" Marcus sneered.

"What are you talking about?" Max was confused, and he had a bad feeling in his gut.

"She dragged me in here, saying you were looking for me, and then she attacked me! She was trying to pull my clothes off. When I told her I wasn't going to do it here, she went postal. That bitch is crazy!"

Ed said nothing. Max just stared.

Jenna did this?

Eric stepped closer to Max. "I have an ambulance on the way, I think his arm is broken, and maybe his leg." Max nodded.

None of this made any sense. Jenna wouldn't try to pick up Marcus, his whole story sounded bogus. He knew she could inflict this type of damage, but why would she? What did he do? He leaned into Eric.

"Have them bring him down to the garage, level one. I'll meet you all there. Oh, and have someone pull the video from in here earlier." Eric nodded and left to radio the crew.

"Don't worry, Marcus, I'll get to the bottom of this," Max stated calmly.

"I want that fucking cunt arrested!" Marcus growled, and Max had all he could do not to break Marcus's other arm and leg for him.

Instead he turned and stormed down the hallway, stopping in a quiet office and closing the door.

He dialed Jenna's number.

◆ ◆ ◆

Jenna

Jenna stumbled through the slick streets for a few blocks before finally stopping to think. She was freezing in her tiny dress, and her heels weren't cut out for snow and ice. She just wanted to curl up into a ball and cry.

She had lost it. For the first time in a long time, she had lost control; she had hurt someone. Yes, he deserved it, but that wasn't the point. She had done it without being aware she was doing it. She didn't want to go back to psychiatric care. She didn't want to be hospitalized.

Why the fuck had she ever thought she could do a 'normal' relationship?

She looked around her nervously. She had no idea where she was. She had to get home.

Which home? Andrew's home... would he take her, knowing she might be going to jail?

Max's home?... He would probably never talk to her again, after what she did.

Defeated, she dropped onto a snow covered park bench and buried her face in her hands and cried. She had hit a dead end.

Her phone rang in her purse, and she looked up startled.

Probably the police, wanting to question me before they arrest me.

She pulled it out, relieved to see it was Max calling, and then instantly dreading it. She knew she had to face the end sooner or later, she would go with her head up.

"Hello...," She whispered.

"Blue! Baby! Where are you?! Are you okay?!" He sounded panicked.

"I... I don't know where I am, Max." She looked around. "There's a Starbucks... and a bookstore..."

"Are you OUTSIDE?!" He sounded beyond panicked. "Baby, go into Starbucks, ask them the address. I'm coming to get you. DON'T LEAVE. Just wait for me, get a coffee and warm up, okay, Baby! I'm on my way, text me the address."

Jenna stood up stiffly and moved numbly toward the Starbucks. She wrapped her arms around her shaking shoulders. She saw crowds of holiday shoppers moving to and fro under the festive holiday lights which were strung everywhere. Couples walked gloved hand in gloved hand. She saw couples through the windows in the bars, drinking, laughing; their whole futures ahead of them. It made her sad.

She took a seat by the window and sipped her coffee. She had sent Max the address, and she was waiting. It felt like a march to the gallows. When he found out what she had done to a friend of his, he was going to lose it. Not because she had hurt him, but the degree to which she had hurt him. She could have slapped his face. She could have kneed him in the balls. Those things he deserved.

But she knew she had broken an arm, a leg, and probably two to three ribs. She had lost control. And that was all that ever mattered in the end.

Max flew through the door, his face a picture of panic, and ran to her, skidding on the slippery floor tiles. "JENNA!" He dropped and wrapped his arms around her, sloshing her coffee. He buried his head in her neck and squeezed her.

Then he looked up, his eyes wide, and he held her face in his hands, inspecting her. "Jenna, are you okay? Are you hurt?! Did he hurt you?!"

"Who?" she asked, genuinely confused.

"Marcus, did he hurt you?" Max held her, searching, and Jenna could see his heart breaking. He was worried about her wellbeing, again.

Jenna threw her head back and laughed, and laughed, and laughed. It came out sounding manic. She knew she must look crazy. Max just stared at her, his mouth agape, confusion in his eyes.

"Max, do you really think Marcus could hurt me?" She hic-coughed. "No, he implied I was a prostitute, tried to bribe me to leave you, and then he tried to grope me.... inappropriately." At this, she hung her head in shame.

"Oh my fucking GOD. I will fucking kill him." Max's rage was radiating off of him in waves.

"I don't think you need to, I already kind of took care of that." Jenna whispered softly.

Max's eyes softened immediately, realizing that Jenna needed him more than he needed to get Marcus.

"Tell me everything, Baby." He sat and waited.

◆ ◆ ◆

Max

Max didn't like the idea at all, but Jenna seemed to think that it was the only way to uncover the truth of the situation. As much as he didn't like it, he didn't want to see Jenna locked up for defending herself either.

"Leave the call open, Baby. I'll hear everything. Scream if you need help, we'll be right there." Max repeated.

"Max, Baby, even with both arms and both legs, Marcus is no threat to me. Just what do you think he's going to do to me while he's half broken?" Her matter-of-fact delivery had Max chuckling.

"Right... so, good luck, then." He chuckled again as he watched her walk to the elevator while he stayed out of sight.

The EMT's had moved Marcus on a gurney to the parking garage level one, where the ambulance was waiting. Jenna approached them, and the EMT's all suddenly remembered they had to go back inside and get some things they had left: effectively leaving Jenna and Marcus, who was strapped to the gurney, alone.

Marcus looked around confused, until he saw her. He heard Marcus's voice through his phone, which Jenna had called and left open.

"You fucking psycho cunt! I'm going to make sure you rot in prison you crazy bitch!" Spittle flew from his mouth as he screamed.

"Why, Marcus? Why were you sharing girls with Max? Why did you want to double what he was paying me? Why?" She stood a few feet away, her hands in the pocket of the coat Max had brought for her.

"That's none of your fucking business, cunt! Your job is to spread your legs, not ask questions. If you had just done your fucking job and distracted him, I would be partner by now. You fucking bitches can't even fuck worth a damn! What fucking use are you?!" He thrashed on the gurney.

"So Max was stopping you from making partner?" She asked calmly.

"That position should have been mine! My own fucking father was a partner! But no, Max has to come in with his perfect record, sucking up, staying late to get all the glory! If he thinks he can just step in and take my partnership, he's got another thing coming! I spent four fucking years 'coming up through the ranks', while he just gets fast-tracked to Partner.

"He's going down. And when he does, guess who'll be there, ready to take the position that should have been mine in the FIRST place?! This isn't over bitch. I'd fucking kill you if I could get up right now!"

"Is that why you tried to grab my crotch, to take ownership of something that belongs to Max?" she asked evenly.

"You aren't listening!" Marcus screamed, becoming more and more unglued. "Max doesn't own SHIT. If I want it, I'm taking it. I make it a point to ruin all of his girls. You're next! I know how he likes it, so you should be fine with me chocking you out or knocking you around, you fucking whore! I'm going to enjoy fucking you, and making you hurt!"

Max watched from fifty feet away, his blood boiling. He wanted to kill Marcus.

"That's enough." Max watched as Jenna turned and saw a couple of policemen headed her way. Her head fell immediately. Tears started to leak down her cheeks. One of the officers stopped next to her, while the paramedics miraculously reappeared and converged on Marcus with the other officer. Max rushed from his concealed spot to Jenna's side.

"Ma'am, are you okay? Do you need medical help?" The officer seemed sincere and caring.

"No... I'm good. I'm ready." Jenna breathed out a slow resolved breath. Max placed his hand on her lower back and she turned to see him standing beside her, his eyes full of concern as he stared at her.

"Blue, Baby, you ready to go home?" He spoke gently.

She looked at the police officer, then back to Max, with confusion. "Uh... don't I need to go down to the station?" she asked hesitantly.

"Ma'am, we will need a statement from you in order to charge Marcus, but we can get that tomorrow if you'd rather rest."

Jenna seemed shocked, but quietly agreed to go home.

Max silently beat himself up for leaving her alone at the party. He should have protected her. He couldn't believe that he had essentially brought her right to Marcus.

Suddenly all of Max's lingering questions made sense. Marcus had given Max the number for the agency, the girls... All the times Marcus had insisted he go out for a "guys night" right before Max had to appear in court for a high profile case. There were so many little things... Marcus had been trying to sabotage him.

Max watched as Jenna looked between them with confusion written all over her face. She was distraught. He would have to deal with Marcus tomorrow, right now, his Blue needed him.

Chapter 13

Max

Max settled Jenna into the tub of hot water to relax. When she closed her eyes and laid back he sat with her, watching her. She had been quiet on the way home, and it worried him.

He expected her to be furious, after what she'd done to Marcus. He expected her to be in full warrior mode. He expected her to be swearing and cursing when he found her. Instead, she looked defeated. She kept her head down as if she had accepted some terrible fate. Had Marcus done more to her than she had admitted? She seemed... broken.

When her breaths gentled in the tub he quietly extracted himself from the room and headed to his home office. He dialed Eric from the security team, and had them send him the video feed from his office. He checked in on Jenna one more time, before settling in front of his computer to watch.

Rage boiled up in him as he watched Marcus block her into the room. There was no audio, but he could see by Jenna's body language that she was uncomfortable. He saw the moment her body realized Marcus was a threat; she straightened, her eyes intent and aware. He saw the moment Marcus reached out and grabbed her crotch with his hand, grabbed and held, a sneer on his face.

And then he saw Jenna snap.

She never looked angry; she had a look of devastating focus as she did what she had to do. Her shots were lethal as she rained them down on Marcus. She was right, he was completely outmatched. She handed him his ass in seconds flat.

Max watched as she slowly came to, watched her searching around her with panic in her eyes, before bolting out of the room. She must have been terrified... but Max wasn't sure of what.

It was late as Max laid in bed behind Jenna, holding her close. He couldn't fall asleep, remembering the terrorized look in her eyes as she bolted out of his office and away from Marcus. He wished he could take that from her. He wished that he could make her world a peaceful place, like she made his; he wondered what demons haunted her to make her look like that.

Jenna twitched in his arms, hard; then she thrashed.

"Williams! NO!" she cried out, thrashing harder against his body. "Brady! OH MY GOD! BRADY!!!!" she wailed, kicking out and scratching to get out of his hold. Instinctively he rolled on top of her gently with his body weight, rolling her under him.

"Jenna... Baby... wake up. Jenna, it's a nightmare. I'm here, Baby!" he whispered urgently in her ear.

Her eyes flew open wide, haunted. Her breathing was ragged, and she searched around her frantically to try to understand where she was, what was going on. When her eyes finally met his, she let out a keening wail and broke into sobs, her whole body convulsing with the force.

Max rolled off of her and held her close as she shattered in his arms. His heart broke watching her internal suffering, not understanding what was going on. He rocked her gently and just whispered reassurances in her ear. If it had been any other girl, he might have been turned off by the drama and waterworks, but he found he wanted to be the one to fix Jenna. He wanted to be the one she shared her pain with. He sat with her for hours as she slowly poured her pain out in his arms.

◆ ◆ ◆

Jenna

I sat in the back, too pissed to even look at him. Rob Williams, my squad leader, and fiance... former fiance... sat in the front, making conversation with Brady. We had been engaged to be married, he even gave me a ring. It was tiny, but I hadn't cared; we didn't get paid much, and it had meant everything to me. He had made life bearable while we were on duty in the "sandbox."

And then I found out he'd been fucking around. We'd had a huge argument, and I refused to talk to him anymore. He'd begged for a chance to explain, but what was there to explain? He'd stuck his dick in a dozen other women while we were together. We were over.

The humvee rolled along, and I kept my eye on the surroundings. Williams and Brady joked as we went. Rage boiled through me.

Suddenly I was in the air, a sonic boom tearing through my body like thunder, pain searing through my gut. I hit the ground hard, and my vision started to darken around the edges. I rolled my head and saw Brady... half of Brady... her eyes lifeless. Williams was crawling toward her. I screamed and screamed and screamed for him to take cover, but he didn't listen. I watched as the bullet tore through his skull, right before my vision went black.

Jenna seemed to suddenly come to, her sobbing fit having passed. Looking up, she was surprised to see Max holding her quietly. He looked down at her with concern in his eyes, and kissed her forehead.

"I'm with you, Baby. You're ok now." He whispered.

A part of Jenna wanted to be mortified, finding herself so weak and vulnerable, but she was exhausted. She was tired of fighting this fight over and over, with the same result. It was a war she couldn't win. And it took a piece of her every time she tried.

"I was in the humvee again...," she whispered.

"Shhh, Baby. You don't have to talk about it if you don't want to," Max soothed into her ear.

But she continued, staring straight ahead.

"I had just found out my fiance had been cheating on me, and I broke up with him. I wouldn't even talk to him. But we were on the same squad, I couldn't get out of working with him everyday, and it killed me.

"He was in the humvee with me and Brady when we hit the bomb. I was thrown, Brady was ripped in half. Williams was trying to... I don't know, recover her? I told him to take cover. I told him... but he wouldn't listen. I watched him die.

"I watched them both die. I never got the chance to tell him how he had destroyed me. And I never got the chance to hear him out. I just shut him out... and then I watched him die.

"It's all I see. You'll leave too. You'll leave me."

She ended in a haunted whisper. Her shoulders started to tremble, and Max saw her eyes starting to take the faraway look.

"Blue, Baby, I can't leave you," he asserted. "My reptile is in love with your little Muffy Mammal. He can't survive without her. He'd rather die than lose you."

She dropped her head on his chest, but her look was still far away. He gently picked up her chin and brought her eyes to his, although she didn't seem to focus on him.

"Blue, Baby... I love you. I'm not going anywhere." He leaned down and kissed her lips tenderly. At first she didn't respond, but soon her lips moved ever so slightly, and then she was kissing him fully back. He held her tightly, and her arms slowly made their way around him as well. It was tender and comforting. It was like feeling home.

He'd said he loved her? Did he say that? He couldn't mean it. He just felt bad for her. She chose to let it go. She wasn't ready to deal with everything that meant at that moment.

◆ ◆ ◆

Max

Max's heart constricted as he kissed Jenna with all of the passion that he felt. He'd fucking said it. He'd told her he loved her. And he'd chosen to do it when she was all fucked-over with trauma, instead of waiting for a tender moment. But she had needed to hear it, right then. He just felt like it was right.

God, he hoped he hadn't made the ultimate mistake saying that to her! What if she didn't feel the same?!

Their kisses became more urgent, and soon she was moaning into his mouth. He wasn't sure that sex was a good idea, based on her emotional state, but she wasn't giving him much say in the matter. She crawled up to straddle him, kissing him with a deep need for closeness, connection, contact. He gave in and gave her what she wanted.

He brought his fingers up between her legs and felt her wetness. She groaned loudly as she kissed him more fervently. Very cautiously, he brought himself to her entrance, and slowly pushed inside her. After their blowout about condoms, he had never gone back to using them; nothing felt as good as her wet walls squeezing his naked cock inside of her. His movements were more lovemaking, and less animal fucking. He slowly pumped his cock in and out of her wetness, kissing her deeply; hoping she could feel the love and adoration he felt for her.

He had never wanted to be like this with any other woman. He was worshiping her body with his cock, with his hands, with his mouth. He had come to worship at the temple of her divinity, and he could only hope she found him worthy. She became restless, groaning for more, squirming on his cock, but he continued deep slow plunges, pacing them through the sexual high that was slowly climbing over them both. It was a whole new experience for them both, together.

The sensations grew overwhelming, fogging both of their minds, but still he pumped with slow paced movements, deep inside her, relishing the feel of her tightness sucking him in and milking him. When she started to clamp down hard, he started to lose control. Her groaning became louder, her body convulsing and thrusting against him; his hips took over. He slammed into her deeply, then again, and again. Her screams tore through the room, her nails clawing into his chest. Again and again he took her deeply, until she clenched around him so tightly that he was locked deep in her wet channel.

They screamed their release in unison, their bodies locked together in passion. He held her close, as he pumped them through their orgasms, their juices sticking to their skin as it leaked around them. He had never felt more peace.

◆ ◆ ◆

Jenna

She laid with her head over his chest, listening to his heart beating. She was basking in the sexual bliss that was Max, his arms around her, his scent all over her, his juices running down her thigh. She could still feel his cock inside her, no longer fully hard.

He had said he loved her.

It lit her up inside. She knew he was probably only saying it to make her feel better, because she was such an emotional basket case, but it still made her glow with joy. She knew he didn't really mean it... but a part of her wished he did. A part of her wanted to be everything to this man. She had not allowed herself to grow attached to anyone for so long, but he had just gotten around her walls and embedded himself deep inside her. She wanted him. She loved him.

But history had proven that we don't all get what we want.

She would bask for a few more minutes, feeling his warmth, savoring the moment. But once the tender moment was over, it was back to life. Once he was alone, and had time to think, he would reconsider, and backpedal away from her, and her crazy, as fast as he could.

She might get a text saying "it just wasn't working out" between them... or she might just never hear from him again.

She knew what to expect.

Jenna wouldn't let herself dwell; she would live in the warmth of denial for as long as she could. There would be time to fall apart later.

Jenna woke with a start. She must have fallen back asleep. She was groggy, and her head was foggy. She looked beside her to find Max gone.

Regretting it already?

Her heart ached as she dragged herself out of his bed and headed for the shower. She should make herself ready to be scarce, she didn't want drama, she was just too exhausted. She ran the shower and stepped under the heads, letting the hot water streak down her body and carry away her tension.

"You're up!" She turned to see Max standing in the doorway with a huge smile on his face, pulling his clothing off. "Mind if I join you?"

Don't be fooled, he wants a quickie before it's over. That's all.

"Sure." She smiled, but she knew it didn't reach her eyes.

Dammit, don't cry! Don't you dare be emotional!

Max stepped into the spray of water and collected her into his arms. He showered her face with kisses, and then stopped, holding her face and staring into her eyes.

"I love you, Blue." It was a declaration. He wanted her to see him, to hear him; to understand. "I love you. I know we haven't been together long, but I can't help the way I feel. I want to protect you, I want to claim you, I want you to be mine... I don't want to live without you with me.

"I.Love.You." He punctuated kisses on her mouth as he spoke his words of adoration on them.

Jenna stood frozen in shock. This is not what she had foreseen. It was messing with her head, giving her false hope. Terror seized her. Max watched her reaction and slowly pulled back.

"Blue, Baby, I don't need for you to say it back to me, but what are you thinking right now? Talk to me. Help me under-stand." He spoke calmly, but she saw the fear in his eyes.

Was he afraid of losing her? Was it true?!

"I... I'm terrified," she admitted with a gulp, her eyes wide.

"Why?!" he asked, still cupping her face.

"B... because last night... I..." She exhaled a staggered breath. "I lost it... Max, I lost control. I hurt Marcus, really hurt him. I was out of control.

"And then... the flashback... I..." Tears streamed down her face and she tried to duck her head. "I'm broken. You'll leave me."

Max pulled her into a tight hug; she tried to resist, tried to protect her heart, but in the end she could do nothing but wrap her arms around him.

"Blue, I told you. I'm not going anywhere. I love you." He nuzzled his head into her neck, his breath warm on her wet skin.

"I don't want to let you go, Max!" She gripped him tightly. He gripped her back just as tightly, and they stood under the water until they finally fell away naturally.

Max grabbed the soap and lathered his hands. He washed her body gently and adoringly, paying attention to every last part of her. Then he washed and conditioned her hair, taking great joy in combing it out. When they were finished he turned the water off and stepped out to get a towel to wrap her in, and dry her.

She noticed that he was instantly hard again, running his hands over her with the soap, and later the towel; but he did nothing about it, and seemed happy to just take care of her.

She watched him as he moved to towel dry, and then comb her hair. He smiled a ridiculous smile, and she knew she mirrored it.

He said he wouldn't leave. He said he loved her.

◆ ◆ ◆

Max

Max talked Jenna out of going to church. He felt a little guilty, but truthfully, they needed to stop by the police station to make their statements, and so that Max could give them the video footage that would hopefully exonerate Jenna of any wrongdoing.

Marcus had accosted her first.

It disturbed him that he hadn't seen through Marcus's act, that he considered him a friend. Looking back, he recognized all the times that Marcus tried to sabotage him, tried to talk him into bad behaviors, tried to take him down. Yes, he'd willingly gone along with a lot of it, but he should have seen Marcus's ulterior motive.

He was just glad that Jenna was okay. He didn't care if Marcus ruined his reputation, as long as Jenna was safe.

He glanced over at her in the passenger seat, his hand in hers as he drove. They would get through their statements with the police, and enjoy the rest of their day together.

◆ ◆ ◆

Jenna

The police station wasn't as bad as Jenna had expected. Everyone was professional, and there was none of the cold accusation she was anticipating. It was very official, actually. She had to tell her side of the story; she filled them in on the conversation they saw on video. Then they covered the audio she had from the parking garage, which Max had recorded.

There was enough evidence to arrest Marcus for assault and battery, but the police warned her that he would probably not realistically see jail time, as it would be perceived that he hadn't caused her "lasting harm"... and of course because she proved she could beat the shit out of him. He would probably get a hefty fine, and be ordered to stay away from her. Honestly, it was what she expected. He was rich; even if he had full on raped her, he'd probably never see jail time.

Max seemed furious, but she understood it was the way it was. She loved to see that he was so protective of her, and she wondered if she couldn't channel any of that anger later in the bedroom. She grinned at him stupidly, and he caught himself; his frown immediately changing to his devilish smirk.

Later that evening they snuggled in bed with the television on; Max had even lit a fire in the bedroom fireplace. She was exhausted from hours of rage fucking and tender love-making with Max. Her body was sore in all of the best ways.

"Christmas Eve is Friday," he mentioned.

"It is.. What are you plans for the holiday?" She looked up into his eyes.

"Well..." He hesitated. "My boys are coming to visit for a few days from Europe." He looked down at her, unsure.

"Oh," she whispered, then added, "Do you need me to stay at Andrew's?"

She could see his eyes flick back and forth, a debate running in his head, and she waited.

"Well," he sighed, "to be honest, I had thought it was a little early to introduce you."

Her heart sank.

"But I just can't imagine spending Christmas without you. Would you feel comfortable being here, with the boys here too? We might have to... uh... modify our activity level." He smirked down at her.

Her smile beamed.

"I can't not care for my anaconda, baby, you can't ask me to do that." She smirked.

Max laughed. "I wouldn't dream of it. And I can't neglect my Muffy. But while the boys are here, no screaming orgasms. I get enough shit from their mother already."

"Tell me about her," Jenna said, full of curiosity. She wanted to know what kind of a woman could be married to Max, and ever let him go.

"Not much to tell, really, it was a long time ago." He breathed out. "We got married young. I was just out of law school. She was beautiful, and so smart. And she gave me my sons, so I can't regret it all."

"Why did you end it with her?" Jenna pushed.

Max thought for a moment. "Well, even then I had certain sexual appetites... Virginia was a good girl, a virgin when I met her. I tried to be who she needed me to be. It's not that I didn't love her..." He paused. "I think she came to resent me. I was young and stupid, I pushed her to be more of what I needed in the bedroom. She did anything I asked, but I knew she really didn't enjoy it. I guess she finally got sick of it, because she started having affairs.

"I would have gone to couples counseling, I would have worked on saving our marriage, before she brought someone else into it. Once she cheated, I was done. I wasn't going to share her, and I could never trust her not to do it again. We just slowly drifted apart.

"I threw myself into my work, and she took the boys and moved to Europe to punish me. It killed me to let them go."

His jaw was set in a hard line. Jenna leaned up and kissed him on his jaw.

"Thank you for telling me," she said simply. He seemed startled and looked down at her as she leaned up to take his lips with hers, tenderly.

That started up another sexual feeding frenzy. Max reached between her thighs urgently, pulling his fingers roughly between her folds and spreading her moisture over her mound, where the lightest bit of hair was starting to grow back in.

He pulled his fingers back and stuck them in his mouth to suck them clean. Jenna watched him intently, her mouth watering.

"You're wet for me, Blue," he stated, heat in his eyes.

"Are you wet for me?" she asked him.

"Why don't you find out?" He challenged her.

Without pause she ripped the comforter and sheets back to see his large engorged cock nestled proudly between his legs. She could see every vein over his thick muscled tool. She brought her head down quickly, and darted her warm pink tongue over the tip of his shaft, where a bead of his fluid waited for her. His salty taste in her mouth only made her want more, and she wasted no time hungrily taking him deep into her throat, sucking him in deep, pushing him back out, laving him with her tongue in the way that she knew drove him crazy.

Max groaned loudly, spreading his legs wide for her, his eyes glued to her as she lowered her mouth over his cock again and again, her eyes wide.

"FUCK, Blue... I love the way you fuck my cock with your mouth. You're going to make me blow down that beautiful throat, Baby." He groaned, his eyes half-lidded. His mouth fell open, gasps escaping his panting chest as she worked his cock with her mouth and hands.

She could tell he was holding out, trying to make it last longer, trying to savor the feelings. She wasn't having any of that. She wanted him to lose control, violate her mouth with his cock, explode down her throat with a roar. A slow smile crossed her mouth, even as she swallowed him down again.

The hand that she was using to caress and massage his balls was already slick with her saliva, as it dripped down his shaft. She slowly pushed it lower, between his ass cheeks, spreading the wetness. His cock immediately swelled in her mouth, and he groaned loud and long. Her fingers pulsed over his hole, applying subtle pressure.

"What are you doing?" Max asked, suddenly wary.

"Trust me, Baby." She purred over his cock.

He gave her one last unsure glance, and then let his head fall back, his eyes closed, trusting.

She worked his cock harder, sucking him deep and kneading his balls. When he was groaning with her movement she slowly pushed her finger into his ass, pressing around the walls. He jumped, tightening. She worked his cock more, bringing his attention back to his pleasure, and then slowly worked her finger in his ass in rhythm with her mouth taking his cock. He slowly loosened up, until she had her finger all the way in him. Then she curled her finger and pressed.

Max roared to life, his body tight; his hands fisted violently in her hair as he rammed his cock into her throat with abandon. His abs were clenched with the force of his hips moving to crush her mouth and drive his cock deeper. His noises were animalistic groans and grunts. He lost all control, and Jenna felt his cock swelling incredibly hard and firm, spasming deep; followed by the hot release of his juices down her open throat. His body spasmed with the effort as his hips plungered her mouth unconsciously, relentlessly, spilling his release deep inside her.

Jenna gently withdrew her finger from his back end, which sent him into another spasming series of pistoning his cock down her throat, roaring; until finally he fell back on the bed, boneless and quivering.

"Blue... you fucking devious bitch. I love you." He panted hard.

Chapter 14

Max

It was the week of Christmas, and Max finally had a Christmas to look forward to. He had gone out Monday at lunch and visited the Diamond District, and by Wednesday he had the ring in a tiny velvet box, ready.

It was Friday afternoon, and he sat at his desk, staring at the open box with the beautiful solitaire diamond ring sparkling. He wanted this. After only two months, he wanted her to promise to stay with him forever. He wanted to wake up with her every day, and fuck her every night.

He just didn't know if she felt the same.

She was slower to let him in, she held on too closely to her own mind and heart. Would she be willing to make this commitment, so soon? Hell, she hadn't even met his boys yet, and her introduction to his coworkers and his brother hadn't exactly gone smoothly. He frowned at the ring.

Why would she agree to marry him? He was a workaholic. He was demanding, and stubborn. What could he offer her that she didn't already have other than his money, which she made abundantly clear she didn't want.

But he had to ask. He wanted her like he had never wanted anyone else. He wanted all of her smiles, all of her warmth, all of her heart, and yes, all of her sex. She saw herself as fucked up, but he saw her as the strongest person he'd ever met. She made him want to be a better man.

He looked at the clock. Five pm, time to go and collect his sweetheart. It was showtime.

◆ ◆ ◆

Jenna

It was Friday, Christmas Eve, and Max would be home any minute. Jenna chewed her thumbnail, a sure sign she was nervous. She was having serious second thoughts about her Christmas gift for Max. She had gotten him a framed picture of them together that she had taken when they went to the last charity ball; he loved that dress on her. They both looked so happy; it was taken at the beginning of the night, not the end.

But she had another, more personal, gift for him to open in private. And that was the one she was turning in circles in her mind.

Was it appropriate? Would he like it? Would he be offended? Would he use it?...

She didn't have the resources he did, but she could be thoughtful. She would have to hope he received it in the spirit in which she gave it.

She heard the door close loudly and jogged out to the foyer. Max threw his briefcase down and wrapped his arms around her, picking her up and swinging her in a circle.

"Merry Christmas, Baby!" He was giddy.

Jenna laughed with him, before he placed her back on her feet and smothered her in a hot deep kiss, his hands pulling her ass into his erection.

"I bought some mistletoe for Muffy." He chuckled as he nibbled on her lips. This set her off into another fit of giggles.

"Oh yeah, well I got something for your anaconda… but I swallowed it. He's going to have to go down after it, I'm afraid," she said with a straight face.

Max groaned, his eyes coming alive with heat.

"Don't start with me, woman. If I put my cock in you right now, we'll never make our dinner reservation," he warned, teasingly.

"Doesn't matter to me. I'll eat either way," she replied casually, a smirk on her face.

Max growled and bent her over so that he could spank her ass over her clothing, but she just groaned with pleasure each time until he had to stop because it was torturing him worse than it was her. She won that round.

Max turned for the coat closet, seeming to want to get them out of the house before he changed his mind.

They sat in the upscale restaurant across from each other an hour later. As it was Christmas Eve, the place was packed, every table reserved in advance. The lighting was low, with candles on each table to create a romantic atmosphere. The room was loud with conversation, but when Max looked at her, it was like there was no one else but the two of them.

He was unusually quiet, and seemed a little nervous. She knew his sons were arriving the next day, and chalked it up to introduction jitters. She was nervous about meeting them. She knew they lived in Europe, so even if they didn't get along, she doubted that it would interfere much with their relationship… But she wanted them to like her. She didn't want there to be yet another hurdle in their life.

Dinner was wonderful, and they laughed and talked. They sat over their deserts, and Jenna watched Max's mouth move. He was speaking, but she was lost in watching him. He was so expressive. He could be a cold distant lawyer, but when he wasn't he had the greatest range of expressions and feelings, and they all played center stage through his eyes. She smiled at him with all of the tenderness that she felt in her heart.

And then he got up suddenly. She looked at him with surprise. He rushed to kneel beside her and take her hand, and she looked at him with confusion. Had she missed something important in their conversation? She really should have been listening better!

"Blue, Baby, I..." He seemed to be choking on his words. "I know I've only known you a short while, but you have completely turned my life around. I didn't know how sad and lonely I was until I met you. I didn't even know what I had been missing."

The noise of the restaurant seemed to still, and everyone stopped to watch Max.

"But now that I do know, I also know I can't live without it. I want to give you all of my nights, and all of my mornings, and every day in between. I want to see you looking at me, the exact way you've been looking at me all night, for the rest of my life.

"I know I don't have much to offer you. I know I'm not perfect, and I don't always say the right thing. But I hope I'm saying this right.

"Will you please make me the happiest man in the world and marry me?"

He pulled a small black velvet box out of his pocket and popped it open to display the large solitaire diamond ring nestled inside. Applause and "Aaawwwws" broke out around them.

Jenna froze, she felt like her heart stopped. She felt terror, as all of the eyes in the restaurant were watching her, waiting for her. Max stared at her hopefully... his eyes begging... She couldn't breathe.

I need to get out of here!

◆ ◆ ◆

Max

Jenna's eyes opened wide, with fear, not with excitement. Max knew. She wasn't ready. She leapt from her chair and raced out of the restaurant, not caring that people were watching her openly running. Max struggled to get his wallet out of his pocket, dropped a credit card on the table, and ran after her.

She had a head start, and once he got through the double doors and into the cold night air he realized he'd lost her. He looked around wildly, but she was nowhere to be seen. Devastation filled him and his heart ached like it had been wrenched out of his chest.

She couldn't even say no to him, she just ran. What the hell was so horrible about the thought of being married to him that she couldn't even talk about it?

A piece of him died as he stared at the traffic.

He made his way back inside to pay the check and get his coat. On his way back to the door Mia stepped in front of him.

"Max, you didn't deserve that," she said quietly.

"Get lost, Mia," he growled, as he tried to move around her.

Of course she was there, and had seen everything. Of course she did.

He didn't want to deal with her shit on top of everything else he was feeling.

"Max, Baby... I can make you feel better. You know I can. She wasn't the one... I am." She smiled up at him with a hungry grin, stretching her arms around his neck.

It was the wrong thing to say. He flung her hands away from him, and charged out of the restaurant to be alone.

◆ ◆ ◆

Jenna

"He fucking asked me to marry him!" Jenna screeched. Tears were rolling down her cheeks. Andrew sat beside her, running his hand down her back to comfort her.

"So you ran?" Andrew concluded.

Jenna just stared at him through her tears, before sobbing loudly and nodding. Andrew pulled her in close and held her.

"If you don't want to marry him, Jenna, you need to tell him with words. You can't just ghost him like this." He spoke firmly but gently. Andrew would never whitewash the truth, and he called Jenna on her bullshit, just like she did for him.

"It's not that I don't want to..." She hiccoughed through sobs.

"Then why did you run?" he asked.

"Be... Because I was scared!" She lost it again, devolving into sobs.

"So... you DO want to marry him?" Andrew asked, confused.

"I... I ... yes. No. I don't know, Andrew." She sobbed again. "I can't make a decision that fast!"

"Alright, Baby-Girl. I think you need a stiff drink. I'll be right back." Andrew stood and walked into the kitchen.

He returned, handed her the drink, and then his cell phone.

"I texted Max. I know it's not really my place, but you guys need to work this out. I only started the conversation. I just wanted you to know what was being said, Baby-Girl."

Jenna read the exchange.

"Andrew: I know you're probably not in a good place right now. Neither is she. I just thought you should know, the answer isn't no, she just needs time to process."

"Max: Thanks, Man. I appreciate it. Is she okay?"

"Andrew: She will be. She needs to talk to you. She'll come around, it just shocked her. She doesn't deal well with sudden change."

"Max: I'm here, when she's ready."

Andrew sat next to her.

"Jenna, you know you need to call him and tell him what's going on with you, even if it's to say you need time or space. He cares about you, just send him a text. Don't make him suffer anymore than he already is." Andrew squeezed her hand.

Guilt sat like lead in her gut.

Andrew left the room, and she picked her phone up.

"Blue: So, an amazing thing happened today."

A few seconds later Max replied.

"Max: Yeah? What was that, Baby?"

Tears formed in Jenna's eyes. He still called her Baby. He didn't tell her to fuck off, and never contact him again.

"Blue: So I was having this amazing date with Prince Charming, and he kissed me and woke me from my sleep!"

"Max: Really? And then what happened?"

"Blue: And then, when I was about to get my 'happily ever after', I was possessed by a demon and ran away, to save him. But now that I've battled the demon, I don't know if he even wants me back. I just ran, without an explanation, but it was because I was possessed... I couldn't tell him that."

She sniffed back tears as she hit "send."

"Max: He'd have to be a real moron not to want you back after you fought off a demon and saved him, don't you think?"

"Blue: God I hope so! I can't imagine never seeing him again. I fucked this up so badly."

"Max: But Blue, the story isn't over yet. This is just the plot challenge. Now that you've battled the demon, you have to fall into Prince Charming's arms again."

Hope welled in Jenna's heart.

"Blue: Do you want me to come over? Muffy would love to give you some reptile therapy."

There was a brief delay as the three dots appeared and disappeared.

"Max: Blue, I think I need the night to think. Please give Muffy a little extra love for me. Why don't you come over tomorrow and meet the boys?"

Jenna's heart slammed as she read the message. He'd never put her off before. She had fucked up royally.

"Blue: Of course, Baby. Whatever you want."

"Max: I love you, Blue. Merry Christmas."

"Blue: Merry Christmas." The words felt empty to her. It wasn't merry at all. She was hollow inside, and she knew he was gutted on his end. She had to fix this.

◆ ◆ ◆

Max

Max looked at all of the Christmas decorations he and Jenna had put up over the previous week. It felt hollow. He had put them up with hopes that she would be his wife, that this was the start of their life together. Now, he wasn't sure what she wanted. And he wasn't sure that he could just see her as a date, knowing she would never feel more for him. It tore him apart.

He had finally given his heart to someone, and they didn't want it all.

He heard the loud thumping of footsteps coming down the stairs. Damned, teenagers moved like a herd of elephants.

He embraced them both, messing Eddie's hair and smiling at Charlie. They were both so tall. Eddie looked just like his Uncle Ed had at his age, awkward and gangly, growing quickly. Charlie was rounder, softer, more sensitive. He loved these boys. They settled down over coffee and cocoa when his phone rang.

The caller ID read Virginia: his ex-wife.

"I need to take this. You boys get comfortable, I'll be right back." Max answered and took his cell phone upstairs to his office. He didn't want the boys to hear them squabble, which is the only reason she ever called.

"Ginny," he said.

"Max! Merry Christmas! How are you and the boys?" She chirped.

Max put her on speaker, after making sure his door was shut. He put the phone down on the desk and started clearing off work folders. He needed to keep his hands busy.

"We're fine. What's up?" he asked flatly, not really wanting her story.

◆ ◆ ◆

Jenna

Jenna put her key in the lock and opened the door. The house was warm and cheery, a far cry from what she was feeling. Anxiety twisted in her gut. She walked in to see two tall teenagers in the living room; their heads came up to see her at the same time.

"Hi." She waved. "I'm Jenna." She smiled politely, and the boys both grinned back as they stood and rushed to meet her.

"I'm Eddie," the blond boy answered, putting out his hand to shake hers, "and this is Charlie."

She shook both of their hands. Charlie had Max's eyes, and Eddie looked just like Max's brother, Ed. It was like getting to meet them when they were younger, and her smile grew.

"You're named after your uncle?" she asked the tall blond boy. "You look like him."

Eddie smiled as his cheeks turned pink.

"Dad's just upstairs for a minute." Charlie smiled shyly.

Did they know about her? Had he told them?

"Oh, well, I need to drop something off up there anyway, I'll be right back!" She smiled, and then turned and climbed the stairs. The boys went back to their conversation in the living room.

Jenna could hear voices coming from Max's office, and she assumed he was on a work call. She crept quietly up the stairs so as not to intrude. She just wanted to put her gift in his bedroom. She snuck it into his night table drawer and headed back. As she got to his door she could hear he was arguing with a woman.

"Ginny, we're not doing this," he demanded.

"Max, we were MARRIED. We are family. We have babies together. You can't dismiss me so out of hand. Look, I know I made mistakes, but we were kids. You made mistakes too. I've grown, and learned. I'm ready to give you what you always wanted, Max. Give me a chance. We could be a family again. Think of the boys. I'll be in Boston on Tuesday; all I ask is that you meet me for dinner," she begged.

"Ginny, things have changed. I can't just-"

"Just meet me for dinner, Max. That's all I ask. I'm ready to give you everything that you've asked for, everything I wasn't willing to give you before. I'm braver now."

"Fine, I'll meet you," Max answered, sounding annoyed. "Send me the information."

Jenna gasped silently. He was talking to his ex-wife. He had agreed to meet her. What the fuck?! She quietly scurried down the stairs, tears starting to form. When she got to the bottom, she saw the boys both look up, and she panicked.

"Uh... I forgot I have an appointment. I'm sorry, I need to go. It was so nice meeting you both!" She rushed to the door and out into the night, hailing a cab.

◆ ◆ ◆

Max

Max climbed down the stairs and found the boys both staring at the front door.

"What's going on?" he asked looking at the door, and then them.

"Uuuhh… We met Jenna." Eddie volunteered, his cheeks growing red.

"You did? Where is she?" Max asked, looking around.

"Uhhh…" Eddie stammered.

"She left in a hurry." Charlie spoke up. "She went upstairs to leave something, and then came down and left; said she had an appointment."

Max stared in horror.

"She was really pretty." Eddie offered, apologetically.

"I'll give her a call a little later. What do you boys want to eat?" Max changed the subject quickly, trying to ignore the sinking feeling in his gut.

Had she heard him? Of course she heard him! She wouldn't have flown out of here like her ass was on fire unless she had. Jesus fucking Christ this was turning into a nightmare. He couldn't catch a break! How was he ever going to get her to come back after he hit her with a diamond ring, and followed it up with meeting with his ex?!

He settled in to spend time with his boys, and try to plan a strategy.

Max spent Christmas Day and the following day with his boys. He loved getting to see them, and he was so proud of the young men they were becoming. Time just got away from him.

He had the rest of the week off, and once the boys flew home he no longer had a distraction to keep his mind from thinking about Jenna. When Tuesday rolled around, and he hadn't heard from her yet he started to panic. He was meeting his ex for dinner that night, and he decided not to call Jenna until he had gotten it over with.

Dread pooled in his stomach.

Dinner with Virginia went better than expected. Max was no fool, he knew she only wanted to rekindle a relationship with him, but by the end of dinner he had stuck to his guns and told her the answer was no. In years passed, he would have wound up in bed with her again, only to feel used and foolish afterwards, but this time he could only think of Jenna.

He had set firm boundaries, and after much wheedling and manipulation, she had finally caved.

He should have felt good about that but he couldn't, not with so much left unsaid between him and Jenna. He tried texting her on Wednesday, but she didn't respond. He tried again Wednesday night, asking to talk with her, and she shut him out completely.

He knew that they would never make it if they couldn't communicate, but it was impossible to communicate if she kept running and hiding. He considered showing up at the coffee shop, and then decided against it; they didn't need all the drama at her workplace. But the longer they went without talking, the worse it was getting. He needed to see her.

Max put his coat on and got ready to go out to the store. He opened his front door and saw a basket on his stoop. He picked it up and brought it to the dining room table. Inside the basket was a bottle of red wine with a red ribbon, and a typed note.

> "My dearest Max,
>
> I am completely devastated. I've tried to get over you, and I just can't. Please, I want to marry you. I want to have our life together back. I am so sorry for the way I've behaved. I'll be over at five tonight to talk.
>
> I love you,
> M"

"Ooooh, Muffy..." he whispered. Joy filled his heart.

She wanted to talk to him, she wanted to see him. She wanted to MARRY him!

He looked at the clock, it was already three thirty. He threw his coat over a chair, not even bothering to hang it up. He went upstairs and pulled out the black velvet box with her ring, and brought it down to the table, beside the basket. He was going to explode having to wait until five to see her.

Chapter 15

Jenna

Christmas had been horrific. The rest of the week wasn't much better. Jenna dragged herself to work everyday, close to losing it and bawling. He had texted her Wednesday, but she couldn't bring herself to answer. She just wanted to scream and demand he tell her about his meeting with his ex.

It was Thursday afternoon, and she stood like a zombie in front of the cappuccino machine. She wasn't eating, she couldn't sleep. All she could think about was Max.

Max, meeting his ex-wife for dinner.

What was it she was going to give him? He had always wanted anal with Jenna, maybe that was what she was offering him? Maybe she was holding that last sexual fetish over his head to entice him back?

Max had said she was beautiful and smart, that he had been willing to work on their marriage... so maybe she was taking him up on it? Maybe Jenna had ruined her opportunity, and he was running back to the wife he knew?

Jenna swallowed a bout of nausea, but she couldn't stop her mind from picturing Max happy with a beautiful ex-wife in his bed, giving herself to him wholly, letting him have everything he ever wanted, something even Jenna hadn't given him.

Jenna ran into the ladies room and vomited in the toilet. When there was nothing left, she just dry heaved until the convulsions finally stopped. She sat on the floor in the stall, her sweaty head leaning against the cold tiled wall and groaned. She couldn't do this anymore. She couldn't torture herself with visions of what Max might be doing. She heaved herself off of the floor and cleaned herself up. She was going to see him.

It was a little after four in the afternoon when she stood in front of Max's door. She had a key. She just didn't feel right using it, not now. Instead she rang the bell.

The door flew open seconds later, and Max grabbed her and hugged her for dear life.

"You're here!" he yelped.

He looked as bad as she felt. She felt her arms wrap around him, hugging him back, before visions of him and his ex swamped her mind.

She pushed herself back, away from him.

"Do you want to tell me about your dinner date?" she asked him sharply.

His face fell immediately.

"Come inside, I'll need a drink for this." He turned and walked into the dining room. He opened a bottle of red wine, and Jenna noticed her ring box on the table. She said nothing.

Max filled a glass, and held the bottle in offering to her, but she shook her head no. She wanted answers on a clear head. Max drained half of his glass and refilled it before leading Jenna into the living room. They each sat down, Jenna chose an armchair opposite him, and she noticed the sad frown on his face when she didn't sit next to him.

Too fucking bad.

"I met with Ginny because I needed her to sign the final divorce papers," he finally confessed, his eyes down.

"DIVORCE PAPERS?! You were still MARRIED when you proposed to me?!" she demanded.

Max physically winced. "Jenna, we've been separated for ten years, legally separated... lived on different continents. I've been begging her to just sign the divorce papers ever since, but she's had this crazy idea that we would get back together one day. I would never meet her in person because I had no desire to see her, but now I needed that divorce. I needed to be free for you. So I met with her."

"Don't you DARE put this on me!" Jenna hissed. "Did you fuck her too?""

Max snapped his head up. "NO. I didn't fucking TOUCH her, Jenna. I am exclusive with you. I didn't consider this dinner a date: it was a business meeting to me, nothing more."

"So she didn't try to seduce you?" Jenna snarled.

"Of course she did. She pulled out all the stops. Five years ago, Jenna, she might have swayed me, but last night she had zero power over me. You know why? Because all I could think about was getting back to see you. All I could think about was how much I had fucked it up with you, and how desperately I wanted you back.

"Jenna, I'm telling you the truth. I don't want her. I haven't wanted her in a long time. I only want you. I don't know how to unfuck this. If you don't want to marry me, I will accept that. I'm sorry I sprang it on you like I did; the only thing I could think about was having you in my life, not letting you get away. And all I did was push you further. Please tell me there's something we can do to fix this, Jenna, because I'm miserable. I don't want to live a life without you in it. I need you, and it scares the ever living shit out of me."

He swallowed his whole glass of wine, and went back to the dining room to refill it before she could answer.

Jenna sat in shock. Of all the things she expected him to say, hearing that he was still married blew her mind.

But it's not like he and his ex were a happy family; hell, she'd been staying with him for more than a month, and the ex was never mentioned. She really wasn't a part of his life. And now he was free and clear of her. Could they make this work?

Max came shuffling back into the room, he turned, unsteady and wobbled on his feet.

"Max, are you ok?" Jenna looked up, an eyebrow cocked in concern.

"Yeaaaahhhhh... I.. I'mmm ffffffffffiinnnne." He was slurring, and his eyes were glassy.

"Just how much wine have you had?" Jenna demanded.

"Jussshhht opennnned it." He wobbled in place.

Jenna rolled her eyes. "Let's get you up to bed, Max." She stood and put his arm over her shoulder to steady him.

"Noooo!" He demanded, pulling back sluggishly. "No sexxxxx. Wee neeeed, we neeeed to talk." He looked smashed. Jenna had seen him open the bottle of wine, but she didn't know if he'd been drinking scotch before she got there... but he hadn't smelled of alcohol.

She pulled him back to her and started to herd him up the stairs. "No sex, big boy. You need sleep. Then we talk."

He leaned on her heavily as he struggled to maneuver up the stairs.

"You'll ssshhhhlleeep with meee?" He grinned a big dopey grin, stopping on the stairs. Jenna grabbed him around the chest and began heaving him upwards.

When they got to the top he seemed to lose his coordination. He got one foot on the top stair, leaned forward, and dragged the other foot after himself but didn't manage to get it flat on the landing. When he stood up, his bodyweight overcompensated backwards and he pitched. Jenna panicked and grabbed his arm, but that only swung him around, his momentum pulled him back down the stairs. Jenna dug her feet in, but they slid forward, forcing her to release his arm as the bulk of his weight slammed down the stairs.

Jenna screamed and ran down after him. He hit his head on one of the treads, leaving a messy bloody splatter, and landed in an unconscious heap at the bottom, his arm sticking out at an uncomfortable angle.

Jenna checked his pulse. He was breathing. He wasn't dead! She tried waking him, but his eyes were rolled back in his head. She dashed for the dining room table for her cell and dialed 911.

It felt like it took forever before the ambulance and police showed up. Jenna told them what happened, and it took four paramedics to lift Max's muscular body onto a gurney. Jenna was an anxious mess, her makeup running down her face with her tears. The policeman asked her again to walk her through what had happened, since she arrived. She felt a flush come to her cheeks as she explained that they had a fight, and then he started acting 'off'.

"You fucking bitch! You pushed him!" A piercing scream cut through the room, and all heads turned to see Mia, standing behind the paramedics by the dining room table.

"And who are you?" the officer asked her.

"I am his FIANCE!" she announced, waving her hand which was wearing Jenna's ring.

Jenna's eyes flashed to the table, to see that the ring box was open, and empty.

"What do you know about this?" The officer turned to Mia.

"She's lying! That's MY ring!" Jenna screamed, but the officer told her to back off as he questioned Mia.

"She was jealous!" Mia started crying dramatically. "She's been stalking him. He asked me to marry him, and she told me she'd end me. I never thought she'd attack him. Was he drugged?!" She looked around and then headed straight for the wine bottle. "Did you test this?!"

The police officer took the bottle from her and put it into an evidence bag, and Mia smiled at her smugly behind his back. Jenna's world went red.

She remembered leaping around the table onto Mia, but the next thing she remembered was being handcuffed and stuffed into the backseat of a squad car by five police officers, her heartbeat rocketing, her rage boiling. Apparently, she had hurt a couple of officers pretty badly in her struggle to get back to Mia.

The slamming of the police car door suddenly cooled her temper. She looked around with wide eyes at the crowd that had gathered on the street around Max's house. People stared at her, in the back of the car, in judgment. Police were stopping traffic, and a second ambulance sat waiting.

She was in really deep shit.

It seemed like hours before an officer came to her cell door and opened it with a metal clang.

"Miss Jones, you've made bail, come with me." She rolled off of the concrete bench and made her way to the door, then followed the officer down the hallway to a window. She turned and saw Andrew standing in a waiting area, looking like shit.

She imagined she looked like hell herself.

The man at the window gave her a bag with her purse and her shoes, and had her sign several forms, before they released her to Andrew.

Without saying a word Andrew wrapped his arms around her and just held her. She was too stunned to be able to hug him back.

On the drive home Andrew finally broke the silence. "I never thought I'd really have to bail you out of jail, Baby-Girl." He smirked at her, but there was sadness in his eyes. Jenna felt like she had let him down. She had let everyone down, and she still didn't know what the hell was going on.

When they got home Andrew held her as they sat on the sofa, while she relayed everything that had happened.

"Sounds like he was drugged," Andrew commented. "Do you know where he got the wine?"

"No, it was in a basket, with a bow, on his table," Jenna answered sullenly. She was worried to death about Max, but the police had ordered her to stay away from him and Mia.

She was beside herself with fear for him. It was too much to ask.

"So, it was probably a gift. Maybe he knows who he got it from, and once he recovers, he will tell the police it wasn't you." Andrew added hopefully.

"Maybe." Jenna added quietly.

"Look, I know that bitch has them all believing this fairytale, but once he comes to, he's going to clear everything up, and she will get hers." Andrew added fiercely.

Jenna just looked at him. Her gut told her it was over. That bitch was wearing her ring. She never got to resolve things with Max. Now she was looking at a court date and jail time for assaulting officers and Mia. There was no happily ever after at the end of this fairy tale.

◆ ◆ ◆

Max

The room was dark, and Max was aware of a deep thrumming pain in his head. It didn't help that there were beeping noises going off around him, annoying the hell out of him. He groaned and tried to open his eyes. It wasn't easy.

He wasn't in his bed. He looked around the room until it finally seemed to come into focus. He was in a hospital room. There was an IV hooked into his arm, and monitors making all of the annoying noises.

He had no idea how he'd gotten there. He went to look to his left and a jarring pain stabbed into his shoulder. He cried out as he looked down to see his arm in a sling.

What the hell had happened?

He tried to remember what he did last. He was home. He had done some housework... Jenna had come over!

Then nothing.

Was Jenna alright?! His heart rate skyrocketed, setting off the machine beside him, and a nurse ran into his room immediately.

"Oh good, you're awake, Mr. Thurston. I'll need you to lie back please, you still need to recover." She spoke firmly but warmly, pushing him back down by his good shoulder; he was as weak as a kitten.

"What happened?! Is Jenna ok?!" His voice was raspy, his throat as dry as the desert. He was going to go crazy if he couldn't find out.

The nurse smiled sympathetically.

"I'll tell the doctor you're up. He'll come in and check you out, and then you can have a conversation with the officers outside, okay. I promise you'll get your answers, you just need to be patient and let us do our jobs, Mr. Thurston."

With that she breezed back out of the door.

Max's mind ran in circles as he tried to remember what happened, tried to figure out where Jenna was. He had told her about Ginny, hadn't he? She was mad... Dammit! It was like a part of his life had been vacuumed out of his head.

A tall man in a white medical coat came in and introduced himself as Dr. Klavian. He went through his full routine, shining lights in Max's eyes, asking him the date and his name, and checking his vitals. He explained to Max that he had been drugged and fallen down a flight of stairs, resulting in a mild concussion, and a dislocated shoulder. They were keeping him for one night, but he should make a full recovery.

When Max tried to ask him about Jenna the doctor just put his hands up.

"I don't have those answers, Mr. Thurston. If you're up to it, I'll send the police in."

Max nodded, eager to get some answers. His shoulder throbbed.

It wasn't long before a police officer stepped into the room in full uniform, notepad in hand.

"Hi, I'm Detective Trace. How are you feeling, Mr. Thurston?" The detective asked.

"Like shit, thanks for asking. Where is Jenna?" The officer seemed to balk.

"You mean Miss Jones?" he asked carefully.

"Yes, Jenna Jones, my girlfriend, where is she? Is she ok?!" He was getting aggravated.

"Well, she's in lockup right now, Mr. Thurston," he stated calmly. After Max exploded he continued, "She beat the shit out of Mia Westry, and three of our officers as they tried to subdue her. Miss Westry is in the hospital, and claiming to be your fiance." The detective was watching Max for a reaction.

Max just tipped his head back and laughed. He laughed so hard, he hurt his shoulder and winced through his laughter.

"Something funny?" the detective asked, not seeing the humor at all.

"If Mia claimed to be my fiance, she's lucky she's still alive, Detective. My girlfriend is fiercely protective." Max claimed proudly.

"Yeah, well that protective girlfriend of yours is also under investigation for drugging you, and potentially pushing you down the stairs. Did you two fight, before the incident?" the detective asked knowingly.

The color drained from Max's face. "No... We.. We talked."

"About what, Mr. Thurston" The detective prompted.

"About my ex-wife," he answered quietly.

"And you told Miss Jones that you were still married at that time?" he asked.

"I want my lawyer." Was all Max would say.

Two days later Max was resting at home. The police had gotten the engagement ring back, but Max hadn't pressed burglary charges because Mia was already suffering severe disfigurement and humiliation at Jenna's hands. The police, however, did charge her with making false statements.

Max put the ring back into the black velvet box on the table. There was a basket there with a red ribbon. Where had the basket come from? He searched his mind. He seemed to recall a bottle of wine in it. Jenna's statement had said he took a bottle of wine out of it and drank it; the lab later confirmed it was drugged, heavily. Did she bring it?

Something kept gnawing in the back of his mind. He wanted to say there was a card with the basket, he was sure of it. *Signed by Muffy?* Jenna never signed with "Muffy," but that's what he remembered.

He couldn't believe she would hurt him. Sure he hadn't told her he was still technically married; to be honest, he had largely forgotten about it.

She had warned him she was violent. The police had shared her history with him. She had put several men into the hospital in different states, some in critical condition. She had brutally attacked Marcus. Granted, he was a prick, and deserved it.

But if she brought the wine, then she was planning to attack him; she was planning to weaken him first. What kind of psychopath was she? And he had wanted to *marry* her!

His heart turned to stone.

◆ ◆ ◆

Jenna

Jenna sat on the sofa. She was numb. She couldn't get any answers, she couldn't reach out to Max. She sat on the sofa, day after day, dying a little more inside. She couldn't even pick up and move, it would violate her bail. She felt like her life was over, and she was just waiting for her body to catch up.

The newspapers had splashed the story all over the front pages. They didn't say she HAD drugged and attacked Max, but they certainly painted a telling picture. They dug up things from her past to cast her as a black widow, attacking ex-boyfriends out of jealousy. Mia gave them a whole page of bullshit to print, all of it lies, to make herself look like the heroine and Jenna like the psycho ex.

That's me, Psycho ex.

She was going to go crazy staring at the same four walls.

Her phone beeped.

"Max: I need to see you, you are neglecting your reptile."

"Jenna: Are you alright?! I have been so worried! I was so scared! The police told me I'm not allowed to talk to you or see you."

"Max: Come over, I won't tell."

Jenna didn't even stop to consider, she called an Uber and grabbed her bag.

Twenty minutes later she knocked on his door, looking around nervously, remembering all the people staring at her in the back of the police car. The door swung open, and she rushed in and threw her arms around Max, carefully avoiding his sling.

"Oh my god I have been so worried!" Her voice was cracking.

Max wrapped one arm around her loosely. "I'm fine, as you can see." He smirked at her.

She looked up at him. Something was off. There was no tenderness in his look. Was he still mad about their argument?

"I've missed your attention, Jenna." He purred.

She looked at him unsurely. He only called her Blue when he was romantic, he saved Jenna for factual conversations... he was mixing them. Did he hit his head harder than they thought?

"I... I've missed you too, Max," she answered.

He ushered her into the living room. When he didn't ask, she took off her own coat, and draped it carefully over the side of a chair. He was usually so attentive.

"I need you, Jenna, I need you now," he called to her, his voice deep with need and command.

"I'm here, Baby," she said, walking up to him.

"Here's what's going to happen, Jenna. You are going to get on your knees, and suck my cock for me like a good girl. Do it."

Her eyes widened in shock, and he brought his hand up to her head to push her down to her knees.

"Don't make me ask twice. Don't make me doubt you." His eyes had a cold hard edge to them.

But his words smacked against the guilt that Jenna felt. She didn't want him to doubt her. She quickly undid his pants, and pulled him out, taking him tentatively into her mouth, looking up to gauge his reaction.

Max's eyes were closed, and he grunted his approval, his hand still on the back of her head. Then suddenly his hand fisted her hair painfully as he dragged her mouth over his cock, slamming his hips forward roughly.

He groaned as he worked his cock in her throat, taking what he needed from her, not saying a word to her; he climaxed quickly, forcing his cock as far into her mouth as he could, spilling down her throat, gagging her in the process.

After a few more pumps he pulled his cock out of her mouth suddenly, releasing her head so that she fell back onto the floor as he walked away.

"Wh-where are you going?" she asked in a panic.

"I have to take a piss," he answered, and shut the bathroom door behind him.

Jenna sat on the floor in stunned silence. Tears streamed down her face. That was not role play; that was him using her body without caring. He had never treated her like that before, and she suddenly felt cheap.

Max strolled back into the room, his pants done back up.

"I'm really tired. You should go." He spoke indifferently, not looking at her, as if she was beneath him. He started climbing the stairs.

"Oh, and Jenna?... Leave the key." He climbed, never looking back, effectively dismissing her.

Jenna left the key on his table, got her coat and purse, and left, shutting the door behind her with a snap.

Whatever spark of life had been left inside her had just been snuffed.

Chapter 16

Max

It was New Year's Eve. Max straightened his tie in the mirror. He didn't want to go out and act happy, but he couldn't sit around his house any longer. Everywhere he turned he saw memories of Jenna. She haunted him.

Anger rose in his gut. He had trusted her. He had *loved* her. How had he not recognized what a psychopath she was? She was damaged and broken, and she had nearly killed him. She had even warned him! She had told him up front what she was, and he had just refused to see it.

He tugged at his tie aggressively. He didn't want to think about her anymore.

As he turned to get his wallet his phone rang. He flipped it over to see it was the detective, so he answered it.

"Mr. Thurston, this is Detective Trace; we spoke at the hospital." His voice was curt and professional.

"I remember," Max answered.

"I just wanted to update you on your case. We never recovered the note you said you thought was with the wine, but we did lift fingerprints from it. They belong to Miss Westry. We are going to charge her. I just wanted you to be aware."

Max's jaw went slack with confusion.

"But... wait, the police report said she picked the bottle up to hand it to you, of course her prints are on it." Max snapped.

"Yes, but the partial print we picked up was on the *bottom* of the bottle, where she had not touched it. As Miss Jones had such a ... violent... response to Miss Westry's presence, it will be hard to prove that they worked together on this; at least we can prove that the drugs came from Miss Westry. Whether or not a jury believes that Miss Jones then attacked you, I can't say."

Max remained silent. He was shocked.

Very slowly, an image came to his mind... a note.

> "My dearest Max,
>
> I am completely devastated. I've tried to get over you, and I just can't. Please, I want to marry you. I want to have our life together back. I am so sorry for the way I've behaved. I'll be over at five tonight to talk.
>
> I love you,
>
> M"

Maybe it was "M" for Mia?

Max hung up the phone without acknowledging the detective and rushed to pull out his copies of the police statements. Jenna had arrived a little after four, not five. The paramedics arrived at four forty seven, and Mia shortly after.

Cold terror swam in his gut. It hadn't been Jenna. It was Mia all along. Jenna just found him first.

Max called the detective back, and relayed what he had just figured out. The detective didn't say anything about it, only thanked him and ended the call.

Max fell heavily into his chair.

What the fuck have I done?!

◆ ◆ ◆

Andrew

Andrew wiped down the furniture in his treatment room. He checked his watch. He had one more client for the day, and then he could go home. It was already the second week of January, and the snow was coming down hard. It had been touch and go for a long time, and he just wanted to go and visit Jenna. She needed him.

Looking at his watch again, he made his way out to the waiting room. A tall man in an expensive business suit stood looking at the artwork on the wall, his back to Andrew.

"We're all set for you," Andrew announced, and then stopped short as the man turned around.

"What the FUCK are YOU doing here?!" Andrew roared.

Max slumped his shoulders in defeat, but it did nothing to tame the rage that was building inside of Andrew.

"Andrew, I fucked up. I love her. I need to see her," Max answered. "She's not answering my texts."

Andrew crossed the room in three large steps and slammed his fist into Max's jaw, snapping his head back, and sending him reeling into the line of chairs.

"I warned you!" Andrew seethed. "I told you that if you hurt her, I would end you, you pretentious prick! I don't care how rich you are, or how big your dick is, I will put you into the motherfucking ground for what you did to her."

Max put his hands up in surrender. "I know. I know Andrew. I'm here to fix it, tell me what I can do." Max was begging.

Andrew glared down at him, his chest heaving, his fists clenched tight. He seemed poised to spring at the slightest movement.

"You listen to me, and you listen good. Do you have any idea what she is going through because of you? No, she's not answering you, she has NO PHONE. She's in a fucking psychiatric ward because she attacked that whore that drugged you, did you know that? Because she DEFENDED you. She was so enraged on YOUR behalf, that she attacked the officers who tried to protect that fucking slut. So now Jenna is on a suicide watch, at the request of the motherfucking shrink she has by court order. All because of YOU. If you really want to help her, you will stay the FUCK away from her. Because so help me God, if I find out you are screwing with her again, I won't hold back; I don't care if I do go to prison!"

Andrew stormed out of the room, slamming the door behind him.

Max picked himself up with a shudder and pulled himself out of the door.

◆ ◆ ◆

Jenna

Two hours later Andrew sat in the concrete block room with Jenna. She was starting to get some color back in her cheeks. The hospital was forcing her to eat, but her cheeks were still gaunt.

"Look what I brought you!" Andrew teased, and pulled out two boxes of hair color for her.

Jenna smiled a sedated smile and wrapped her arms around Andrew.

"You're the BEST friend, EVER," she said.

"Well, DUH," he responded with a laugh.

"So how are you doing, Baby-Girl?" He held her close.

"I'm starting to see things clearly, Drew," she answered slowly. "I just wish I fucking understood. I know closure is bullshit, but it really fucking makes me insane that I was somehow pegged for attempted murder of my supposed boyfriend. I didn't need to drug him if I had wanted to kill him." She looked up at the camera on the ceiling and added, "Hypothetically speaking."

Drew just nodded, his brows drawn together.

"I mean, yah, I'll totally take the credit for beating the crap out of Mia. I'll even admit to accidentally involving those cops... But HOW could Max believe I would do that to him? I can even deal with the way he treated me afterwards."

Andrew started to interrupt her but she put her hand up to silence him.

"Andrew, if he REALLY thought I was a psycho who drugged him and tried to kill him, and who was alone with his KIDS? Yeah, I can understand his mindset; not saying I agree with it, but I can understand it.

"What will haunt me for the rest of my life is how he could ask me to marry him... and not a week later believe that I would kill him.

"I really love him, Andrew, and I thought he really loved me."

Andrew stared at his hands. He looked angry, conflicted.

"Jenna... I have something I want to tell you."

◆ ◆ ◆

Max

Max sat in his office and re-read the same page for a third time, before finally dropping it in disgust. It was pointless. He couldn't focus. He replayed Andrew's words from two days prior.

"She's in a fucking psychiatric ward... on a suicide watch"

He was so tempted to search out all of the psychiatric hospitals, to see if he could find her, but that was the most selfish thing he could think of. She was already in enough pain because of him. How could he push his way into her life again, especially now, after all she'd been through? No matter how much it hurt, he had to leave her alone. He had to let her heal.

He had to let her go.

The thought was physically painful. His chest ached. He felt like a shell of a person walking through his days. There was no love, no happiness. His world was a swath of gray without her sunshine.

He tried to bury himself in his work, but he couldn't stop the freight train in his head from steaming down the track, bringing her back front and center.

It was his punishment. He deserved it. He would never forgive himself.

His cell phone beeped and he pulled it out of his pocket.

"Andrew: Against my better judgment, I am letting you know that Jenna will be released from the hospital on the twentieth. God help her, she still loves you. My statement still stands."

Tears formed in Max's eyes. She still loved him?! He was afraid to hope.

"Max: Thank you for telling me. I'm a mess without her. So, is it safe to contact her when she's out?"

"Andrew: Baby steps."

Max stared at the screen. Baby steps? He could do baby steps, for Jenna he could low-crawl.

◆ ◆ ◆

Jenna

Nothing had ever felt as good to Jenna as sleeping in her own bed and using her own shower. She had a contingency release; if she lost more weight, they would throw her right back in the hospital again, so she was having hot-fudge sundaes every night. Andrew had gotten them pizza and she was sitting relaxing in front of the fireplace.

"Mail's here," Andrew called and dropped an envelope in her lap. Her face scrunched in confusion until she saw the return address: "Not Keats"

Her heart started pounding and tears started to fall; she looked up to see Andrew watching her carefully. She ripped the envelope open.

"My dearest Jenna,

While I am not a poet, I feel as though I have a huge debt to you to atone for, so I shall endeavor to pay it, partially at least, through poetry for you. I can only hope that this does not make your situation worse.

Ode to a Dumbass
The caveman with his head so thick
More often thinking with his dick
Had fallen for the vixen's trick
And pushed his love away.
And then to add a worse offense
He lured her back with false pretense
And being that he's just so dense
He hurt his love away
Once the deed was said and done
The caveman did proceed to run
Shunning his only light and sun
He turned his love away
And then when in the darkness sat
Wondering how it came to that
He realized he was the prat
He sent his love away
Caveman wanders dire and doomed
Where once the flowers grew and bloomed
But now his heart alone is tombed
Until his love comes to stay

I know, it's vomit-inducing, right?

I promised to never run. I promised to talk it out. So this is me saying I'm beyond sorry; I can't live with myself. Even my reptile parts hate me and are on strike. I was wrong, and I hurt you.

I don't even know how I could ever make it up to you.

But I want to... if you would let me.

Warmest regards,

RBF NK (and anaconda)"

◆ ◆ ◆

Max

It had been a week since Jenna should have received her letter, and Max had heard nothing back. He became more depressed as the days passed, still unwilling to admit that it was finally over. He just couldn't let her go.

Court kept him busy. Work kept him occupied. But at night he dreamed of Jenna. Of making love to her body, of hearing her sigh, of seeing her smile... and then seeing the look of horror on her face when he betrayed her. He felt the stab in his heart every night.

He got home late on a Friday night and dropped his briefcase on the floor, he rifled through his mail until he held a hand-written envelope, with the return address "Jenna." His hands started shaking, as he tore it open with anticipation and dread.

"My dearest RBF NK,

You are correct in asserting that you are not a poet. Please stop torturing me with bad prose. I think I have suffered enough.

I would like to learn more about you, so I thought I might ask you questions to determine whether or not I thought we should ever meet.

So here is my first question: If you love someone, I mean truly love someone, do you think it's possible to ever truly forgive them for losing faith in you?

I eagerly await your answer.

Best regards,

Jenna"

Max dropped into his chair, stunned. He was afraid to read too much into it. Was she really open to dialog about this, or was this a subtle way of saying she was never going to be able to overlook what he did?

What had started as an opening had turned into torture by introspection.

He went up to his office and started writing.

It took two days, and fifteen revisions before he had something he was willing to send back. Each letter carried a prayer with it, that at the end of the correspondence, there could be reconciliation.

Jenna

Five days later the next letter arrived. Jenna tore it open. There was none of the giddiness she had experienced when they first met, now it was her heart searching, wondering what still remained of the joy she had found. The joy he had taken back.

"My dearest Jenna,

Again, I am humbled by receiving your letter. You will never know how truly grateful I am for any small piece of you in my life, even if it is only so that you can spit on me.

As to your question 'Do you think it is possible to ever truly forgive someone you love for losing faith in you?'

My answer is, God, I hope so.

I say that because I have failed at it. My first wife lost faith in me, and I was never willing to forgive. Marcus lost faith in me, and I am not willing to forgive. I have lost faith in myself because I took the only good person I have ever met and hurt her out of misguided spite, and for that I will never be able to forgive myself.

In all of these situations, someone who I loved betrayed my love, and I could not be a bigger man and forgive them.

But it gets worse. I am a selfish man. When I realized that I myself lost faith in the only person who had ever earned it from me, I had the audacity to hope, to pray, that I might one day be forgiven. Not because I deserve it; I don't. But because she is a better human being than I ever was.

Maybe the most I can hope for is that one day I can be that kind of human being.

Let me ask you a question: If you knew that the person you were in love with was really a monster, could you ever consider being with them?

Please feel free to ask me anything. If you feel compelled to send nude photos, I would welcome those as well.

Warmly,

RBF NK"

Tears ran down Jenna's face. Where once these letters made her giddy with anticipation, she read nothing but heartache and pain in them now. She didn't want to live like this, continuing to beat each other up, or allow each other to beat themselves up.

As she no longer had a job, she had plenty of time to sit and consider how she would answer.

◆ ◆ ◆

Max

Another week had come and gone, and Valentine's day was fast approaching. Max hadn't received a response from Jenna yet, and doubt was starting to fester in him. Had he answered her question wrong? Had he just made himself seem pathetic? Was he expecting too much from her?

His court cases were starting to thin out again, and he had hoped that he might get to see Jenna for Valentine's Day, but he was beginning to realize that he had, again, put the cart before the horse.

She may never forgive him. He might spent years chasing her, only to have her treat him as an intellectual curiosity, and nothing more.

Could he blame her?

When he saw the envelope in his mail the next day his heart swelled. He always got emotional when he held the envelope in his hand, and realized that she had held it first. It was almost like getting to feel her, indirectly. And that was sadly pathetic in itself.

> "My Dearest RBF NK,
>
> You make some strong arguments, although they are emotional arguments.
>
> I would like to think that the answer to my question is: yes. I suppose I will have to ponder it further, and apply it practically to ever truly know. But you know how adventurous I am; I'm sure I will have the opportunity.
>
> In answer to your question: 'If you knew that the person you were in love with was really a monster, could you ever consider being with them?'
>
> My answer is no.
>
> Because true monsters are rare. The sociopaths who kill without remorse, who are completely and permanently devoid of empathy, they are almost never to be found. More than often, the people we think are monsters are not unfeeling creatures; they are deeply feeling beings who lash out due to misunderstanding or pain. I am more inclined to judge those who judge the monsters and label them, because they have never hurt enough

to understand how someone could do something that they, themselves, consider 'unthinkable.' I understand the temporary lapse of judgment that makes someone hurt another through blind passion; only to regret it later in privacy.

You cannot love a true monster; they are incapable of returning it.

But you can adore a wounded creature who acts like a monster, and perhaps help them to heal that part of themself.

I feel I should take this opportunity to warn you, I will be shopping at Lady Saks on February 10th at 2 pm. I warn you because somehow I always attract ass-holes, and I would hate for you to find yourself in that situation.

Have a wonderful weekend,

Jenna"

Max checked his calendar. Shit! Tomorrow was the 10th. He was supposed to be in court all day, but he already knew he'd be calling in a junior associate to sit in.

His heart sang. She wanted to see him!

◆ ◆ ◆

Jenna

It was two o'clock when Jenna rode the escalator up to ladies' evening wear in the expensive department store. She saw Max immediately, standing by some racks in the back of the department. He was openly staring at her, looking fearful, and she chuckled to herself.

A few weeks ago he was afraid I tried to kill him, now he's afraid I'll reject him. Irony?

Jenna pretended she didn't see him, and instead headed to the nearest rack to look at dresses. She pulled a hanger out, looked the dress over, and then put it back, pulling out another one. When Max didn't move, she moved to another rack closer to him and made a show of looking at each dress, occasionally pulling one out.

She saw him out of the corner of her eye start approaching her slowly, like she was a vicious animal. She waited until he was only a few steps away before turning to him suddenly with a dress in hand.

"Excuse me, BOY, I need this in a size six. Chop chop, go fetch it." She waved the dress haughtily.

Max smirked. "I'm sorry, Miss, I don't work-"

"Excuses! Excuses!" Jenna waved him off. "You men think that just because you have large penises you can stand around all day doing nothing but look good?! Make yourself useful and GET TO WORK," she demanded with mock anger.

"Miss," Max began, trying not to chuckle. "That dress is hideous and overpriced. Don't you know hookers shop here? You should try a boutique, and leave me to my large penis and looking good."

Jenna dropped her jaw in mock outrage. "Well I NEVER!" she demanded.

"Bullshit, you haven't." Max laughed.

"I'll have you fired for this!" she teased, losing her character.

"That's fine. There's only one job I want, only one person I will work under," he replied, completely seriously.

Jenna looked at the dress in her hand, and back at Max. "I got nothing," she replied with a smile.

"That's not true at all," Max answered and pulled her into his body. He looked down into her eyes. "May I kiss you, Blue?" he asked quietly.

Jenna just nodded dumbly, lost in his eyes. Max bent down, eyes closed, and kissed her lips tenderly. It was all there: the passion, the longing, the hope... their emotions burned like sparks on their lips as their tongues rose to duck and stroke.

And just like that, everything else ceased to exist. It was just Max, his mouth on Jenna's, breathing each other's breaths.

A loud throat clearing behind them finally pulled Jenna out of her stupor, and she turned to see an older woman who worked for the department store a few racks away, giving them both a dirty look. Max burst out laughing, and Jenna followed.

Max grabbed her hand and pulled her toward the escalator.

◆ ◆ ◆

Max

Max held her hand tightly as they rode down the escalator. He had no idea where he should take her next, only that he couldn't let her go. He was never letting her go again.

When they got to the main floor, Max headed for the door.

"Where are we going?" Jenna asked, a huge smile on her face.

"Uh... Are you hungry?" he asked hopefully.

"Starved!" she answered quickly.

"Okay, what are you in the mood for? There's Indian, Italian, Thai-"

"Anaconda." She smirked at him as he almost creamed his pants.

Max opened the door to his house for her and ushered her in. Guilt settled deep in his gut. He wanted her, God knew he wanted her... but bringing her back here after he had... He really couldn't live with himself, he was so ashamed. His cock was only semi-rigid, and shrinking by the minute.

He hung their coats up, trying to think of some way to slow things down, but her body slammed his up against the wall, her mouth on his, needy, hungry. She moaned into his mouth and he groaned in response.

Finally, she pulled away and dragged him toward the living room. His heart stopped as he eyed the spot.

"Drink?" he asked her nervously.

"Whatever you're having." she answered, smiling up at him with nothing but unadulterated joy.

My God, how can she even stand in this room without reliving the horror?

Max poured them both a glass of scotch with a shaking hand and sat on the couch, as far away from the spot of shame as he could. Jenna followed and sat sideways on his lap. He sipped his scotch and looked at her in awe.

She sipped her scotch, and then looked at him curiously.

"Max, what's the matter?" She was so observant.

"I..." He hung his head, his cheeks flaming.

"You don't want me?" she asked quietly.

His head whipped up. "NO. No. I DO want you. You have no idea how much I want you... I just..." He couldn't say it.

"Can you talk about it if your anaconda is warmer?" She smiled warmly. His cock stiffened briefly under her legs, giving its opinion.

"Maybe." He smirked shyly.

She leaned in so that her lips were by his earlobe. "I'll tell you a secret. My mammal is a little rusty, so you may need to get some lubrication if we're nesting reptiles today." She nipped his earlobe softly between her teeth.

He leaned into the crook of her neck, his breath hot on her skin. "I would love to take care of your little mammal. Would she prefer I bring some down here, or would she be more comfortable upstairs?" he asked eloquently.

"Hmmm. I think she prefers the privacy of your boudoir, there's more space to ... spread out there." She purred

Max's cock twitched in approval.

Max led her up the stairs, to his room, praying that he didn't have an embarrassing malfunction.

"So, how would you like to..." Max started uncomfortably, and then turned around to see Jenna stripping her clothing off.

"Well, yeah, that will do just fine," he said, and started pulling his clothing off as well.

Jenna stood before him, fully nude, her pussy shaved clean. Max's cock responded without hesitation, and Max was silently relieved. Jenna pushed him toward the bed, and had him sit against the headboard. He reached into his nightstand for the lube, and then reached back in to pull out the wrapped gift that had been sitting there since Christmas.

"You didn't open it?" she asked.

"How could I? I had to be able to thank you. I know how I love it when you thank me for my package." He grinned at her.

"Maybe, after we've finished our chat, you'll want to open it." She winked at him.

"Baby, I will open anything of yours." He pulled her closer and kissed her deeply. His need was obvious. His cock strained against her belly.

She took the lube from him and drizzled it over his cock, and then worked it in with her hands. Max groaned in appreciation.

"Blue, Baby, it's been a while. If you want to have a conversation you need to stop that." He groaned.

"It's been a while for me, too, Baby. How bout you let me get your reptile warm, and we can talk?" she negotiated.

Max groaned again. "Blue, you're touching my cock. You can literally have anything you want right now."

Jenna laughed and pulled herself up onto her knees. Max held the base of his cock under her, and she slowly slipped down. Again, she only got a him in a few inches before he stuck. Max threw his head back again and groaned out loud, his hands grabbing her hips.

"Fuck! Blue, you are so fucking tight!" He could feel the head of his cock throbbing inside her walls, and her pussy grabbing at him.

Jenna lifted slightly and then pushed down hard, taking him several inches deeper. She moaned, her mouth open with pleasure, and Max damn near exploded right there. She was the most erotic woman he had ever seen; he wasn't even all the way in her, and she wasn't even moving, and she had him a hairs-breath away from losing all control.

Her eyes were closed in bliss. "I love the way you stretch me! I love the burrrn...," she whispered. Max grabbed the base of his cock, to hold off ending the session too soon.

"So what did you want to talk about?" she asked sweetly, as she adjusted to his girth filling her and stretching her.

"Oh..." Reality crashed back into him, and he felt his cock deflate.

Jenna took the opportunity to pull herself up and slam back down onto him, seating him fully. Max grabbed at her hips while he groaned, his cock swelling again feeling itself deep inside her. Jenna ground her hips into him, getting him where she wanted him.

Jenna leaned in and kissed Max, her tongue running over his lips.

"Max, Honey, I know that whatever your thinking is upsetting your reptile, so I'm going to need to administer some TLC while you talk, is that ok?"

His cock instantly twitched inside of her, and she giggled as she lifted gently and dropped back down a few inches. She did it a few times until Max had to hold her hips in place, for fear of coming too soon.

"Talk to me, Baby," she whispered huskily.

Chapter 17

Jenna

Goddamn I missed that cock.

Jenna pulled herself up a few inches, to slam back down. He swelled even more inside her, getting incredibly harder. She did it again. Then again. He hit all the right places!

Max grabbed her hips to still her. He was on the edge, and could go at any moment. As much as she loved to tease him, he needed this space to communicate.

"Talk to me, Baby," she whispered huskily.

He did fine when they were being sexual, but when he thought about his emotions, it just shut him down. As he started to formulate his words, and she felt his shaft start to wither, she clenched tightly, making it spring back inside her.

Max looked at her in wonder.

Then he cleared his throat. "I.. uh... When I first walked you back in, I felt so ashamed of what I had done to you. I hated myself. My body wants you, but I can't stand the thought of enjoying your body... knowing..." He hanged his head, unable to meet her eyes.

"Hey, hey, hey..." Jenna picked his chin up, he had tears in his eyes. She held his face in her hands and smiled at him warmly.

"Remember I told you that you would never force me. Remember I told you that I would stop you if you hurt me. Just like anal, that hurt me that day."

Tears ran down Max's face, and his erection began to completely wither.

"None of that," Jenna commanded on a laugh, and clenched her pussy around him again. "Just like anal it hurt for a while... but that's because you were hurting. I chose to share that with you. I could have told you to stop. I could have made you stop. So quit beating yourself up over it. If you really want to make up for it, replace that memory for me. Take me to that place and give me an amazing memory to think about instead." She smiled at him, and began to ride his cock in short strokes.

She could see he was conflicted. He wanted to beat himself up. He wanted to hate himself.

"I don't deserve you," he whispered.

"So make yourself worthy," she whispered back as she kissed him deeply. She ground her hips around him, letting him press against all of her walls as he slowly grew and hardened again inside of her. He was amazingly huge, and when he was fully engorged he could send her completely over the edge in seconds.

But he was still struggling emotionally.

Jenna looked into his eyes.

"Max, Baby, do you love this pussy?" she asked him plainly.

"I adore your pussy," he answered without hesitation.

"Then show me. Take that big cock of yours and love this pussy, and fuck this pussy until it weeps all over you. Make it come on your cock, until it has no control anymore. Take my pussy, Max. Claim my pussy," she urged, nipping his neck and sucking.

His breathing grew raspier, his groans deeper. He grabbed her hips and lifted them to rocket them down on his cock.

Jenna groaned. "That's it baby!"

He did it again, and again, but Jenna still felt him holding back.

"Baby, I need more. Can you get behind me, Baby? I want to feel you take me from behind," she purred.

He launched her up and flipped her over, kneeling behind her. She dropped her chest to the mattress and looked back over her shoulder to watch him.

"Fuck me, Max. Claim my pussy." Her eyes were heavy with lust.

◆ ◆ ◆

Max

Max lined himself up and launched his cock deep into her. She screamed her pleasure, as he slammed into her again and again, harder and harder. He picked one of his knees up, his foot on the bed beside her, to change the angle, and Jenna keened. The new angle brought him deeper, and the pressure that deep made her convulse and groan. Instantly she was coming, her body jerked and squeezed down hard on Max's cock as he thrust. Her low long wail came out deeper and louder until she was screaming, overwhelmed.

Max leaned forward over her, thrusting like an animal, until his balls tightened and retracted, the sensation moving through his cock, making it hard as steel. He was rammed as deep into her pussy as he could get and her body gripped his cock there, squeezing it, milking it, sucking him dry into her. He screamed as his world went dark with fireworks behind his eyes. His hips pulled back and slammed into her again and again, the sensations too good. He just wanted to bury his cock in her, feel her sucking him from the inside. There was no thought. There was only the perfect blissful feeling of her taking his cock inside her.

Finally he collapsed on her, his breathing was harsh, matching hers. He wrapped his arms around her and pulled her close. He still felt guilty, but he felt better about her being intimate with him. Instantly, he felt like he was home.

"Now open your gift." She breathed into his ear.

He didn't want to move, but he forced himself to reach into his nightstand drawer and pull the gift out. It was heavy in his hand. He unwrapped it, and then stared at the buttplug.

"Next round?" Jenna purred.

◆ ◆ ◆

Jenna

Jenna woke surrounded by roses in bed. She rubbed the back of her hand over her eyes and tried to take it all in. The bedroom door opened, and Max strolled in with a tray in his hands, a huge smile on his face.

"Good Morning, my dearest Blue!" he sang. He placed the tray of food in front of her, and leaned in for a searing kiss.

"What is all this?" She laughed.

"Making up for lost time." He smirked. "Now, what would you like for Valentine's Day, Sweetheart?" he asked.

Jenna thought about it for a minute, and her eyes caught on the small wrapped gift on his fireplace mantle. It was the 'family appropriate' gift she had bought for him at Christmas.

"I'd like for you to open that gift," she said, pointing.

Max turned around, and then walked to the mantle to bring it back.

"That hardly seems like a gift for YOU." He smiled.

"I know, but it's all I want." She smiled back.

Max tore the paper off, and his eyes opened wide when he took in the frame and the photo of them together. She was wearing the blue dress he had bought for her, and they looked perfect together. Jenna could see he was getting emotional.

"Damn," he said low. "I thought I had outdone you by filling the bed with roses. Back to square one." He chuckled.

Jenna had the biggest smile on her face.

"Boy, I'm glad I didn't open this at Christmas." He chuckled. "The boys would have gone ape."

Jenna's face fell. Immediately a look of regret sprang into Max's face.

"Oh, Blue, I didn't mean... I'm just glad I have it now. That's what I meant."

Jenna tried to appear happy, but it was clear there was sadness welling in her eyes. "I never got a chance to spend time with them," she said, "Eddie looks so much like your brother, and I can see you in Charlie's face."

Max smiled softly. "Eddie. Yeah... With a little planning, we can visit them anytime you'd like. They really like you, you know. I think Eddie might even have a crush on you."

He was trying really hard to smooth over the fiasco that had been Christmas; Jenna didn't want to ruin it by pointing out she couldn't travel due to her court order, and the impending case with Marcus. Instead she smiled gratefully.

She enjoyed her breakfast in bed, and then she enjoyed Max in bed. They spent hours discovering each other's pleasure, and she made one of the best Valentine's Days that she could remember.

◆ ◆ ◆

Max

Max sat in the small office in the courthouse and waited with Jenna. His thoughts drifted as he thought about his life with Jenna now, and how happy he was. He had been seeing her since December; other than their brief separation at Christmas, a little over three months. In that time he had invited her to stay over, which recently had been more like having her move in, and he couldn't be more happy. He had never wanted a woman to sleep over, and now he got antsy if she didn't.

He had rushed to ask her to marry him, and after Mia's failed attempt to break them up he had never brought it up again. He still had the ring, sitting in his safe. He still wanted her to marry him, but he was giving her time and space. Maybe she would even surprise him and ask him? She certainly seemed happy enough with him. He made sure of that.

He watched her out of the corner of his eye. She looked tired, distracted. As the court date for Marcus's trial had grown closer she had experienced more night terrors, and she never seemed hungry. She was more snappish and withdrawn. He watched her like a hawk, trying to take care of her as she stressed out.

Today the case was being heard, and she sat clutching her hands in her lap, looking afraid and exhausted. Essentially, she had filed a battery charge against Marcus, and he had countered. Max couldn't wait for it to just be over, so that she could go back to being happy and carefree. His heart ached to see her like this.

The court officer leaned his head into the room and told them, "It's time." Jenna popped out of her chair nervously, and Max placed his hand on the small of her back as they followed the man into the courtroom. Jenna was seated at a table to the right with the lawyer Max had hired for her, Bill Altworth; Marcus was seated with his attorney to the left.

Jenna stared straight ahead, occasionally looking at her lawyer to answer a question. Max sat in the first row, behind her. He noticed she avoided looking at Marcus at all costs. Marcus seemed to have no problem glaring or sneering at her.

Once the judge arrived the show was on the road. Jenna was questioned and Marcus was questioned. The tone took an immediate downturn once the video from the security footage was shown. Arguments were made back and forth, as there was no audio, no way to know what was said other than Jenna and Marcus's word. The audio recorded in the parking lot couldn't be used because Marcus had not been informed he was being recorded. It looked an awful lot like the judge was leaning heavily toward Marcus's version of the story, as he overruled any objection to the contrary.

The point was made that at no point in the video, except the very beginning when Jenna couldn't get past Marcus, did she ever look "afraid." In the video she stood with a blank face, back straight, head up, until Marcus grabbed her crotch and held. The judge dismissed the notion that she was putting on a brave face out of self preservation, outright. Max knew she was just responding to a perceived predator by not looking like prey, but the judge wasn't listening.

Then, at the end of the video, her face had contorted with controlled rage as she proceeded to pound the living daylights out of him. Marcus's team argued that at no point was she actually afraid; in fact, they claimed, she was goading him into a fight.

Marcus's lawyer painted a picture of them negotiating a tryst, and when the terms weren't good enough for Jenna, of her having a mental break. Every time Jenna's lawyer pointed out the sneering condescending looks made by Marcus they were downplayed, or outright overruled.

Max watched as Jenna's shoulders and head fell lower and lower.

At the end of the day, the court found Marcus and Jenna both guilty of battery; Marcus was ordered to pay a $500 fine. It was the mildest of slaps on the wrist for a man as wealthy as he was. Jenna was ordered to continue court ordered psychiatric counseling weekly and three hundred hours of community service, as her attack had been more violent; she was warned that she would be institutionalized if she should be deemed a danger to society.

It didn't feel like a win.

Marcus was all smug smiles as he shook his lawyer's hand, and before making his way past Jenna he leaned in and told her point blank, "This isn't over yet." before making his way out of the courtroom, flashing his smile in triumph.

Max gathered Jenna into his arms and took her home.

◆ ◆ ◆

Jenna

The court case had been an emotional wrecking ball. Jenna held it together when Max was with her, but when he was at work she would break down and bawl. There just didn't seem to be any justice. She was willing to admit she took it too far, but it didn't matter; because it seemed like whatever he did to her first was completely okay with the court. In the end they painted her as a whore, and made her the bad guy.

At least Marcus wasn't working with Max any longer. After Marcus's father heard the audio, and found out about the charges against him, the firm decided to distance itself from Marcus, and he found a position with another firm. No real loss for him, minimal inconvenience on his life.

A few days after the trial Jenna's phone rang with an incoming call from an unfamiliar number, and she let it go to voicemail. She took a shower, and cleaned the bedroom up, before remembering to check her phone again. She listened to the message.

"Miss Jones, My name is Dr. Oscar Tilden, and I have been assigned as your new psychiatric counselor by the courts. I have arranged an appointment with you on Friday at 4:30 pm. Your attendance to these sessions weekly is mandatory. I look forward to meeting you. Here is the address..."

Jenna stared at her phone. After the incident at Christmas she had been assigned to a shrink named Carol. She liked Carol.

Carol was less psychologist, more hippy grandmother, and she felt good about seeing her. This guy didn't sound nice at all.

Jenna sighed loudly, and promised herself she would not judge him before she had even met him; she just had to get him to sign off and say that she was managing her anger better. Hopefully, in a few visits, he would clear her. She was just pissed, because Carol had said she was close to releasing her; now she had to start all over.

Maybe he would use Carol's notes? She could hope.

Friday afternoon at 4:25 Jenna stood in the waiting room at the address she had been given. The office was awfully swanky for a court appointed shrink. She was used to bare-bones beige walls and dated carpeting, with mis-matched chairs and ancient artwork. This office boasted nice seating areas, fresh flowers, and beautiful framed art. The receptionist sat behind a tall cherry wood desk with a partition.

Jenna checked in and sat to wait for her appointment. Right at 4:30 a shorter middle-aged man came into the waiting area. He was chubby, and balding, but wore an expensive suit. Jenna took an immediate dislike to him. From the way he looked down his nose, and his rat-like facial expression, it was clear he thought highly of himself. He introduced himself as Dr. Tilden and brought her down a long hallway to his office at the end.

Jenna's nerves were heightened as Dr. Tilden closed the door behind them and then proceeded to sit on a large sofa in his office instead of behind his desk. Jenna just stood, wondering what to do.

Dr. Tilden turned to her with a smile. "Jennifer, come sit here next to me so we can learn about each other." He patted the cushion next to him.

"Call me Jenna," she said, but didn't move.

Dr. Tilden gave a small smile, but it was creepy; it was a smile that said he had a secret and she wasn't going to like it.

"Jennifer, this is a part of our court-appointed time together. It is my job to determine if you are stable enough to be able to live independently in society, or whether you are a danger to yourself and others. I cannot do that if you cannot follow instructions," he said coolly, his smug smirk still twisting his lips.

"You were in the military, yes?" he asked.

She knew damned well he already knew she had been. "Yes," she answered curtly.

"Well then, you are no stranger to taking orders. While we are here, I will be giving the orders, and you will be following them. Do you understand?" His smile widened.

"No. I don't understand. How are you going to be evaluating me if you are giving me orders?" she asked, trying to keep her face blank and her panic out of her voice.

The smug shit smiled openly.

"You see? If you had simply followed my orders, you would already know, because we would have moved on to conversation. But here we sit, discussing orders, instead of following them. Now, Jennifer, *come* and *sit*." He patted the cushion beside him again.

Jenna's mind screamed. Warning bells blared in her head. If she did as he said, he would walk all over her each week, if she didn't, she may prolong the process of him releasing her. Even though it pissed her off to no end, she slowly made her way over to the couch and sat down, leaving a foot of space between them.

"Have you always had this disdain for authority figures?" He chuckled.

Jenna sat deadpan and didn't answer him. Dr. Tilden just rolled his eyes as he leaned beside him to pick something up.

"I can already see how this is going to go," he stated quietly. In the next moment he had lifted his clipboard with a thick folder on it and notes. There was also a dog collar contraption on it.

"Now, Jennifer, it is my understanding that you have a history of violence. For that reason I will need you to wear this while we are in these sessions, for my protection. It will only be activated if you become *unstable*." He held the collar out to her, his expression cold.

"I'm not putting that fucking thing on," Jenna stated flatly.

"You ARE putting that fucking thing on, Jennifer, or you are spending the weekend in the hospital for psychiatric surveillance. Don't test me again." There was a cold malice in his eyes that told Jenna that he was never going to clear her for release.

"You do what you have to do. I'm not wearing that." She fired back at him.

He sighed, a small smile twisting his mouth, as he made his way to his phone on his desk. Pushing the button, Jenna heard the receptionist pick up.

"Vicky, send two officers in. Miss Jones is non-compliant. Call down to the ward and have a room prepared for her for a 48-hour evaluation for her safety." He looked gleeful as he made the order, staring Jenna in the eye with challenge.

"Right away, Doctor." And the line went dead.

Jenna didn't move from the couch, her arms crossed over her chest defiantly. It had to be illegal?! You couldn't make psych patients wear shock collars, could you?! It was horrific.

The door opened suddenly, and two uniformed security officers stepped in and headed for Jenna. Her first instinct was to put up a fight, defend herself, but she looked at Dr. Tilden, who was watching her expectantly. Waiting.

And then she knew.

This was what was going to happen every week. He was going to humiliate her and dominate her, push her to fight back. Because if she did, if she lost control, he could lock her up for good. This was just the first test.

Lifting her head, she stood and walked to the guards. She offered no resistance as they wrestled her to the floor, unnecessarily, and handcuffed her. She made sure her face was blank of all emotion; at that point, it wasn't difficult.

As they dragged her out of the room roughly she heard Dr. Tilden behind her call out, "I'll see you next week, same time." before his door shut with a bang.

◆ ◆ ◆

Max

Max paced the living room floor, panic was starting to set in. It was already after seven, Jenna's appointment had been at 4:30, and she hadn't come home. He had texted and called her, but got no answer. Snow was falling hard outside, and the only thing he could think was that she had been in an accident driving back.

He picked up his phone and called Andrew, hoping that she had maybe gone to his house to pick something up and forgotten to tell him.

"Max," Andrew answered on the first ring.

"Andrew, have you seen Jenna?" Max blurted.

"No... Not since we sparred Tuesday, she's been with you. What's going on?" Andrew's concern was evident.

"It's probably nothing... but she hasn't come home from her psych appointment. It was at 4:30, and she's not answering my calls." Max knew he sounded paranoid.

"Did... did you two fight?" Andrew hedged.

"What? NO, we didn't fight. THAT'S why I'm worried. Other than court, things have been good. She had no reason not to come home!" Max exploded.

"Alright, alright... I had to ask." Andrew blew out a breath. "Okay, look, I'll check around some of the places she hangs around. Why don't you call the police and notify them?"

"The police?!" Max whispered, his heart pounding in his ribcage.

"Yes, if something's happened to her, they need to know sooner than later. Call the police Max, I'll search around here. Call me if you find anything, I'll do likewise." Andrew hung up.

Max stared at his phone, catatonic. This couldn't be happening. She couldn't be gone. Andrew's words finally filtered through the cold fog in his mind and he dialed 911.

A half hour later, Max was desperate for any piece of information. He was not a religious man, but he was ready to sell his soul to get Jenna back in one piece. He prayed. He bargained. He threatened. His mind kept picturing her dead off the side of the road, or kidnapped and sold into sex trafficking. The longer it went on, the worse his assumptions became.

His phone rang and he leapt to answer it, almost dropping it in the process.

"HELLO!" he answered, his panic obvious.

"Mr. Thurston, we have located Miss Jones. She's safe," the officer reported.

"OH THANK GOD! Where is she? Is she hurt? Wh-"

"Mr. Thurston, she's been admitted to the hospital under the orders of her doctor. I cannot give you any further information about her." The officer finished.

"What do you mean you can't-"

"Sir, are you her family?" the officer asked.

"NO! I'm-"

"Unless you are her family or spouse, I cannot give you confidential medical information. I'm sorry. I can only tell you that she's safe. Goodnight, Mr. Thurston."

Max screamed and resisted the urge to launch the cell phone into the wall. Instead he called Andrew to fill him in.

"Why the fuck would Carol have sent her back to that fucking hell hole?!" Andrew screamed.

"I don't know, but I'm going over there." Max ground out.

"I'll meet you there. I'll text you the address." Andrew spit before hanging up.

Forty five minutes later Max and Andrew were still arguing with the chief nurse on the psych floor. They were refused admission to see Jenna, and because they weren't related they were not given any information, other than she was on a 48-hour hold, and would be released Sunday night. They were both ready to kill someone by the time security "suggested" they leave.

Max at least felt like he had someone who understood how tortured he felt by this whole situation, as Andrew was as crazed and desperate as he was to get to her. They stopped at a restaurant nearby to discuss what they could do about the situation; but without much information, they were both pretty well fucked.

Chapter 18

Jenna

Jenna was equally pissed off royally, and more depressed than she could ever remember being. She had been treated like a prisoner over the weekend. They had actually restrained her to the bed, so she had to beg to use the bathroom. She didn't know what that fucking doctor had told them about her, but she was essentially tied down and abandoned for two days, heavily sedated.

They had strip-searched her upon arrival, taking her clothing and personal items; to include her phone. She never got a chance to call Max or Andrew to warn them. She spent Friday night howling with rage and sorrow, worried sick about them; she knew they would lose it if she just didn't show up. That fucking doctor had engineered quite the little torture for her.

She wanted to kill him. She wanted to choke him to death. But she knew that was playing right into his hands. What the fuck had she ever done to him to make him want to destroy her?

And she had no way out.

Who would believe her? If she said her psychologist was too tough, she would be accused of being non-compliant: she already had been. If she told anyone about the collar, or using lock-up as punishment... well, he was the doctor, she was the fucked up patient. She knew how that ended.

By Sunday she was empty again, facing a hopeless situation. She didn't want to let Andrew and Max down. She didn't want to go to jail, or be institutionalized. If this weekend had taught her anything, it's that she could be made to disappear, and everyone around her would be forced to move on with their lives while she rotted, alone.

The large male goon of a nurse pulled her along the hallway behind him to get her belongings. She saw Andrew and Max both spring out of their chairs and rush to her. She couldn't even hold up a brave face, she was too broken down. She collapsed into a puddle and bawled.

Max brought them both back to his place; Jenna was appreciative that he made space for Andrew, when she was sure he wanted her alone. At that moment, she didn't want to be alone with anyone; she just felt like she was letting everyone down.

Max changed her into some fuzzy pajamas, and got her a scotch, and then snuggled with her on the couch while they asked her what had happened.

Andrew started off, he spoke calmly, soothingly. "Jenna, why would Carol do this to you? Did something happen at your appointment?"

Jenna stared into her glass. "The court replaced Carol. I'm seeing this fuckwit, Dr. Tilden. He's a control freak. He demands that I follow his orders. He insisted I had to wear a shock collar: when I refused, he had me put away."

Max and Andrew stared at each other in horror.

◆ ◆ ◆

Max

WHAT.THE.FUCK?!

Max stared at Andrew, then at Jenna. Was she serious? It sounded like something out of a horror movie. Doctors don't make patients wear shock collars, and they don't lock them up to make them do their bidding. There must be some misunderstanding.

Maybe she had another break with reality?

Andrew was the first to break the silence. "Baby-girl, are you sure about that?"

Jenna's face contorted with rage as she looked up at him. "I fucking know what I saw, Andrew! He fucking threatened to lock me up if I ever refuse his orders. He's trying to get me locked away for good!" At that she started bawling uncontrollably, her shoulders heaving.

Max grabbed for her and pulled her into him, rubbing his hands down her back. They let her cry herself out, and then Max carried her up and put her to bed.

Max sat with Andrew for a few hours, discussing what Jenna had told them. They were both at a loss to explain it.

"She wouldn't lie, not about this," Max said with certainty.

"Yeah, but... it's so fucked up, Max. No doctor would risk their license doing something like that. Do you think she just doesn't want to see him? Is this just her way of rebelling because Marcus got off scot free?" Andrew thought out loud.

Max grunted. "Maybe somewhere in the middle; maybe she resents having to see him, and he's an asshole control freak?"

"So what can we do?" Andrew asked, looking pointedly at Max. "This guy isn't going to help her; he's only going to make her worse. Can they assign her another shrink?"

"I don't know." Max sighed. "I'll call tomorrow and see what I can find out. I have some friends, I can try to pull some strings. Look, I'm going to plan some time off to be with her, but until I can, can I have her stay at your place when I'm not here during the day?"

"Yeah, Man, we'll have to work out a schedule. I'll schedule off around your days, so one of us is available." Andrew stared at the floor, his jaw set in a hard line.

"I'm calling out tomorrow. Let me know what your schedule looks like, okay?" Max looked as grim as Andrew about the whole situation, his eyebrows were furrowed with confusion and anger.

"Will do. And Max, I'm sorry about what I said before-"

"Don't be. You were right. I would still expect you to hand me my ass if I hurt her. I'd have done the same. You're a good friend." Max held his hand out, and the two men shook over their shared love for Jenna.

◆ ◆ ◆

Jenna

The world was silent, with only the thrumming pain in her eardrums. Jenna saw Brady on the ground. Brady was dead. Williams was crawling toward her. There was blood spattered everywhere, and the humvee was on its side. She tried to crawl to them, to help them; she tried to scream.

"See what you did, Jennifer? This is your fault. This is what happens when you don't follow orders." A stern voice said beside her.

She turned to see Dr. Tilden sitting beside her, a loaded gun aimed at her head.

Jenna woke with a scream in her throat. Hands grabbed her and pulled her tight and she flailed and fought to get free.

"Sshhh ssshhhh ssshhhhh... Blue! It's just me. It's Max. It's okay. You're okay." His arms wrapped her snugly against his hard body.

I'm not okay.

Her heartbeat slowly settled, and her pulse followed. She was slick with sweat, and suddenly too hot. She pulled the covers off of her so she could breathe. Max stroked his hands over her soothingly, whispering words of comfort in her ear.

Like an aftershock her heartbeat spiked again, this time with need.

She rolled in his arms suddenly and launched her body onto his, devouring his mouth with hers, clawing at his body.

She needed him inside of her, immediately, NOW. She couldn't wait. She needed to feel all of him. She needed him stretching her body, pounding roughly into her. She needed all of him inside of her or she was going to explode.

The more erratic and panicked her movements became, the more Max tried to gently ease her back, slow her down; but she wasn't having any of it. She bit him hard and he yelped, jumping back.

"Blue, Baby..." He heaved in panted breaths, "What's going on? What's happening with you right now?"

She launched herself back on top of him, pulling and clawing desperately. "I need you inside me, Max. I need you right now. I need you. Please Max, fill me. PLEASE MAX!" She ripped her pajama top off over her head and flung it, and then reached down to pull her bottoms off.

Max held his hands on her hips, eyeing her unsurely.

"Baby, I'll give you everything you need, but you have to help me understand. Blue..." His eyes searched hers, but she wouldn't meet his.

"Just... just put it in. I'll talk! I need your cock!" she demanded as she finally met his eyes; hers were large and wild.

"Baby, you're not warmed up, it will be uncomfortable... let me..." He reached for his lube; but she took matters into her own hands, positioning herself over him and forcing her pussy onto his shaft in a series of up and down pumps of her hips.

He winced a little at the friction as her skin pulled against his a little. She tried to continue to ride him, but he stilled her by pulling her hips down and holding.

"Blue, Baby. Tell me." He looked into her eyes, and she stopped struggling.

Jenna dropped her head onto his chest and started to cry, overwhelmed. Max just held her and stoked her back with his fingers.

"What's going on, Baby? You can tell me. I can't make it better if you don't tell me," he whispered softly.

"He...He's going to kill me!" she choked out through her crying. "He wants to hurt me, and I can't fight back, or he wins. I can't win!" she ended with a wail.

"Who? Blue, Who wants to hurt you?" Max asked.

"That... That ... doctor!" Her body shook with tremors as the tears streamed down her face and collected on Max's chest. She clutched onto him for dear life.

"I won't let him hurt you, Blue." Max promised her.

Jenna wanted to believe that. She wanted to believe Max would protect her; but he couldn't. No one could. Not even her. She knew it was a hopeless situation.

"Max..." She sniffled. "I know how fucked up this is right now, but I really need you to fuck me hard. I need to feel you. I need to know you're with me. Please." She whimpered. "I need this right now."

Max picked her face up to look into her eyes. He must have seen something that told him she was more stable, because he sighed deeply and pulled her closer.

"Okay, Baby. I'll give you whatever you need, but you have to let me warm you up. That's the only way I can do it, Baby. Okay?" He searched her eyes.

She looked up at him with her big glazed doe eyes, and then nodded, as her eyes started to fill with heat instead of fear. He reached into his nightstand to pull out the lube, and gently lifted her off of him. He poured the lube into his hands to warm it, and then rubbed his cock down until it was smooth and slippery. Then he rubbed his hands up through her folds, stopping to flick quickly over her clit.

Her body responded to his every move, leaning into his hand, her lips opening to receive him, her body jerking and groaning as he worked her clit. He pressed three fingers inside of her to draw out her own wetness, and pumped her gently a few times to expand her tight channel. Jenna moaned and rode his fingers, her head thrown back, her eyes closed as she lost herself to the feeling.

Max withdrew his hand and slowly pulled her hips down onto him tight. Jenna moaned loudly, her mouth in a blissful "O".

"Blue, Baby, look at me. Look at me while I love your gorgeous body, Baby," he whispered. Her pussy clenched around him tightly as she opened her eyes with a gasp and met his hooded eyes. They just stared intensely at each other for a moment, until Jenna suddenly lifted up on her knees and slammed herself back down, impaling herself on his cock with a loud groan. Max groaned with her. She did it again, and again, each time harder, more brutal.

Max just watched her take her pleasure. She was feeling their connection, but he also knew she wasn't building toward climax, she was savoring each thrust deep inside of her, like she couldn't get it deep enough.

"Baby...," He panted, "pick your knees up, Blue. Squat over me. Yes! JUST like THAT!"

He helped her maneuver, and the new position sunk him incredibly deep inside her. She screamed the first time she slammed her ass down on him with her full body weight. Max shuddered, seeming lost in the intense feeling of having her grip him so tightly while being so deep inside her body. She slammed into him over, and over, dropping her body onto his cock like a sheath, her pussy trying to suck him further inside as she rose off of him each time.

It was slow and brutal and fucking amazing.

Jenna could feel Max getting close, but she didn't want it to end. She wanted to ride him forever, feel him deep inside of her endlessly. When his cock split her wide open, when she burned from his girth and his depth, when she ached with the fullness of it; then she knew. Then she was one with him. She needed that union. He grounded her in what was real and true.

"Baby,... Blue... If you keep doing that... I'm going to blow, Baby. ... I can't fucking control it... You're too fucking tight. You're too fucking hot..." Max was panting and heaving, struggling not to let it go.

Jenna stopped moving, settling over him, she leaned down to kiss him deeply. It was the first time she had that night. She really kissed him, not just devoured him for her own needs. She put all of her love and caring into that kiss, as if she could breathe her emotion into him through their mouths.

She wanted him deeper inside of her, so deep it hurt, and she didn't know how to do that.

Max gently turned so she moved off of him onto the bed. She whimpered with displeasure, but he pulled her ass up into the air, pushing her chest down to the mattress.

"I need you deep, Baby..." She groaned. "I need you to hurt me."

Max froze for a moment, every muscle tense, and then leaned down to kiss her back. He ran his hands up her sides and then down her ass, until he settled them on her hips.

"You know I can't do that, Baby," he whispered. "but I can give you what you need."

He reached under her, plunging three fingers inside of her wetness and pumping her hard, while he flicked her clit. With his other hand he grabbed the bottle of lube and poured some down between the cheeks of her ass. With his first hand still plundering her tight pussy, he fingered her puckered hole with his other, pushing more and more firmly, until he had a finger in.

Jenna yelped and then moaned, rocking her hips back onto his fingers, riding them. She also tilted her hips up and back, trying to ride the finger in her ass while she mewled and whimpered. Max smiled in relief, and pushed the finger in farther, pressing the walls of her ass, while his hand fucked her pussy.

Jenna looked over her shoulder to see how aroused Max was becoming, watching her take in the new sensation. She clawed at the blankets and squirmed, trying to get him into her deeper. He gently pushed a second finger into her ass and she gasped out loud before groaning. She was starting to come undone. He pumped her ass and pussy hard a few more minutes before adding a third finger into her ass, making her scream and throw her head back with ecstasy. She was throwing her hips back at him, grinding on him, panting and heaving like a wild beast.

Finally, he slowly pulled his fingers out of her ass. She chased him with her hips, whining in frustration, until she felt him push the head of his cock against her back hole. She froze.

"Do you want me to, Baby?" he asked, concerned.

"FUCK YES!" she screamed and launched her hips backwards. Max chuckled, as she only pushed him back, her hole too tight for her to take him that way.

He lined himself up again, poured more lube on, and then gently and slowly pressed the head into her, while his other hand still worked her pussy and clit hard.

"OOOhh... ooohhhhh... ohhhhhhh" Jenna's body seemed to stagger, not knowing what to do. Max kept the pressure on her pussy hard, as he worked his cock into her ass inch by slow inch, until he was finally fully seated. Max was clearly using all of his self control to hold back, as his cock seemed ready to blow. He held himself there, letting her adjust; until she finally squirmed, circling her hips, needing the friction.

And then he let her have it.

He pulled back and pounded his hips forward, fucking her ass with all that he had. She knew he was close, and she could feel her own greedy pussy milking his hand into her, wanting more. He lifted one knee beside her and jackhammered into her with a roar. He wrapped his free hand around her waist, securing her to him as he thrust like an animal into her tight ass.

Jenna screamed each gasping breath, and her legs and back locked up, the orgasm overtaking her. Her entire body trembled as if every muscle had been pulled tight, she was a live wire about to burst. Her pussy latched onto his hand, wringing it; while her ass tightened around his engorged shaft.

He exploded as she did. He was locked inside her for just a moment, and then he was thrusting and thrusting, shooting his juices deep into her ass, roaring and groaning. She was lost in the euphoric bliss that connected them in that moment.

He fell on top of her, both of them like throbbing masses of jello, completely blissed out and riding the afterglow.

Jenna smiled up at Max adoringly. "That was what I needed," she whispered. Max kissed her long and deep, gently and slowly pulling out of her. He held her and kissed her, until she finally fell back asleep in his arms, completely sated.

Chapter 19

Max

Andrew and Max threw together a schedule to be with Jenna around the clock. On the rare day that neither could get out of going to work, Jenna accompanied Andrew to his spa. This was a win-win because one of them would always be with her, and they could get her relaxation treatments.

At first she was livid about them "babysitting" her... but as the days went on, she really seemed to love the amount of time and attention she was getting. She was not a demanding woman, she would never expect them to spend more time than they could; so it was a gift to her that they devoted this time to her and her wellbeing, and she appreciated it.

Max sat in contemplation. *Or maybe she finally realized that being alone was too painful?*

The three of them spent some time together as well, and Max had to admit that he liked Andrew. While they ran in very different circles, Andrew was a take-no-shit kind of man, and yet still fun-loving and carefree, completely comfortable in his own skin. And Max knew he could trust Andrew with Jenna's wellbeing.

It was Thursday, and Jenna had her next psych appointment the next afternoon. Andrew was home with her, while Max had gone into work. Max closed his office door to keep his conversation private from the rest of his office, when he called Dr. Tilden. He wanted to get to the bottom of the situation.

The receptionist told Max that Dr. Tilden was with a client, but that she would give him the message. A half hour later, his phone rang.

"Mr. Thurston, this is Dr. Tilden, returning your call. How can I help you?" His voice was professional, but warm.

"Doctor, I have some questions about your treatment of Jenna Jones." Max began.

"Mr. Thurston, I need to remind you that due to confidentiality laws, I am not permitted to share anything of our sessions together. Unless you are her husband?..."

Max knew that even if he was married to Jenna the doctor wouldn't give him anything, but he had to try.

"No, we're not married. But I am concerned about some of the things she has told me. She said you insisted she wear a shock collar, and of course you had her sent to the hospital for the weekend. I question whether either of those things are really in her best interest," Max stated coldly.

The doctor sighed and then answered. "Mr. Thurston, I understand your concern about Miss Jones. What I *can* tell you is this: I have never asked a patient to wear a collar of any sort, that would be unethical and illegal." His voice sounded concerned and disappointed.

"While I can't give you particulars about her, you must know she is in a very fragile state. Part of therapy involves diving deep into the traumas of the past to uncover why people become unstable and choose to be violent. She is very resistant to therapy, and I have no doubt that in her mind I am a monster. I represent years of suppression, and the fear of unlocking all of that trauma can be overwhelming.

"I would not have sent Miss Jones to the hospital unless she was so unstable that I thought it was absolutely necessary. She attacked two of my security staff while trying to attack me.

"I ask you to consider this, as she seems to trust you, do you find that violence is her go-to? Does she engage in risky or dangerous hobbies? I noticed some bruising on her arms. Does she push for painful physical contact?

"I don't want you to answer me, I want you to consider that people like Jenna engage in self-violence as a way of avoiding painful emotions. And until they uncover the roots of those emotions, they will forever engage in self-harm as a way of life. It is easier to understand physical pain than it is emotional overwhelm.

"I can only advise that encouraging or participating in those activities will only undermine her in the long-run. She needs to be able to access her own vulnerability, to be open and honest about her feelings, without running to pain to distract her from them. People like her often downward spiral, as no pain can be great enough. They seek more and more risky or dangerous contact, until they completely implode, or explode. They wind up in hospitals, prisons, or morgues.

"I really need the people who love her the most to cooperate in her recovery; because anything less is enabling her to fail." He ended sadly.

"I see," Max stated flatly. "I understand what you're saying, but I don't want for her to be restrained, and I'd like to have a witness with her when you see her."

"I agree, I can have a security guard on hand to ensure both of our safety, if that would make you feel better? It would actually be helpful." The doctor added.

"Yes." Max blew out a breath. "I think that would be for the best. Thank you for your time, Doctor." They said their good-byes, and hung up.

Max sat at his desk completely confused. He ran over the conversation again and again. The doctor had outright denied what Jenna had told him. Would Jenna lie to that degree? Was she so damaged that she would imagine or make-up a threat to get out of therapy?

He refused to believe it. He had doubted her before, and regretted it. She had been seeing Carol, happily. It wasn't the therapy that scared her.

And having someone else in the room meant she would be safer, so it would be easier for her. He felt good about that, at least.

As to the rest of it, it hit a little too close to home. She was having night terrors all the time now, and wanting extremely rough sex afterwards. She kept pushing for more and more. She wasn't sleeping much at night, but was sleeping a lot during the day.

She had also trained with Andrew, and had come home with dark new bruises. Was she hurting herself on purpose? Was she punishing herself in some way? If so, would this doctor be able to help her, before she became someone Max didn't even recognize? After only one appointment, and a weekend in lock-up, she had regressed significantly into herself. She rarely smiled or laughed, and was uncharacteristically fearful, jumpy.

Once again he cursed that he didn't know more about her; he felt like there were too many unknowns. He didn't have a clue how to deal with it. Maybe he should try holding back on the rough sex? He didn't want to enable her if she was just doing it to hurt herself. And while he was never a fan of plain vanilla sex, he would do it for her.

But would this be a permanent change? He couldn't imagine a life with Jenna as a shell of herself, and tepid lovemaking on top of it. He loved her, but what if she was becoming someone other than the woman he met, the woman he'd asked to marry him. Was he tying himself to a zombie?

But he also couldn't abandon her in her time of need! Holy fuck this was complicated. He just wanted his Blue back.

◆ ◆ ◆

Jenna

Jenna woke with a scream, her eyes wide, clawing to free herself. Max's arms pulled her close as he whispered words of comfort into her ears until she recovered herself and realized where she was.

She was safe.

Instantly she turned in his arms, pouncing on him like a feral beast.

It was her sanctuary. Only his hard body ramming deep inside of her brought her comfort, brought her connection, and pulled her out of the dark place in her head... the place where people never really died, they just haunted her to no end.

She kissed him urgently, her hands raking his body; but instead of relaxing back into her Max pulled away slowly, holding her, slowing her. Her breaths were ragged pants, on the edge of a growl.

"Blue, Baby... slow down. It's okay," he whispered, as he kissed her tenderly.

She deepened the kiss, biting his lip and sucking it into her mouth with a groan. Again, he pulled back, slowing her.

"Eeeaaaasssy, Baby." He cooed, stroking her gently.

It was probably supposed to be comforting, but the light finger touches on her skin only felt annoying. It was not what she wanted. It was not what she *needed*!

"Max..." She gasped, "Max, I need you to fuck me! I need you!" She groaned desperately, clutching at him.

He pulled back again.

"Baby, can't we do this slow? Can't I love and appreciate your body? What's the rush?" He smiled down at her, still foggy from sleep.

Her eyes were wide, with anger. "NO. Max, I don't want slow. I need you deep inside of me. I need to feel your connection to me. I need you to ground me. Why won't you just take me?" Her ragged breaths and angry eyes spoke of her frustration.

Max just sat looking at her, a look of concern held in his eyes as he took her in.

"Why, Blue?" he whispered. "Help me to understand."

"NEVERMIND." She snapped, rolling away from him, giving him her back as she laid on her side.

"Blue... talk to me?" he whispered, running his hands over her hip, before she shoved it away. She said nothing, but he could see the tremors running through her shoulders and knew she was crying. He wrapped his arms around her strongly.

"You won't talk to me, Blue?" he asked gently.

Jenna's heart was pounding. When she was this over-whelmed, there was no talking, there was only feeling. This was the first time he had ever denied her what she needed, questioned her. He had always trusted her to tell him what she needed; now, suddenly, he was acting like her therapist, wanting to discuss her thoughts and feelings, instead of being with her.

There was nothing to discuss! She had seen countless therapists and discussed the dreams. They got worse when she was anxious or fearful; they served as a barometer to her emotional wellbeing. She knew that. She knew she was fucked in the head over having to see this new therapist; it scared the ever living shit out of her.

Before Max, she learned to live in the haze of the pain for days after night terrors; but Max had been such sweet relief! She had found someone who anchored her like no one else ever had. Sure, she'd had sex after night terrors before, but they had never given her the peace that Max did. She assumed it was because she and Max cared so deeply for each other. She had taken refuge in that tiny warm place that was them, and it made her feel whole.

But now, now he was shutting the door on her. Now he was asking her to relive the terror of the dreams, to go through it again. Why wouldn't he let her in when she needed it so desperately? WHY? WHY was he doing this to her?

She said nothing.

Max held her while she cried in silence, until at last she seemed to calm, and then eventually to fall asleep. She knew he must be exhausted from being woken every night, but she savored the fact that he watched over her.

Friday afternoon came far too fast. Jenna had a meltdown at Max's, crying and begging him to keep her home, to get her out of her appointment, but Max could only shake his head sadly and say that the court would put her back in the hospital if she didn't go through with it.

In the end, he dropped her off at the office; she was completely numb.

The receptionist sent her back to Dr. Tilden's office, and she was surprised to see that one of the security guards who had manhandled her the week before stood in the room as well. Dr. Tilden sat on the sofa as he had before.

Jenna was aware of the rage growing in her body, but not in her mind; she felt nothing emotionally. It was bizarre to feel your heart rate pick up, your muscles bunch and tense, and yet feel nothing emotionally.

"Ah, Jennifer, here you are. Come *sit*." He patted the seat beside him with a smug smirk.

Jenna looked at the security guard, who was also smirking, watching her.

"Why is HE here?" She jerked her thumb at the guard.

"We will get to that, in time. Now SIT. I don't like having to repeat myself." The doctor said with aggravation.

Looking between the guard and the doctor, and seeing no alternative, Jenna walked over and sat on the sofa, again leaving space between them.

"As you felt it necessary to *divulge* the personal details of our sessions together," the doctor looked at her pointedly with anger, "it has become necessary for me to have certain protections in place." The doctor spoke conversationally and pointed to the guard. "Scott, here, will be on hand, in case you become... unstable." A small smile twisted his lips.

Jenna looked back and saw that "Scott" crossed his arms over his chest, a blatant evil smile on his face.

"So let's begin, shall we, Jennifer? We know you have a history of rage and violence; I need to know just how insidious it is with you. I see bruises on you... do you engage in painful sports or hobbies?" He asked curiously.

"No," Jenna responded through grit teeth, her jaw hard. Her anger was burning through her numbness.

"Don't lie to me!" The doctor hissed, "Or I shall be forced to punish you. You need to learn sooner than later that you are not in control here, I am. I give the orders, you follow them, immediately. You *will* be honest with me. So I will give you this one chance: do you engage in painful sports or hobbies? Answer me truthfully." He demanded.

"No." Jenna repeated.

"I see a weekend observation was not long enough, Jennifer? Maybe you'd prefer a week away from your boyfriend next time?" he asked coldly.

"I don't engage in painful hobbies. They don't hurt, they're not painful," she answered back.

"So, those bruises don't hurt?" he asked mockingly, and then reached out and grabbed her arm hard over a large purple bruise.

She yelped and jumped, but Scott was on her in a blink of an eye, his arms holding her around hers, keeping her immobile.

She glared at the doctor, but said nothing. She knew she couldn't win this.

"What about your sex life?" he asked conversationally again.

"I'm not discussing my sex life with you," she said seething, her anger rising into her awareness.

"I beg to differ. You are going to tell me every detail about anything I ask, Jennifer, starting with your sex life. Tell me, do you and your boyfriend have rough sex?" He smiled pleasantly.

"I am NOT telling you what my boyfriend and I do," she shouted. "and when he finds out about this..."

"Oh I can assure you, Jennifer, he knows all about this." He seemed to be enjoying pressing her buttons.

"*You're* lying now." She threw back at him.

"Not at all. I spoke with him just yesterday, in fact. Who do you think arranged for me to be your therapist?" He smiled broadly.

"What the fuck are you talking about?" Jenna yelled.

"Jennifer..." The doctor sighed with frustration. "No man likes to be emasculated. It is such a turn off to have the woman that you want to marry behave so recklessly. He can't take you out in public without you causing a scene or getting arrested. You even humiliated him when he tried to propose to you. How do you imagine that feels for a wealthy powerful man who is used to getting what he wants? Hmmm?" His words were delivered condescendingly down his nose at her.

Jenna sat in stunned silence. *How did he know those things?*

"And the fact that you need to control him in the bedroom is really the final straw. Jennifer, MEN like to be in control, especially men like Mr. Thurston. They don't need to be bossed around or outshined. To them, women are for their pleasure, and it ruins the fantasy to have someone who runs their mouth and believes they are in control. You are not marriage material the way you are. I am just here to help you."

"I don't fucking need your help," she yelled. Her anger warred with the panic rising in her chest.

Had Max talked to him? Had Max told them their most intimate details? Was Max unhappy with her? Why wouldn't he just talk to her? She couldn't believe he would resort to having this animal torturing her weekly.

"That's not what he said." Doctor Tilden dropped the hammer, and despite herself, Jenna's heart sank into her stomach.

"You're lying." She spit, but it didn't have the heat it had the last time.

"Tell me, has he fucked your ass yet?" he asked calmly, interest in his eyes.

"Fuck you." She spit.

"Did you initiate it?" he continued.

"It's none of your fucking business." She seethed.

"Everything is my business," he answered coldly. "You see, Jennifer, men like Mr. Thurston need to be the one to set the bar in the bedroom. You need to be made to become more submissive if you ever hope to hold onto a man like him. Your careless attitude is only going to push him away."

Jenna was refusing to look at him. Tears streamed down her cheeks while Scott still held her down, occasionally leaning in to sniff her hair in a way that was invasive and creepy. His hands also wandered on her body, a fact about which she was painfully aware that she could do nothing.

The doctor continued as if she was a perfectly attentive student. "I am not your enemy, Jennifer. I am only trying to help you. What good are you to him if you are in jail? Hmmm? What do you think that would do for his reputation as a well respected attorney and partner in his firm? Do you think he wants a wife who goes rogue and beats people up? Or flies into a jealous rage? Or commands him in the bedroom, when he commands courtrooms and powerful men alike?

"No, Jennifer, you need to be brought to heel, and the sooner you learn that the better." He finished, putting his clipboard down on the coffee table.

"We have just a few minutes left, so let's discuss your punishment for your transgressions today. You have two options: you can either allow me to administer your punishment, or you can go back to the hospital for another visit, longer this time, I think."

When she said nothing, and didn't look at him, he made a grunting noise to Scott, who stood immediately picking her up with him. She squeaked as Scott carried her over to stand in front of the doctor.

"Jennifer, you are going to lay across my lap, and take your punishments like a big girl. I know you like pain, but I guarantee that this will not be enjoyable for you. It's either that, or 72 hours away from Mr. Thurston."

"Why are you doing this?" she whispered, tears running down her face.

"Why, for Mr. Thurston, of course. We'll have you trained up in no time!" He smirked. "Now, LIE DOWN." His voice was suddenly forceful.

Jenna hesitated, and Scott was on her again, lifting her and dropping her over the doctor's lap. Then he took both of her wrists into his and held them over her head.

"This is for your own good," the doctor said, before bringing the flat of his hand down hard on her ass.

◆ ◆ ◆

Max

As soon as he dropped Jenna off at her appointment Max dialed Andrew immediately. He had been wanting to talk to him all day, after his conversation with his doctor the day before, and her behavior the night before.

"Max," Andrew answered, "is everything okay?"

Max filled him in on the conversation he had with Dr. Tilden the day before, and then bashfully went into the details of their personal sex life, as it related. Jenna had told him that she shared everything with Andrew, so Andrew knew her completely. He had to get a read on what was true and what was not.

"I don't believe for a second that he didn't ask her to wear a collar. Jenna is no pushover, if something freaks her out she says so. I also don't believe that she attacked anyone, Max. If she had, they'd have been sent to the hospital, she would have done serious damage to that doctor before security could even get to her. I saw the bruises on her when we picked her up; those weren't from sparring. She had handprints on her arms: if they grabbed her, she let them. I know she could have stopped them otherwise."

"What about her... uh... sexual preferences?" Max asked sheepishly. It absolutely killed him that he had to discuss something so personal and private about her without her knowing.

"Jenna has always liked it rough, for as long as I've known her. She has trouble hanging on to boyfriends because they either can't provide what she wants, or they take it as a free-for-all and assume they can beat and demean her, and she doesn't allow that.

"You're a rare breed, Max, you and she are compatible that way, without being too much or too little. She's told me so." Andrew finished.

"Yeah, but lately, she's been looking for more... She even asked me to hurt her." Max said with uncertainty, his guilt rising to the surface.

"I know that's what it looks like, Max, but I know Jenna. This thing she has with you, it's a trust bond she hasn't been able to forge with anyone else. If I know her, it's probably her way of connecting with you to allow herself to be vulnerable. Kinda like sharing your pain, but in a good way. She channels a lot of her healing through sex," Andrew stated.

"Sooo, you don't think what the doctor said…"

"Max, that doctor is an evil fuckwit. What you have with Jenna was working, before she saw him. Don't let him plant any thoughts in your mind. Jenna is brilliant, and knows what she needs, she'd tell you. You can trust her. I don't trust that bastard as far as I can throw him, he's on some fucking authority high, and I'm going to find a way to get her out of seeing him."

Max breathed a sigh of relief. Andrew knew her. Andrew said he could trust her.

Now, they just had to figure out how to get that fucking doctor away from her.

At five thirty Max sat in the empty parking lot where Jenna was having her appointment. It bothered him that there were no other cars. Did that mean that there was no one else in the building… that they were alone? Warning bells went off in his head.

Just then the front door opened, and Jenna walked out. She was the picture of defeat. Her head hung low, her shoulders curled down, her hands clutching her purse in a death grip. Max got out and opened her door for her, and she didn't even look up. She didn't kiss him, she didn't greet him, she only slid into the car and hissed as she sat, curling on her hip as if she was trying to go fetal.

Max's eyes widened, watching her. She was worse. She was not okay.

As he walked back around the car, he pulled his cell phone out and texted Andrew, telling him to meet them at his house. That doctor was going to kill her, he had to find a way to put a stop to it.

Chapter 20

Jenna

Jenna was silent the whole ride back to Max's house. The numbness had taken her again, replacing the pain and hopelessness that she felt. It was preferable to the questions that taunted her, as if the doctor had gotten into her head and planted doubt.

Was Max behind this? Did he know? Did HE condone it? Was this some sort of punishment because she hadn't agreed to marry him, or because of her recent violent outbursts? How else did the doctor know those private things about her?

She couldn't believe that. The Max she knew wasn't the Max the doctor described. He took care of her... or at least he had until the night before. The doctor said they had spoken yesterday, right before Max's behavior toward her changed. *Were they working together? Was that the reason?*

She let the thoughts float out of her mind, and allowed the foggy haze to fill her. Her ass HURT. He had beaten her pretty good, and she couldn't even sit down. She shifted her hip underneath her.

When Max opened the door and let her into the house, she made a beeline for the stairs and up to the bedroom. She needed some space. And she wanted a shower. Max got her some towels, and then gave her some privacy, and she was grateful. She wasn't ready to let him see what the doctor had done to her. While her heart screamed that she should tell him, her mind insisted to keep it to herself... just in case.

Just in case... the thought made her want to cry.

She let the scalding water flow over her as she cried, finally letting the emotions out. She scrubbed her body hard, as if she could erase the doctor from her system. She felt dirty, tainted.

She had never felt so helpless in her life, she had always been able to take care of herself. And now she was in a relationship, with someone she thought she would be able to count on... but he did nothing. He did nothing to stop it. He might be behind it...

He also doesn't know everything. Her heart told her.

She shook her head against it. If he WAS involved, she couldn't show him weakness. She only wished she could know for sure. She WANTED to trust him; she wanted to believe he would be her knight in shining armor...

But she didn't trust him. She'd trusted people in the past, and look where it had gotten her. No.

Max wouldn't be her savior. She'd have to find a way, herself, and unfortunately, the most immediate solution would land her in a hospital, or prison. Either way, she wasn't going to be free, and she was already losing Max.

◆ ◆ ◆

Max

Andrew arrived shortly after Jenna got into the shower. Once Max could hear the water running he filled Andrew in. Seeing her after her appointment had cemented that something seriously wrong was happening with the doctor, but they needed a strategy for getting her a new therapist, or getting her out of therapy altogether.

They went round and round, brainstorming out loud back and forth, but the court system was always an issue. Both men agreed that the judge clearly had a bias toward Marcus, and had filed an appeal on behalf of Jenna... but court took time: time Jenna didn't have. There were also no guarantees another judge wouldn't find the same way.

In the end, they both agreed to call friends and contacts that they had in high places, to try to call in favors, or create new ones. Whatever it took, they were going to put a stop to whatever was going on with Dr. Tilden.

Jenna came down the stairs forty minutes later, wearing oversized fuzzy pajamas, her hair pulled into a messy bun. Her eyes were red and puffy, Max noticed. She seemed despondent, lifeless.

The two men watched as she came into the living room like a zombie. They were seated on either end of the sofa, and she laid down on her side between them, with her head on Andrew's lap, her feet in Max's. The two men looked at each other over her, both seeing her preference to be closer to Andrew, which was unusual. She usually clung to Max.

"How are you feeling, Baby-Girl?" Andrew asked gently, as he stroked her hair.

"Mmmmphh." She mumbled, shrugging her shoulder.

Max and Andrew shared another look.

"Can you tell us what you and that doctor talked about?" Andrew asked carefully, trying to seem curious.

"I'd rather not," she whispered. She stared straight ahead, her eyes were large and haunted, as if she was seeing a terror no one else could see.

Max cleared his throat, and then tried. "Blue, Baby... we have concerns about this doctor, and how he's treating you. Can you help us understand?" There was a gentle pleading in his voice.

Jenna's eyes swiveled to his, although her head didn't move. She watched him with slightly narrowed eyes, before answering.

"I told you about him last week," she hissed, accusatorially. "You didn't seem concerned then. How was your conversation with him yesterday? Did you fill him in on everything?" He could hear the pain and anger in her voice: betrayal.

"I did speak to him yesterday. I told him I didn't want you restrained, and I wanted a witness in the room with you," he stated. There was a slight edge to his voice. He was being defensive. What was she accusing him of, exactly? How was this HIS fault? He was only trying to help!

Andrew soothed her, stroking her hair. He must have understood what was going through Max's mind. "Baby-girl, we're trying to help. We're on your side."

"Whatever..." she growled, and went back to staring straight ahead.

Max and Andrew exchanged worried looks over her.

◆ ◆ ◆

Jenna

Jenna was immobilized with terror. Her body wouldn't respond, but her mind was overwhelmed. It was her worst nightmare realized all over again. She was trapped! She tried to scream, again and again, but no sound came out. The explosions boomed around her. Bullets tore through the air, whizzing by her. She could hear the screams of the dying, and see lifeless eyes all around her amidst the gore and blood. She was trapped.

A strong arm wrapped around her tightly, and she fought to free herself. Sobs ripped from her body, which moved in slow motion, as if underwater.

A voice spoke in her ear, clearly, "Blue... it's okay Baby... it's just me, Max. You're okay. I've got you. You're safe." It just kept repeating like a mantra.

Finally she managed to get her heavy eyelids to open. She was in Max's bedroom. His arm was around her. He was with her. She was safe.

Relief flooded her system, followed by loud wracking sobs convulsing her chest. She couldn't stop. It was just too much for her system to process. Max held her closely, talking her through it gently, stroking her back, until she finally regained some control. She took a deep breath, and willed herself to relax.

Immediately she wanted to roll into Max, to take him inside her and find her relief, her anchor. But as soon as the thought hit her, her body stiffened.

What if he refused her again?

She was too close to coming unhinged again, she couldn't deal with that. Instead, she took another deep breath, which broke as she exhaled. It was grief she was feeling, the loss of something so precious between them. She was losing him, one way or another.

Max seemed to understand, because he pulled her against him tightly, forcefully.

"Blue, Baby, I'm here. Take what you need. I'm here for you," he whispered into her ear, nipping her earlobe.

Her head whipped to him, her eyes wide in question. He covered her mouth with his and kissed her deeply, giving her permission. She didn't waste a minute.

She climbed on top of him, devouring his mouth in hers, while her hands ran all over his body feverishly. They kissed endlessly, and Max reached his hand up to knead her breast under her pajama top firmly, pinching her nipple. Jenna moaned into his mouth, her sex rubbing against his now hard erection through her pajamas.

Max broke the kiss long enough to pull her pajama top off of her, and she followed by pulling her bottoms off next. Then she was back on top of him, dominating him, devouring him, while he let her. She could feel her wetness gliding over his naked cock as she ground herself against it, hitting her clit and sending her higher.

"I need to be inside of you." Max groaned. "Take me how you need me, Baby. This cock is all yours."

She reached between them, holding his cock at the base, as she placed her opening over its head; then she pushed back onto him, hard. They both groaned loudly. She wiggled her hips and then lifted and pumped back down, again and again, until she had him fully seated.

She stopped her movement then, and just moaned in satisfaction, before dropping down to kiss Max again, this time tenderly.

"Thank you..." She breathed over his mouth, her eyes closed.

"Blue... look at me, Baby," Max said gently.

Jenna opened her eyes and focused on his.

"You don't ever have to thank me for this. I meant it. This cock is yours. I'm sorry I didn't give you what you needed last night; I was an idiot, and over thought it. I will never make that mistake again. If you want it, you take it. This is yours, Baby. No one's, but yours. I promise to give you whatever you need from now on."

Tears welled in her eyes as she looked down at his sincere face, and she leaned down to kiss him tenderly again. They sat locked in their embrace, kissing and teasing, his cock still deep inside of her, until she felt him twitch with desire in her core. Her hips immediately bucked in response, eliciting a long low groan from Max.

With her eyes locked on his, she sat upright, and launched herself up and back on his cock, ramming him deep inside of her. She cried out with each thrust deeper into her, this position giving her the most pleasure.

She leaned lower, hovering over his body, her weight on her arms. Slamming herself back onto his hardness, she could feel her own wetness seeping out of her and down onto his body. She ground her clit into him as she tucked her hips, lifted, and slammed back again. Over and over, she rode his cock hard, as she built up to the blissful climax.

She could feel he was close too, both of them sucking in ragged gasps of air. And suddenly it overtook her, her orgasm springing from inside of her, clamping her down tight while her muscles trembled. She threw her head back and screamed as the most mind-blowing orgasm she had ever had took her over completely. Blackness filled her vision for a moment, and then she was back.

Max was still locked deep inside her, spilling into her with a loud groan. When she fell on top of him, they were both sweaty and panting, his cock still buried in her warm body. He kissed the top of her head tenderly and stroked her hair, and she was sound asleep minutes later.

Jenna woke to find herself alone in bed. Sitting up with a wince of pain on her backside, she heard the sound of the water running in the bathroom, just before it shut off. A few moments later Max appeared in the bathroom door with only a towel wrapped around his waist.

Jenna openly ogled his muscular body, his fine muscles on full display. He was an amazing example of a man, and she had the urge to run her hands over all of the planes and curves of him. Max must have noticed, because he smiled broadly before dropping the towel from his waist, and strutting into the room like a damn peacock.

He made his way over to her on the bed, snaking his hand gently behind her head and kissing her tenderly. At first Jenna stiffened, but soon she relaxed into his kiss, kissing him back.

The doctor was wrong. He doesn't mind me being the instigator.

She smiled to herself as he slowly got dressed, and she watched his fine ass as he did.

◆ ◆ ◆

Max

The week passed in a blur. Jenna got quieter, and more de-pressed as the week passed, and by Friday afternoon she was an emotional wreck.

Max knew that her therapy sessions were upsetting her, but they still hadn't been able to get any leverage to get her out of them. It gutted him to see her so emotional, she cried uncontrollably, and he finally resorted to giving her a valium before they had to leave for her appointment.

At first she stared at him resentfully when he tried to con-vince her that the therapy was supposed to help her. Finally she just seemed to accept her fate. She stared out the window as he drove her, not speaking to him. He couldn't understand what this doctor was saying to her that affected her this much; it clearly wasn't making her better. He could only hope that having someone else in the room made her feel safer, but she wasn't acting like that was the case.

When he dropped her off she gave him one last longing look, tears in her eyes, before heading into the building with her head down. It was so unlike his fiery Blue.

As he drove away he called a friend of his who was a judge, it was his last resort.

"Max! I haven't heard from you in forever! How the hell are you?!" The voice boomed over his car speakers.

"Bruce! Yeah, I know, I'm sorry. Look... I have a ... situation. I need your professional help," Max answered.

"Professional, huh? Does this involve strippers and Vegas?" He chuckled.

Max chuckled, "No, nothing like that. I have a girlfriend, and she's seeing a court appointed shrink. I hate to ask this of you, but I don't trust this doctor. She had another doctor before her case was heard, and she got along well with her, but this guy... Bruce, something's not right. I'd like to know if there's anything I can do to get her re-appointed. I'm not trying to get her out of the therapy... just with someone else."

"Hmmm. I don't know, Max. Do you have any evidence of wrongdoing? I mean, what are you basing this on?" Bruce questioned back.

"(Sigh) Bruce, all I can say is that she's a strong independent woman, but when she leaves his office it's like she's been beaten down. Her mental health is spiraling, and I'm seriously worried he's doing more harm than good. If I could even get her a second opinion, I'd be grateful."

"We don't have as much pull with these things as you may think, Max, but I will make some confidential inquiries. Can you send me all of her information, and the case information? I don't need to tell you that this stays between us, do I?" Bruce answered, his tone serious.

"No, of course not," Max answered quickly. "And Bruce, thank you. I really appreciate it."

◆ ◆ ◆

Jenna

"So, Jennifer, did you take my advice and let your boyfriend take the lead in the bedroom this week?" Dr. Tilden smirked smugly.

"I've told you, I'm not discussing that," Jenna said firmly, staring at the wall.

"Did you still engage in rough sex?" He asked casually, ignoring her tone.

"That's NONE of your business," she hissed.

"I'll take that as a yes... so, you let him initiate?" he continued on, goading.

Jenna didn't answer. But as her mind wandered back to that night after her last session... the night that she wasn't going to ask Max for what she needed... She was suddenly very aware that he HAD initiated it, and been fine with it. Because it was HIS idea.

She could feel the color draining from her cheeks, as a lump formed in her throat. She could feel the tears starting to rise and she willed them out of existence. She wouldn't cry in front of this monster. She wouldn't give him anything.

But he saw it. A huge grin lit his face.

"See?!" He laughed. "Progress! You'll be ready to marry him in no time!" He laughed, and Scott chuckled in her ear, his arms wrapped around her as usual. Today she was forced to sit on his lap, to save him bending over her, behind her.

"Has he fucked your ass again?" The doctor chuckled, enjoying her discomfort.

Jenna finally lost her cool. "FUCK YOU, YOU PIG!"

The doctor only laughed harder. "Oh, oh my... Are you becoming unstable, Jennifer? Do we need to have Scott intercede on your behalf to keep you safe? I'm sure he would be glad to do so." Scott grabbed her breast roughly and started to squeeze it, while moaning softly in her ear.

Jenna brought her stare to the far wall again and remained silent.

"Answer me, Jennifer," the doctor demanded sternly.

"No," she gritted out between clenched teeth. Her hands were balled into fists at her side, useless, as Scott continued to grope her more aggressively and rub his erection into her ass.

"Well, I would say we have made some good progress today, wouldn't you agree?" The doctor smiled pleasantly and put his clipboard down. He stood up then, and started to pull the belt out of his suit pants.

"I think it's time for your punishment. Scott, you'll need to remove her pants for this."

◆ ◆ ◆

Max

Max waited in the parking lot, again surprised that there were so few cars. Instead of waiting in the lot, he let himself into the building and found the office suite where Jenna had her meetings. There seemed to be no one around. She was just walking out of the door, her head down, as she ran into him with an alarmed screech. She never walked around unaware of her surroundings, so the fact that she had run into him was not a good sign.

Max wrapped her in a hug, and noticed instantly that she was not alright. And when he put his arms around her, she just stood still, unmoving. He could see the numbness in her again.

How the hell could this be helping her?

He spoke comforting words into her ear quietly, until at last her hands came up around his hips limply. Slowly he ushered her to the elevators and down to the waiting car. He wanted to go back to the doctor's office and demand answers, but she needed him right then. It would have to wait.

He opened her car door, and noticed that again she seemed to curl up on her side in a fetal position. His anxiety was starting to ramp up. Therapy wasn't supposed to leave people like this, was it? He called Andrew again to meet them at his place. It looked like this was going to be a weekly thing until they could get her a different doctor.

Once home Jenna headed straight upstairs for the shower again. Max realized she'd done it the last week as well, and it set off warning bells in his head. He waited for Andrew to arrive, and then made his way upstairs to check on her.

Pushing the door open into the steamy bathroom Max walked cautiously to the shower. Jenna was leaning against the tiled wall, and he could hear her crying quietly. His heart broke seeing her like that, his beautiful wildcat so fractured. But before he could say a word his eyes took in the color across her backside and he froze.

Black bruises and red welts marred her otherwise perfect bottom. The air stuck in Max's lungs. The bastard had beaten her! In an instant his mind replayed her trip back from her appointment, how she had curled on her side... just like she did the week BEFORE.

Rage filled him. His fists clenched at his side. His breathing heaved through flared nostrils.

"JENNA!" He tried not to shout, but there was no containing the absolute fury that was consuming him.

Jenna jumped in the shower, hands over her mouth to keep from screaming. But the sight of her body trembling in fear, tears streaming from her red eyes, instantly cooled Max.

"Blue... Baby..." His voice cracked. "Why didn't you tell me?!"

But Jenna couldn't say anything, she only started sobbing out loud, her whole upper body heaving as she slid to the floor. Max rushed to the shower, clothes and all, and shut the water off so that he could pick her up and carry her out. He sat on the floor, wrapping as much of his body around her as he could, his instinct to protect her, to help her.

"ANDREW!" he bellowed, and moments later Andrew appeared through the door.

"HOLY FUCK! WHAT...?!" Andrew's jaw fell as he took in her injured ass cheeks. "NO... NO... no... Baby-Girl!" He dropped to the floor beside them, tears streaming down his cheeks.

"We need to get her to a hospital," Max gritted out. His whole body was shaking with rage, but he didn't dare let go of Jenna.

How did that Motherfucker think he could do this to her? How did he think he could get away with this?!

Max got her up slowly and dried her, even as he held her closely. Her sobbing had not died down and she was shaking violently. Andrew rushed out of the bathroom to get her clothing, and then reappeared with it. Together they got her dressed, and Max carried her back down the stairs. Andrew offered to drive so that Max could hold her in the backseat, as they sped through the streets of Boston to the hospital Emergency Room.

Hours later Max sat beside her in her hospital bed. Andrew pulled the curtain back and handed a cup of coffee to Max as they waited for the doctor to return. In the end they had to sedate Jenna to get her to calm down, and she was out cold, on her side, in the hospital bed.

Max had taken photos and sent them to his friend Bruce, the judge, for probable cause. One thing was for sure, Jenna was never going back to that office again, with or without court approval.

That's if the doctor was even still alive after Max got through with him.

Chapter 21

Max

The hospital kept Jenna for observation, and Max and Andrew camped out in her room to wait for her to wake up.

Somewhere in the early hours of the morning she slowly blinked her eyes open to find Andrew beside her, staring at her with worried red eyes.

"What happened?" she asked, her lip pouting out involuntarily.

"You happened, Baby-Girl," Andrew whispered, his voice breaking as new tears ran down his cheeks. He looked over to see Max waking at hearing their voices.

Max walked up to the side of her bed and cupped her face in his hands.

"Blue: NO ONE... and I mean NO ONE gets to hurt you. Do you understand me? This is NOT your fault, and I'm not going to tolerate ANYONE hurting my girl. Do you hear me?" He knew his anger wasn't directed at her, and he tried to keep his words supportive. Involuntary tears leaked from his eyes.

"Why didn't you tell us?" Andrew pleaded. "Jenna, we never would have made you go back. Why? Why didn't you tell me?" Andrew's composure slipped as his face crumpled with anguish.

Fresh tears fell from Jenna's eyes as she looked down, unable to face them. "I... He told me Max had set this up. I was confused."

"WHAT?!" Max whispered in outrage, his jaw open. "Blue, how could you think I would ever do anything like this to you?!" There was anger, but it was the hurt reflecting out of his eyes that kept Jenna looking down. "I have always been on your side," he stated flatly.

"On MY side?!" She choked. "By telling him about our sex life?! About our private moments?! How is THAT on my side?"

Max and Andrew both stopped moving instantly, and then Andrew shot a questioning look to Max, who immediately shook his head 'no'.

"And that 'witness' you insisted on...," she continued, her voice cracking as it got louder, "was one of the security guards who manhandled me the first week, thank you very much. Now he gets to paw me all hour, and there's not a fucking thing I can do about it. So THANKS for that!" Tears streamed down her face as she pulled herself fetal, losing control of her emotions.

"WHAT?!!!" He and Andrew both roared in unison.

Jenna devolved into a sobbing mess, and Max kneeled on the floor in front of her.

"Jenna, Baby, I need you to tell me everything, right fucking now, because I am going to fucking kill him!" Max was outraged, his hands shaking. He felt a hair's breath away from losing it.

Jenna looked up through blurry tear-streaked eyes and saw undiluted rage in his. She seemed to startle. Andrew held her close, keeping her protected.

"He... he told me you knew..." She sobbed. "He told me you wanted him to do this to me!" She devolved into sobs again, unable to continue.

Max and Andrew stared at each other, both murderous. Had it not been for Jenna's fragile state, they would both have been out the door hunting that doctor down. But neither was willing to leave Jenna, not while she was falling apart. And so they held her, clung to her really, while she cried.

Max's heart broke open, seeing her in so much pain.

I am going to fucking kill that doctor with my bare hands.

They all stayed that way, hunched over Jenna on the bed, as her tears slowly subsided into whimpers, the machines beeping gently in the background. Max got her another sedative pill, hoping she would get some rest, and she took it without even asking what it was. After another half hour, her eyes were closed, and her breathing was soft and regulated. She was asleep.

Max and Andrew slipped out of her room. Max left the door open a crack as he left, in case she cried out. He didn't want her to wake alone, but he needed to finish his conversation with Andrew.

Andrew ran his hand roughly through his hair and blew out a long breath as he sat back down. "This is fucked up," he started. "I am going to kill that motherfucker."

"Get in line," Max growled.

They shared a look, and Max continued. "We need evidence. If we get a dickhead judge like we did last time, her word won't hold water against his."

"Does he tape his sessions?" Andrew wondered out loud.

"That would be helpful." Max grunted. "We'd have instant proof. But we can't count on that. He'd be an idiot to keep that kind of evidence."

"Then we need a witness," Andrew suggested.

"We can't get anyone else in the room with them, and we can't put a wire or camera on her; it won't be admissible in court," Max gritted through a clenched jaw, remembering the last case against Marcus.

"Unless we have probable cause, then we could get a warrant," Andrew replied.

"Wouldn't matter," Max growled. "The bastard would remove any proof before he could be served. And then we'd have tipped our hand."

"Not if we caught him in the act," Andrew said sharply, his look piercing with meaning.

"I don't want her going back!" Max demanded. "We can't ask her to do that."

"I don't want her anywhere near him either, but shouldn't that be her decision?" Andrew countered. "Shouldn't she have the choice to take him down? What's the alternative? Going back to that asshole every week? Max, she's the toughest woman I have ever met, but this will kill her." Andrew rubbed his chin between his index finger and thumb, a frown on his face as he contemplated. "I think I have a solution."

"What are you thinking?" Max asked him.

Max paced in the small hospital room, damn near wearing out a path in the linoleum.

The policeman had been questioning Jenna for over forty-five minutes, and Max barely had his rage under control. Andrew sat beside Jenna, holding her clutched hand, but Max could see his own rage burning beneath the surface too.

Max had heard Jenna recount how the doctor had told her that Max had put him up to this, how he was "training" her to be more submissive, and "better wife material." He felt like an absolute asshole now, as he realized the doctor had planted seeds in his mind as well to plant a wedge between them. He shared those with the officer, after he had finished questioning Jenna.

Max felt like the biggest asshole on the planet. She had tried to tell them, but they had downplayed her reaction. They had assumed he was a real and professional doctor, and not the fucking sadist he was. He should have listened! He should have believed her! No wonder she hadn't trusted him.

The doctor had given Jenna a prescription for valium, to help her with her anxiety, but she refused it. Max couldn't understand why she wouldn't take it; it was only for a small amount, and they were low dose. Andrew took the bottle and told Max to step out of the room, once the doctor left. Max raised an eyebrow, but did as he was asked, stopping a few feet away from the door; he could still hear everything.

"You will take these," Andrew insisted forcefully.

"I don't need that shit, Andrew." Jenna fired back. "I'm not going to pop pills to make my problems go away."

"Jenna, *I* am the addict here, not YOU. And I am telling you, as your friend, you need this right now. This is such a small dose, it's only going to help to calm you, not take your problems away. You need rest, and you need peace. Don't be so damned stubborn. Just take the fucking pills."

Jenna must have conceded, because shortly after that the door opened quickly, and Andrew looked up in surprise to see Max standing a few feet away. Andrew's eyes fell quickly, as he stepped into the corridor and closed the door behind him so that Jenna could get dressed.

Max said nothing about what he had just heard. It made sense now... why he never saw Andrew with a drink in his hand. Oddly, he had more respect for him, not less.

◆ ◆ ◆

Jenna

Jenna yawned and stretched, and then realized that she was drooling... not on her pillow. *OH GOD! She was drooling on Max's muscular chest!*

The hospital had released her after examination, labs, police, and a day of observation. She had taken the pills that the doctor had prescribed, and slept soundly through the night, apparently drooling all over her boyfriend.

She immediately went to lift herself off of him, but his strong hands came around her and held her gently against him.

"Morning, Blue." He smiled down at her warmly, his hair all mussed, and his eyes sleepy and red as she looked up at him.

"Morning, Lover." She smiled back sleepily.

"I need to wake up like this every morning." He smiled down at her, stroking her hair behind her ear.

"Wake up? Did you even sleep?" she asked, suddenly self conscious.

Max just chuckled deeply and leaned down to kiss her forehead.

"No," he said, "I was staying up to make sure you were safe. Andrew and I have some ideas we'd like to discuss with you today."

"You and Andrew?" she asked warily.

"Yes, the three of us. He's on his way over. I texted him a while ago. But first... Blue... I need to ask you a favor. Well... a few, actually," he said gently, peppering her head with small kisses.

"Sure, Max, what do you need?" She looked up at him, open and exposed, with her heart right there for him to see.

"Well... first, I'd like to take some pictures of your backside, if that's okay with you?" he asked hesitantly, watching her reaction.

At first she looked confused. "What?... Why- Ooooohhhh." Then she blushed a deep crimson and looked down.

"Because I'd like to have evidence," he stated, again, watchful to see her response.

"Evidence?" she questioned.

"I'll need the photos as evidence. Can you do that for me, Baby?" he asked her gently, there was a gentle plea in his voice, as if it meant a lot to him.

Jenna sighed. "Max... What difference will it make? He's going to get away with it. It's only going to be used against me." Tears were already forming in her eyes again. "It's hopeless."

Jesus... how much can one person cry? She swiped her eyes angrily.

"Not this time," Max said. "Andrew and I have a plan. We want to stop Dr. Tilden, and exonerate you at the same time. I want this nightmare to be over for you."

"You have a plan?" Her head came up, tears still streaming, but there was hope lighting her eyes.

He looked down at her, his eyes hard, "NO ONE hurts my girl," He stated, and then softened and kissed her tenderly on her quivering lips, his arms wrapped around her.

Max had her put a pair of thong panties on, to somewhat protect her modesty, before snapping several photos of her ass. He made sure that he had a good picture of the bruising, and the belt-print. Jenna was relieved when he finally said he had enough, and took her into the bathroom to take a shower together.

He didn't make love to her in the shower, instead choosing to lather up and rub her body down gently. He massaged and caressed her, avoiding any tender spots. He smothered her with sweet kisses from head to toe. His caresses were soft and thorough. He even washed and conditioned her hair like she was precious to him, before turning off the shower and drying her off. He went out of his way to show her how loved she was... even if they didn't say the words.

As he dried her off, after their shower, he leaned into her ear. "Favor number two," he stated, "no secrets between us, no omissions, no half-truths. I need you to tell me in the future if you feel you have a reason not to trust me. And I need you to tell me if anyone is hurting you, even if it's me." He took her face in his hand so that they were eye to eye.

"I need that from you, Blue. I need that like you need to connect after night terrors. Can you do that for me?"

Butterflies danced in Jenna's stomach. She realized he was asking her to be accountable; he was asking her to trust him to fix issues and to let him in. Sex was easy... letting a man into your body was simple. Letting a man into your heart and mind... that was harder.

What if he didn't like what he saw?

She searched his eyes, as he waited for her answer. She was still fucked up after what the doctor had told her, but her heart knew she wanted Max on her side. Her heart said to trust him. It scared her to put her faith in him, almost as afraid as she was of Dr. Tilden, but she wanted there to be more between them. She wanted to believe she could trust him, that this time she wouldn't be let down. And if she was honest, she was already too far gone to just walk away from him now. She should at least give him a chance, maybe he was the one who could look into her darkness, and not be afraid?

She nodded her head slowly.

"I need to hear it, Blue. Tell me. Complete honesty, no holding back." He spoke gently but firmly.

"Complete honesty," she said, her voice cracking, "No holding back." She looked up at him with her big doe eyes.

Max smiled, and it was like the sun shining on her. She hadn't realized how much she wanted for him to approve of her, how much she needed for him to be on her side. Suddenly, she was no longer alone in her battles. A huge sense of relief seeped into her letting her shoulders drop, relaxed. Max leaned down and kissed her tenderly, but deeply- drying her off, momentarily forgotten.

◆ ◆ ◆

Max

Andrew arrived with pastries for breakfast, and Max had a pot of coffee ready. Jenna walked down the stairs as Andrew was walking into the dining room. He stopped and course-corrected, heading right for Jenna. He pulled her into a big hug and smiled down at her.

"How's my Baby-Girl today?" He grinned warmly.

Max smiled as he poured their coffees; seeing Jenna happy always made him happy.

He had shown Andrew the pictures of Jenna's bruises before she had come downstairs, and he had nearly punched a hole in Max's wall. It was amazing how he could smother that rage and hold her so sweetly only moments later.

Because she needs us first. Max reminded himself.

Max had put a deep soft cushion on Jenna's chair for her, and he saw the wetness rising to her eyes as she silently thanked him with a nod, before gingerly sitting with them for breakfast.

Once they were all eating, and drinking their coffees, Andrew laid out the plan.

Once they had medical documentation, Max would contact Bruce, his judge friend, who had agreed to authorize a search warrant for the doctor's office and home, contingent on medical findings.

They told Jenna that what they would like to do is trap him in the act: which would require her to go back to see him the following Friday. They would hold the charges and warrant until she was in her appointment. They would serve the warrant while she was with him.

"I don't understand," Jenna said over her coffee, clearly nervous about going back. "If you knock, they're just going to step back and act like everything is normal.

"Who said anything about knocking?" Andrew asked flatly. There was violence in his look, it was the same look Max was wearing whenever they talked about Dr. Tilden.

"And..." Max added, "We'll have other witnesses with us. Police." They were leaving zero to chance with this asshole walking away from this. "I'm going to have you call me before you go in, so we can hear everything. I want to be in there before he lays a hand on you."

Andrew looked at Jenna. "Baby-Girl, we won't make you do this; I don't even like having to ask you to do this... but I want him nailed to the wall so fucking hard that there is no chance of him ever seeing the light of day again. Can you do this? We'll be right there."

Jenna looked between Max and Andrew; both of them were leaning in, watching her, with a deep look of concern etched on each of their faces.

"This motherfucker is going down," she said, as she picked up her coffee.

◆ ◆ ◆

Jenna

The three of them rode in silence to the restaurant, no one saying a word about all of the things they had heard Jenna confess.

There was a part of her that wanted Max alone. She wanted to hear him assure her that all of the things the doctor said weren't true. She knew they weren't. In her head she knew. But doubt was a poison, and once it had a foothold, it seemed to always linger around the edges, waiting to be proven true, growing stronger and taking root like a weed.

They made small talk over their meal, and eventually the three of them found their way back to Max's house. It was mid-March, and the air was still bitter cold, despite Spring's imminent arrival. Andrew and Max shook hands, and then Andrew swept Jenna up into a hug, as he said his goodbye's and made his way home.

Jenna felt sad watching Andrew get into his car, and pull out into traffic. She loved having her two men together. They were all the people she had in her life, and until recently, it had only been her and Andrew. She wished that he had someone to go home to, but she was also, selfishly, glad that he was available for her in her time of need.

She looked up to see Max watching him drive away, as well. A small smile came to her face. They had really come together over her, in a way she never thought imaginable. She had never met most of Andrew's dates, and Andrew had never met most of hers... their relationships usually didn't last long enough for "meet the family" moments. This was nice. The three of them were family.

Max placed his hand on her lower back gently, ushering her toward the warmth of the house. Soon, they would be able to go outside with only light jackets, but that definitely wasn't happening yet. She shivered, and headed up the steps with Max at her side.

It was late in the evening, and Jenna and Max sat in bed with the television on. Neither was watching too intently. Jenna peeked over at Max; she had been watching him lost in thought for a while, a small frown on his face. She was about to turn back to the television when he spoke.

"You know nothing he said was true, right?" Max was looking at her, pain in his eyes.

Jenna's heart lit up.

"Yeah." She breathed, looking back at him and taking his hand in hers.

"What he said was... it's not what I want, Blue. I don't ever expect you to be anything other than the woman I pissed off that day in the store. I don't want you to be some simpering bimbo for me to fuck. I love the fact that you can be just as in control as I am. I told you before how I like my sex, and you are a rare woman because you meet me right where I am, without judgment."

His eyes rose to meet hers.

"And I couldn't give a shit about how other people perceive you at events. You mean everything to me, and if they don't like it, tough shit. I love to dress you up, yes, but it's not because I want you to be something that you're not. In my mind, you are the most beautiful woman in the world. You deserve to have beautiful clothing, and to be treated with luxury. But I'd be just as happy having you on my arm in jeans and a t-shirt.

"And, honestly, it is a huge turn on having a girlfriend who is as kick-ass as you are. I never have to worry about someone taking advantage of you, or trying to steal you away because you are a strong, outspoken woman. You have no idea what a relief that is to me. And if anyone ever mistreated you, I would expect you to lay a smackdown on them. I'm impressed that you can, and you do.

"Please don't ever change who you are. That doctor didn't know shit. I would gladly bow down to you any time you asked."

Max's eyes were full of tenderness, and it looked like he wanted to say more, and just couldn't get the words out. But Jenna heard the unspoken words. She leaned in and kissed him deeply.

"How about right now?" she asked teasingly.

Chapter 22

Jenna

"How about what right now?" Max asked, confused.

"Would you bow down to me right now? Would you let me dominate you?" Her eyes sparkled with mischief, and Max smiled slowly.

"You know I would," he said seductively.

"Alright, then, Max. Go stand over there." Jenna pointed beside the bed. Max smiled at her and slowly climbed off of the bed to stand beside it, on her side. Jenna muted the television, so they were surrounded by silence.

"Right here, Mistress?" he asked, trying to suppress his smile.

"Yes, right there," she answered haughtily, her own smile on full display. "Now, I want you to take off your clothing... slowly," she commanded.

Max moved slowly, sliding his robe off of his shoulders so that it fell in a satin heap on the floor. Then he inched his thumbs into the waistband of his silk boxers and ever so slowly eased them down his legs, until they too were piled with the robe. Then he stood back up, his massive cock hanging firm between his muscular thighs.

Jenna licked her lips, and she noticed Max's eyes tracking her tongue.

"Stroke yourself," she commanded, her eyes heating.

Max smirked again, but took his cock into his hand and began to stroke it slowly but firmly.

"Like this, Mistress?" he teased.

"Less talking, more stroking," she answered, her eyes fixed on his hand, as it shuttled from base to tip. She reached back, opening his side drawer, and pulled the bottle of lube out. "Use this," she commanded, as she gently tossed it to him.

He slowly drizzled the flavored gel over his hand, before rubbing his two hands together, and then taking his cock into both hands he made a great show of massaging it all over himself, as he groaned.

Jenna watched his cock growing, becoming more reddish purple as he tugged on it. His breathing was becoming more ragged, with the occasional moan for her benefit, until finally she couldn't stand it any longer.

"Come here, sit with your back against the headboard," she instructed. Max immediately headed for the bed, one hand still pulling his cock slowly. She could see the bead of his juices on the end. He sat back for her, clearly proud, as he shuttled his hand up and down his cock, the 'thucking' sound filling the silence of the room.

"Spread your legs wide," she commanded, and he complied, opening up to her, his hard cock on full display.

"I'm going to suck that wonderful cock of yours, and you are not going to come until I say you can," she instructed. Max groaned loudly.

"I don't know if I can do that, Mistress." He hissed, but she ignored him.

Lying down on her stomach, she took him into her mouth, and he groaned, his hands coming to her head. She immediately pulled off of him.

"No touching," she said up to him wickedly. She could see the desire in his eyes. His groan was tortured.

She looked at his cock as she cooed, "Your cock is so big... I wonder how I will ever fit it all in my mouth? Mmmmmmm."

She took him deeply into her mouth again, pulling and sucking just the way she knew he liked. At first she teased him with short bobs of her head, but then she would sink down deep onto him, feeling him jump in her mouth as he hissed. Then she would pull off of him, just running her tongue over his shaft, laving his head around the sides.

"Don't tease me, Blue." He groaned impatiently.

"Silence," she snapped. "You will take it how I give it to you." She grinned up at him evilly, and he dropped his head back trying to control himself. His hands were gripping the sheets around him firmly. His cock was amazingly hard.

She took him deeply again, hollowing her cheeks and sucking on the up-swing. She moved faster, getting into a rhythm. Despite himself, his hips tried desperately to thrust up into her mouth, but she clamped her hands down onto his thighs. He groaned in frustration as she continued to work his cock with her mouth.

She would get him close... and then slow back down, gentling him back while he snorted in frustration. Then she would speed up, getting him back to close again, and repeat. On the third time around, as she was getting him closer she pulled off of him, but kept her hand working him as she talked.

"Do you think you have been a good servant?" she asked him with a small smile.

"That... That is for you to decide... Mistress." He panted, his eyes pleading.

"I think you've been very good." She smiled at him with satisfaction. "So here's what's going to happen," she continued, "I am going to take you in my mouth, and you are going to fuck my mouth with this magnificent cock of yours while you watch me, and then you are going to blow right down my throat."

Max groaned loudly and his cock lurched in Jenna's hand. She had to admit that having this power over his body made her feel good. She slowly brought her mouth down over his cock, looking up at him. Once she had him fully seated, to the back of her throat, he lost all control.

His hands flew into her hair and fisted hard as his hips jerked upward into her mouth with a pounding rhythm. Max again groaned loudly, his eyes fixed on her, as he watched his cock fucking her mouth, her lips tight around him. He didn't last very long before his hips shot upwards, his back bowing. He groaned a keening rumble, and Jenna could feel his cock spasming on her tongue as he released his juices down her throat. When his body fell back to the bed he continued thrusting into her, riding out the orgasm. She tasted his fluids on her tongue, salty and oh-so-Max.

She ran her tongue over him, around him, getting all of him and licking him clean. She even sucked his balls into her mouth and ran her tongue over them, which elicited another long groan.

"Blue…" He groaned through half-lidded eyes, "You are fucking amazing."

"Good," she answered proudly. "I'm glad you enjoyed it, because we're doing it again."

◆ ◆ ◆

Max

Max was being tortured in the best possible of ways. Jenna had teased him and sucked him off, giving him a mind-blowing orgasm with her talented little mouth. Then she proceeded to suck him off again… for forty five minutes. She would bring him close to the edge, and then slow back down, or stop altogether to kiss him and grind her wet pussy against him.

Max was on the verge of exploding, and she didn't seem to be getting tired. He literally had nothing left in him to ejaculate, but his cock was still hard and ready, and wanting it. Max wasn't sure he could handle anymore. That was something he never thought he would catch himself saying.

He winced as another orgasm tore through him, his balls contracting tight. It was the strangest feeling, like overstimulation. But Jenna was loving it. He wanted to take a picture of her with her lips wrapped around his girth, she looked so fucking erotic, but he would never do it.

Once he calmed, and she gave him yet another tongue bath she retreated from him, laying on her back with her knees up and spread. Max grinned wide.

"Now it's your turn. Eat my pussy and make me scream your name, servant," she ordered seductively.

Max moved to pounce on her, but his dick was still too sensitive. He carefully pulled himself up, and then placed an open mouth kiss over her pussy and found it already warm and wet for him.

At feeling how ready she was for him, his dick was got hard again, and he groaned over her pussy, which caused Jenna to groan. He used his fingers to pull her lips open to him, so he could access all parts of her with his tongue, before finally settling on her clit, one finger sliding into her wetness.

She was always so fucking amazingly tight!

She groaned and mewled, grabbing him by the hair and pressing his face down onto her clit.

"Right there! Right there, Baby! OOOOhhhhh," she crowed, her hips swiveling up to meet his mouth and his hand. He put another finger into her and she groaned louder, trying to fuck his hand while she rode his mouth. Her dialog got dirtier and dirtier as he sucked and nipped at her clit before flicking it quickly, his hands ramming her walls.

"MAX! Oh my god!... your mouth feels so amazing on my pussy! YES! Suck it! Suck it!" She groaned loud and long. Max added a third finger, pressing the walls inside her and stretching her out while he attended her clit like a man on a mission.

The added girth only seemed to drive her into a further frenzy. Her hips came up off of the bed, trying to fuck his hand into her further.

With a wicked grin he flexed his fingertips into her G-spot, and she was screaming in ecstasy. Within seconds her pussy clamped tight around his hands, the inner walls milking him, trying to drag him further into her body as a scream tore out of her. And then she was convulsing with pleasure, incoherent.

Max continued to pump her, and she continued to pulse around him. When the sensations started to die down, he began to pull his hand out of her.

"What are you doing?" she demanded.

"Well-"

"I didn't say stop! Did I scream your name?!" she demanded wickedly.

Max groaned, but smiled a wide smile as he went back down on her. "No, Mistress," was all he could say, before his tongue was all over her.

Twenty minutes later, Max's jaw was sore and stiff, but he was proud of himself. He had given her multiple orgasms, and the blissed out look on her face made him feel accomplished. Just seeing her coming had his cock hard and ready to go again, but the rest of him was needing a break.

Jenna looked up at him with a grin. "Tired yet, servant?" she teased.

"Never, Mistress," Max lied.

"Good, because now you fuck me hard with that big cock of yours."

Max smiled and shook his head, but he pulled himself between her knees and pressed his cock into her waiting channel. Immediately his hips slammed forward, having a mind of their own. He braced himself on his hands over her as his cock slammed deep inside her at a punishing pace. Jenna was groaning and grinding in time with his thrusts. They were both breathing heavily, covered in a thin layer of sweat.

Max pushed her legs up beside her, giving him better access. He was careful not to hit her tender backside with his thighs as he plowed into her ruthlessly. She screamed out, throwing her hands around his neck and raking her nails into his muscles.

"YES! YES! OH GOD! FUCK ME HARD!" She was spewing dirty talk, overcome with the intense feelings of having his cock ravaging her swollen wet pussy. What started as a low moaning wail turned into a screaming roar of release as she again clamped down on him, her body locking and trembling.

"MAAAAAAAAAAAAAAXXXXXXX... AAAAAAAAAAAAAAAAAAAAAAAAAAGGGHHHH!"

Max was not immune. Just hearing the words come out of her mouth brought him close to losing his last bit of control, until finally he was roaring, his body seizing.

"Fuck! FUCK! You're so damned TIGHT! FUCK! I love you, Blue! I LOVE YOU! FUCK! I LOVE YOU!..." He went on and on until his speech was strangled by the orgasm pulling his whole body tight and snapping back. As he pumped roughly through his orgasm he picked right back up.

"I love you! God, I love you. I love you so fucking much, Blue. I love you!" He continued on until he was only whispering it, the sweat dripping off of his wet hair and forehead and spattering down onto her. He collapsed onto her, his head buried in the curve of her neck, still whispering, "I love you, Blue. I love you so much. I love you..."

He laid there, panting. He had told her he loved her before, and he had promised himself he wouldn't smother her with his feelings. He had wanted to give her time to say it back on her terms. But with their hormones raging, and their bodily fluids all over each other, their energies intertwined, he couldn't help it.

He lived her. He breathed her. He loved her.

Would she say it back? Would she ignore it? Would she back away from what they had?

He had told her in the beginning he wasn't a relationship kind of guy; it was supposed to be just fucking. But it had stopped being just fucking really fast. She had somehow gotten through all of his walls, passed all of his tests, checked all of his boxes. She was a unicorn: damned near extinct, impossible to find, and perfect. Perfect for him. He could never let her go.

◆ ◆ ◆

Jenna

"I love you, Blue," he whispered desperately, over and over.

Jenna was a fog of emotions, feelings, and sensations. It was like Max was all over her, inside her, surrounding her, in her heart and mind... it was like they co-existed in the same warm space. She heard him say it again, and at the edges of her consciousness she felt the stabbing cold spike of fear.

"I love you...," he whispered.

She was in her safe place, her afterglow, in the strength of his arms. So she allowed herself to look at her fear, and not to bury it. Why did she fear those words?

She knew immediately, as another face appeared in her mind.

Williams.

He had sworn he loved her. They had lived and worked in a life and death environment, and had clung to each other, gotten each other through. He had looked her in the eye after they had shared their mutual suffering physically, roughly, and told her the same thing; "I love you." He had the same tenderness in his eyes.

When things got tough, when people died, when it didn't seem like she would make it through, those three words on his lips carried her. "I love you." They gave her strength, they gave her a reason to push through.

Until the day she discovered it was all a lie. He may have been sincere in the moment, but it hadn't stopped him from giving himself to plenty of other women. Maybe he did love her?... but he gave his love away so easily, and to so many... it was diluted. Worthless.

She had trusted him, believed in him, not just to love her but for her actual life and safety. He was supposed to have her back, just like she had his.

And when she'd realized she had let herself be exposed and vulnerable, all that time, believing he was watching out for her too...

It seemed like another lifetime to Jenna. But it felt like right now.

Max was still snuggled into her, they were sticky, wet, and hot, but neither one wanted to move and ruin the moment of peace that ran between them. Jenna looked over at him, his eyes were closed with a warm smile on his face. He looked so genuinely happy and peaceful.

She gave him that.

The pieces slowly started to click into place for her. The same sense of security, comfort, protection that she had needed from Williams... Max was offering her, even without her offering it back. With no guarantee she would ever love him the same way, he extended his heart to shield hers.

It was unfair. It was not right to take this comfort from him, but withhold it back. That was what Williams did, although he lied and said he returned it. Jenna couldn't bear to have the same inequity with Max.

But saying it meant committing to it. It made it real.

Her mind spun. She knew she felt it, so wasn't she committed? Did she truly think she could just turn and walk away tomorrow? No, she couldn't... she wouldn't. She didn't ever want to let go of Max. The thought of a lifetime ahead of her without him in it suddenly terrified her more than telling him she loved him. She knew what she had to do, and swallowed her fear.

"Max..." She shook his shoulder gently until he slowly opened his eyes and looked at her. She had a strange look in her eyes as they were reflected in his; they were wide, fearful, wary... so many emotions as she took him in.

Max said nothing, waiting for her to continue. A small look of concern started to build in his brows, but he held space for her while she pulled together what she wanted to communicate.

Her eyes flicked down, and then back up to his, clearly unsure.

"I.... I love you too," she whispered.

A small smile bloomed on Max's kissable lips, his sleepy eyes were full of joy. "I know you do, Blue," was all he said. Then he pulled her down and kissed her deeply.

Chapter 23

Max

It was already Tuesday night, and Max was anxious; he was running late, and his brother and sister-in-law were coming over for dinner with him and Jenna. He had gotten tied up on the phone with a client, and then traffic to the liquor store had been heavy. He rushed into the house, hanging his coat quickly, and saw that they had already arrived. He just wanted the night to go perfectly.

Jenna pounced around the corner, and a big smile lit her face. She was wearing an apron over her dress, and her hair was pulled back into a ponytail. She bounced on the balls of her feet like a little kid as she waited for him to give her a kiss, and he smiled to himself. He would never get tired of this. The weight of anxiety fell off of his shoulders as he took her in.

He stopped to kiss Jenna first, wrapping his arms around her. Walking into the dining room he wrapped his brother in a quick hug, and kissed Joelle on the cheek. He couldn't remember the last time he'd had them over... God, had it been years already? Time seemed to be flying faster and faster. He missed the closeness he once had with his family. Yes, he saw Ed at work, but not much, and it was different having them in his home. Jenna was having a really good effect on him, he was ready to let go of his bachelor ways.

He brought the bottles of wine he had picked up into the kitchen, where Jenna had returned, and was in her glory cooking up a storm. As she stirred a pot he walked up behind her and pulled her back into him for a hug, kissing her cheek over her shoulder. He could picture himself doing this every night, with her as his wife.

Wife. His heart sank as he realized what he had thought. His mind flashed to the tiny black velvet box, sitting untouched in his safe upstairs.

Max tried to push the thought away. He didn't want to be a moody bitch when they had family over. He could talk to her later about marriage, but not right now. Unaware of his inner dialog, Jenna stirred and looked up at him with adoring eyes.

It was a formal dining room, but Max had never really utilized it as such. Jenna had pulled out his fine china, and the table was decked out like a supper for royalty. His crystal glasses and fine silver were polished and sparkling. She had really gone over the top, making a roast leg of lamb, side dishes, gravies and mint jelly. She had baked homemade bread, and a pie for dessert. The smell of rich food hung in the air, making his stomach growl in appreciation.

Jenna and Joelle brought the platters out to the table, joking between themselves as they set the feast out. Max was happy to see that they got along so well. He wanted Jenna to feel comfortable with his family; hell, he wanted her to BE his family. She fit right in. Conversation flowed easily, as the four of them ate and chatted, and Max couldn't help but feel proud. He would have never been able to do this with the other girls he had taken out. Jenna really was the one.

◆ ◆ ◆

Jenna

Once dinner was finished, Joelle and Jenna started to clear the plates, but Max and Ed were quick to get up and get to them first. Joelle stared at Jenna, and then burst out laughing. Even Jenna found it humorous how the boys were catering to them.

"I wish I got this treatment at home," Joelle teased, before she excused herself to "powder her nose." Jenna stepped into the kitchen to start coffee for dessert, and top off her wine glass. She could hear Ed talking to Max in the dining room a few steps away as they gathered plates.

"So, where did you order from tonight, this was amazing," Ed complimented.

"Order? Jenna made it." Max laughed.

There was a brief pause, and then Ed replied, "She's that fucking hot and she cooks too? Holy shit, Max, you need to marry this one!"

Another pause...

"(Sigh) I tried. She doesn't want that," Max answered sadly.

Jenna jerked and sloshed the wine all over the counter.

Is that what he thinks?... Of course it's what he thinks! I ran out of there like he was a serial killer; what was he supposed to think?

A heaviness filled her heart. She still had fears about getting married, but they'd never had an actual conversation about it. She hated that he believed she didn't want him that way. She grabbed a cloth to wipe up the wine, and made a mental note to bring it up after all of the nastiness with her shrink was over.

Ed picked the conversation back up in the dining room as she put the towel away. "Well, Max, she's not the only fish in the sea. Have you tried making her jealous? Worked with Joelle."

The room went eerily quiet and Jenna froze, she could barely hear Max's whispered response, clearly strained with anger.

"I wouldn't disrespect her like that, Ed. Whether she marries me or not, she's it for me. I won't manipulate her insecurity to force her into committing to me, and frankly I'm kind of shocked that you would."

"Give it another couple of years." Ed chuckled. "You will."

Jenna held her breath, but before Max could say anything else she heard Joelle return to the room; the conversation changed to a new topic. She smoothed her sweaty hands down her skirt and brought the coffee service into the dining room; avoiding eye contact with Ed.

The next morning Jenna was running on a treadmill next to Andrew at the gym. She wanted to run faster, to burn off her anxiety, but she couldn't keep a conversation going with her huffing and puffing. The clank of weights in the background echoed off of the mirrored walls, jarring her frazzled nerves.

"I'm confused." Andrew blew out, hardly winded. "DO you want to marry him?" He shot her a sideways glance.

"I... (huff)... don't know." Jenna slowed her pace a little more, taking a few more deep breaths before continuing. It was not fair that she was soaking wet with sweat, and he was hardly moist. "I love him. I want to be with him... But a part of me feels like it's too soon to make a 'rest of your life' decision."

"But you're living with him," Andrew stated flatly. "That's kind of committed. I mean, you're not going to accidentally NOT live with him at some point."

"Yes, but I can leave if it doesn't work out. Really, Andrew, I'm not sure I'm really ready to marry anyone, if I'm honest. I don't know if I ever will be..." She paused in thought. "But if I was, it would be with him," she added thoughtfully.

"So what is it about marriage that has you so shaken?" Andrew asked, still able to hold a conversation as he ran.

"I'm not sure," she answered, looking straight ahead. "I just saw that ring, and I felt nothing but terror. The whole restaurant was watching. They all expected me to say yes; I felt the pressure like a glacier on my shoulders."

"Do you think this has to do with Williams?" Andrew asked her outright.

Jenna stumbled on the treadmill, caught herself, and loped back into pace.

"I don't know..." She mumbled. "Maybe?"

"Alright, so what are you going to do about it Baby-Girl? If you have a shot at happiness, are you going to let that fuck-head take your future as well as your past? Or are you going to meet this head on?" He challenged.

"What's wrong with just living in denial?" She whined.

"Denial solves nothing, Jenna, and it will only push him away. You need to at least tell him what's going on in your head. Didn't you promise him that?"

"When did you become my dad?" she whined again, but there was a small smile on her face, before she huffed another breath.

"Look, all I'm saying is that if the dick is as good as you're saying it is, I would be trying to work this out a little more. Waking up to that everyday is a gift from Heaven, trust me on this." He laughed out loud, and Jenna groaned.

Later that afternoon Jenna was sitting in Andrew's office while he worked with a client; she was spending the day with him at work, as Max had a court case he needed to work on and Andrew was booked solid. She had done the filing, and tidied up the waiting room, trying to make herself useful. As she sat to scroll through her social media her phone rang, the caller ID identifying Joelle.

"Hey Joelle!" Jenna smiled as she answered.

"Hey, Jenna! How is your day going? I hope I'm not interrupting anything?"

"No, just enjoying some down time." Jenna spun in the office chair like a child as she talked.

"Look, I know it's none of my business, but I really feel like you're family already, so I wanted to volunteer to help you plan your wedding.... If that's okay?" Jenna stopped the chair hard and nearly flew off of it.

"W..wedding? Joelle, we're not getting married. I mean... not yet... I mean... we're not engaged yet," Jenna stammered, suddenly feeling on the spot.

"Oh... well, I know he got you a ring, so it's only a matter of time, and these things take a while to put together; so now is a good time to get started, don't you think? I know some great event planners- OH, and I know some really darling locations, perfect for both the ceremony and reception... Unless... you want to do a destination wedding, which is a great idea too! Have you thought of Italy?..." Joelle babbled on and on.

Jenna felt herself starting to hyperventilate.

Why the fuck is everyone insisting I get married?

Joelle was still talking. "... Because there's this adorable place in Florence-"

"Joelle, I have to go. Bye!" Jenna hung up before Joelle could say another word. The overwhelm hit her again, and she had to close her eyes and take deep breaths in through her nose, and breathe out through her mouth to try to calm her panicking body down.

Clearly Spirit was trying to deliver her a message. She needed to figure this shit out sooner than later.

◆ ◆ ◆

Max

Max closed the door and breathed a sigh of relief. Coming home was now his new favorite time of the day, well, maybe after going to bed with Jenna. It was a definite second, though.

"I'm hooooooommme." He sang as he hung his coat up and left his briefcase in the hallway.

"In here!" Andrew called from the living room.

Max rushed in to see Andrew watching a movie, while Jenna napped on the sofa.

"How was she today?" Max lowered his voice to a whisper, although Jenna tended to sleep deeply when she did sleep.

Andrew had a pained expression. "We had a little... setback... today. I gave her a few valium to calm down, thus she's sleeping now."

"What kind of setback?" Max asked, his body on alert.

"I'm not entirely sure... but it has to do with marriage. We had discussed it this morning in the gym, and then she was freaking out when I got back into my office. I couldn't figure out if something else had triggered the panic attack, or if it was a delayed reaction to our conversation; but she was pretty upset.

"I probably shouldn't share this, but I think you need to know: she was engaged once when she was in the Army to a guy named Williams. She was completely devoted to him, made him her world, and she found out he cheated on her... a lot." Andrew confided.

"She told me a little about him, but I thought it was seeing him dying that had bothered her," Max said.

"Partially, it was. But the reason they were there was because she refused orders to remain assigned with him after she found out. They were driving back to headquarters ahead of schedule to get reassigned by her request. She blames herself for his death; she said she was in such a hurry to get away from him that she put them into a dangerous situation that never should have happened. Had she accepted the orders and stayed there, they wouldn't have been in that vehicle that day, on that road. She's never been able to let go of the guilt. She was the only survivor.

"I don't know what it is about him and marriage that freaks her out so much. She did get married for a very brief time after her service, but I know for a fact that she never took that seriously, it was a convenience thing that lasted like five minutes." Andrew finished.

Max thanked Andrew, and Andrew made his way home for the night. Max looked down to watch Jenna breathing softly, her blue hair spilled out over the cushion on the sofa. She looked so small and fragile, so different from her confident bad-ass self. Occasionally her brows would scrunch and she would pucker her mouth slightly, before her features would smooth back out peacefully. She looked angelic with her blue halo.

He lifted Jenna up and carried her upstairs to bed, gently undressing her and tucking her in. He took a quick shower and had a bite to eat before getting comfortable beside her, reading a book. Just having her beside him was heaven. A few hours of silence passed before he felt her roll over, her eyes blinking slowly open.

"I don't remember coming to bed," she stated groggily, her mouth drawn into a small pout that made Max smile instantly. She was adorable when she first woke up, with her hair looking freshly fucked, and her eyes blinking wearily.

"I tucked you in, Baby. You were tired." He smiled down at her and kissed her on the forehead as she struggled to focus her eyes.

"I took pills, didn't I?" she asked flatly. "I only get cotton mouth and brain fog when I take those freaking pills."

"Yeah, Blue, you did. But Andrew felt like you needed them, Baby. You had a hard day. Want to talk about it?" Max gently put his book aside.

Jenna sighed grumpily, a look of resolve coming over her before she nodded. "Yeah." She breathed out weakly, clearly not excited about it.

"Come here, Baby. Hop on my talking stick." He grinned at her.

She shot him a look with a raised brow that said she didn't find it amusing, but did climb onto his lap. He lubed himself up for her, and then they worked together to get her seated with him deep inside of her. It was like their couples counseling technique.

"So what's got you upset, my dearest Blue?" Max asked softly, his voice velvety and deep.

Jenna leaned into him, her head resting on his shoulder. "I just got overwhelmed. Why the hell is everyone insisting I get married. Why don't I get to decide that?" she asked heatedly.

"Who's 'everybody'?" Max asked, suddenly confused.

"Well, you asked me, and the whole fucking restaurant watched on expectantly. Then that fucking doctor was telling me I wasn't marriage material and he needed to train me up. Then Ed was talking about manipulating me into it sooner or later. Then Andrew is asking why I don't like the idea of marriage. And then Joelle calls and she's already planning a fucking wedding I never said yes to!" Tears were streaming down Jenna's cheek and onto Max's shoulder.

"It's not that I don't want to marry you, Max. I'm terrified of getting married. It scares the hell out of me. And I don't like everyone having more of an opinion on whether I do it or not than I do! I feel like I'm being railroaded before I can really get a handle on my own feelings." Her voice cracked as her words choked out.

"Oh, Baby!" Max wrapped his arms around her and let her cry. She was still groggy and overwhelmed, so he held her until she finally seemed to calm down and snuggle into him.

"Blue, nobody's opinion matters more than yours and mine when it comes to marriage. I don't give a fuck what anyone else thinks about it.

"Please don't take anything that doctor said as having any relevance at all. His opinion counts less than nothing as far as I'm concerned.

"I'm pissed with Ed about what he said, and I'm sorry you had to hear that; I'm ashamed that he's my brother and he feels that way.

"I think Andrew was just trying to be a good friend to you and help you process, Baby; I don't think he was trying to sway you one way or another. But you could ask him. He loves you.

"And Joelle... Boy... I have no idea what the hell climbed up her ass. All I can say is, I'm sorry.

"Blue, I will never expect you to marry me. I love what we have, and if marriage bothers you that much, I could be happy just doing what we are doing. Don't feel like you'll lose me if you don't want to get married. I'm happy, if you're happy." He kissed her temple tenderly.

"I feel like I'm going to lose you either way, Max," she whispered into his shoulder.

"What?! WHY?" His voice pitched up with concern.

"Because I'm fucked up, Max. I play the housewife, but I'm not Suzy Homemaker. I'm independent, and I'm not some polished woman you can show off without the risk of me embarrassing you. I get into fights. I have bruises. Right now my life is one big dumpster fire, other than you.

"Hell... I can't even give you kids!" Her voice was getting louder, panic starting to creep in. "What happens if you decide a few years later that you want more kids, but you're tied to me?!

"Sooner or later you're going to realize that I'm really *not* marriage material. And then you're going to want an exit strategy out of my life as fast as you can, Max."

There was a sense of outrage in Max at her resolved tone, that she thought so little of herself and her worth to him. Did she really think he was so shallow? He had to take a few breaths before he lashed out his anger at her.

"Well... We're all fucked up, Blue. So you don't get bragging rights for that. I'm a sexual deviant with two estranged kids and an ex-wife who felt it necessary to leave the continent because of me.

"As for being Suzy Homemaker, I never asked for that. I'd get bored with a traditional housewife, and you know it. You're a great cook, and I love that you do that, but if you never wanted to cook again I would still love you. Don't put that burden on me: I never asked you to play that role in my life. I told you, I already have staff.

"Yes, you have bruises, a temper, and you're independent. I happen to like all of those qualities. If those fragile glass bitches at events can't appreciate the rockstar that you are, then fuck them. I'll take you just like this.

"As for kids... Have you ever even *asked* me if I thought I wanted more? Because I wasn't planning on it. I have two already. IF you were to somehow get pregnant, I would be overjoyed and love the hell out of that baby, because it was something that we made together, but no I'm not planning on it, and I won't miss it when it doesn't happen.

"Blue, Baby, I don't know what bill of goods you've been sold, but there is no check list for 'marriage material.' Marriage is whatever you make it. For some, it's riding Harleys all over the country in leathers. For others, it's life on the farm. For some, it's having sex with as many other people as you can... which I am totally not okay with, by the way, in case you're getting any ideas.

"If you agreed to marry me, we would make OUR marriage whatever we wanted it to be. I don't assume you'd become a 1950's housewife, and you don't assume I become a 1950's husband. I want you to be the wild, impulsive, kick-ass, dumpster-fire-starting little wildcat that you are, always. THAT'S who I would be marrying. That would define our marriage.

"And besides, I'm not exactly traditional marriage material myself. Sure I have money, but you have to admit that I have issues too. I paid for dates. I hardly know my kids. My ex thinks I'm a sexual fiend. I have very few friends, and I am a workaholic.

"We just bring what we have to the table, and agree to live with that. Does that sound reasonable to you?"

Jenna looked up at him with awe in her eyes. "I... yeah... I think so. Can I think on that?" she whispered.

"Blue, take all the time you need. I don't need for you to marry me. I need for you to be happy, and to be you." Max leaned down and took her mouth in a tender kiss, stroking his tongue into hers, and holding her in his arms. He wished that she could see inside his heart, that she understood he didn't expect her to change. If anything, he would die a happy man if she would just remain exactly the same, and choose to be with him.

Chapter 24

Jenna

The week flew by uneventfully, their routine finally becoming somewhat normal. Jenna was laying on the couch, trying to nap while Max was working in his home office, but she couldn't shut off the dialog in her head. With no job, Jenna was feeling frustrated with being babysat by her guys everyday. At the same time, she couldn't deny that she was on an emotional rollercoaster: fine one minute, bawling the next. She had never been so frail, and it bothered her. She missed her kick-ass confident self. She missed working, earning her own money, and she missed her church community.

While Max had his work to do, she considered what her life would look like going forward.

Would Max expect her not to work? Would she become some bored trophy wife, relying on his income until he got tired of her once she was older and losing her beauty?

She couldn't ever imagine ever allowing that to happen to her. She had put herself in the backseat for a man before, and she would never let it happen again. Rolling onto her side, she decided then and there that she needed to find a job for herself... once they dealt with Dr. Tilden.

The drive to Dr. Tilden's office was quiet. Jenna stared out the window solemnly while Max drove and Andrew sat in the backseat. Both men had wary eyes and exuded anxiety. Jenna looked between them nervously as they drove in silence.

In a strange turn of events, it wasn't Jenna begging to get out of the appointment that week; instead, Max had rounded on her hours before and told her that he really didn't want her to go. His clenching jaw and fists showed Jenna how furious he was with the doctor, but when he turned his eyes on her, there was nothing but fear for her safety. His eyes were wide, pleading, but his hands were gentle as they tucked a blue curl behind her ear.

She knew he didn't want her to go as much as she herself didn't want to, and she wished that she could just give in and ease his anxiety. But she held strong, even though she felt like her stomach wanted to vacate her body cavity. She wanted this over. Better to face it head on; the sooner they went, the sooner it could be over, and she could get her life back. Max had dropped his head and accepted her decision, but she could see the pain written all over his face.

When they parked it didn't surprise her at all that both men got out of the car with her and walked her up to the office. Max had her show them which office she would be in, and with a kiss goodbye she sat to wait while they regrouped at the car. Jenna called Max's cell, and then turned her volume off, so that if he spoke it wouldn't be heard. She put her phone in the top part of her purse, out of sight, but able to hear. Her nerves spiked. Jenna tapped her foot nervously until she saw the doctor appear in the waiting room to collect her.

They made their way into the room, and Jenna made sure that the door wasn't locked before she took her mandatory seat on Scott's lap on the other end of the sofa from the doctor. He beamed widely when she didn't argue, and she wondered if she should have made more of a scene. Her nerves were on high alert, and she was trying to act like nothing was going on, which made her feel like she was not acting like her normal self at all.

GAH! This is too much fucking drama!

She must have made a face at her own thoughts because the doctor immediately picked up on it. "Jennifer..." he cooed, "Is something the matter today?" He smiled smugly, as if the thought pleased him. "You seem... distracted."

"No more than any other day I have to be here," she answered shortly. Behind her Scott chuckled. Her eyes swept around the small office, taking in the high end chairs and sofa, the bookshelf filled with books, and the many awards framed on the walls. She wanted to never see this room again.

"You do realize that the more you run that smart mouth of yours, Jennifer, the worse it will be for you, right?" the doctor shot back flatly, his smug smile vanishing.

Jenna shifted her eyes back to him. "You're going to beat me regardless of what I say or do, so why be nice to you, *Doctor?*" There was a slight sneer in her voice, but she kept her eyes focused on the wall as she usually did, not giving him the benefit of looking back at him.

"Not so," Dr. Tilden fired back. "I told you before, you make the choice. You can take your punishment like a big girl with me... OR... you can spend a week in the hospital away from all that good rough sex with your boyfriend. You just let me know if you change your mind, but we both know you enjoy being punished by me, now don't we?" He winked at her.

"No. I don't," she answered flatly, eyes boring a hole into the wall. "And I don't think it's fair that you get to beat me, or lock me up, just to entertain yourself," she added.

She heard the doctor grunt, and Scott's arms immediately wrapped around her to "restrain her," groping her breasts and waist, trying to get into her shirt. Jenna tried to jerk away from him, before finally giving up and holding herself stiffly.

"And why the fuck does he get to grope me?! Isn't he supposed to be in here for MY protection?" she demanded, frustrated.

Doctor Tilden shot up out of his seat pulling his arm back and backhanded her face hard, knocking her head to the side with a THWAP.

"I have warned you, Jennifer, YOU are not the one in control here: I am. When you act unstable, it is necessary for ME to have some protection." His anger dissipated as he straightened his suit jacket and sat back down.

"And how is he protecting you by groping me?" she fired at him. She knew she was antagonizing him, but she wanted every fucking detail on record. Her face still flared with pain, and she could feel the swelling starting in her cheek.

The doctor just chuckled and ignored her question.

"So, Jennifer, now that you have wasted my valuable time, let's begin shall we? How was your progress this week? How many times has he fucked your ass this week? Did he make you scream?" The doctor leaned in, clearly excited to hear her response. Behind her Scott was moaning softly as he fondled her breasts, and he rubbed his erection into her ass through their clothing. Jenna gagged a little.

A small shuffling sound outside the door alerted Jenna that Max and Andrew must be getting ready to barge in, and as much as she wanted out, she wanted the doctor to get caught with his hands in the cookie jar.

"Not yet!" she answered quickly, and then recovered, "I mean... no, he hasn't yet this week." Her cheeks flamed red, as she knew Max could hear the entire conversation.

"Good! Good!" the doctor encouraged. "You're finally opening up to me. That's progress! So tell me, what is it about him hurting you that excites you so much? Does he have a huge cock, or does he just punish you harshly to get you off?" Again the doctor looked far too invested in her answer.

Jenna said nothing, and stared at the wall.

"Tell me..." The doctor licked his lips with anticipation, "does he fuck your mouth forcefully? Does he make you gag to quiet that never-ending snark of yours?"

Jenna stared straight ahead, silent.

"Does he restrain you?" The doctor tried again, but Jenna refused to acknowledge him.

The doctor continued to ask her about her sexual preferences, positions, styles, and even if she played with toys, before finally sighing and giving up. With a deep frown on his face, he put his clipboard down in a huff. He looked at his watch as he slowly stood up, drawing his belt out of his pant loops.

"I had thought we were making progress...," he stated slowly.

"Wait, you don't need the belt," Jenna blurted, panic rising in her.

"As I've said, Jennifer, YOU are not in charge here. Scott..." The doctor sat back down as Scott stood with Jenna and forced her down onto his lap, then Scott forced her jeans down so that her ass was exposed, the bruises from the previous week still present.

"I see that last week's lesson, while still evident on that tasty ass, was not enough to teach you to behave," the doctor said with hunger in his voice. "However, I am glad to see that you have stopped disclosing our session details. It would be best if you didn't share, Jennifer, as I'm sure you know that Mr. Thurston would probably believe me if I told him I had no idea where these marks came from... or perhaps if I told him that you had confessed to having dirty rough sex with other men? Wouldn't that be exciting?" There was a deepness to his voice that gave away just how much he was enjoying holding her life in his hands, and torturing her, as if he was savoring these fantasies.

Scott clamped her hands over her head, and Jenna thrashed and screamed; with the first CRACK of the leather on her skin the door exploded open with a BOOM as it hit the wall. Suddenly the room was full of people, and chaos ensued.

"What is the meaning of this?!" Dr. Tilden roared, standing abruptly and dumping Jenna's body onto the floor. She ducked into a ball, trying to pull her pants back up, and taking in all of the feet she could see at floor level.

Scott moved to grab the nearest body, but unfortunately for him it was a police officer; when Scott moved to hit him, the officer simply tazed him to the ground and then cuffed him. Another officer stepped up to Dr. Tilden.

"You are under arrest…," he stated, as the doctor tried to talk over him. The officer forcefully turned the sputtering doctor around, putting cuffs on his wrists, as he read him his Miranda Rights.

Max was in front of the doctor instantly, fists flying at the doctor's face.

"You sick FUCK!" he roared as he landed a series of quick but violent punches on the restrained doctor, before the officer pulled the screeching doctor away from him, and another two officers pulled Max back. Doctor Tilden was doubled over and bleeding as he was pushed toward the door, and away from Max's fury.

Andrew was already picking Jenna up, pulling her clothing back in place, and soothing her sobs.

Max finally managed to regain control of his anger, and straightening up he stepped away from the officers, who both eyed him warily but released him. Max stepped up to a very pale Bruce, who stood beside him with a stunned expression on his face.

"Have you seen enough, *Your Honor?*" Max asked Bruce loudly, keeping his eyes on the doctor.

Instantly the doctor stopped wailing and spun his head. Realization hit him like a two-by-four. His boiling anger was replaced by fear as all of the color drained from his face.

"What?! No! NO! This is all a mistake! She attacked me!" he stuttered. "Scott! Scott! Tell them!" he roared as they half-dragged him out of the room. Scott was in no shape to answer, as he himself was half-carried behind the doctor in handcuffs.

One of the remaining officers turned to Max. "I'm going to need a formal statement." The officers worked quickly and efficiently, having Jenna walk them through the recording and telling them what was happening that they couldn't see. They took photos around the room, and of Jenna's newest injuries, and within thirty minutes they released her to Max, again advising she get medical care. But Max's eyes were already watching as Jenna slowly calmed on Andrew's lap, his arms around her.

"Can we go now?" He never once took his eyes off of Jenna.

"That will be fine, if Judge Haskins is okay with it?" The officer looked to Bruce, and he nodded sullenly. There were unshed tears in the corners of his eyes, the scene he had witnessed seemingly too unthinkable.

One by one Bruce and the remaining officers slowly filed out of the room. Max sat beside Andrew, and Jenna scrambled into his lap, her arms flung around him. Her breathing was heavy as she clung to Max's shoulders, making herself small, flush against his body.

"Look, I'm going to catch a ride with one of the guys, okay? You two need some alone time tonight." Andrew volunteered, as he backed slowly toward the door.

"Thank you." Jenna hiccoughed as she looked up to catch his eyes.

Andrew stopped, his eyes locked on hers. "You did good, Baby-Girl. I'm proud of you." He smiled, as he slipped through the door, closing it behind him.

Only Jenna and Max remained in the room, sitting on the couch on which she had only just been held prisoner.

She was free!

◆ ◆ ◆

Max

The door clicked shut and it was like a switch was flipped in Max. Without everyone around he finally gave in and allowed himself to break down. He clutched at Jenna roughly, burying his face in her hair and neck, holding on for dear life.

Every minute he had been made to listen to that man abuse her had ripped a piece of his soul out. He knew why they were doing it, but his heart considered him a traitor for allowing it to happen. There was some primal need inside of him, over-flowing; he had to protect her. He had to claim her. He had to own her.

Suddenly he couldn't get close enough. No matter how hard he held her, it felt too fragile, as if she could be torn away at any moment. He needed her closer, like they needed to be inside of each other, sharing one space.

Jenna looked up at him with big sad eyes. "Now you under-stand," she said to him intently, the wet tracks of her tears still on her swelling face.

He looked into her eyes, and in that moment... he did. He did understand. All those times that she had launched her body onto his after her night terrors, all of those times that she needed him to ground her back into reality; suddenly he understood.

His mouth came down on hers, hard, their teeth knocking; as he took her mouth in his and devoured it. Her arms were around him in an instant, and within seconds they were claw-ing their clothing off.

It was wild and sexual, but it also wasn't. It was a primal drive. It was the drive to own, to claim, to protect. No amount of closeness was close enough. Clothing separated them, distance separated them. He needed to be one with her, in her, on her, all over her.

They came at each other like animals, each fighting for dominance, until finally Max flipped her onto her back on the sofa and pushed his body over hers. Still he devoured her with searing kisses, even as they clawed and groaned into each other.

With one hard thrust he was inside her. There was no thought. There was only the animalistic surging of his hips as he fucked into her harder and harder. One of his hands crept up to her throat, holding it there. He didn't squeeze to cut off her air supply, only held her in a position of dominance as he fucked her roughly. She arched her back into him with a moan.

"No one touches this body, or fucks this pussy but ME!" he roared, slamming his cock into her. "You are MINE!"

Jenna groaned and whimpered, her body writhing underneath his.

"TELL ME! TELL ME YOU ARE MINE!" he demanded, bringing a leg up to thrust into her deeper, harder.

"I'm... I'm yours!" she gasped, followed by a long low moan.

He pulled her legs up higher, her legs over his shoulders. "No one will ever fucking touch you again, Blue! NO ONE. You are MINE." He was screaming, raging, fucking... it was all a haze of raw emotion and sensation. "I own you. You are mine! You are mine!" He roared this like a mantra between heaving breaths. His hands latched onto her, fingers digging into her soft flesh, as he fucked his frustration and rage out. His face was contorted, and there was no humanity in the deep blue depths of his eyes. He was an animal, and his primal instinct drove him harder, deeper, faster, rougher.

"Yes.. YES! All yours!" Jenna moaned. Her head fell back, her blue hair spilling over the sofa. There was only the wet slapping noise of their bodies pounding together, and their ragged breaths and groans, as their bodies wound tighter and tighter.

And then it was like time stood still, as their euphoria built to a crescendo, bringing them to the top edge of the peak, perfectly balanced and just waiting to tumble over. Their eyes met in a moment of clarity. Both of them lost in the fog of the passion... aware and joined together, before they burst over the edge and roared into bliss, their bodies surging and convulsing in perfect unison.

As their sweaty bodies collapsed together, Max gathered Jenna into his arms protectively; his primal need still not fully sated.

He thought he may never let her go again.

◆ ◆ ◆

Jenna

Max was like a mother hen all night. He practically carried Jenna to the car, and then into the house. He ordered dinner in, and ran her a hot bath; then he proceeded to both feed and bathe her in the tub as if she was precious. She had to order him out of the room so that she could use the toilet in privacy.

Jenna had never seen him so clingy... no, clingy was the wrong word... attached? Tenacious?

She was out of danger, so she knew it wasn't her safety driving him. This was a whole new side of him she had never experienced before, his caveman side. It seemed like he wanted to carry her around, and club anyone who approached her. And once home, he was providing for her, feeding her, caring for her.

She loved him, but she really just needed a minute to herself to wrap her head around everything. Was she like this after their post-night-terror sex? Usually, she just fell asleep. But Max was hyper-attentive, never taking his eyes off of her, constantly fluffing her pillow, offering a blanket, asking if she needed more food... In truth, it was a little exhausting.

Jenna sighed.

This was probably just as traumatic for him as it had been for her, and everyone processes differently.

They ended the night cuddled in bed under a thick comforter watching a movie... until the caveman and his anaconda came out to play again.

And again, roughly.

And again, tenderly.

And... again, blissfully.

◆ ◆ ◆

Max

Max peeked back into the bedroom again. Jenna was still asleep, all spread out in his bed like a vision. She had starfished to take up the entire center of the bed, the comforter and sheets wrapped haphazardly around her body while her limbs stretched in all directions.

He had showered fast, to be able to look in on her quickly before drying himself off. Then he just decided to dry off with the door open, so he could keep a line of sight on her.

He didn't know where this sudden urge was coming from, but he literally had to fight himself to let her out of his sight. He wanted to guard her, protect her. He wanted her to need him, to look to him to provide for her and make her feel safe. He knew it was unhealthy, but it was overwhelming.

He looked to the bed again, before pulling on some sweats to head downstairs to make breakfast for her, but before he could pull the door closed, he instead opened it to check on her again.

Get a grip!

Shaking his head at himself he rushed down the stairs to make breakfast as quickly as possible and get back to her.

Chapter 25

Jenna

In the weeks following the doctor's arrest things between Max and Jenna were awkward. While Jenna struggled with letting go of the anxiety, hurt, and a false sense of betrayal, Max struggled with his own possessive instincts, which he had never experienced before. While nothing had changed between them, they had each changed individually, and that changed everything. They waltzed gracefully around the elephant in the room.

It was like they were back at the awkward getting-to-know-you dating stage; they approached each other tentatively, cautiously. The only thing that remained a constant was their sex life, and they relied on that like a life-line to help them through the rest of their emotional overwhelm.

Max reconnected with his therapist, to help him to process, and Jenna saw Carol again to help her. With enough time, enough communication, and enough orgasms, they were making progress to strengthen their relationship again.

Jenna stared at the silent living room, suddenly aware of how alone she was when Max had to return to working his long hours. It had never bothered her before, in fact, she had looked forward to her alone time. She had always been content knowing Max would come home in the evening, and they would enjoy their few hours together.

Suddenly she found herself missing him when he wasn't home. She felt lonely, and this new emotion caused her to war with her own independent nature; she didn't want to be clingy or needy... but there it was. She resisted the urge to ask him to stay home with her, or to take her out, or to call or text him constantly during the day... although she still did text him quite often.

But as her eyes floated over the same leather furniture, expensive carpet, and design touches, she knew she needed to find something for herself, something to keep her busy. Maybe it was time to go back to work?

◆ ◆ ◆

Max

Max sat at his desk, not seeing anything on his computer screen. He tried to re-read the documents again, and his eyes glazed over. It was no use. Getting up to give himself a break, he headed for the kitchen for a fresh cup of coffee, his morning cup cold and unappetizing.

As he poured his fresh cup, his thoughts wandered back to his house and Jenna.

He hated leaving her there alone everyday, even though her mental health was dramatically improved. If he was honest, it wasn't her mental health that made him want to stay. He wanted to be with her all the time, skin to skin, wrapped in her scent.

Ever since that fucking doctor's office, he had changed. He couldn't touch her enough, see her enough, feel her enough. It's like he had become a damned puppy, following her around. He preferred when they stayed home, because if any other man came near her, it was like he turned into an alphahole, he would suddenly become paranoid that some other guy was going to get her attention and lure her away. He had never been insecure over a woman, never.

He knew their relationship was solid, but fuck, it was like he couldn't control himself. While he'd always had a dominant alpha personality he'd never really felt the need to control someone the way he wanted to own Jenna completely. He wanted all of her, body, mind, and soul. He didn't want her to feel stifled at home, but he was far less anxious when it was only him and her together.

To add to his anxiety the long hours and stress at work were making him moody and snappish, something he never wanted to be with Jenna. Even when he got home, he needed time alone to decompress, and she seemed starved for attention and just wanted to latch onto him the moment he walked through the door. He hated the wounded look in her eyes when he would shut himself away in his home office for a moment of peace before he could come back to her and be the boyfriend she deserved.

He wanted to keep her, but he also wanted space from her. Maybe it had been a mistake asking her to move in so soon. But he couldn't imagine her not being at his house waiting for him. Selfishly, he didn't want her to be anywhere else. It didn't make any sense to him. It was like he wanted to lock her up so he knew she was safe, and then live his life. Definitely not healthy.

Max sighed deeply before taking a deep swallow of coffee. He didn't need to work, he had plenty of money to last him and Jenna both for the rest of their life, but he had commitments. He had become a partner in the firm to help to grow the firm and usher in the next generation of lawyers. It had always been his goal and his dream, but now he felt himself becoming resentful.

Was he resentful of the job, for keeping him away from Jenna, or was he resentful of Jenna for making him question his life purpose? He needed to figure his shit out, before he sabotaged both of them.

◆ ◆ ◆

Jenna

It was late May, and the snow was long gone from the streets. The weather was becoming warmer, and the flowers were poking out of their flower boxes up and down the streets. Jenna had texted with Joelle and Andrew for a while after Max had left for work, but she couldn't seem to shake her restlessness. She was used to being busy, being useful. At Max's house, she was neither.

She made a snap decision to visit her church and work on the mural. It was Wednesday, but she called one of the ministers to see if he could let her into the building. She hadn't painted in months, and her hands were itching to finish the mural she had started so long ago. She dialed the number, and waited as the phone rang, before Mark answered.

"Jenna! What a pleasant surprise!" She could hear Mark's smile over the line. He was a kind person, and one of her favorite Ministers at the church.

"Hi Reverend Mark! I'm sorry I've been away so long, a lot has happened. Look... I was wondering if I could get into the church today? I've been wanting to get back and finish that mural. I'm sorry it's not done already."

There was a pause on the other end of the line before Mark cautiously replied. "Err... Jenna, the mural is finished. An anonymous donor gave us the money and specifically requested that we hire a team to come out and finish it. I hope you're not upset. When we didn't hear from you... well, I assumed you had a lot going on in your life, so I didn't want to bother you with the news."

Jenna could tell he was trying to let her down gently; he knew how much that project had meant to her. Still, she couldn't keep her voice from cracking as she replied.

"Oh... uh... yeah... Well, I'm glad you got it finished then," she trailed off to a whisper.

"I'm sorry I didn't call you, Jenna. Will we see you on Sunday?" he asked hopefully.

"I'm not sure right now, Mark. But I will be back, I promise." They ended the call, and Jenna's heart hurt.

The words stuck in her mind, *anonymous donor...* Who would do that? No one had ever come forward to help the church in that way before. Maybe they were just sick of seeing the mural half done, and had taken matters into their own hands? She knew she had no right to be upset, she had all but abandoned the work in the whirlwind that was her new relationship with Max.

But she was upset. That mural had been her baby, her project; it had given her a goal to accomplish. And now it was gone.

She stared at the phone in her hand. She wondered what other parts of her life had she walked away from in her frenzy to have a boyfriend. In that moment of clarity she decided that she would start looking for a job, immediately. She had become far too complacent living like a fixture in her boyfriend's apartment, she needed something of her own.

Jenna spent the afternoon going through the online want ads and local recruiting ads. Nothing jumped out at her, and it was making her depressed. She knew better than to settle for a customer service job; she and the public didn't get along well. She needed something fast-paced, where she could blend into the background.

By the time evening rolled around Jenna had only seen one or two ads that even vaguely interested her. She sighed as she logged off of the computer and headed downstairs to get dinner ready. Max would be home soon.

She had learned to kiss him hello, and let him go. It killed her a little bit. She was starved for conversation, she missed seeing him, but when he got home he looked wiped out and distracted. All he wanted was to get away from her. So she had learned to kiss him and get out of his way, but it felt wrong.

Maybe she had moved in with him too soon. Now she was stuck; she liked being with him, missed him in fact. But he was moody and tired, in a way she hadn't seen when they were first dating. Was this what their future was going to look like? Jenna thought that when the nonsense with the doctor was over they would return to their happy-go-lucky relationship, but it was not working out that way.

◆ ◆ ◆

Max

Max put his coat in the closet and set his briefcase on the floor in the hallway. Jenna wasn't right there to greet him like she usually was, and inwardly he inhaled with relief. He loved her, but he also didn't have the energy she had when he got home. He just needed a few minutes to unwind.

He looked into the kitchen on his way by, expecting to find her, but the kitchen was empty. The timer on the stove read an hour remaining for whatever she had in there. It was unusual... she normally couldn't wait to see him.

A cold ball of steel formed in his gut.

Did she get tired of me being so moody and absent? Is she pulling away? Did she find someone else? Oh God... what if she wants to end it?!

He knew his thoughts were irrational, but it didn't change the cold tingle of fear that snaked down his spine as he rushed up the stairs toward the bedroom.

"Blue?!" he called loudly, his voice pitchy, as he tugged at his tie before ripping it off and tossing it.

"In here…" Her voice was muffled through the bathroom door.

He knocked, before cautiously walking in to find her laid out in the sunken tub. Seeing her sprawled out, wet and naked, in the hot water brought an instant reaction in him; his dick throbbed and hardened and his heart rate sped up. While his body wanted full-steam ahead, his fear still held his mind captive.

"Taking a bath?" he asked, trying to sound curious instead of relieved.

"I was just waiting for you." She smiled up at him seductively. "Get naked and join me. My mammal needs attention." Jenna ran her hands down her sides into the water, hovering over her mound.

Fatigue, fear, and moodiness were instantly forgotten as Max quickly stripped off his clothing, tossing it all in a pile on the floor carelessly. Jenna sat up, away from the back of the tub, so that Max could climb in behind her. The water sloshed over the sides as he settled in with his legs around her, and she leaned back into him.

Her warm wet body against his chest instantly calmed him of any fears, and ignited his hunger for her. He pulled her wet blue locks away from her neck so that he could place an open-mouth kiss where her neck and shoulder met. He worked his kisses up her throat, and to her jaw, nipping and suckling gently as he went. His hands snaked around her body to wrap around her warm moist breasts and tease her nipples.

"I like this greeting." He breathed enthusiastically into her neck.

"I thought you might," she answered with amusement. "You've been so tense lately, I thought I might surprise you with a little reptile therapy."

With that she leaned forward and twisted her body around until she straddled him, facing him. Jenna leaned in, but before she could kiss him he cupped her face in his hands, looking into her eyes.

"I have been tense lately, haven't I?" he asked, his earlier insecurity rising to the surface.

"We both have," she answered, but her tone didn't say any more.

"Have I been a neglectful boyfriend, Blue? You know I don't mean to be. I told you my work hours can be-"

"No." She cut him off before he could take the conversation down that dark path. "You are doing just what you told me you would do. I have no issue with you. I think it's me," she answered sadly.

"What do you mean?" he asked quickly, his eyebrows rising with alarm. He didn't like the way that sounded at all.

Jenna sighed. Then she picked herself up, grabbing his semi-erect cock at the base, and pushed down onto him. It was her signal they needed to talk.

"I mean... I need to do something with myself all day," Jenna answered, searching his eyes with hers.

"Something... like what?" Max asked, still holding her face, his stomach clenching as the acid from the fear started building.

"I don't know... a job. I need to keep busy, Max. I'm not used to this lifestyle. I don't have a club to hang out in with all of your associates' wives, and play tennis or golf all day. I need a purpose.

"I called the church today, the one I told you about. They finished my mural without me." There was sadness in her eyes.

Max stared at her, his brows crossing in confusion. This is not what he had expected her to say, and he didn't understand how a job and her mural at the church were related.

"I wanted to surprise you," he stated. "I knew how much painting that mural was hurting you, so I paid to have a team finish it for you. I thought you'd be happy."

Her eyes flew open wide. "Max. I LOVED that mural. It was a piece of my heart. I was devastated when I found out they had moved on and finished it without me. Why would you do that without telling me?" Tears formed in the corners of her eyes.

All of the hunger leached out of Max's body, to be replaced by a wary irritation.

"Blue, like I said, I wanted to surprise you. I remember how hurt you were whenever you came back from painting. Andrew even had to work on you a few times. I was trying to help, not take it away from you." He knew his voice was not as sympathetic as it should have been, but he hadn't been prepared to be thrown into an emotional conversation; it felt like a bait-and-switch.

Max redirected the conversation. "And why do you want to get a job? Honey, I have money, if there's anything you need-"

"I don't *need* money, Max." Jenna interrupted, her own irritation rising to the surface. "I need something to do all day. I can't sit around your house doing nothing. I need to earn my keep. I don't want to be a homemaker, I need to get out."

Max could see that she was frustrated. He knew she was right, but he also had to fight his own instincts that just wanted to lock her away in the house and protect her. It was unreasonable, but it was how he felt.

"Well, if you want a job, you don't need my permission, Baby. If you want, I can get you a job in my firm. We're always looking for people, and we could ride in together."

If she wanted to work somewhere, Max liked the idea of her being close to him doing it. He would make sure she didn't work in his office, otherwise they'd be on top of each other day and night, and he didn't think he could handle that. But having her in the building? That could work. Problem solved.

"No," Jenna answered flatly.

"Why not?" he asked, trying to keep the irritation out of his voice, but losing the battle.

"I don't do well in office environments. Plus... I think it wouldn't give you enough alone time,... away from me. I'll find something." Her eyes didn't meet his as they said it.

Max didn't know how to respond to that. Partially because he didn't really want her going out and getting a job, but he also knew that it was unfair to her; the whole thing left him feeling pissed off and stressed. If she left the house, he wouldn't know she was safe.

They both sat in the tub in silence for a few minutes before Jenna finally broke the quiet.

"What's happening to us?" she whispered, looking into Max's eyes.

"What do you mean?" he asked with a little snap in his voice.

"This. This is what I mean," she answered him back. Her eyes reflected sadness, hurt.

A part of him wanted to grab her to his body and hold her close and comfort her, but another part was tired and itching for a fight to end the low-level buzz of anxiety that always seemed to be humming just below his skin.

When he didn't say anything she continued. "Things are changing between us, I feel it. It scares me."

"What do you want me to say?" he answered coolly. "I told you I'm a workaholic when we met, Jenna. My work is very stressful. I can't always be in the honeymoon phase; I have obligations."

Jenna didn't give him the argument he was looking for. Instead she leaned in and kissed him tenderly. With his anger already flaring, he quickly took the kiss deeper.

◆ ◆ ◆

Jenna

Jenna let him push his tongue into her mouth as his hands tightened around her hips.

I know you have obligations, I just don't want to be treated like one of them.

She was still hurt that he had stepped in and taken her art project away, but she could see his side of it too. It didn't make it hurt less, but at least she could understand it. But the rest of his attitude? She felt like she was a burden to him, like he didn't want to be with her but put up with her. That hurt her the most.

He had always been so attentive, he had treated her like she was something precious. In only a few months she had been relegated to "daily," almost taken for granted. She couldn't have conversations without him getting irritated or shutting down. Little by little he was pushing her away, and she didn't know how to stop it.

The most she could do was try to get back to carving her own life, so that when he did finally push her out she had somewhere to land.

She moved her hips up and back, riding the length of his cock as he plundered her mouth. This was something they could do. While they were joined, they were together, unified. It had become the last good place in their relationship; there was no debate, no hurt feelings. She dug her nails into his biceps as his length hit her at just the right spot, causing her to groan out loud, her eyes floating shut in bliss. His cock responded as her pussy clamped down on him, her arousal growing quicker. He thrust his hips up into her, the bathwater sloshing everywhere, as he held her hips tightly.

Their groans grew deeper. She reached a hand up to pinch her own nipple, rolling her head back with a loud groan. His cock grew incredibly hard as he watched her work her nipple between her finger and thumb; her body responded instantly to his. Within seconds they were heaving breaths and thrusting wildly, chasing their release together before both of them threw their heads back with a scream, their bodies convulsing on each other.

As they gently rode out the aftershocks, Jenna leaned in and kissed Max tenderly again. He returned her tenderness, the stiffness gone from his shoulders, his demeanor more relaxed, happier. But Jenna was still tight with worry.

Yes, they had talked... but nothing had really been accomplished. It worried her for the days to come.

Chapter 26

Jenna

Max had gotten up early to go into the office and prep for court. Jenna was still in her pajamas in the late morning as she dragged herself downstairs to get coffee and look over the want ads again. Not having a job also meant she had no reason to get out of bed most days, and she berated herself for allowing herself to get soft. If she got a job, she'd have to get back onto a daily schedule, but she looked forward to that.

She sipped her coffee as she sorted through more ads; there really wasn't a lot that called to her, and it was frustrating her. She picked up her head and took in the quiet house around her. She could hear her own breathing. It was unnerving.

After a few moments of contemplation she felt like she had had enough. She snapped her laptop shut and marched up the stairs with her coffee mug. She would take a shower and make herself presentable, and then she would go to Andrew's house. At least there she felt like she belonged, like she was home, and not a guest staying in someone else's home.

It was just after noon when her Uber driver dropped her off at Andrew's place. She rushed up the stairs quickly and let herself in. She knew he would probably be at work, but she just wanted to sit in his space and think. Shutting the front door behind her, she made her way through the living room and dining room, heading for her bedroom, and squealed as she bounced off of a wet muscular chest belonging to a very hot and very naked man.

"Andy, where's the- Oh my God, I'm so sorry!" The man took several steps back, his face turning red, as his hands flew to his groin to cover himself. The motion only drew Jenna's eyes there, seeing him in all of his glory, before she could pull them away. This man was beautiful! He was in great shape, like a bodybuilder, his broad chest narrowing into a slender 'V', leading to a thick cock hanging between well muscled thighs. He dripped water on the floor, and it was clear he had just come out of the shower.

"Um.. who are you?" she asked, trying to look anywhere but at his crotch.

"Oh, yeah, sorry. I'm Daniel. I'd shake your hand, but..." His cheeks flamed redder.

"Baby Girl!" Andrew laughed as he rounded the corner and lifted her in a bear hug.

"You must be Jenna." Daniel smiled behind Andrew. It was then that Andrew turned and noticed that Daniel was dripping wet and bare-assed naked. Andrew stepped in front of him, blocking Jenna's view of the goods.

"I see you've met my boyfriend," Andrew said with a cheeky smile.

"Your... *boyfriend?*" Jenna asked, a huge grin spreading across her face.

"I'll just-" Daniel started, but Andrew cut him off.

"Go put some clothing on, before my roomie jumps you and turns you." He swatted Daniel on the ass as Daniel ducked behind him and into Andrew's bedroom with a laugh.

"Boyfriend?!" Jenna mouthed to Andrew as the bedroom door shut.

Andrew smiled, a smug look of satisfaction on his face. Jenna beamed. Andrew never introduced men as his boyfriend, in fact, he never brought them home. It thrilled Jenna to think that Andrew finally had someone in his life, while simultaneously rubbing salt in her own relationship wound.

"I want deets!" Jenna whispered, narrowing her eyes.

Andrew just laughed as he pulled her into the kitchen.

"He's a pitcher for the Red Sox. I saw him as a client, and he kept asking me out."

"But you don't date clients," Jenna admonished him.

"True, I don't. After his issue was resolved, he booked an appointment to tell me I was fired, and then asked me out again." Andrew chuckled. "Honestly, we just hit it off really well, so we're seeing where it takes us."

Jenna grabbed Andrew into a big hug. "I am so happy for you, Drew. You deserve something good in your life."

"I have something good, Chica. I have you!" He smiled down at her. "And now I have great sex too. Win-win!" His smile grew wider as Jenna slapped him on the chest half-heartedly.

Daniel strode into the room, this time dressed, and threw an arm around Andrew's shoulders. "Sorry about that." He smiled shyly. "It's nice to finally meet you," he said to Jenna. "I've heard so much about you!"

"Lies! All lies!" Jenna laughed.

"Not all lies!" Andrew chuckled mischievously. "Let's go out to lunch, and I can really fill you in!"

Jenna sipped her coffee with a smile as she watched Daniel regale them with stories about locker room scandals over lunch in the cafe. She noticed how Andrew watched Daniel with a look so tender it made her teeth ache.

Was that how Max used to look at her?

Shaking her head to clear those emotions out, she tuned back into the conversation. She didn't want to make today about her, not when Andrew was so happy.

Daniel seemed like just the right guy for him. He was an athlete, and they shared a love of martial arts. More than that though was the tenderness and admiration in their eyes when they looked at each other. Jenna could feel the emotions they sent to one another, and it warmed her heart. It was obvious they were both smitten.

"Sorry you had to find out this way, Baby Girl." Andrew's voice brought Jenna out of her stupor. "What brought you over today?"

Jenna looked up to see both sets of eyes on her. She nibbled her lower lip uncomfortably, not sure how much to say. Everything felt so unsettled within her.

"I just needed to get out of the house. I'm trying to find a job. I can't sit around all day anymore," she finally confessed. It was true, and it didn't go into the darker emotions that she felt were starting to infect her relationship.

"What do you do for work?" Daniel asked, curious.

"Jenna is great with behind-the-scenes, but she doesn't do well with customer service or office environments," Andrew offered quickly.

Jenna smiled at Andrew's protectiveness. "I can deal with the public, just in small doses," she quickly added.

Daniel dragged his finger over his lower lip as he stared in contemplation at the table, and Jenna noticed that Andrew's eyes were tracking their movement. A knowing smirk pulled at the corner of her mouth.

"Well, I don't know if it interests you or not, but I'm part owner of a private gym, and we're looking for staff. There would be some interacting with gym members; but as it's a private gym, they pretty much know what they need. I can take you by there if you'd like to check it out. Ruth is the manager, and a good friend of mine; I know she'd give you an interview. I mean, it's not glamorous, but it does pay really well." Daniel's eyes swung to Andrew first, as if asking permission, before settling on Jenna.

Jenna was smiling ear to ear. "Yes, I'd love that. When is a good time for you?" She was eager to get a job already, and have somewhere to be on a daily basis.

"What do you have going on after lunch?" Daniel asked, looking between Andrew and her. "I could take you over there today. I know Ruth is in. She's always in." He laughed.

"I'd love that!" Jenna clapped happily, and then quickly looked to Andrew, "That is, unless you two have plans! I don't want to interrupt your time together."

Andrew smirked at her. "As if you could... No, today is good, Baby Girl. Let's do this."

After a ten minute heated alphahole debate between Daniel and Andrew as to who would get to pay the bill, the three of them headed out to Andrew's SUV to check out the gym.

The usual sounds surrounded them as they walked between the cardio machines and around the free weight benches. The clang of weights and the grunts of men working out filled the large space. Light bounced off of the mirrored walls, but was absorbed in the black matting on the floor. The place was immaculate, and didn't have the stale sweat smell most gyms were notorious for. It didn't look like a gym to Jenna, every-thing was high-end; it felt more like a private health club. Largely, because it was, she realized.

In addition to the workout facilities, there was a member sauna, hot tub and lap pool, changing and showering area, makeup area, small cafe with health smoothies, and they were in the process of adding tanning and massage areas. There was even a small business area for those who needed to see to urgent emails or faxes that interrupted their workouts.

Daniel introduced Jenna to Ruth, and then he and Andrew left them alone to talk.

Ruth walked Jenna around, touring the facilities, and dis-cussing what they would need from staff. Daniel had been honest, it wasn't a glamorous job; Jenna would be wiping down machines, answering member questions, refilling supplies, making smoothies... basically anything members needed. While it wasn't exciting, it was just what Jenna was looking for, and Daniel was right: it did pay well.

With a smile and a handshake, Ruth welcomed Jenna to the team, and they agreed she would start the next day.

She couldn't wait to tell Max.

◆ ◆ ◆

Max

Max sipped his scotch. The bar wasn't too loud, but was filling quickly as the workforce of Boston got out and filled the space around him with men and women in suits and office attire. This had been a good idea, he decided.

Before leaving work he had texted Jenna to tell her he would be home a little later. Then he'd gone to the bar not far from his building to relax and unwind. While he wasn't thrilled with paying for scotch in a public bar when he had a perfectly good bottle in the privacy of his home, he was glad that he could sit and collect his thoughts, undisturbed. This way he could mellow out, and then go home to see Jenna, without being a moody bitch.

Perfect.

His mind drifted as he watched more people make their way into the bar, the tables filling quickly, and the noise level becoming louder. He took another sip, and sat back on his bar stool, letting his shoulders relax.

He had just gotten his second scotch when a small hand landed gently on his shoulder.

"Max?" The feminine voice could hardly be heard above the now rowdy noise.

Max turned his head to see Mia standing behind him, her hand still on his shoulder, her look uncertain. His anger rose to the surface immediately, fueled in part by the scotch.

"You're not supposed to be within one hundred feet of me, Mia. I'd suggest you leave," he spit out coldly, before turning back to his scotch.

"I need to talk to you, Max. It's important! It's about Jenna-" she blurted quickly.

He swung his head back to face her, his eyes narrowed and his jaw tight. "Don't you fucking say her name. I have nothing to say to you, and I'm not interested in anything you have to say. Get the fuck out of here, before I call the cops. This is your last warning." This time he didn't turn away from her, but kept his glare on her.

Her eyes filled with shock, and slowly morphed into sadness. She jerked her hand back, sucking in a breath, and then turned and slowly walked out of the bar. Once she had walked through the doors Max finally turned back and swallowed the glass of scotch in front of him, his peaceful state shot to hell.

It had seemed like a good idea.

◆ ◆ ◆

Jenna

Jenna gave the gravy one last stir before turning off the heat under it. She was excited about her new job, but she was also a little nervous to tell Max. He had been so weirdly protective lately, and she didn't want to argue with him about it. She chewed her lip nervously as she considered how to tell him, when she heard the front door open and close.

It took all of her willpower not to run into the foyer and bounce with excitement; she still got butterflies whenever she saw him, but she knew he would be moody and restless. Instead, she focused on dinner, and waited for him to find her.

In a few minutes he was behind her in the kitchen. She turned with a smile, and he pulled her in for a deep kiss. He tasted of scotch. She didn't know why, but it bothered her on some level she couldn't put her finger on. Nonetheless, she said nothing about it. She didn't need yet another battle.

Max smiled down at her warmly, not pulling away as he usually did to run to his office. "How was your day my beautiful Blue?" His hands stroked through her hair behind her ears.

She smiled back up at him, happy to have HER Max with her for a change.

"I've had a great day! Andrew has a boyfriend!" she informed him happily, a silly grin on her face.

"Does he now?" Max asked, surprised. "Is he nice?"

"Yes, he really is..." Jenna answered, a sly look forming on her face. "But not as nice as MY boyfriend," she teased wickedly, before slowly sinking to her knees in front of him.

Max hissed out a breath as she unbuckled his belt and undid his suit pants to retrieve his eager cock from its confines.

"You know... I think I'm really going to like the fact that Andrew has a nice boyfriend." Max said in a deep gravelly voice as Jenna stroked his length firmly a few times in her hands.

"You're going to love him!" Jenna said to him, looking up at him through her lashes, just before her mouth plunged over him, taking him deeply.

Jenna sucked his cock deep into her mouth, working the base with her hands, while watching his face. His eyes were heavy with lust as he watched her intently; the sight of himself submerging into her mouth always got him off, and she knew just how to make him explode. Already, she could feel him reaching that level of hard that told her it wouldn't be long. He groaned as his hands clawed at her hair, his breathing becoming more ragged.

"Fuck, Blue. Your mouth is amazing on my cock!" He groaned out, his eyes closing for a moment to savor the sensation, but opening again so he could watch her devour him.

She reached with one hand to cup and massage his balls, and felt them tighten in her hand, as Max threw his head back with a loud groan. His body went rigid, his hands clutching her head over his cock, and then she felt the telltale spasms on her tongue as he drained into her mouth with loud groans.

She worked him with her mouth, drawing every last bit of him into her, wanting to relieve every last bit of tension from his body, until his breathing calmed. She tucked him back into his briefs and slacks, zipping it up, before standing in front of him again.

He pulled her into a tight embrace, his head buried in her neck with a soft groan.

"What would I do without you, Blue?" he whispered.

"Let's hope you never find out," she whispered back.

As they started to eat dinner Jenna clumsily announced, "I got a job." There was a cautious smile on her face.

"You did?" Max asked in surprise as he passed her the vegetables. "Where will you be working? Doing what?"

"I got a job at a private health club. I.. uh... I guess I'll be doing everything." She chuckled nervously. "I take care of whatever needs doing. It's a great place, and I get to use the facilities," she finished. She chewed her bottom lip, waiting to see if he was going to argue with her.

Max looked up from his plate and smiled at her. "That's great, Sweetheart! If it's what you want to do, I'm happy for you."

She reached over the table to take his hand, suddenly overcome with emotion. She hadn't realized she had been so worried about bringing it up, and she was desperately glad that she didn't have to defend her position with him about it. She needed to work. Sensing her emotional state, Max stopped what he was doing to pick her hand up and gently kiss the back of it.

For the first time in a long time, they had a quiet laid-back night together, and just basked in each other's company.

The next morning Jenna was at Peak Performance, her new employer, at eight in the morning sharp. Daniel greeted her himself and gave her several shirts with the company logo to wear while working. She was delighted that she had a job where she could wear yoga pants and sneakers as a part of her work attire.

At first she was a little star struck, being around Daniel Black, pitcher for the Boston Red Sox, but as the morning wore on she almost forgot about his celebrity status. He was so much like Andrew that it was like having Andrew with her. He joked and teased with her, just like Andrew did, and even called her "Baby Girl." It felt like she had always known him. She knew she and Daniel were going to be close friends.

The job wasn't exciting, but it also wasn't difficult. She made several rounds, wiping down machines, weight bars, and benches. She learned how to use the smoothie machine and work the cafe counter, and just generally kept herself busy. The members were nice, and kept to themselves, many of them local celebrities in their own right. They came to work out in peace, and she left them alone unless they asked for something. The job was just what she had been hoping for.

As she made another round of wiping down cardio machines the news on one of the tv sets mounted on the wall caught her eye. There was a picture of a woman, and the crawl mentioned that the woman had been murdered the day before. Jenna knew she had seen the woman somewhere, but couldn't place her. Stopping her cleaning, she turned the volume up.

"... Ashley Myers. The twenty-four year-old was found in an alley in downtown Boston. Police are still investigating the exact cause of death. Miss Myers was known to have worked for a high-end call girl service in Boston, but police aren't speculating as to whether that played a role in her death or not..." The newscaster's voice rang passionately.

The screen showed picture after picture of the woman, Ashley. She had blond hair and a pretty smile. Photos showed her in Boston Common, a scene in a kitchen holding a puppy, and then a scene at a charity event.

Jenna's heart stopped. Ashley was wearing the horrible dress she had seen in the department store. She was the woman Jenna had interrupted talking with Mia in the bathroom! Jenna's hand flew over her mouth as a shocked gasp escaped. She was the woman who had been seeing Marcus, the one Marcus wouldn't leave his wife for!

Her hands started shaking as she stared at the screen. The story ended abruptly and the program turned to weather and traffic, but Jenna could only stand transfixed, staring. Jenna knew what a monster Marcus was, but would he have murdered her? Her gut told her *yes*, but she had no proof whatsoever, and Marcus had already proven that even the court system couldn't beat him.

Whether he had killed her or not, Jenna suddenly didn't feel safe. She hadn't thought of Marcus since she had been forced to deal with the much bigger threat of Doctor Tilden, but now all of her fear and anxiety came back to her in a tidal wave. Luckily, her shift was ending soon, because she needed to get the hell out of there and get back to the safety of Max!

She pushed her cleaning supplies back into the cabinet, grabbed her bag, and rushed out the door without even finding Daniel to say goodbye. It was the longest train ride, ever, as she scanned the faces on the packed subway nervously. It wasn't until she closed and locked Max's door behind her that she let out a deep breath, finally feeling safe again.

◆ ◆ ◆

Max

Max hung his coat in the closet and moved his briefcase to the wall in the hallway. As he stood up he had to jump back in surprise. Jenna was right in front of him, almost touching him, and he hadn't seen her there when he came in. He smiled and was about to kiss her hello when he took in the haunted look on her face. His smile fell immediately.

"What happened?" he asked nervously.

Jenna's cheeks flushed, she seemed nervous, which only put Max more on edge.

"Do you remember the charity ball, the one where I crashed into you?" she asked nervously.

"Yes," he answered, still not understanding.

"You remember how I told you I interrupted Mia and her friend in the bathroom, talking about their 'boyfriends?'" Her eyes were wide.

"I do. What's going on, Blue?" He was starting to get impatient, as his nerves were all on end.

"Mia's friend, Ashley was her name... she was murdered yesterday. She's... dead." Jenna squeaked.

Max frowned, his eyebrows drawing together. He didn't know if there was more to the story, as it seemed to have upset Jenna deeply, but neither of them were good friends with Ashley. Max had seen her with Marcus a few times at events, and Marcus had bragged about fucking her... but he didn't *know* her.

"Oookaaay," he volunteered, hoping Jenna would fill in the missing blanks.

"Max... she was seeing Marcus! Do you think...?" She didn't finish her question, her cheeks flaming pink.

Max pulled her into his chest and held her. "I don't know, Honey. I would never peg Marcus as a murderer. He has status and money. I mean, what would be his motivation? He could easily just fire her. It's not like she was even his only girlfriend," he spoke his thoughts out loud.

"I know... It's just..." Again, Jenna let the sentence fall flat.

"I get it. He's a prick. But it doesn't mean he killed her, Blue. Her lifestyle choices could have easily put her into a dangerous position. For that matter, it could have been that she was just in the wrong place at the wrong time. We don't know what happened for sure."

Max placed a finger under her chin to tip it up to look at him. "Don't get stressed out about this Baby; I'm not going to let anything or anyone hurt you again. You are safe." He placed a tender kiss on her forehead, before leaning down to place another on her lips. He could feel her slowly relaxing in his grip.

Later that evening Max looked down to see Jenna curled up on his shoulder, sound asleep. Her blue hair fell like a waterfall, cascading over her shoulder and spilling onto his chest as well. He very slowly and carefully slid himself out from under her, propping a pillow under her head. Once he was sure she was still sleeping soundly, he quietly made his way to his office. Closing the door he pulled out his cell and dialed.

"Max," A voice answered.

"Mooch, I have a job for you," Max stated flatly.

"Yeah, boss, whatever you need," the voice answered.

"I need you to look into the murder that happened yesterday in Boston, a blond by the name of Ashley. Find out what the detectives aren't releasing to the public, and keep it on the down low. I don't want anyone to know I'm poking into this." Max whispered into the phone.

"Sure thing, boss. You in some trouble?" the voice inquired.

"No, not me. I'm thinking of someone else. Just get me what you can as fast as you can. You know how to get a hold of me," Max finished.

"Will do, boss." With that, the line went dead.

Chapter 27

Max

Max walked into the kitchen and Jenna turned and handed him a mug of coffee. She looked adorable in her yoga pants and company shirt, with her hair pulled into a messy blue ponytail. She looked absolutely fuckable.

Max smirked as he leaned down to kiss her lips.

"What's that look for?" she asked him knowingly, kissing him back.

Max feigned ignorance, placing his hand dramatically on his chest. "What look?" he asked innocently.

"That look that says I am going to chase you down and eat you alive," she answered with a smirk.

"You've answered your own question," he stated, as he took a long swig of his coffee.

"I've got to get going," Jenna said suddenly as she put her cup in the sink and reached for her bag. "I don't want to miss the train and be late. Where are my keys?!"

Max stilled. "Jenna, why don't you get an Uber?" he asked.

The thought of her being out in public with that recent murder still unsolved left him uneasy. While there was no direct tie to Marcus, or to Jenna, it just hit too close to home.

"Why spend money to make money?" Jenna answered simply, still searching for her keys.

"Well, if it's an issue of money, I can pay for it," he volunteered.

When she shot him her 'that's not going to happen' look, he changed tacks, "Or you could just take one of mine."

"One of your what?" she asked, still distracted with looking through her purse for her keys.

"One of my cars," he clarified.

Jenna stopped shuffling through her purse and brought her eyes up to meet Max's.

"Are you kidding me? Max, those cars cost almost as much as most people's houses. I can't drive one of those. What if I scratched it?!" She seemed horrified.

"They are insured, Jenna. They can be, and have been, replaced. YOU are not replaceable, and I would feel a lot better knowing that you are safe in your own vehicle, rather than crammed into public transportation." He wouldn't tell her he was worried that there could potentially be someone out there who wanted to hurt her, but he had to let her know it was a line he was drawing in the sand. This was non-negotiable.

"Max, I-" she started, but was instantly cut off.

"Blue, I am *asking* you... PLEASE... do this for me. I am already dealing with my own issues about your safety, knowing you are out there working somewhere, and I can't be there to protect you. PLEASE give me this. Take my damn car." His words were firm but gentle, and he knew he couldn't hide all of the anxiety that was coming out of him.

She must have seen it on his face as well because she paused, her mouth set in a little angry pout, but in the end she nodded her head yes. Max breathed out a sigh of relief, and turned to grab her keys from the counter behind him before walking her to the garage where he parked his cars.

It had been two weeks since the news of Ashley's murder had broken. There had been no news about any breakthroughs on the case, and other than a news piece about a small memorial set up where Ashley had died, it seemed the public didn't give a shit about a call girl winding up dead.

Max's phone vibrated in his pocket, and when he pulled it out and saw the caller ID he answered it immediately.

"Mooch, tell me you've heard something," he answered quickly.

"I have," the voice replied. "Seems Ashley got on the wrong side of the Giovanni family, someone ordered her hit. I haven't been able to find out who, though."

"The mob?" Max asked incredulously. "Why would they want to kill a call girl?"

"Well, that's where it gets interesting," Mooch supplied. "It turns out that her agency is one of theirs."

"That makes no sense then," Max thought out loud. "Why would they kill one of their own money-makers? Was she skimming?"

"It's possible, but not likely. The agency got paid first, and then paid her. The family helped provide housing and protection for the girls, so they were kept loyal. Near as I can figure it, she must have seen something she wasn't supposed to. That's one of the only things that would make them take out one of their own; I mean, let's face it, they're pretty replaceable, otherwise. I'll call you if I can get more."

The call went dead and Max tucked his phone back into his pocket. Max didn't know what to make of the situation. He couldn't see anything that would tie this to Marcus, or indicate that Jenna was in any danger, but it just didn't sit right. Something just didn't add up.

What he did know was that he suddenly felt like an asshole for all of those years of hiring girls to be his date and meet his needs. They were essentially owned by the mob, kept like cattle. Mooch was right, they were treated like they were expendable, and he had done it to them as well. Something in his gut warned him that karma was going to take Jenna away from him for all of the women that he had overlooked so arrogantly.

◆ ◆ ◆

Jenna

Jenna sat behind the computer at the desk on the counter at the gym. She had cleaned everything she could find to clean, and it was slow so there was nothing more she could busy herself with. She searched the internet for information on Ashley's investigation again.

It had been four weeks since Ashley's murder, and police hadn't been able to discover much. She had been shot, and that was about all they were saying. It made Jenna sad. She didn't have any love for Ashley, but she certainly didn't want her life to be snuffed out without an afterthought. Everyone deserved to be loved and recognized, sex worker or not.

When her shift was over she grabbed her bag and headed out to the parking lot down the block to get Max's Audi. As she approached it, she noticed a figure standing near the car: a woman, with a long coat too warm for the weather, with a scarf over her head and large sunglasses. Jenna slowed her pace.

The woman turned and looked at her, and then removed her sunglasses. It was Mia. Her expression broadcast her terror, and Jenna noticed that the hand she held her sunglasses in was shaking. Mia noticed too, as she quickly stuffed her hands into her coat pocket.

"What the fuck do YOU want?" Jenna growled, still approaching the car, but keeping a good distance away from Mia.

Mia made a small noise in her throat, and then cleared it before lifting her chin. "Look, I know I'm not your favorite person, but I'm not here for you. I need you to give something to Max-"

"You have a lot of goddamn nerve!" Jenna bellowed, her rage flowing freely.

"Will you shut up and listen?!" Mia bellowed back, her own rage on display. "He killed Ashley. And he wants to kill you too. Maybe even Max. You need to give Max this drive. It has all of the information."

Tears rolled down her angry cheeks. She held up her hand, showing a small jump drive in her palm. "I don't care if you don't like me. But I do love Max, and I don't want anything to happen to him."

Jenna was stunned, and stood, immobile. "Who? Who killed Ashley?" she whispered.

Mia marched toward her, and Jenna prepared herself to defend against the attack, but Mia just dropped the jump drive into her hand as she hurried past, pulling her sunglasses on.

"Marcus," was all she said as she disappeared around the corner.

◆ ◆ ◆

Max

Max and Jenna sat with Mort from IT staring at him as he typed away. When Jenna had called Max, hysterical, he had told her to meet him at the office. It had taken two glasses of scotch before she calmed down enough to tell him what had happened with Mia. Max barely had his rage contained at the thought of Mia bothering Jenna again, but Jenna needed him more than his anger.

He had called Mort, a trusted employee from the IT department, to check out the jump drive. He expected it to have some nasty computer virus that would wipe out his systems, so having Mort open it in a contained computer seemed the best option.

"What did you find?" Max asked, as he walked up behind Mort to look at the screen.

"I'm not really sure," Mort answered. "There's no virus, nor malware. Just a bunch of documents and records, some photos and videos."

Mort clicked on one of the documents. "It looks like a legal document for a company called Frasier Holdings, out of Dorchester..." he offered.

Max's eyes flicked down the document, taking in all of the details. He clicked to the next page, reading further. Finally, when he finished, he let out a breath.

"You're sure the drive is safe, Mort?" he asked again.

"Positive," Mort answered.

"Alright. Thanks for the help." Max effectively dismissed Mort, and once the door closed he and Jenna were alone again.

"What is it?" Jenna asked.

"What it looks like is a lot of documentation that implicates Marcus in connection with the Giovanni family and their illegal businesses," Max stated simply. "Also, it appears he had the family influence the judge at your trial with him, and it was him who had Doctor Tilden assigned to your case. It seems the good doctor works for the family as well."

Jenna's eyes bulged wide. Her mind went back over all of the small details she knew about Marcus, and in retrospect, it made sense. This was how he got the judge to basically ignore his assault and battery charge. It explained why she was given a sadistic psychopath for a therapist. It explained how Dr. Tilden knew all of her personal information, as Mia had been there the night Max proposed. This was how he was getting away with everything, including murdering Ashley. The jump drive itself might be the very thing that had gotten her killed.

Jenna jumped back from the computer like it was on fire.

"You have to give that to the police!" she insisted, never taking her eyes off of the screen.

"No, I can't trust the police, I don't know who he's bought off. I'll bring it to Bruce. I know he will make sure it gets into the right hands. I'll also keep a copy for the newspaper, in case it gets stopped by one of the family's goons." Max continued opening documents, reading them over.

"Max, won't they come after us if they know we have this?" Jenna's eyes were wide with fear as Max looked up to meet them.

"Don't worry, Blue. They will never know we have this. I will keep you safe," he promised her.

He looked back to the screen to continue looking like he was reading. He couldn't tell her that it looked like Marcus had already started inquiring about a hit on her. He tried to keep his face neutral, but he could feel the blood pooling in his gut.

◆ ◆ ◆

Jenna

Max had taken Jenna with him when he visited Bruce at home, but they left her sitting in the living room while the men went into Bruce's home office to discuss the drive. Jenna's heart was beating wildly in her chest.

If Marcus knew that Ashley had that drive... did he know it got passed to Mia? Did he know she had passed it to Jenna? Were they out there, right now, looking to murder her?

Jenna was a strong woman, who could defend herself against most shit in this world, but even she understood the danger of a cowardly hit man, hiding unseen, waiting to take her out anywhere, anytime. She was no longer in Afghanistan; she didn't have her flack vest and helmet to help protect her. Just walking down the street, she was vulnerable, and so was Max.

A thought rose to her consciousness, and as much as she wanted to push it down and never consider it, it fought its way back again and again. She knew what she needed to do.

The next day Jenna paced in Max's living room. He had insisted she call out of work, and she was smart enough to know what he wasn't telling her. She was in danger. She had insisted he stay with her, but he seemed to think he was fine to go into work, so long as he was careful. They had argued for a half hour, before he had finally just stormed out of the house, shouting strict orders for her not to leave.

Tears ran down her face as she pulled her phone out and stared at Nat's contact info. She hadn't spoken to Nat since before she had met Max, and just seeing her name on the screen brought her memories flooding back to her.

Jenna met Nat in high school. Renatta Giovanni was a head-strong fifteen year-old, born into the Giovanni mob family. Jenna's family life had been pretty fucked up, so she never judged Nat. They had naturally gravitated toward one another, both dealing with abusive overbearing males in their families, both dealing with violence as a way of life. It was Nat who had introduced Jenna to martial arts, and taught her how to be a bad-ass. Nat had disappeared soon after graduating high school, when her father tried to marry her off to a much older member of the "family business" as a political strategy. But Nat had always kept in touch with Jenna, secretly.

Jenna pressed the send button and waited.

"Jenna!" Nat's cheerful voice huffed into the line. She was breathing heavy.

"Nat... am I calling at a bad time?" Jenna asked. She was dreading the conversation, and almost welcomed an excuse to hang up.

"No... (huff)... I'm at the gym. Are you ok? (huff)" Nat asked.

"I..." Jenna hesitated. "I need a really big favor, Nat," she whispered.

"Hold on (huff)... let me get somewhere private." There were a few moments of muffled noise, and then Nat was back on the line. "What's going on, Jenna?"

"I hate to ask, but I need your help," Jenna began. "You remember that *family*?... the one on the corner?" Jenna used the code words they had established whenever they wanted to discuss Nat's family. Not that they'd needed to for many years.

"The one on the corner?... yeah... I remember them," Nat said warily.

"Well, somehow I have managed to piss off a friend of theirs. Actually, my boyfriend did. He... uh, he got in that friend's way, and stopped him from getting something that he wanted. So now that friend is mad, and wants to get back at my boyfriend," Jenna continued, hating herself even as she laid it out for Nat. Nat had worked so hard to get away from that family and that life, but Jenna didn't see another choice.

"Let me guess, that friend thinks if he can get to you, he can get to your boyfriend." Nat spoke it as a statement, not a question. She understood how the family operated.

"Exactly. I think they want to teach him a lesson," Jenna whispered again.

There was silence on the other end of the line for a breath, and then Nat breathed out heavily. "Oh, Jenna... I don't know what I can do, if anything, but I'll try. I still have a friend in that family. I can try calling him and seeing if he will meet with you. Can I give him your number?"

"No," Jenna answered quickly. "I have another number he can reach me on."

Jenna wasn't stupid. She had gone out and gotten a burner phone as soon as Max had stormed out that morning. As soon as her dealings with the family were done, she would destroy it, and any way anyone could connect her to them.

"Okay, give me that number," Nat spoke calmly.

Jenna sent her a picture of the number, written down, so that Nat could later delete the photo.

"Honey, it will be ok. I don't know how, but I promise, I will do what I can. I have to warn you though, it may be expensive."

Nat was all business. She had seen enough of their dealings to understand what was going to be involved.

"Money's not an object," Jenna answered.

"Okay," Nat answered. "Jenna, when this is all over, I want the whole story. You may have to come down to Richmond to visit!"

Jenna knew she was trying to cheer her up, but she couldn't lose sight of the task at hand.

"I will, I promise," she answered. "I love you, Nat."

"I love you too, Jenna." It felt like goodbye.

With nothing else to say, they let the call end.

Jenna got up and paced again. It had been hours since she talked to Nat, and there were only a few hours left before Max came home. She didn't want to have this conversation in front of him; he couldn't know.

As she turned and paced in the other direction, the burner phone in her other pocket vibrated. She pulled it out quickly and answered it.

"Hello?" Her voice was small.

"Jenna, I'm assuming? Our mutual friend has asked me to call you to make some arrangements. Can we meet?" The male voice was warm and professional.

"Is it safe to meet?" Jenna's eyes scanned the room, as if there was danger lurking all around her.

"It is. Can you meet me at Castle Island, by the play structure, in forty five minutes?" the man asked.

"I can," she answered simply, her stomach tying itself into knots. "How will I know you?"

"What will you be wearing?" he asked, deflecting her question.

Breathing out a labored breath she answered, "I have cobalt blue hair, you can't miss me." She winced at her own unfortunate choice of words.

"See you then," he answered sharply, and the call ended.

Forty five minutes later Jenna sat on a bench near the playground at Castle Island. It was an old Revolutionary War era fort that now served as a place for people to go and walk and explore. The day was warm, and families were everywhere, many enjoying food from the clam stand nearby.

Jenna looked at her phone again, and then noticed a man about her age approaching her with two ice cream cones. He walked right up to her.

"Jenna, I hope you like chocolate," he stated, as he handed her a cone and then sat beside her, throwing his arm around the back of the bench like they were good friends.

"I do, thank you." She tried to smile gratefully, but the thought of eating the ice cream made her want to vomit.

"I'm Victor. Our friend has told me that a mutual acquaintance of ours has been bothering you." He ate his ice cream, and looked out over the water as he spoke.

"Yes." Was all Jenna could say. Her nerves were shot.

"I can arrange it so that this acquaintance is no longer a problem for you. As it turns out, this person is also a problem for us now, as he somehow managed to leak important information to the public that we would rather have kept private; so it is in all of our best interests to resolve this issue."

"Oh." Was Jenna's only comment. She sat in stunned silence at the news. Apparently the jump drive had already made its way into the legal system.

"This is good news for you, as it means that it won't cost you quite as much." Victor continued casually.

"How much?" Jenna asked, gaining more control of her voice.

"Thirty." Victor answered, his eyes never leaving the water.

"Thousand?" she whispered.

His eyes slowly rotated until they met hers. "Yes."

"Okay," she stated. "How and when?"

"Can you meet me here tomorrow? Same time?" He asked.

Jenna nodded at him, and started eating the ice cream that was slowly melting down her hand and creating a chocolate mess.

"Do you know Mike's Pastries, the bakery in the North End? They make amazing cannolis. I think a box big enough to hold a dozen cannolis would be a lovely gift to bring to me, don't you?" He looked at her knowingly.

"Yes," she answered, "I think it would."

"I will see you tomorrow then." Without another word, Victor got up and walked off, leaving Jenna to sop up the chocolate that had soaked down her arm and into her dress.

◆ ◆ ◆

Max

Jenna was a nervous wreck all night. Max hadn't told her about the hit put on her, but she must have put it together that something was going on. They stayed inside all night, ordering dinner in, and drinking while watching a movie. But she would jump at the slightest sound or movement. Max just held her close, hoping she could feel safer in his arms.

Bruce had called him earlier that day to say that the drive had found its way to several different departments within the police, to ensure that no one individual could make it disappear. He expected an arrest warrant for Marcus the next day.

Max held Jenna tightly as she watched the movie. He would be glad when all of this was over. Why the hell was the Universe so hell bent on taking Jenna away from him? It just made him want to push back; it appealed to that primal side of him that wanted to lock her in a cave so no one could touch her ever again. He was ready to fight for her. He wasn't letting her go.

The next morning Max looked up from the shower to see Jenna at the sink brushing her teeth.

"What are you doing up?" he asked her, blowing water off of his face.

"Getting ready for work." Her words were all muffled by the toothbrush in her mouth.

"I think you should stay home today too. Just one more day. I'd feel better if you waited until tomorrow to go back." He spoke loudly to be heard above the shower.

"Max, I can't hide forever." Was all she said, spitting out the last of the toothpaste and rinsing her mouth.

"I really don't want you to go," he finally said, his tone softer.

"I know, Baby, but I need to." She met his eyes and then strolled over, leaning into the shower to kiss him, getting herself wet in the process.

Max reached to pull her into the water as their kiss deepened, but she groaned and pulled away reluctantly.

"If you do that, neither of us will get anything done today." She teased, and then grabbed a towel to dry herself with, before leaving the bathroom.

Max went through his day on autopilot. He shuffled files on his desk, and grunted responses at co-workers. At least he didn't have any court appearances, he wasn't sure he could hold it together for that. His thoughts revolved around Jenna, and he was in a state of near panic all day, thinking something bad was going to happen to her any minute.

He couldn't concentrate, and was effectively useless for most of the day. At about two in the afternoon he couldn't take it any longer. He had been texting with her all day, but he needed to see her. He needed to see that she was in a safe environment.

As he hurried out to his car he was still arguing with himself. He had never been this pussy-whipped for a woman before, but even that knowledge wouldn't stop him from driving to her work and checking in on her.

When had he gone over the edge?

Max parked in the nearest lot to Peak Performance and rushed to their building. He made his way inside, and got into the line of people waiting at the counter. There was a large display of a blond bodybuilder with no shirt on, standing by the counter, and several of the women were openly ogling it.

"Oh my God he's so hot. Do you think he'd do a little one on one coaching with me?" one woman asked on a laugh.

Her girlfriend replied, "Somehow I doubt it. I heard he's with someone now, lucky bitch. I keep hoping to run into him here, but he's always out."

"He was here earlier," the first woman responded. "I watched his magnificent ass as he was working out. You just missed him." She shrugged her shoulders at her friend, and they both eventually moved along.

"Can I help you?" Max looked back to the counter, where a middle aged woman waited for him.

"I'm looking for Jenna," he answered simply, trying not to look like a tourist in the enormous club.

"Oh, I'm sorry. She's left for the day. You just missed her," the woman answered.

Max stared at her blankly.

Why would she have left without telling him? She knew how crazy he had been all day worrying about her.

He could feel his nerves and anxiety ramping up. The *"You just missed her"* echoed in his head from the previous woman's conversation.

Probably a coincidence.

He couldn't help the sinking feeling in his gut.

◆ ◆ ◆

Jenna

Jenna sat on the bench with a few minutes to spare. Her fingers played with the string on the small white box in her lap filled with thirty thousand dollars. She had gone to the bakery and asked if she could just have an empty box; they looked at her like she was strange, but she'd hated to put cash in a box that had ricotta and chocolate all over it.

The five minutes seemed to drag on for hours, but soon she saw Victor's familiar face approaching her again. He sat beside her without a word.

"I have your cannolis," she said simply, indicating the box.

"Very good," he said smiling. "Then you can rest assured our mutual friend will not be bothering you any longer."

Jenna smiled and handed the box to Victor, who promptly stood with it, and left the way he had come.

Jenna sat and stared after him.

That just seemed too easy.

◆ ◆ ◆

Max

Max paced in the living room. He had texted Jenna several times, and hadn't heard anything back. He was trying to remain sensible, trying to convince himself that it was all just a misunderstanding and he was blowing things out of proportion.

His heart pounded like a drum in his chest, positive that the worst had happened. His imagination spun stories of her being gunned down in the street, or kidnapped and tortured. He pushed away the visions of himself screaming in grief, having lost her forever.

Get a grip on yourself he commanded himself firmly.

Just then his phone beeped a notification. He whipped it out, and breathed out heavily when he saw it was from her.

"Blue: Sorry, Sweetie, I had some personal errands to run this afternoon. I should be home shortly!"

His relief flared into rage. She knew how upset he was for her safety, and she'd left work to "run errands?" He wanted to choke her. Did she have no idea of how he was being eaten alive worrying about her? What "errands" did she have to run that were so important that she had to do them today, of all days?!

His mind went back to the conversation at the gym.

"He was here earlier. I watched his magnificent ass as he was working out. You just missed him."

And then *"Oh, I'm sorry. She's left for the day. You just missed her."*

No.

He wouldn't believe that.

She wouldn't have left to be with another guy.

Would she?

He tried to force the thought down, to not let it get a foothold, but the doubt lingered like a shadow that could never be shaken loose.

Twenty minutes later Jenna bounced through the doors. She hung her coat up and turned her huge smile on Max.

But Max was sitting in one of his living room chairs, his fingers digging into the arms, a glass of scotch by his side. The look on his face spoke murder.

"Where have you been?" Max grated out.

"I told you...," she answered warily. "I had some personal errands to run."

"And you didn't feel the need to let me know about this?" His jaw clenched tighter, although his voice didn't rise. "I've been a fucking mess all day, Jenna, worrying about your safety... only to find you skipped out of work early to suddenly run errands. You didn't think to text me, to let me know, so I wouldn't worry?"

Jenna could smell the scotch, the glass beside him was clearly not his first.

She carefully made her way over to him and knelt in front of him on the floor. "Baby, I am so so sorry. I didn't think-"

"NO. YOU DIDN'T THINK!" he bellowed, his rage tangible. "I have been such a fucking idiot for you, Jenna. I am consumed, worried sick, always worrying about your safety and wellbeing, and you could just stroll off?! I have been getting nothing done at work, Jenna. Every minute of every day is spent worrying about you. That you could just take off, and not even have the consideration to call me..." He stopped suddenly, and shook his head.

"Max-" Before she could say more Max jumped out of the chair and stormed to the door, slamming it behind him after he left.

Chapter 28

Jenna

Jenna looked blankly at the door. She was too stunned to even react. After worrying that someone was trying to kill her, and potentially Max, and having to reach out to the mob to solve that, she simply didn't have an ounce of energy left to deal with Max's tantrums.

Things had felt like they were finally getting better between them, but apparently they weren't. This sick obsession he had with being her protector needed to be addressed. Yes, it had been inconsiderate of her not to have called him and told him that she was leaving early, but what the fuck?! It's not like he owned her! She had the right to live her life.

On any other day he would have been at work and never noticed that she had left hers. She was willing to see his point of view, in lieu of the recent danger to both of them, but he also had to take responsibility for his bullshit caveman attitude.

When Max hadn't returned in a half an hour, Jenna sat down and had her dinner alone. She was tired and hungry, and she wasn't going to play games with Max. Hours passed, and still Max hadn't returned. She tried to distract herself, but the tension in her gut grew with each passing hour. At midnight Jenna finally went to bed on her own.

If this is some bullshit way of teaching me a lesson...

In her heart she knew he was hurt and angry, but he had always accused her of running away. They had both agreed: no running. So where was he?

At ten the next morning Jenna saw the news announcement that Marcus had been arrested with a string of counts against him. She watched in morbid fascination as the police marched him in handcuffs out of his work building. He still wore his smug smile, as if he knew no one could touch him. It made Jenna sick to her stomach.

The gym grew quiet as most people went back to their jobs. She knew she would have another hour before the lunch rush would sweep in next. Daniel appeared at her side.

"How you doin' Baby Girl?" He flashed his million dollar smile.

"I've been better. How's Drew treating you?" She smiled back, not nearly as wide as his.

"I have no complaints there." Daniel chuckled. "What's got you down?" He looked at her with sympathetic denim eyes.

She tried to smile back at him again. "It's nothing, it will pass. Hey, do you want to see this video I found?" she asked, changing the subject.

"Sure! Watcha got?" He brushed the hair off of her neck so that he could bring his chin right down onto her shoulder and look at her phone.

Jenna pressed the play button, and the video of two guys in a gym absolutely destroying themselves began to play. Jenna and Daniel laughed out loud, and Jenna turned her head to Daniel.

"I knew you would appreciate this." She laughed, going back to the video.

Daniel turned to look at her, his mouth so close to her cheek, before turning to the video again. They both burst out laughing again, as the men in the video just kept making one mistake after another. There was nothing sexual about their closeness; Jenna really felt like they were family. She hoped that he and Andrew worked out for the long-term.

◆ ◆ ◆

Max

Max pulled the doors of the gym open. He had rushed right over to see Jenna when they had announced that Marcus had been arrested. He wanted to apologize to her for his reaction last night. It wasn't her fault he worried so much. Yes, she could have called and told him she was leaving early, but she shouldn't have had to. Given the situation, it definitely would have helped, but he was out of line.

He stopped short just inside the doors. Behind the desk, he could see Jenna holding her phone up, while "Mr. Universe" with the "magnificent ass" rested his head on her shoulder. He watched as they laughed, and then Jenna turned to him, her mouth right next to his... almost like...

He saw red.

He ran to the counter, arm cocked, ready to take that son of a bitch out for touching his woman. Jenna saw him first and screamed, but he was in a fog of fury, and nothing would stop him. He launched his arm right at the guy's face, but suddenly Jenna was between them, her arm deflecting his, so that his whole body surged over the counter and he wound up in a pile on the floor.

Immediately he jumped up, ready to charge again, but again Jenna was between them, her hands up, in his face.

"MAX! STOP!" she shouted.

His breathing was ragged, like he had just run a marathon; his heart was pounding in his chest, and a light sheen of sweat was gathering on his forehead and neck.

"You know this guy?" Mr. Universe asked behind her, a sneer on his face. Max just wanted to punch that pretty face and give him a nice bruise.

"Daniel, this is my boyfriend Max. Max, this is Daniel..." Jenna hesitated. There were plenty of eyes on them from the few people still in the gym, and she didn't know if Daniel wanted to be outed in front of strangers. "I know him through Andrew." She finished.

"Was he one of your 'errands' yesterday?" Max growled.

He knew he shouldn't be having this conversation in public, but at that moment all he wanted to do was tear that guy apart. If he had stolen Jenna from him, he would kill him.

"WHAT?" Jenna and Daniel both asked in unison.

And then Daniel tipped his head back and laughed, hard. He couldn't seem to stop laughing. Max stood frozen on the spot, his fists clenched in rage but his stomach suddenly unsure.

Jenna wiped her hand down over her flushed face.

"Why don't you take off, Baby Girl. Spend some time with your man." Daniel said to her, still chuckling, as he walked away like he didn't have a care in the world. Jenna ran into a back room and grabbed her bag, and then headed for the door like her ass was on fire.

"Jenna!" Max called after her, suddenly panicked.

Had he called it wrong?!

He caught up with her outside, on the street, and grabbed her arm to stop her.

"Let go of me!" She spit, her eyes narrowed in fury.

"Jenna I..." Max started, but didn't know how to explain himself.

"Do you have ANY idea how embarrassed I am right now?!" She demanded. "Daniel is Andrew's BOYFRIEND. I am not having sex with him! I can't believe you would storm in here and do that!"

Max stared at her, slack-jawed. A cold sense of sickness crept into his stomach.

"Jenna, I saw him leaning on you, and it looked like-"

"It looked like NOTHING! We are friends! I am allowed to have friends, Max. I'm allowed to live my life without getting your permission! You don't own me!" she screamed.

"I DO OWN YOU!" Max screamed back. "After that fucking doctor, you said it. You said you were mine. So just knock off the bullshit, put my ring on, and make it official for fuck's sake. You're making me crazy with this passive aggressive yes-no bullshit. I can't take not knowing any longer, Jenna. Either marry me now or-" His breaths were heaving.

"Or what?!" Jenna hissed. "What happened to 'take all the time you need?' Talk about passive-aggressive? You know what, Max? I can't take this any longer either. We're done."

Jenna turned on her heel and stormed down the sidewalk. Max stood in shock as the reality of the situation started to break through his angry fog.

"Wait! JENNA!"

Before he could run after her a shot rang out in the air. Then another shot rang out. Jenna's shoulders spun with the impact, and she collapsed in a heap on the sidewalk. Max crouched low and scanned his surroundings, trying to find the shooter, before finally giving up and running to Jenna.

"NO NO NO NO NO JENNA!!!!"

He dialed 911 as he reached for her neck to feel for a pulse. Already a river of blood was soaking her shirt and pooling on the sidewalk underneath her.

Four hours later Jenna was still in surgery. Max sat in the waiting room of the hospital with his head in his hands. The room felt artificially cheerful, with cranberries and blues splashed on the walls, and framed artwork standing sentinel over utilitarian and very uncomfortable chairs.

He felt like a piece of him had died. If she didn't make it...

He couldn't even process the thought.

Andrew and Daniel sat in chairs nearby, consoling each other. Max didn't feel like he deserved consoling, and it wouldn't help him anyway.

Out of nowhere, Daniel's voice broke through the silence. "Why would you think she was with me yesterday?" His voice was soft.

Max shook his head sadly. He was so embarrassed that he had even considered that she would cheat on him.

"She said she had to 'run errands'; you both left the gym about the same time." Was all he could answer. It sounded stupid, even as it hit his own ears.

"She went to the bank." Andrew supplied, and Max looked up to meet his eyes.

"What?" Max hadn't actually considered that she really *was* running errands. Shame consumed him.

"Yeah, she inherited a large amount of money before she left the Army, and she put it in a joint account in both of our names, in case anything ever happened to her. She has no family left. She was making a large withdrawal yesterday; I thought maybe she was finally getting herself a car. She always refused to touch that money. It's been sitting there for almost fifteen years." Andrew finished.

Max stared at him blankly. This was all news to him. He had always assumed she was scraping by, working as a barista, and now in a gym.

"She didn't tell you why she withdrew the money?" Max asked curiously.

"No. And I didn't ask. She would tell me if she wanted me to know," Andrew replied simply. Daniel put his arm around him.

The door at the other side of the room opened, and the surgeon made his way in. All three men jumped out of their chairs.

"She's going to be fine. Luckily the bullet missed her major organs. She will need some rehab for her shoulder, but she will live." The surgeon informed them.

All three men sighed with relief, Andrew and Daniel collapsing into each other.

"Thank you, Doctor. When can we see her?" Max asked.

"She'll be in recovery for a few hours, and even when she comes out she's going to be groggy. Why don't you go get something to eat while you can? Let me have your phone numbers, and I can call you when she's awake." The doctor offered.

"No, I'll wait here," Max said resolutely, dropping back into his chair.

Andrew walked past him and gave his card to the surgeon. "Call us when we can see her." Then he turned to Max and Daniel. "Come on, you two, let's eat while we can."

Max didn't want to take a step away from her, but he knew it was pointless to sit and wait while she was sleeping. Begrudgingly he let Andrew pull him out of his chair and followed them to the elevators.

◆ ◆ ◆

Jenna

Jenna was aware of... something... everything was foggy. She could hear a beeping noise, but it sounded like it was far away. It suddenly felt brighter too. She tried to open her eyes, but they didn't want to cooperate. She tried again, and her eyelids slowly crept open. They felt dry. She felt dry... and foggy.

"She's awake!" a voice spoke beside her. She knew the voice, it made her feel safe... but she couldn't figure out who it was.

She could see movement around her, blobs of color moving toward her. She slowly willed her eyes to open all the way, and after a few seconds the blobs started to come into focus.

Max, Andrew, and Daniel stood beside her bed. Max held her hand in his. All three of them had tear tracks down their faces.

"You guys look like shit," she croaked through her parched throat.

All three of the guys gave a humorless chuckle for her benefit.

"Where am I? What happened?" She tried to turn her head and take in her surroundings, but her muscles were still sloggy and slow. Out of the corner of her eye she could make out the medical equipment. "Why am I in the hospital?" She croaked.

"Blue, you've been shot, Baby. But you're going to be fine. The bullet didn't hit anything important, so you'll recover." Max whispered down to her. He was clearly trying to hold back a deluge of tears as his lips trembled.

"How are you feeling, Baby Girl?" Andrew asked softly.

"Thirsty," she croaked. Daniel whipped out of the room to find a nurse and get her something to drink. In a few moments Daniel was back with a small cup of water and a straw. Andrew helped her to take a few sips and clear her throat.

"Did they get the shooter?" Jenna asked hopefully.

"Someone did," Andrew answered cryptically. "No one is coming after you anymore, so you just rest and recover, okay?" He smiled down at her, but it didn't quite reach his eyes.

Slowly her eyes began to close, despite her desire to keep them open, and soon everything was black.

Brightness. Too much brightness. Jenna slowly opened her eyes to the glare. When she could focus, she could see sunlight streaming in through a window. She turned and looked next to her to find Max asleep in the chair next to her, still holding her hand. She sat in silence and watched as he breathed peacefully. She loved to see him sleeping. Other than after sex, it was one of the only times he truly looked calm.

The door to the room opened, and a doctor in a white coat breezed in with a smile.

"You're awake!" he said warmly.

Max startled awake, jumping in his chair, and Jenna giggled despite herself.

"I am." She turned her attention back to the doctor.

He started with the normal patient tests, asking what her name was, the date, etc. And once he had taken her vitals and looked at her shoulder dressing he sat in a stool on the other side of her bed.

"The surgery removed the bullet from your shoulder blade, but not without some damage. You're going to need some rehab while it heals. You were lucky that your heart or lung weren't punctured. As soon as I have all of my labs back, we can process you to release you," the doctor informed her with a smile. "I'll be back later with some paperwork."

With that the doctor got up and made his way back out the door.

"I'm so sorry." Max said beside her. His eyes were red and puffy.

"It's not your fault, Max," Jenna answered. Her heart was hurting seeing him in so much pain. She wanted to comfort him, but she remembered the conversation they had right before she was shot. Technically, they weren't even a couple any longer.

"Will you come back home with me?" he asked hopefully, his eyes still brimming with tears.

The sight was like a knife to her heart.

"Max... I don't think that's a good idea. We still have some unresolved issues. I think I need some space." Tears ran down her own face as she said it.

Her heart was screaming at her to take it back, to just go with him and forget everything they had said. But she knew that if she did that, she would be owned by him forever. She would never be her own person. She would never be free.

Max closed his eyes with a wince as fresh tears fell. "I don't want it to be over. I love you, Blue."

"I love you too, Max. But we need to figure some things out." She was forcing herself to stay strong, but it was silently killing her inside.

Luckily, the door opened again, revealing Andrew and Daniel.

"Baby Girl!" Andrew pulled out his biggest forced smile.

Jenna put on her biggest forced smile in return.

The three guys sat in Jenna's room, fixing her starched white sheet and thin blanket, and feeding her hospital food, while they waited for her discharge paperwork.

At one point in the conversation Max asked, "Do you think the shooting had anything to do with your withdrawal yesterday?"

Everyone stopped and stared at him.

"You know, like a robbery? Maybe someone knew she had the money and planned to steal it?" Max continued.

Jenna's heart pounded in her chest like a war drum. She didn't know how he'd found out about her making the withdrawal, but she didn't want him to know she had put a hit on Marcus.

Her chest tightened.

Oh, God! He can never find out about that! It would destroy his reputation!

"I doubt it...," she answered shakily. "I spent it."

"On what?" Max asked.

Jenna just shrugged her shoulders. Luckily, the doctor chose that moment to come back in with her discharge papers, and the conversation was dropped. As Jenna gathered up her belongings Max reached down and kissed her gently on the forehead.

"You know where to find me, Blue. Please, come home," he whispered over her, before turning and pushing out the door.

Andrew and Daniel helped her out of bed, and they all slowly made their way out of the hospital.

Several weeks had passed and Jenna was recovering quickly. She had moved back into Andrew's house, and so had Daniel. It was a little crowded with the three of them there, but she loved it. She felt surrounded by love.

She had her daily rehab visits to work her shoulder, and already she had most of her mobility back. The strength would take longer to build. She also still saw Carol, remotely, to work through the pain of losing Max.

At first, she was so preoccupied with the pain and the exercise, it was easy not to focus on missing Max, but as she improved, her alone time started to build to overwhelming. Most days she was in a depressive funk from the minute she woke up to the moment she could finally fall asleep. Her shoulder was feeling better, but her heart was shattered.

She kept waiting for the day that she realized she had "gotten over him" or moved on... but it never came. She dreamt of him every night. She still missed him every day. She was living in her own hell, and pasting on a smile for Andrew and Daniel, who were still blissfully in their own Honeymoon phase.

A part of her realized that it was time for her to move out and get a place of her own. Andrew and Daniel deserved to have their relationship, without her hanging around all the time. And honestly, it hurt her so much to see them so happy, and know that she wasn't.

◆ ◆ ◆

Max

It was two months of pure hell. Max had packed up all of Jenna's clothing and personal items and brought them over to Andrew's for her, except her shampoo and conditioner. And there he sat, like a junkie in the shower, sniffing her shampoo just to feel the closeness of her scent.

Two months.

And every day was torture.

Why hadn't he cut down his work hours to spend more time with her? Why hadn't he prioritized her? Would it have made the difference? Would she still be there?

There was no point in "what if's." She was gone.

Max dragged himself out of the shower and dried off. As he got dressed he turned the news on in the background. He slid his leg into his slacks when he heard the announcement: apparently Marcus had been murdered in jail, waiting for his criminal trial. The police were in an uproar, trying to find out who had killed him behind bars.

Max pulled his other pant leg on. He thought he would be happy when Marcus died. After all the bastard had put Jenna through, he thought he would feel like celebrating. But he didn't. He felt hollow, void. None of it made a difference if Jenna wasn't with him.

He could be happy on her behalf, at least.

He pulled on his shirt and buttoned it, and then put in his cufflinks, before tying his bowtie. He hated charity events like the one he was attending tonight, but he understood the value in them as well. He'd rather contribute quietly.

Tonight there would be no woman on his arm. He would go alone, put in an appearance, and then leave early. If he couldn't go with Jenna, he would prefer no one.

The driver dropped Max off at the front of the venue, where a red carpet had been rolled out. He made his way into the event, stopping for a glass of champagne. Already people he knew were gravitating towards him, making small talk. He pinned his best fake smile on and walked in.

Dinner was served, and speeches were made. Max sat through it all, acting like he was participating, but his mind was still in the dark funk that was his new norm. Once the floor was open for dancing he strategically headed for the exit.

Suddenly he was tackled from the right, a small body bumping gently into his. He turned in surprise to see the blue hair and startled eyes that haunted his dreams. Her mouth was a perfect "O" in shock, as her eyes widened with realization.

"MAX! I am SO sorry!" She scrambled to pull herself away from him, but Max held her close instead.

"I didn't know you'd be here." He offered lamely, trying to grasp for an excuse to keep her for just another few moments.

"Yeah… Andrew… How have you been?" she asked, sadness evident in her eyes.

"You know…" He couldn't lie to her and say he was fine, but he also couldn't tell her she had devastated him. "You?" He tacked on weakly.

"Same," she answered with a sad smile. "How are the boys?" she asked, changing the subject.

"Oh… uh, they're good," he said casually. "I fly out on Christmas Day to visit them in Europe." For a long moment they stood in awkward silence.

Finally Max pulled her into him tightly, holding her against his body, and whispered into her ear, "Blue, I miss you. Please… come home." She stayed in his arms for a few breaths, and he savored every second, before she finally pulled herself away. Tears were forming in her eyes as she backed away from him.

"It was good seeing you again," she whispered, before she turned and practically ran into the crowd.

Chapter 29

Jenna

Jenna paced in her small bedroom, she still hadn't moved out. Andrew was out at a Christmas party, Daniel had flown out of state for a charity event with the team, and she couldn't bring herself to go out. She couldn't put on her happy face, or drink her pain away. Not if she might run into Max again. She was dying inside. It wasn't just depression, she was actively grieving.

She knew she was fucked up. And she knew she'd made the biggest mistake of her life letting Max get away. No matter how much she tried to "man up" and live with the fallout, she just couldn't. Her own traitorous heart was deeply invested in Team Max, and every day was torture without him.

She wasn't eating, she wasn't sleeping, she went through her days like a zombie. It was only a year ago that they had met, when she thought she could fuck her way through him. How had he changed her heart so much in such a short time?

She'd spent the day crying, her eyes swollen and red, and she just couldn't seem to stop. An idea crept back into her mind, as it had so many times before, and rather than trying to shove it back down, she let it play out. She was exhausted trying to deny that she could get over him.

What if she did marry him?

He knew who she was, surely he didn't really think she was white-picket fence and baked pies material. What would marriage to him look like? No matter what fucked up version of marriage it was, it would mean waking up with him every day. It would mean getting his smiles when he got home. It would mean having his body all to herself. Really, did anything else matter? She could hang off of his arm at events. She could try to be presentable, and wear expensive clothing if that was what was expected of a spouse of Max Thurston. She could even deal with the loneliness while he worked long hours; wasn't it better than the eternal loneliness of knowing he was never coming back? Of knowing she had pushed him away?

But she still couldn't give him children. Did he even want children? He said he didn't, but what if he changed his mind? She didn't, or at least she was used to the idea that there wouldn't be any. But if he did? Was he open to other options, like adoption? Could she do that? If it made him happy?

And Marcus... *could she ever tell him she had...* She hissed out loud. She could try.

Slowly the questions circled her mind. She looked at the clock. It was two o'clock, Christmas Eve. She knew he was flying out later that night to see his sons in Europe. It was now or never.

She pulled out her phone, like she had so many times over the last few months, and this time she sent a text before she could stop herself.

◆ ◆ ◆

Max

Max sat staring at his phone. She had texted him. He was tempted to put it on silent, but it was Christmas Eve. They hadn't talked in months. As much as he wanted to put this behind him, there *was no* putting this behind them. He was miserable without her.

But he couldn't accept having her back on her terms, without a commitment.

Or could he?

They were so good together. He knew she loved him, he had no doubt. She had gone above and beyond to be there for him. Why did he need a piece of paper to say that she had to stay with him? His ex-wife had cheated on him and left him, and they had the piece of paper, so clearly it didn't mean anything.

But it wasn't the piece of paper. He didn't want her running away from him again. He couldn't live through it again; he was barely surviving now. She couldn't just bail every time she got scared. He was scared too. He couldn't live with her, knowing she could just cut him off and leave him, never knowing if she'd be back or not. Each time, he had been the one to pursue her. She needed to be the one to come back to him. Maybe they didn't need to be married. Maybe they didn't need to have kids, but he needed to know that she was on his side, that she had his back.

His phone beeped in his hand again.

Maybe this was her trying to come back? Shouldn't he give her the chance? It was Christmas, after all.

He looked down at the screen:

"Blue: Hey, RBFNK, I wanted to wish you a Merry Christmas."

He stared at the screen, anger boiling up in him. "Merry Christmas?" Nothing more? Disappointment tasted sour on his tongue.

"Max: Merry Christmas, Jenna. What do you want?"

He watched the three dots appear and disappear.

"Blue: What I want is... I want to write you poetry. Really BAD poetry. Vomit-inducing poetry that would make Keats roll over in his grave, but which I would be so proud of."

Max rolled his eyes, his heart squeezing. He couldn't go through this again.

"Max: Jenna…"

Another message popped up quickly.

"Blue: I would like to give you the biggest most impressive flower arrangement you've ever seen; when in reality what I wanted to give you was my heart, my soul, and all of my tomorrows."

Max stared at the screen with his heart in his stomach. Tears started to build in his eyes, but he refused to let them fall.

◆ ◆ ◆

Jenna

Jenna typed quickly, trying to get it all out before he shut her down. She just had to say it. She just had to let him know, and then let him decide. He could save her, or he could destroy her; but she had to tell him.

She hit 'send.'

"Blue: But what I really want, more than anything, is to marry you. I want to try not to fuck up married life, to try to be a good wife and partner for you because you deserve that. I deserve that too. It may not be white picket fences, but we could have -2.4 kids. If it's not too late to get on Santa's Good list, that's what I want… more than anything in the world, Max."

She sat and stared at her screen, which was becoming hard to see through the tears that were freely flowing down her cheeks again. She worried her lower lip between her teeth as the seconds passed and there was no response. The longer she waited, the harder the tears fell. It felt like her heart was going to explode out of her chest.

No answer came back. She waited, watching the clock tick.

Why wasn't he answering?

She had told him. She had conceded... but it wasn't enough. He wasn't answering. He wasn't coming back. The clock ticked. The silence was deafening. She was too late. It was over. She dropped her phone and her face fell into her hands as she sobbed out loud.

Suddenly there was a pounding at her front door. She wondered if Andrew had forgotten his keys, as she wiped her face quickly and rushed to let him in. She knew she must look like death warmed over, and she didn't want him to see her in the middle of a breakdown, not at Christmas. She swung the door open and was shocked to find Max in her doorway leaning against the frame, tears leaving trails down his cheeks. He looked just as miserable as she was, with dark rings under his eyes, and he was still the best damned thing she had ever seen.

"Max!" She looked up at him in shock. She wanted to throw herself at him, beg him to take her back, but she could only stand there stupidly and stare.

"Still going right for the balls, I see," he whispered with a small smile.

"Always," she whispered back, hope filling her heart.

"How do you have negative 2.4 kids?!" he asked.

"Oh that's easy," she said, wiping her eyes, "you pre-order them for the next lifetime, silly."

And then she was surrounded by him, his strong arms circling her tightly in a death grip, her arms just as tight around him. His aftershave making her high, his presence filling her. For long minutes they just stood there, rooting themselves into the security of each other, of their 'them-ness'. Until finally Max whispered, "Aren't you going to ask me in? I'm freezing my balls off out here."

With a small laugh, Jenna pulled him into the room and shut the door. She kept her arm locked around him like she was afraid he would disappear, as she pulled him over to the sofa. He fell back onto it, pulling her down into his lap with both arms around her. His eyes searched hers as his hands came up to frame her face delicately. He gently pulled her down and kissed her sweetly, reverently, like he was memorizing her. Jenna's arms were locked around his neck, still in a death grip.

Finally Max pulled back, placing a gentle peck on the end of her nose.

"Blue, we don't have to get married if you don't want to. I'm sorry that I made it into an ultimatum. I love what we have. I just don't want to lose it, to lose you. I'm just afraid...

You're such a strong woman, Blue, you don't need me. You don't need anyone. What's to keep you from running away from me, leaving me?

"I couldn't take it. I have been dying without you. Life isn't worth living without you. I thought if we got married you might stay out of obligation... but I realize how stupid that sounds now. I love you so much... I have just never felt this powerless in my life." His eyes searched hers, imploring her to understand. His vulnerability was right there on the surface.

Tears were flowing from each of their eyes as they looked at each other with intention.

"Max, Baby, you're wrong. I do need you. I need you more than anything. It scares me shitless. I didn't want to need you. I didn't want to be that helpless. I was afraid of losing you, like I lost my squad. I panicked. What if you died too? What if you left me? It was easier to be the one leaving... until it wasn't.

"I died the day I left you. It was terrifying. I could live, broken, miserable, and alone, for the rest of my life; or I could face you, and run the risk that you would be gone one day. And then it hit me; it's really not a choice. Even if I only get one day with you, it's worth it. Every minute with you is worth the pain and the risk. I can't pretend that I can get over you, I can't. I can't pretend to be indifferent, because I am jealous as hell of any woman who gets your smiles, or your time, when I want them all. You are my everything, and my heart lives with you now. I can never go back to who I was before; she died and was reborn with you. I will always belong to you, whether you love me back or not. I have no control over that anymore.

"I would gladly marry you, if it would make you feel more secure with me. I would wear the fancy clothing, and go to your snooty events. I would even try not to attack the bimbos who throw themselves at you. Nothing is more terrifying than the thought of waking up without you, of knowing you are choosing to never come back to me. Please don't ask me to accept that, because I don't think I'm capable of that."

Max pulled her back down for a kiss, deepening it with a sweep of his tongue over her soft pink lips. They sat, locked in a hungry kiss that spoke of their pain and their loss, of their love and their relief. Max rested his forehead on Jenna's and blew out a breath.

"Well, you've done it now, Blue. You're stuck with me. My reptile won't accept anyone else."

Jenna's watery smile met his eyes. "Well that's good, because my mammal is starving."

◆ ◆ ◆

Max

It was crazy how quickly things just fell back together. Max bought Jenna a ticket to join him in Europe, so she could finally spend some time with his boys, even though he really wanted her all to himself. Of course the boys adored her. Truth be told, Max was pretty sure they liked her more than their own mother; there was no denying she was good for him. It was their first proper vacation together, without obligations or worries.

Max worried that when they got home they would have to deal with anything left unspoken, any issue they hadn't tackled. But he was pleasantly surprised. When they returned,

Jenna moved back in with him, for good this time. She was tearful as she cleaned out her room at Andrew's, but he helped her to haul everything out... after he apologized to Daniel for looking like a crazy stalker and trying to attack him in his own gym.

Jenna was just putting the finishing touches on some of the decorating she was doing to make the house more "both of theirs" and less "all his."

"You've forgotten one very important piece." Max called to her.

"I have?" she asked, as she left the mantle she had just been adorning with pictures of them together from Europe.

"Yes." He smiled at her as he held out her ring. "I was hoping you would decorate my life forever."

"I don't know..." She teased. "You tied the house key to a ribbon around your cock. You're just going to hand me the ring?" She gave him a disapproving look.

"Make you a deal, I'll tie it to my cock, if you'll take it off with your teeth." He countered.

"Let me put it on for now, but I want that later tonight." She laughed and then quieted.

"Max..." She began, suddenly more serious.

He turned to look at her, as she worried her lip between her teeth.

"Yeah, Baby," he answered as dread crept up his spine.

"There's something I need to talk to you about." She dropped her gaze and fidgeted with her hands in front of her, her ring sparkling. "It's not easy for me to talk about it, so I'm just going to spit it out.

"Williams and I were married in secret. I found out right after the wedding that he'd been fucking my best friend for months. We never even got our wedding night; I wouldn't talk to him. I wanted nothing to do with him. I spent the week avoiding him until we had to leave a week later for the appointment for me to get reassigned so I'd never have to see him again, and I could file for divorce.

"But he got killed on the way there. It was so fucked up. He betrayed me when I loved him with all of my heart; but once he was gone, I couldn't forgive myself for not having given him the chance to explain. I never heard him out. He died after begging me to forgive him and take him back.

"I was unconscious, in the hospital, when they processed his death. Apparently he had a lot of money. I was still legally his wife, so it all got transferred to me. I never wanted a dime of it. I put it into an account, and had Andrew co-sign so that if I didn't make it out of Afghanistan, he would get it. I've never used any of it... until now." She paused, looking to him before she could continue.

"When you told me that Marcus was involved with the Giovanni's... Well, I have a contact with them, a friend from my childhood. I couldn't take the chance Marcus would kill you... I pulled out thirty thousand dollars to have him eliminated as a threat. I guess they didn't get the hitman out on me until after he got a shot off. I just think you deserve to know this, before you agree to marry me." She eyed him nervously.

Max was speechless. Finally he cleared his throat and ran his hand through his hair.

"You hired a hit man to take out Marcus?" he asked.

"Uh-huh." She nodded her head, scrunching her nose and chewing her bottom lip nervously.

"Damn... and here I was running around worried about how I was going to protect you." Max shook his head. "Holy shit. I should make you MY bodyguard." He laughed.

"So you're not upset?" Jenna asked, blowing out a breath, clearly relieved.

"Blue, I have so much goddamn respect for you right now I can't even put it into words. But I think my reptile can...."

Max wiggled his eyebrows, before pulling Jenna by the hand up the stairs.

Chapter 30

Epilogue

December 31, the following year

Max

Max and Jenna kissed feverishly as they made their way clumsily to the bed. Their hands tore at their clothing, while they refused to release their lips from their contact. Maybe it was all the champagne, or maybe it was that they had finally done it.

Jenna pulled herself out of Max's grip, her hand on his chest to keep him from chasing her. His eyes were wild with need.

"Strip," she commanded.

He smirked and made quick work of the rest of his buttons, ripping his shirt off of his body. He then undid his pants quickly, shucking them down his legs with his briefs. He put his hands on his hips as he stood before her, nude, his arousal on full display.

"Is this what you want?" he asked her, his voice deep with desire.

"What I want is for you to get me out of this dress." She smirked, before turning so he could pull her zipper down in the back. She pulled the heavy strapless gown down until it pooled in a satin heap at her feet. Max reached out instinctively to release her from the strapless bra. She turned, and stepped out of the fabric puddle, wearing only her heels, garter belt, and stockings.

"You really aren't wearing panties!" He laughed, remembering how she had whispered that to him right after he kissed her at the end of their wedding. He had damned near desecrated the event right then and there. And then she had made him sit through the reception, dinner, dancing, and drinks, before finally allowing him to drag her back to their room and have his naughty way with her.

"A girl scout is always prepared," she whispered huskily, bringing his attention back. "Now... I want to suck my husband's cock."

Jenna dropped to her knees, as Max groaned. She wasted no time taking him into her mouth, and running her tongue up and down his length. She loved teasing him.

"More sucking... less teasing." He breathed out on a groan.

"So pushy!" She laughed, before swallowing him into her mouth and sucking hard.

"HOLY FUCKING SHIT, BLUE!" He gasped loudly, his hands shooting into her hair as his hips bucked into her mouth. "I will never get tired of looking down and seeing your beautiful mouth sucking my cock. Holy fuck! How did I get so goddamn lucky?"

Unable to answer with her mouth full, Jenna just moaned, causing Max to release another string of obscenities. She paced her strokes, long and languid. She worked her tongue over his shaft in her mouth, and around the tip when she pulled back. Max groaned loudly.

"So fucking good, Blue! AAAAArrrrrrgggghhh" He was lost in the sensation of her lips, her tongue, her teeth on him.

She worked him faster, harder. His breathing began to catch, and his groans grew louder. She put one finger into her mouth with his cock, and then pulled it back out wet. Slowly she brought it up between his legs, and then between the cheeks of his ass.

"BLUE?!" He looked down at her in warning, but she only chuckled, mouth full and all. She pressed her finger against his hole, working the moisture around. Instantly his hips slammed into her mouth, his cock jerking hard. She continued to suck him down, as she pushed her finger in further, and he was done.

"Fuck!   Fuck!   FUCK!   BLUE!   FUCK!!! AAAAAAAAAAAAAAAAAAAAA!!!"

He roared his release, his hands pulling her mouth over his cock as he pistoned his hips, fucking her face as his orgasm exploded down her throat. After riding out the orgasm, his knees gave way and he slumped onto the bed, his breathing heavy and ragged.

"Holy... fucking shit!" He huffed. "That was... absolutely... fucking... incredible!" He continued to gasp for breath, his skin coated in sweat.

"Who knew a wedding ring would make giving head so much better?" Jenna asked beside him with a laugh.

"I know what else it will make better!" Max huffed, before rising and tackling Jenna to the bed with a squeal. He kissed his way down her body, letting his fingers move over her skin; massaging her breasts, floating down her sides, stroking over her stomach, and leaving light fingertip touches up the insides of her thighs. Jenna moaned and stilled, taking in all of the sensations.

And then his mouth was on her, his tongue diving and exploring, his hands opening her wide for his tongue to probe. Jenna panted, and bucked her hips up, greedy for more friction.

"My impatient little mammal..." Max teased before nipping her inner thigh.

"That's Mrs. Mammal to you." She returned. "Now eat my pussy before I beat your cock with it." She groaned in frustration.

"So pushy." He laughed, and pushed three fingers inside of her.

Her back arched off of the bed with a long deep groan, and Max could feel her channel squeezing at his fingers, milking them into her. He pumped his hand into her and out, and brought his mouth down to her sensitive clit. While he fucked her with his hand, he teased her clit with a flickering tongue, the way he knew would make her crazy. Within seconds she was gasping and groaning, pushing her pussy into his face, and begging for release. Finally he took her clit gently between his teeth and nipped, before sucking it hard.

Jenna screamed her release, her body rigid beneath him, as he felt her warm juices flowing over his fingers. He pumped his hand into her, riding out the shockwaves that jerked her body. He loved seeing his wife when she climaxed. There was nothing more beautiful or more perfect in the world.

Suddenly Jenna was rolling, and thrusting her hips up into the air, dropping her chest to the mattress. She threw a look over her shoulder.

"I expect you to fuck this pussy hard with that big cock, husband. You'd better give me at least ten orgasms!" She smirked at him playfully.

"Only ten?" He pouted, and then chuckled.

"Yes, only ten... before intermission. AND I expect you to talk dirty to me through all ten." She winked.

"I don't know... seems like an awful lot of talking," he said, as he pulled himself up behind her, stroking the head of his cock through her wetness, which elicited another groan from her.

"Now. Fuck me NOW," she demanded, her voice growing more urgent the more he pushed his cock through her folds, "accidentally" rubbing her clit.

"You want this fat cock in you, Baby? You want me to fuck you with this?" He teased as he rubbed back and forth quickly over her clit. She could only groan incoherently in response.

Finally, Max couldn't take it any longer, and with one hard thrust he pushed his cock deep inside of her, sliding easily in her slick wetness.

"FUCK, BLUE." He stilled for a moment, just savoring the feeling of her walls clasping greedily around his cock, her body trying to suction him in deeper. "Your pussy does amazing things to me." He groaned.

Jenna pushed back hard, snugging her ass up to his abs, and clenched tight onto him. It had the desired effect. Max was instantly pushed into motion, drilling into her hard, his hands grabbing painfully into her hips. He grunted as his thrusts worked deeper, splitting her wider to receive him. Jenna wailed with pleasure.

Max picked one of his knees up, giving him even deeper access, sending Jenna into another fit of long loud groans.

"Get ready, Baby. I'm going to fuck you so hard. I'm going to make you come on my cock hard. Give it to me, Baby!" Max growled as he thrust into her sharply. He was all but climbing onto her, forcing his cock deeper, harder, faster. His hips pistoned with force, and Jenna screamed her pleasure.

"Oh God, Baby, you're so close! Holy fuck! Blue, I'm going to shoot my load into your pussy! Take it, Baby! Come for me! COME NOW!" He was shouting, fucking her as hard as he could, when he felt her walls tighten amazingly onto his cock. Her body locked around his cock, and then her muscles were milking him, drawing him out. His balls tightened, and his back went straight as he thrust hard one last time, before his cock started to spasm, and he could feel himself spilling into her while she milked it out of him. He screamed in release, completely at the mercy of her body.

He moved inside her, more slowly, leaning over to kiss the side of her neck where it met her shoulder.

"I'm so fucking glad you're my wife," he whispered, before collapsing on her spent body and pulling her closer to him.

She rolled her head to face him, a dreamy smile on her face.

"That's one down, nine to go." She gave him her most wicked smile.

Also by this Author

Red in Richmond, the Color of Love Series, book 2
   https://www.amazon.com/dp/B0BWSNPSR7

Want to learn more about Jenna's friend Nat?

The scorching second tale in The Color of Love series of dark and spicy adult romance novels!

Nat was doing her best to just survive and stay under the radar, so pursuing the hottie she saw at the gym was a big no-no. To make matters worse, he's a fed! She knows it can't end well if he discovers who she really is, and what she's done.
Baxter was sent to Richmond to follow a lead on the mob family he investigates for the FBI, but he never expected to meet a seductive redhead whose passion runs hot, and whose secrets run deep. He knows nothing good can come out of pursuing her, but he just can't stop himself.
When the truth about her past is brought to light, and the dust clears, will there be anything left for them together?

Amber in Atlanta, the Color of Love Series, book 3
   (to be released June, 2023)

Amber was always the second choice growing up, paling

next to her extraordinary friends. Secrets drove her away when they were still teenagers, but now its all out in the open. How will she reconcile her past with her present; and will she ever get to be someone's first choice?

Paranormal Romance

Heavenly Scent (Very Little Spice)
https://www.amazon.com/dp/B0BX1D5TCX

When one small-town girl turns out to be a mixed-blood hot commodity for an evil kingdom of Fae; it will take her long-absent Fae Father, and unknown Angel grandfather, as well as her sexy Fae warrior, to secure her freedom. Her life changes in an instant, as she fights to avoid a life of slavery. Is she strong enough to survive one crashing blow after the next? And if she can make it to freedom, can she resist the growing passion which threatens to devour her heart?

Daughter of Swan & Swords, Book 1
https://www.amazon.com/dp/B0C5JW8F7V

A Scorching Romance between two unlikely characters thrown together by fate...

Olwen was the only daughter of Ignar Cygnus, a world-famous maker of enchanted swords, and she lived a life of privilege and happiness until she was married off to a jealous and mediocre man with a gambling problem. Her life took a sudden turn for the worst when she was informed she had been bartered away to pay off his debts.

In a world where women were property, she had no rights when the dark stranger on her doorstep informed her she was leaving with him as HIS wife. But she had a secret, a secret that would give her leverage to secure her freedom. Olwen's new husband needed a swordmaker like her father, and she is the only one that could provide him with that.

Olwen is relying on her practicality and skill to find her way to a life of independence, so why does she feel so insecure and awkward around her confident new husband? Will she be able to leave him when she is finally released? Or will the whole new world he opens up to her entice her to stay? There is more than one secret he's keeping, and some of them just might destroy her.